"Wonderfully fresh, funny, tender and outrageous...
Crusie is one of a kind."

—*Booklist*

JENNIFER CRUSIE

BEDROOM BUSINESS

First Published 1994
Second Australian Paperback Edition 2005
ISBN 1 741 16220 3

GETTING RID OF BRADLEY © 1994 by Jennifer Crusie
CHARLIE ALL NIGHT © 1996 by Jennifer Crusie
Philippine Copyright 1994
Australian Copyright 1994
New Zealand Copyright 1994

Published by
Mira Books
3 Gibbes Street
CHATSWOOD NSW 2067
AUSTRALIA

® and TM are trademarks used under license. Trademarks indicated with ®
are registered in Australia, New Zealand, the United States Patent &
Trademark Office and in other countries.

Printed and bound in Australia by
McPherson's Printing Group

CONTENTS

GETTING
RID OF
BRADLEY

For Betsy Struckman, the perfect friend;
And for Steve Struckman, the perfect man;
And for Murph and Cassie, and Mollie, and
Maggie, and Rose, and Bernie, and Lucy and
Liz, and Annie, and Chuck, and Ed, and Jasper,
and Max, and Mose, and Sam.

One

—▶ ◀—

"I've never known anyone who was stood up for her own divorce before," Tina Savage told her sister. "What's it feel like?"

"Not good." Lucy Savage Porter tried to smooth her flowered skirt with a damp hand. "Can we go? I'm not enjoying this." She gave up on the skirt and clutched her lumpy tapestry bag to her as she glanced around the marble hallway of the Riverbend court-house. "Bradley signed the divorce papers. We don't even need to be here."

Tina shook her head. "Psychologically, we need to be here. You had a ceremony when you got married, you need one when you get divorced. I want you to feel divorced. I want you to feel free. Now sit over there on that bench while I find Benton to tell me why this is taking so long."

I'd feel a lot freer if you'd stop ordering me around, Lucy started to say, and then blinked instead. She'd been having rebellious moments like that a lot lately, but they were hard to hold on to, especially since the only time she'd actually followed through on one, it had been a disaster. Right now she was sitting under a brassy head of curls because she'd decided to go blonde as a symbol of her freedom. Some symbol. She looked like Golden Barbie with crow's-feet.

Maybe the problem was that she wasn't an independent kind of person. Other than the hair fiasco, every time she'd decided to be more independent, logic stopped her cold. After all, Tina was right. She did need the closure of hearing the divorce decree. And the bench was the best place to sit. It would be illogical to disagree just for the sake of disagreeing.

No matter how good it would have felt.

She went over and sat down on the bench.

Tina was gone already, trying to find her hapless attorney in the flood of suits that washed around her. Poor Benton. He'd gone beyond the call of lawyerhood in ramming Lucy's divorce through the courts in two weeks, but that wasn't enough for Tina. Tina wouldn't be satisfied until Benton brought her Bradley's head on a platter. Lucy had a momentary image of Tina, dark and svelte and dressed in her white linen suit, standing in front of a flustered Benton who was offering her Bradley's handsome head on a turkey plate.

She liked it. Tina always did have the best ideas.

Tina suddenly appeared before her, parting the suits before her like the Red Sea. "There's some kind of delay. It'll be another hour, but then we'll go have lunch."

Another hour. "All right. At Harvey's Diner?"

Tina shrugged. "Whatever you want."

"Thank you." Lucy dug her physics textbook out of her bag.

"What are you doing?"

"I have to teach Planck's constant tomorrow." Lucy paged through the book. "It's a tough one to get across. I'm reviewing."

"You know, the next thing I'm getting you is a new job," Tina said, and disappeared back into the suits.

A new job?

"I like my job," Lucy said, but Tina was already gone.

Okay, that's the last straw." Lucy closed her book with a thump. *Nobody's ordering me around anymore. From now on, I'm going to be independent even if it is illogical. I'm going to be a whole new me.*

That's it.

I'm changing.

"OKAY, THAT'S IT. I'M quitting," Zack Warren said to his partner. His shaggy dark hair fell across his forehead, almost into his eyes, but he was too mad to brush it back.

"Don't tell me, tell Jerry." Tall, cool, and controlled, Anthony Taylor nodded toward the man who had just pulled a gun on them.

Zack turned back to the gun, wavering now in the hands of the balding, middle-aged embezzler who stood quivering in his bad suit behind his empty desk. Jerry watched them warily, as warily as a cautious man might regard two big guys he was holding a gun on.

"I'm quitting, Jerry," Zack said. "You can let me go because I'm not going to be a cop anymore. You can have the badge."

He started to reach into his worn black leather jacket, and Jerry squeaked, "No!"

Zack froze. "Okay. Fine. No problem." He gauged the possibilities of taking Jerry there in his office. They weren't good. Jerry was very nervous and the office was very small, leaving them no room to maneuver and nothing to take cover behind. It was furnished only with a metal desk, two plastic chairs, and Jerry. The furniture was marginally more interesting than Jerry, or had been until he'd reached into his desk drawer and pulled out the gun.

They deserved this. Just because the guy was pathetic, they'd gotten careless. Zack looked at the gun wobbling in Jerry's hand with respect. A .45. The office currently had no windows, but Zack knew it could have a couple at any minute, a .45 being the kind of gun that left large holes in walls.

And people.

"Why do we do this?" Zack asked Anthony, scowling at the gun. "Life isn't depressing enough, we have to do this, too? I'm not kidding, I'm quitting."

"Stop complaining." Anthony carefully picked a speck of nonexistent lint off his tailored tweed sleeve, keeping his eyes steadily on Jerry the whole time. "You're the probable cause of this anyway. You walked in here in that black leather jacket, looking like you hadn't shaved in a week, and Jerry probably thought you were some lowlife." He smiled at Jerry, an oasis of perfect calm in a very sweaty situation. "I'd have pulled a gun on him, too, Jerry. I understand. Why don't we talk about this?"

Jerry shook his head, but he kept his eyes on Anthony, listening to his even, relaxed voice. Zack moved very slowly a few inches to his right, taking care to seem as if he were only shifting on his feet.

Jerry suddenly shifted his eyes to Zack, so Zack picked up the conversation. "Oh, and if we'd both been dressed in pimp suits like you, he wouldn't have pulled the gun. I ask you, Jerry, was it the jacket that made you pull the gun? Or the badge?"

Jerry narrowed his eyes at Zack, and Anthony moved slightly to the left.

"Just don't move," Jerry said as he swayed back and forth. "Keep your hands up."

"We're not moving, Jerry," Anthony said soothingly. "You are. Relax. You'll feel better."

"Don't get smart," Jerry said, and the gun wavered between them again. "I'll shoot."

"You don't want to shoot us, Jerry." Zack spread his hands apart. "The hassle from shooting a cop is enormous. You wouldn't believe it."

"Oh, yeah." Jerry looked at Zack as he talked, distracted by the movement, and Anthony eased another couple of inches to the left. "And the hassle from stealing thirty thousand from your boss is nothin'."

"Well, it's not like shooting a cop," Anthony said, and Jerry's eyes darted over to him. Zack moved a little more to the right. "Shooting a cop?" Anthony shook his head slowly. "They throw the key away. We don't want that. Put the gun down, Jerry."

"I don't think so." Jerry breathed a little faster and shifted his eyes to Zack. "I don't think so. And you guys are *moving*." He closed his eyes as he aimed the gun at Zack and squeezed the trigger.

Zack dove for the floor as he fired, and Anthony yelled, *"Jerry!"* and Jerry swung the gun toward where he'd been. Zack threw himself over the desk as Anthony flattened himself on the floor, and Jerry put a bullet neatly through the center of the door.

Then Zack slammed Jerry down on the floor.

Anthony rolled to his feet to help. "You all right?"

"Me? Oh, I'm as good as I get," Zack said, breathing a little heavily as he reached for his handcuffs. "Which is a hell of a lot better than Jerry is right now. How about you?"

"There were people in that hall." Anthony went out the door to see what Jerry had hit on the other side while Zack cuffed him.

"You have the right to remain silent, you jerk," Zack said and finished reciting Miranda sitting on top of him. Anthony came back and lounged in the doorway.

"Congratulations," Anthony said to Jerry when Zack was finished. "You shot a water fountain."

"Up yours," Jerry said, but it came out more embarrassed than defiant.

Zack stood and glared down at him. "We've got to start hanging out with a better class of criminals."

"Actually, this is the cream," Anthony said, checking his jacket for damage. It was, as always, spotless. "You want to work Vice or Homicide?"

"No," Zack said. "I want to arrest polite people who don't point guns at me. In fact, I don't want to arrest anybody anymore. I want to hang out with good people. Is that possible? Are there any good people anymore?"

"Well, there's you and me," Anthony said patiently. "We're supposed to be the good guys. Are you sure you're all right? You've been acting strangely lately."

"Could you guys hurry this up?" Jerry whined from the floor. "I'm not *real* comfortable down here."

"You know, Jerry—" Zack was suddenly soft-spoken as he looked down at him "—I could kick your brains out very easily right now." He gently nudged Jerry's head with his foot. "Resisting arrest. Don't push your luck."

Jerry shut up.

"Here's some advice, Jerry." Anthony reached down and hauled him to his feet with one hand. "Don't get smart with a guy you just pointed a gun at. He's likely to be feeling hostile. And frankly, Jerry, we didn't like you much before you pulled the gun."

Jerry closed his eyes.

"I was kind of hoping he'd resist arrest," Zack said.

"No, you were not," Anthony said. "You have plans for lunch. You're arresting a master embezzler at Harvey's Diner. What's wrong with you?"

"Nothing." Zack pushed Jerry into the hall. "The weather. I hate February. And I hate office buildings." He looked around at the smooth gray walls. "Maybe I will quit. Get a nice job out in the open someplace. No guns. You think I'd make a good forest ranger?"

"You know, you worry me," Anthony said.

"That's your problem." Zack moved down the hall, prodding Jerry in front of him. "So, Jerry, what'd you do with the money?"

LUCY SAT SLUMPED across from her sister in a battered turquoise booth in Harvey's shabby diner and tortured her salad.

Tina scowled down at her own salad. "Are you sure it's safe to eat here? I think turquoise Formica is bad for you, and I'm positive this lettuce is. It's white." She tapped a cigarette from the pack on the table and lit it smoothly, like a forties' movie star.

Lucy leaned forward to put her chin in her hand so she could pretend to listen to Tina, and her brassy hair fell into her face again. Tina smoothed a dark, silky strand of her own precisely cut hair, and Lucy looked at her with envy. Maybe they weren't sisters. Maybe Mother had lied to them. No, they had the same cat face: wide forehead, big eyes, little mouth, pointed chin. It was just that Tina looked like a purebred, and she looked like something condemned at the pound.

Stop it, Lucy told herself. *Stop feeling sorry for yourself. You're just having a bad hair day.*

Well, okay, a bad hair week. And then there was the divorce.

You're just having a bad month. Pull yourself together. Spring is coming.

"You are going to get rid of his name, aren't you?" Tina asked. "Lucy Savage Porter always sounded like you'd married a rabid bellboy."

Shut up, Tina. Lucy blinked. "Could we talk about something else?" She squashed her hair back to peer around the dim restaurant, hoping no one else had heard. Since the place was not only dim but small, it was a real fear, but it was also almost empty. There was only a bored waitress leaning on a chipped plastic counter beside a fly-specked case of doughnuts, and two men in a booth identical to theirs on the opposite side of the room.

Lucy was having a hard time ignoring one of the men.

One was tall, slender, and elegant, leaning calmly back in the booth, not a crease in his beautifully cut tweed suit.

The other man was his antithesis. Shorter, thicker, tense as a coiled spring in a creased black leather jacket, he leaned across the table and stabbed his index finger into the Formica. His unshaven face looked as if it were made of slabs, his hair was dark and shaggy, and his smile came and went like a broken neon sign. He was so intense, he was practically bending the table with the force of his personality. Lucy had been reluctantly aware of him ever since they'd entered the diner, kicking herself for stealing glances at him but stealing them just the same.

This was the kind of man who could leave a woman scarred for life. She wasn't so dumb after all. She could have ended up married to somebody like him instead of Bradley.

But think how much excitement she would have had before the end.

"No, that would have been dumb," she said aloud.

"What would be?" Tina asked.

"Nothing." Lucy turned back to her. "That's a beautiful suit you're wearing."

"It should be. It cost a fortune. You couldn't afford it. If you had to make a bad marriage, and I suppose you did since it runs in the family, couldn't you at least have chosen somebody with money?"

"No." Lucy picked up her fork and jabbed at her salad, spearing a cucumber slice because it was there. "Money isn't important."

"Oh? And what is important? And, whatever it is, why did you think that loser Bradley Porter had it? In fact, why did you marry him at all?"

Lucy thought of several cutting things to say about her sister's second and third husbands and then blinked instead. "I married him because of the second law of thermonuclear dynamics."

"You married him because of a physics theory?" Tina put her cigarette out in one of her salad tomatoes, pushed the bowl away, and lit up another. "Well, at least you didn't say 'for lo-o-ove.'" She blew her smoke away from Lucy. "So what's the second law of thermodynamics?"

"It says that isolated systems move toward disorder until they reach their most probable form, and then they remain constant."

"I don't get it. And what does that have to do with Bradley?"

"Nothing. But it has everything to do with me." Lucy pushed her bowl away with one hand and shoved her hair out of her eyes with the other. "I was an isolated system. I mean, there I was, living alone in that little apartment with Einstein for company, and Einstein is great company, but he's also a dog."

"I wondered if you'd noticed that."

"Well, of course, I noticed. And I'd been teaching science for twelve years. Lecturing to kids all day and then going home alone to grade papers at night. The only real social contacts I had were at your weddings."

Tina stuck her tongue out at her and pulled a pepper strip from Lucy's salad bowl.

"And then one day in class, we got to the second law, and I thought, 'That's me. I'm an isolated system, and I'm just going to get more isolated until I reach my most probable form which is probably where I am now, living in an apartment with Einstein.' So I decided to get un-isolated. And that's when Bradley picked me up in the library and I thought, 'This must be it. Physics has brought us together.' I mean, his timing was so perfect. It was so logical."

Tina shook her head. "No wonder you're so screwed up. Life is not logical, and marriage certainly isn't. Stop analyzing things so much. Try impulse for a change."

"I was impulsive once. I married Bradley after I'd only known him two months." Lucy felt a twinge of shame even as she said the words. She'd been stupid. Really stupid. "So I'm not a fan of impulse anymore. And, no offense, but I don't see impulse doing much for you."

Tina smiled. "I've got twelve and a half million dollars, darling. And what have you got? A moth-eaten house and custody of three dogs. Impulse has done more for me than logic has for you. Just look at you. Do you ever have any fun?"

"Fun?" Lucy's eyes went to the dark-haired man across the room. "Fun." She shifted her gaze back to Tina and picked up her fork to attack her salad again. "I don't think I'm the fun type."

"Well, I think you're taking life too seriously. It's time you cut loose. Do something wild. Something spontaneous."

Lucy frowned at her. "I told you. I did something spontaneous once. I married Bradley. Face it, Tina, I'm not the spontaneous type."

Tina shook her head. "Marrying Bradley was not spontaneous. You just gave me a very sensible reason why you married him.

Spontaneous is when it's not sensible but you do it anyway because you want to."

"That's not spontaneous, that's irresponsible."

"Fine, then do something irresponsible. In fact, do something spontaneous *and* irresponsible. Do something just because you have the urge to do it, because it feels good. Do something selfish, just for you."

Lucy's eyes went back to the dark-haired man across the room. "I don't think so." She stabbed her salad again.

"How do you know unless you've tried it? You've never done anything selfish in your life."

"Well, you know, I did," Lucy said slowly, her fork frozen in her hand. "Once. In fact, I think that's the real reason why I married Bradley. I dated Bradley because of the second law, but I think I married Bradley to get my house."

Tina looked interested. "Really? That's so unlike you."

Lucy nodded. "I think I just convinced myself I loved him because he offered me the house." She poked at her salad again, averting her eyes from Tina. "I love the house more than I ever loved Bradley. I think he knew it finally, and that's why he cheated on me."

"Well, I'll be damned." Tina put her cigarette out and leaned back in the booth. "This explains a lot. Is this what that fight you had last October was about?"

"How did you know…?"

"That's when you moved upstairs to the attic bedroom. I never bought that story about Bradley snoring. I knew there had been a fight."

"No." Lucy frowned. "There wasn't. We never fought. We just had a…disagreement. Over one of the dogs."

Tina winced. "For anyone else that would be a minor disagreement. For you…if Bradley did something to one of those dogs, he couldn't have known you very well. And this explains why you're not brokenhearted over the divorce. You're upset, but it's not because you miss Bradley. You're glad he's gone, aren't you?"

"Yes," Lucy whispered. "That's awful, but I am."

"No, it's not. That's healthy. What I don't understand is what you're so upset about. You're free. You can do anything you want. What's wrong with you?''

"I feel stupid," Lucy said.

"What?" Tina leaned forward. "You? You've got more brains than..."

"Not real-life brains. I have science brains. But real life?" Lucy shook her head. "I don't even know what happened in my marriage. I know it was awful for me, but I would have sworn to you that Bradley was happy and he loved me, and then out of the blue, I come home and find him with a blonde. In my house. And she says they've been having an affair in my bedroom, and he flusters around, obviously guilty, and when I get upset, he leaves." She sat back. "He just leaves."

"Men," Tina said.

"So I don't have a clue where I went wrong. The only thing I've ever known for sure in my whole life is that I'm smart. And now I'm not even sure about that. It's upsetting."

"Well, if you think he was angry about the house..."

"It's not just that he cheated on me. It's that he won't talk to me now. In the lawyer's office, all he said was, 'Is this what you want?' And I said yes, because it was, but..." Lucy bit her lip. "He hasn't even come by to pick up the rest of his papers and things. It's like a chunk of my life just dropped out of sight."

"Oh." Tina shifted uncomfortably. "Well, I may have had something to do with that."

Lucy froze. "What did you do?"

"Well. You know how upset you were when you called me that day and told me that Bradley and the blonde had just been there?"

"What did you do?"

"Well, I had the new locks put on...."

Lucy nodded. "What else did you do?"

"Well, when he came to the door to talk to you..."

"He came to the door to talk to me?"

"You were upstairs in your bedroom crying." Tina paused. "I was...angry."

"Oh, no."

"I know, I know. I lose it when I get angry." Tina lit another cigarette, inhaled, and blew out another stream of smoke before she went on, faster now to get it over with. "Anyway, I told him that if he ever tried to talk to you again, I would have private detectives digging up every slimy thing he'd ever done, and that I would personally see that they all made the front page of the *Inquirer*, and that I would also find every asset he possessed and take it from him."

Lucy looked at her, stunned.

"I think I might also have mentioned bodily harm. I was really upset. You never cry."

"So that's why he hasn't called? You are something else, Tina."

"I'm sorry," Tina said. "But I could just see him talking you back into that damn marriage. I couldn't stand seeing you unhappy anymore."

"I wouldn't have gone back. But I would have liked to have talked to him." Lucy took a deep breath. "I love you, Tine, and I appreciate everything you've done for me, but you've got to get out of my life. It's my life."

"I know, honey." Tina fiddled with her cigarette. "But you need help. I mean, I let you pick the restaurant and look where we ended up." She glanced around at the plastic walls and the chipped Formica. "This place is a dump."

"I had a reason for wanting to come here," Lucy said. "Bradley wrote to me. He said if I'd have lunch here with him, he could explain everything." Lucy looked around the cheap diner again, perplexed. "It doesn't seem like his kind of place."

"Do you want him back?" Tina asked. "I'll get him back if that's what you want."

"No." Lucy pressed her lips together and stabbed her salad again. "That's not what I want."

"Well, what do you want? Just tell me what you want. I'll make it happen."

Lucy smacked her fork down. "You can't. Or you won't. I want to live my own life. I want to make my own mistakes. I want you to be my sister, not my keeper. You don't have to take care of me."

"I know I don't have to." Tina frowned. "But I want to. I want you to be happy. You never have any fun."

"I don't want to have fun." Lucy took a deep breath. "Do you know what I want?"

Tina shook her head, her eyes on Lucy.

"I want to be independent. I want to take care of myself, without you racing to the rescue with money and lawyers. You always tell me what to do, and you're always right, and most of the time I don't mind it, but then I married Bradley, and he was worse than you are. Between you and Bradley, I haven't made a decision on my own in almost a year because everything you told me to do was the sensible thing, and it would have been stupid for me to argue. Only I did all the sensible things, and now look at my life. It's a mess." Lucy stuck her chin out. "So, I'm changing. I want to make my own mistakes and mop up after them myself. I want to talk to my ex-husband without you threatening him with death. And if I want to dye my hair purple or adopt another ten dogs or…or…" Her eyes twitched to the man across the room. "Or go out with inappropriate men. I want you to stay out. It's my life. I want it back."

"Oh."

"I appreciate everything you've done for me. Just stop doing it."

"All right." Tina picked a cucumber slice out of Lucy's salad. "Inappropriate men, huh?"

Lucy slid down a little in her seat. "Probably not. That was just big talk."

"What about that guy across the room you keep looking at?"

"Oh, no." Lucy closed her eyes. "I'm that transparent?"

"Well, he doesn't seem to have noticed." Tina glanced across the room. "He really is attractive, though. Your instincts aren't so bad."

Lucy looked at the two men across the room again out of the corner of her eye. The one in the black was talking, his fingers slashing the air while he spoke.

"He's gorgeous," Lucy said.

"Actually, he looks a little dull. But if that's what you want, let me see what I can do." Tina started to get up.

"Dull?" Lucy said. "He looks insane."

Tina stopped. "You're talking about the one in the tweed, not the one in the black leather, right? You can't be serious about the black leather."

"It's my fantasy," Lucy said. "And sit down. You're not going over there and embarrass me."

Tina sat down. "The black leather would not be good for you."

"I can't tell you how tired I am of things that are good for me," Lucy said.

"I know." Tina nodded sympathetically. "But that doesn't mean you should commit emotional hari-kari. That guy is unstable."

Lucy's eyes went back to the black leather. "Actually, you know, he's just what you ordered. What I'm feeling for him is definitely spontaneous and irresponsible."

Tina looked at him and frowned. "Maybe if you just used him for the cheap thrill and then discarded him."

"I couldn't do that." Lucy tore her eyes away from him. "I could never do that. I'd better just concentrate on being independent without the inappropriate-man part."

But she looked back at the man in black leather one more time and sighed.

"I CAN FEEL IT." In the booth across the room, Zack tapped his fingers on the scarred table. "Bradley's here. Or he's been here. Or somebody he knows is here. Or..."

Anthony leaned back. "All right. He's here. So are we. But it's been an hour and I'm getting bored, so just point him out to me, and we'll arrest him and go. He's disguised as one of those two women, right?"

"Fine." Zack glared at him. "Don't help. I'll do this without you. Fine." He drummed his fingers on the table.

"Zack, I want to get him as much as you do," Anthony said patiently. "He's thumbed his nose at every cop who's tried to nail him in the last nine months. And the million and a half he's traveling on is not chicken feed. But I need more than just one of your instincts to keep me in this dive any longer."

Zack slapped the table and then drummed his fingers again. "Look, we got an honest-to-God phone tip that he'd be here, and it's the best thing we've got so far. It's not like we have anything else on this thing. It's not like—"

"Zack," Anthony interrupted him. "You're driving me crazy."

"What? Oh. The fingers?" Zack stopped drumming on the table. "Sorry."

"No, not the fingers. Although that's got to stop, too. No, it's the way you've been acting lately." Anthony shook his head slowly. "That was a bad moment today with Jerry. I thought you were really going to kick him."

"Me? Naw." Zack paused. "Probably not."

"Exactly." Anthony nailed him with a frown. "That's what I'm talking about. The 'probably' part. And all this rambling about quitting. I don't like it. You've always been nuts. That's fine. I can deal with nuts. But lately, you've been depressed nuts. I can't deal with that."

"I'm not depressed." Zack picked up a package of sugar, tore it savagely across the middle, and dumped it in his coffee. "I'm not *elated* right now, but I'm not depressed."

"You just decapitated a sugar packet. That should tell you something."

Zack stared at the mutilated packet and then tossed it on the table. "I'll tell you something. I was really disappointed in old Jerry today. I mean, I felt sorry for the poor sap, and then he pulled a gun on us, and I thought, damn, nobody's decent anymore. And then he shot at us, and I was really mad." Zack shook his head. "Sometimes I think there aren't any decent people in the world anymore." He tasted his coffee and frowned. "So maybe the job's getting me down a little, but I'm not depressed."

"You are depressed." Anthony spoke clearly and calmly, as if he were speaking to the mentally ill. "And your depression is affecting our work. I know what's wrong."

Zack glared at him. "Have I ever mentioned how much I hate it that you were a psych minor? A minor, for cripes' sake. With a minor, you're not even allowed to psychoanalyze dogs."

"It's because you're worried about getting older. It started when you turned thirty-six."

"I don't want to talk about it." Zack turned his attention back to the restaurant. "Do those two women look guilty to you? There's something strange about the blonde. I think it's her hair. That hair is not real."

"Ever since your birthday, you've been snarling at the younger men on the force. And I have shoes older than the women you've been dating." Anthony shook his head. "You are really transparent on this one."

Zack scowled at him. "It's not age. Hell, you're the same age I am."

"Yes, but I'm not depressed about it."

"Well, you should be." Zack fiddled with his spoon, spattering the scarred tabletop with flecks of coffee. "Remember Falk, the old guy I started out on patrol with? There's a kid on patrol with him right now.... I was in *high school* when he was born. He lived down the block from me."

"Zack, you're thirty-six. These things happen. So there are people who are younger than you are. Deal with it."

"I'm not as fast as I used to be, either." Zack dropped his voice. "When we play one on one? I'm slowing down. A lot."

"This is all in your mind. I haven't noticed you getting any slower."

"That's because you're getting slower, too."

Anthony narrowed his eyes. "Do you mind if we keep this your depression? Personally, I am getting better, not older."

"You're getting older. But you don't care because you've always been the brains. Brains don't age."

"Oh, fine. And that makes you what? The brawn?" Anthony leaned back and folded his arms. "I can take you anytime, turkey."

"No, I'm the instinct. Lightning-fast instinct." Zack sent his eyes around the diner again before he turned back to Anthony. "But lately, I'm losing it. When we were chasing that guy on the fortieth floor yesterday? The one on the roof? For a minute, just for a minute, I thought, 'This is nuts. I'm going to fall off a roof because somebody just boosted somebody else's camcorder. It's not worth it.' And then today with Jerry? I kept looking at that damn desk, thinking, 'That's going to hurt when I have to go over it.' I kept hoping he'd surrender so I wouldn't have to go over that damn desk. I tell you, I'm losing it."

"Look, lightning, you are not getting slower, you are not losing your instincts, and you are not going to die. You are just growing up. And, may I add, not a moment too soon."

"I'm serious—"

"So am I." Anthony pointed his finger at Zack, and Zack shut up. "You have been going ninety miles an hour ever since I met you eighteen years ago. I used to watch you and think, 'How does he do that?' and marvel. Then I grew up, and now I watch you and think, '*Why* does he do that?' You have nothing to prove to anybody, and you're still acting like some hotshot TV cop." Anthony leaned forward. "Not chasing the camcorder off the roof was good. It was a sign of maturity."

"Don't say that word," Zack said. "Maturity means death."

"It does not. What's wrong with you?"

Zack started drumming his fingers again. "I don't know. Sometimes… You know, my brothers are all married. They've got wives, they've got kids, they've got big houses, they've got responsibilities." He scowled at Anthony. "It's like they're living death."

"I've met your family. They're happy. What are you talking about?"

"Responsibility," Zack said. "Maturity. The minute I stopped chasing that camcorder, death said hello."

Anthony started to laugh. "I don't believe this. You've always been a flake, but this, this is new. You know what you need?"

"Nothing. I need nothing. I'll be fine."

"You need to settle down. Look, you used to live for this job, but it's not enough anymore. That's good. But you look at your brothers, and you want what they've got, and it scares you, so you become depressed instead. That's bad. Face it. Maturity is not death. It's just the next step in life. Most people encounter it sooner than you did, but you'll do fine." Anthony sipped his coffee. "You will have to change the kind of women you date, though."

"What's wrong with the kind of women I date?"

"They're younger than your car, they carry knives, and they ride motorcycles naked on I-75."

"Well, they beat those plastic Yuppies you hang out with. What's the latest one's name? Cheryl? Please." Zack rolled his eyes.

"Cheryl has many fine qualities," Anthony said without much enthusiasm.

"Name one."

"She can read. Have you ever dated anyone literate?"

"Look, I don't want to date anybody right now."

"You're not dating?" Anthony frowned at him. "There are no women in your life?"

"I'm resting." Zack leaned back in the booth and tapped his fingers on the cracked upholstery. "I'm concentrating on my career."

"Oh, good for you. So how long has it been since you...dated?"

"New Year's Eve."

Anthony shook his head. "That's two months. That alone could make you depressed."

"I'm not that depressed." Zack's tapping picked up speed. "Could we get off this please?"

"All right, you're not ready for a wife. Start small. Get a dog."

"A dog? A dog?" Zack slapped the table. "A dog. That's all I need is some dopey dog with big sad eyes telepathically telling me he never sees me and where have I been?"

"Zack..."

"Besides, I had a dog once. I got him when I was three."

"Zack..."

"I went away to college and he died. Dogs are a responsibility. You can't leave them."

"You went away to college." Anthony cast an imploring look at the ceiling. "I don't believe this. Zack, if you got him when you were three, he was fifteen by the time you went to college. That's 105 in dog years. He died because he was old, not because you went to college."

Zack wasn't listening. "You start taking responsibility for things, they worry you. I don't need that. Worry slows you down. You start to second-guess everything. And then, pretty soon, the instincts go. That's why I hang out with you. Nothing ever happens to you."

"Thank you," Anthony said. "I think. All right, a dog is not a good idea, but maybe—"

"Look, could we get back to work here? This conversation is really depressing me."

"Fine. But think about what I said." Zack scowled at him and Anthony held up his hand. "All right, back to work. Now, which one of those two women over there does your sixth sense tell you is John Bradley, embezzler?" He studied them. "The hot brunette has a mean look to her, but I suppose the blonde's a possible, too."

"You don't think the blonde's hot?" Zack shook his head. "You have no taste in women. The hair's a little weird, but the face is good, and the body is excellent."

"How do you know? They're sitting down."

"She went to the counter to get another fork. I may be getting older, but I'm not dead yet. The blonde would definitely be worth some time." Zack squinted over at her. "You know, I think she's been looking at me."

"Right."

"Hey. Women look at me. It happens."

"Well, at least you're not depressed anymore." Anthony checked his watch. "We've wasted an hour here for nothing. Would you like to arrest the blonde so you can pat her down, or shall we just leave?"

"Fine. Make fun." Zack shoved his coffee away and tossed some coins on the table as a tip. "But I'm telling you right now, there's something here that would have helped us break this Bradley case. And now we'll never know."

"I can live with that," Anthony said.

"That's because you have no instincts," Zack said.

"OKAY," TINA SAID AS Lucy finished her salad. "Let's concentrate on the basics—getting your new life started."

"Let's not," Lucy said.

"First of all, you've got to get rid of anything of Bradley's that's left. Then we've got to change your hair. And then I'll fix you up with some presentable men I know. Everyone I know has money, so at least you'll be eating in decent restaurants. Not like this dump."

"Tina," Lucy said. "No dating. I will fix my hair because it looks awful, but no dating."

"What about Bradley's papers? I think you should throw whatever he left out on the lawn. Or better yet, burn it and dance around the flames."

"Tina, that's ridiculous. You're blowing this out of proportion."

"No, I'm not. Psychologically, this is a very big deal. Get rid of his things and you'll get rid of him."

"I am rid of him," Lucy protested. "I just want to talk to him so I know what happened. I don't want him back."

"Good. Remember that." Tina stood and took her black silk trench coat from the rack at the end of the booth. Then she handed Lucy her bright blue quilted-cotton jacket and bag. "What have you got in that bag? It weighs a ton."

"My physics book, remember? I brought it so if the divorce got boring, I could review. And sure enough…"

Tina closed her eyes. "I have to save you. This is too painful." She jabbed her finger at Lucy. "You go home and start throwing Bradley out. I'll make an appointment for your hair tomorrow."

"Tina. No. If I want my hair done, I will do it."

"I know this wonderful woman on Court Street.…"

"*No.*"

Tina stopped. "All right. But at least get rid of Bradley."

"Maybe." Lucy took a deep breath, full of independence. "Maybe."

"DAMN IT. I WAS SURE there'd be something about Bradley here." Zack stood.

"Your blonde's leaving," Anthony said and they both turned to watch.

They were splitting up, the brunette heading for the back door to the parking lot, the blonde to the street door. Just before she got to the door, the brunette turned.

"Lucy," she called, and it sounded like an order. "I mean it. As soon as you get home."

"All right, all right," the blonde said. "As soon as I get home, I will get rid of Bradley." Then she turned and walked out the door.

"Instinct," Zack said and took off after her.

"I hate it when you do this," Anthony said, and moved toward the parking-lot door to stop the brunette.

Two

The february wind cut at Lucy's face as she set off at a dead run to find her car, her purse banging heavily into her hip. She'd almost reached the alley next to the lot when somebody grabbed her arm, and she swung around and fell against the brick wall of the building behind her.

It was the black leather from the restaurant. "Excuse me?" he said. "We need to talk." He blocked her against the wall and reached inside his beat-up leather jacket. "I'm—"

"No." Lucy shook her head until the street blurred. "I'm very busy. Really. You probably noticed me staring at you? That was a mistake. I'm sorry. I have to go." She tried to slip away, but he caught at her arm again.

"I have to ask you about Bradley," he said, and Lucy stopped pulling away. "I'm—"

"Bradley? Oh, you mean with my sister back there? Getting rid of him? That was a joke."

He smiled down at her, and Lucy lost her breath. He was too intense to be handsome and too electric to be ignored. "I love jokes," he said. "Tell me about it."

I'd tell you anything, Lucy thought, and then she heard a sound like a car backfiring. There was a pinging sound and a chip of the brick wall behind them struck her on the cheek and the man swore and yanked her into the alley. He shoved her behind a trash bin and pinned her to the metal with his body, so close to her that her heart thudded against his chest. He was solid and a lot stronger than she was, and she tried to push him away, but he didn't budge.

"What are you doing?" Lucy tried to push him off. "Let go."

"Quiet."

He eased himself off her slightly, reached inside his jacket, pulled out a gun, and aimed it carefully at the street.

Lucy froze, part of her mind marvelling at seeing a real gun in the hand of a real felon, the rest of her mind in meltdown. *Move,* she told her feet, but she stayed frozen against him. She shoved her chin up his chest to get a better look at him, trying to decide whether he was just run-of-the-mill violent or totally deranged.

He looked big and tense and concentrated. His anvil-like jaw was clenched and his crazy blue eyes swept up and down the street.

Totally deranged.

She shifted again, and he whispered without looking at her, "Would you hold still, please?"

Please? At least he was polite.

She tried to shove him off her, but he weighed a ton, so she decided to fall back on her former strong suit: brains. "You're squashing me," she said, trying to breath around his jacket, and he eased off her a little more, just enough to give her room to lunge for the street. He caught her by the coat before she could take another step, yanking her back and yelling, "Are you crazy?"

"Me?" Lucy yelled back, trying to jerk her coat away. "What about you? Grabbing women? Let me go."

"Listen, lady," He tried to push her back behind the Dumpster. "I'm..."

"*Let go!*" She swung her purse filled with five pounds of physics book and connected with his solar plexus.

His gasp was an inverted scream, and his grip tightened on her convulsively. She jerked away again, and her shoulder bag swung up hard into his face, catching him solidly on the mouth and neatly splitting his lip. His head jerked up, and then Lucy slugged him along the temple, this time on purpose, not even wincing as his head made a *thock* sound when her book-filled bag connected. After the last blow, he let go of her and lurched back a step, and she ran down the alley in the opposite direction, propelled by so much adrenaline that when she finally rushed out into the next street, she almost ran into the patrol car that was cruising by.

"Some horrible man just grabbed me and dragged me into an alley," she said to the two patrolmen who piled out of the car. She jabbed her finger behind her. "He's big, and he's got dark hair and a big jaw, and he's wearing a horrible old black leather jacket, and he needs a shave, and he's probably a drug dealer or something!"

The two men exploded into action, the taller, younger one pounding down the alley while the older, stockier one yelled at her to wait and then followed him.

Lucy paced back and forth beside the patrol car, vibrating with energy.

Wow, *this* was what Tina was talking about. Spontaneity. This was great. This was wonderful. She felt *good.* Of course, she couldn't go around beating up every man she met, but...oh, she felt good. She felt really good.

She checked her watch. The police had been gone forty-five seconds. Einstein's theory of relativity. Of course. Time passed slower when you were moving. Here she'd been standing still, watching her life rush past her, and all she had to do was *do something* and it slowed down and became this wonderful, rich...

Oh, she felt good.

Sort of.

She slumped suddenly against the side of the patrol car, her adrenaline spent. Maybe she'd killed him. He deserved it, but maybe she really had hurt him. That physics book was heavy. What had she done? What was she doing? She looked at her watch again. A minute gone now. She couldn't stay there. She had to go. She couldn't...

Lucy put her hand up to her face in confusion and when she brought it down again, there was blood on it. Her cheek. She was bleeding.

She tore a piece of paper out of her address book, wrote her name, address and phone number on it, and left it under the windshield wiper of the cruiser. Then she went back to her car and drove home, still vibrating with the aftereffects of the adrenaline, stopping only once along the way, at a drugstore.

"SHE SAID YOU WERE A horrible drug dealer." The young patrolman grinned at Zack.

"Arrest her." Zack tried to breathe normally. He leaned on the wall by the alley, his gaze still searching the street. "Lock her in the back of the car until I can breathe again. She knows something about the Bradley job."

The young cop snorted. "She didn't look like she knew her own name."

Zack looked at him with distaste. He was tall, blond, and reasonably good-looking if you liked the movie-star type, but mostly he was just young. "Look, Junior," Zack said. "When you've been around as long as I have, you'll find out that it isn't what they look like, it's what they do." He touched his lip, and his fingers came away bloody. "Ouch."

"And I heard you were a tough guy." The younger cop grinned again.

Zack stared him down until his grin faded. "You know who you remind me of? The kid cop in *Lethal Weapon 3*. You know, the one who says, 'It's my twenty-first birthday today,' and right away you know he's dead meat? You knew the bad guys were going to drill him." Zack squinted at him. "Of course, in your case, it'll be friendly fire."

"Ha," the young cop said.

"So where's my suspect?" Zack said. "Do *not* tell me you've lost her. She's the only link we've got to an embezzler."

"My partner Falk went to get her." He grinned again. "He said he knew you, and that I shouldn't shoot you even though you were obviously a dangerous drug dealer. They're gonna love this back at the station."

Zack glared at him, and he swallowed and said, "Really, he'll be back any minute." He looked over Zack's shoulder, suddenly relieved. "See? Here he comes now."

Zack eased himself off the wall with great care. Then he looked in the patrol car as it pulled up and straightened quickly. "Where is she?"

"Wait." Falk held up his hand as he got out. He slammed the car door and waved a piece of paper at Zack. "The good news is, she left her address." He handed it over to Zack, who had slumped back against the wall. "You want Matthews and me to go pick her up?"

"'Lucy Savage,'" Zack read. "Well, the last name's right. That woman's damn near feral. No, I don't want you to pick her up. The reason I have to go pick her up now is because the two of you couldn't hold on to her. I'll handle it."

"You want us for backup? She must have been all of five-seven, maybe one thirty-five. You probably only got six inches and sixty pounds on her."

"Very, very funny" Zack pushed himself gingerly away from the wall. "Call Forensics and get some lab people down here. There's a bullet in this wall."

"Your instincts tell you that?"

"No," Zack said with obvious patience. "The chunk of wall that sliced that hellcat's cheek told me that. Somebody was shooting at her."

Matthews went over to the wall. "He's right."

"Well, of course, I'm right. Just what I need—infant cops checking my work. Will you call that in? Please?" Zack glared at the younger man, who stomped back to the car, grumbling.

"Was I ever that obnoxious?" Zack asked Falk.

"What do you mean, 'was'? You still are. You sure they weren't shooting at you? I'm serious," Falk added hastily when Zack turned his glare on him. "Not everybody loves you like we do back at the station."

"No," Zack said. "It was her." Zack looked back at the wall. "Helluva sloppy job, though. Broad daylight, not a chance of hitting her unless he was a lot closer. This guy is either a real amateur, or he was just trying to scare her and didn't care if he picked off an innocent bystander. Like me."

"You sure you don't need backup on this?"

"Yeah." Zack turned back to him. "I think I may just possibly be able to handle one medium-size woman by myself."

"I don't know. She did a nice job on you. I think you need us."

"Oh, yeah, I need you and Junior here." Zack jerked his head at the other cop who'd joined them again. "What was it, Falk? Nobody would work with you, so you stopped by the junior high for help?"

"Hey," Matthews said. "I'm twenty. I got two years of college."

"So do I," Zack said, touching his lip again gingerly. "Fat lot of good it's doing me here. Get on that bullet." He turned and walked toward the parking lot and his own car.

"Hey, Warren," Falk called after him. "Did you have one of those famous instincts of yours right before she nailed you? Or right after?"

"All great men are persecuted," Zack said and kept on walking. He knew he was right about this Bradley thing. And Lucy Savage was very shortly going to be very sorry that she and John Bradley had ever messed with him.

As soon as he took some aspirin and got some ice on his damn lip.

LUCY UNLOCKED HER massive front door with its jewel-colored leaded glass and then crossed the vestibule to unlock the beveled-glass inner door. It immediately burst open under the pressure of the three dog bodies that were pressed against it.

"Easy," Lucy said, still worn-out from her adrenaline surge. She dropped down onto the tiled floor to pet them, and they piled around her in the warm glow of the colored sunlight that streamed through the stained glass.

Einstein, the big sheepdog, flopped down beside her, but Heisenburg, the walking mop, and Maxwell, the little miscellaneous dog, both climbed into her lap to lick her face and burrow under her hands. She gathered them all to her, loving them and the warmth and color of her beautiful old house and, for once, herself.

"I beat up a mugger today," she told the dogs. "He attacked me and I beat him up. I *won*." The dogs looked suitably impressed. That was one of the many great things about dogs. They were easy to impress. Not like Tina.

But even Tina would be impressed with this. Carefully tipping the little dogs off her lap, Lucy stood and went inside the house.

Her house. Every time she walked into it, she felt safe. The living room was papered in huge flowers in shades of rose and edged with wide oak woodwork, and the floors gleamed in the soft sunlight that filtered through her lace curtains. The fat, worn, upholstered furniture was splashed with flowers, too, in roses and blues and golds, and the mantel and tables were crammed with pictures, and flowers in vases, and books. She sank into the big blue overstuffed chair by the wobbly piecrust phone table and looked through the archway into her dining room, warm with the glow of the stained-glass windows there.

Her house. She felt all the tension ease out of her. Her home.

Einstein barked at her for attention, and she remembered Tina. She dropped her purse and the bag from the drugstore on the floor and dialed her sister's number, absentmindedly scratching behind Einstein's ears while she listened to the ring.

"Tina?" she said when the ringing stopped, but it was Tina's machine, so she left a message. "This is Lucy. I wanted you to know, I just beat up a mugger. I really did, and it was *wonderful.* And don't worry, I'm okay. In fact, I'm great. You were right. I love you!"

And then she hung up and relaxed into the threadbare softness of her chair, hugging herself.

She really did feel wonderful. Sort of tired, but wonderful. Good tired.

Her gaze fell on the drugstore bag where she'd dropped it, and she stood, swooping it up as she straightened.

"Look at this," she told the dogs. "I went to the store to get disinfectant for my cheek, and right there, in the checkout line, was a big display that said 'On Sale! Discontinued! 1/2 Off!' and it was this!" With a flourish, she pulled a box out of the bag. "So I bought it."

Einstein squinted at the box, decided it wasn't biscuits, and collapsed with disappointment. Maxwell contemplated the air. Heisenburg rolled over onto his back.

Lucy ignored them to study the photo on the box: the model's hair was a rich cloud of midnight curls and she looked sultry and provocative. "This is the new me," she told the dogs. "It's time I changed. I just made a mistake with this blonde mess because I didn't think it through. I'm not the blonde type, you know?"

Maxwell and Einstein looked at each other. Heisenburg stayed on his back.

"Oh, you may laugh. But I'm changing my hair and I'm changing my life. No more mousy, timid brown or brassy, tacky blonde. I'm going to change into a whole new Lucy. I'm going to be a brunette.

Dark, fascinating, dangerous. Independent. All men will desire me. All men will fear me."

Einstein sighed, Maxwell scratched, and Heisenburg stayed on his back.

Lucy looked back at the picture on the box. "Well, maybe not. But they won't ignore me or stare at my hair in disbelief. And I'll *feel* tougher with this hair. I'll take chances. I'll date exciting men." She remembered the last exciting man she'd been attracted to, the one who had mugged her in an alley. "Well, maybe not. You know, I don't have very good taste in men. Maybe I'll hold off on the dating for a while."

Like maybe forever.

She looked down at the dogs who were staring at her now with adoration. Even Maxwell's usually glazed eyes were shining with puppy love, and Heisenburg had let his head fall back so he could worship her upside down. "I should just stick with you guys. You're the best."

Okay. No men for a while, no matter how lonely she felt. But she could still change. She could still be independent and control her life. She could do it.

"I'll tell you something else," she told the dogs. "I'm really being independent. I'm even taking back my maiden name. In fact, I already did. I just signed a note with it. And not only that, later, when I'm done, we've got *real* fun. Do you know what we're going to do?"

Einstein and Maxwell cocked an ear at the lilt in her voice. Heisenburg lay doggedly on his back.

"All right, all right," Lucy said to him, giving in to canine blackmail. "Dead dog?" Heisenburg jumped up, delirious at finally being noticed.

"You are spoiled rotten," Lucy told him. "Now as I was saying, do you know what we're going to do?"

The dogs waited.

"We're going to get rid of Bradley!" Lucy said, flinging her arms wide.

The dogs went wild with joy.

"My sentiments, exactly," she told them and went upstairs to start transforming herself.

AN HOUR AND A HALF later, Zack pulled up in front of the address Lucy Savage had left on the patrol-car windshield.

It was in an older neighborhood, close to the university and in the throes of gentrification. Some of the big old Victorians were completely restored, some hadn't been touched, and some were in transition. The Savage house was one that someone had begun to make an effort with.

Zack sat in his car and checked the place out. The three-story cream brick house, like all the others around it, was on a hill bisected by the cracked concrete driveways that consumed the narrow side yards separating the houses. A small blue Civic, its windows rolled up tightly in the February cold, sat in the driveway to the left. The drive to the right was empty.

There was no one in sight.

Great. This is why he needed a partner with him so he could say, "It's quiet...too quiet." So where was Anthony? Chasing brunettes. You couldn't trust anybody these days.

He got out of the car and climbed the concrete steps to the house.

He twisted the knob on the antique doorbell, and its hellish scream echoed through the big rooms of the house, followed by the barking of what seemed like a thousand dogs.

His grandmother had once had a doorbell like this one, and he remembered how wonderfully godawful it had sounded, the kind of ring that went right up your spine and out the top of your head. Then one day, his grandmother had had enough and put chimes in instead, and he hadn't felt the same way about his grandmother's house since.

Or his grandmother, for that matter.

And now Lucy Savage had the same godawful doorbell. It figured. Savage woman, savage doorbell.

He twisted it again. A thousand dogs barked again.

The door opened.

She was a brunette, sort of. Actually, she had the blackest hair he'd ever seen in his life on anyone. Or anything. It was the kind of dead, dull black that seemed to absorb light and air, and her face was surrounded and overwhelmed by it. For a moment, he wasn't even sure it was the same woman, and then he recognized the pointed chin and the big eyes, now widening in startled recognition. She started to slam the massive wood door, but he put his foot in it to block her. forgetting that he was wearing canvas shoes, not leather. She slammed the heavy door into his foot and yelled, "Go away. I have vicious dogs. I'm calling the police!"

"I *am* the police!" Zack clenched his teeth against the pain. He shoved his badge in against the shoe-width crack in the door. "Do you know the penalty for assaulting a police officer?"

"What?" She stared at his badge and then slumped against the doorframe, letting the door fall open. "I don't believe this. I just don't believe this."

"Believe it, lady. Can I come in, or do you want to beat on me some more?"

She stood back so he could go in, her eyes wide in her woebegone face, and Zack would have felt sorry for her if he hadn't been in so much pain.

"Thank you." He limped past her into the vestibule. She closed the door behind him and then opened the vesitbule door, and the dogs attacked.

The big sheep dog was the first to reach him. It immediately leaned heavily against his leg, shedding all over his jeans and drooling into his shoe. The little skinny brown one draped itself over Zack's uninjured foot and stared off into space at nothing in particular. And the one that looked like a floor mop barked at him once and then rolled over onto its back with all four short legs in the air arid lay there, motionless.

"These are vicious attack dogs?"

"I thought you were a mugger." She shoved her impossible hair out of her face. "And they sound vicious." They both looked down at the dogs. "Sort of."

"What's wrong with the mop?" Zack asked.

"He's not a mop. That's Heisenburg and... Never mind. Am I under arrest for beating you up?"

"You did not beat me up, lady. The only reason you hit me at all is that I wasn't defending myself because I didn't want to hurt you." Zack looked down at Heisenburg. "Is he sick?"

"No," she said. "It's a dog joke. It's the only one he knows."

"A dog joke."

"Yes. You feed him the setup, and then he does the punch line. Like a knock-knock joke."

"You taught this dog a joke?"

"No." She looked down at the mop with pride. "He thought it up on his own."

Zack looked around the spotless vestibule and through the open door. The next room was spacious, with high ceilings and hardwood floors covered with worn Oriental rugs. It was full of sunlight and comfortable, threadbare, overstuffed furniture, and he could hear a fire crackling cheerfully somewhere close. He looked at the woebegone brunette gazing down at her three dogs, and at the two dogs gazing back adoringly. And finally he looked at the third dog, Heisenburg, waiting patiently on his back for his setup line.

If this woman was a crook, he was Queen of the May. He grinned at her so suddenly that she blinked. "You're not a criminal, are you?" he asked, and she shook her head.

"Not unless you arrest me for mugging you. I deserve it. I know I deserve it. But you scared me." She frowned. "Why did you drag me into that alley?"

"We need to talk." Zack held out his hand. "I'm Detective Zachery Warren."

She took his hand and shook it. "I'm Lucy Savage, and I'm really sorry I beat you up. Your lip looks awful."

"You didn't beat me up. Would you feed this dog his line so we can go sit down?"

"Oh, no!" Lucy said, with so much enthusiasm that Zack looked to see what was wrong. "Dead dog?"

Heisenburg rolled over and jumped to his feet and barked.

Zack looked at Lucy. "That's a dog joke?"

"What did you expect? 'That was no lady, that was my wife'?"

"I don't know," Zack said, confused. "Can we go sit down? My foot is killing me."

"IF YOU DON'T MIND, I'd like to ask you a few questions before I explain about the alley," Zack began when he was finally sitting on the rose-colored love seat across from the blazing fireplace in the living room. So far, he'd turned down coffee, tea, soft drinks, aspirin, and ice for his foot from Lucy, and affectionate approaches from Heisenberg, who wanted to sit in his lap. Now he was anxious to cut to the chase and get some answers before one of the other dogs began a soft shoe or tried to sell him magazines.

"Sure," Lucy said. "Whatever."

She was sitting next to him in a big, ugly olive-green chair that didn't seem to go with the rest of the house, and she looked swallowed up by it somehow, her knees higher than her waist, her shoulders bowing in a little like folded angel wings.

"Are you all right?" Zack said. "You seem...depressed."

"I went to court to get divorced today, and my ex-husband stood me up. Then my sister decided to change my life. Then a drug dealer tried to mug me, so I beat him up, and I thought, at last, I'm doing something right, and then he turned out to be a cop. You." She blinked. "I'm having a bad day. I'll get over it."

"You didn't beat me up. I wasn't even trying to defend myself."

"Sure. Whatever."

Zack gave up. "Tell me about Bradley. Everything you know."

"Bradley?" Lucy sat back, confused. "That's what you said on the street. Why do you want to know about my ex-husband?"

"If he's the man we're looking for, he embezzled a million and a half in government bonds from the bank where he worked."

Lucy's mouth dropped open and she sat up straight. "He embezzled from his bank?"

"Banks are the best places to embezzle from," Zack said. "They usually have the most money. Now, when and where did you meet him?"

"He picked me up at the library," Lucy said, still dazed from his announcement. "I was working on some lesson plans, and I looked up, and there he was, and he asked if he could sit down, and he talked to me and bought me a juice from the vending machines, and then he walked me to my car, and two months later we were married."

"That fast?" Zack said, writing everything down.

"Well, I had my reasons." Lucy sank back in her chair and closed her eyes. "They were the wrong reasons, but I didn't know that then."

Zack wasn't listening. This could be it. The dates matched. He looked over at Lucy, sitting lost in an ugly green chair, and he felt a sudden protectiveness for her that was totally out of character for him. The poor helpless kid was just an innocent bystander. That rat Bradley...

Bradley.

Zack started to tap his notebook again. "And exactly when did you meet him?"

"And besides," Lucy went on, still lost in her own train of thought, "there was the second law of thermonuclear dynamics."

"I'm sure there was. When did you meet him?"

Lucy came back to earth. "Sorry. We got married June first. We met in the middle of March."

"And you got divorced in February." Zack looked up from his notebook. "Any particular reason? Did he begin acting suspiciously? Did you find more money in your checking account than you could account for? Any..."

"It was the blonde," Lucy said.

"Oh." Zack winced for her. "Another woman? Sorry."

"Girl, really. Very young. Maybe twenty."

"That could be his wife," Zack said.

"His wife?" Lucy said faintly.

"Uh, yeah. Sorry to drop it on you like that. He was married."

"Oh," Lucy said.

"Bianca Bradley. Also blonde and young, twenty-four. He must have a thing for blondes." Zack looked at Lucy's impossible black hair and looked back as his notebook. "So..."

"That's funny," Lucy said. "Her maiden name was the same as his Christian name."

"No, her maiden name is Bergman. She..."

"Where did the Bradley come from?"

"What Bradley?" Zack said.

"Her last name."

"When she married John Bradley," Zack said, his patience wearing thin. "The same John Bradley you married."

"I didn't marry John Bradley." Lucy sat up straight. "I married Bradley Porter. I don't believe this. You've been asking me questions about the wrong Bradley. What's going on?"

Three

—◄►—

"This is the dumbest thing I've ever heard," Lucy said. "I mean, first you grab me in an alley—"

"Listen." Zack fixed his eyes her. "John Talbot Bradley is six-five and weighs about two hundred pounds. He has brown hair and brown eyes, and he's in very good physical condition. He used to be a high-school phys-ed teacher. Does he sound like your ex-husband?"

Lucy opened her mouth and Zack held up his hand. "Think about it before you answer. I know it sounds dumb, but think about it."

Lucy shook her head. "No. Bradley's blond and good-looking and a little out of shape. I bought him sweats once so he could run with me, and he told me that physical exertion was for people who didn't use their minds. The height is close. But his eyes are gray."

Zack began to slap his notebook with his pencil. "He still might be able to pull it off. You met him in March and that's when John Bradley went missing in California."

Lucy shook her head again. "Then definitely not. I met him in March, but he'd already been branch manager of his bank for a year."

"Branch manager of a bank?" Zack stopped frowning. "Two Bradleys, two banks. And then the phone tip and the diner. There's got to be a connection here. All my instincts tell me there's a connection."

"All my logic tells me there isn't," Lucy said.

"Your logic is wrong," Zack said absently.

"I beg your pardon?"

"Why were you in that diner today?"

"I told you, I was at the courthouse...."

"Were you supposed to meet Bradley at the diner?"

"Not exactly. I was supposed to meet Bradley at the courthouse. But he'd sent me a note, asking me to have lunch with him at the diner after the hearing, and then when he didn't show up at the courthouse and my sister Tina wanted to talk, I suggested the diner, just in case he'd be there."

"So you went to the diner to meet Bradley."

"No," Lucy said patiently. "I wasn't even sure he'd be there. But Tina insisted on lunch so she could convince me to become spontaneous and irresponsible, and I picked the diner just in case he might be there. And then thanks to her, I beat up a cop."

"You did not beat up a cop. I told you, I wasn't fighting back." Zack leaned forward until he was almost touching her, his blue eyes blazing into hers. "Now, listen. *Concentrate.*"

Lucy blinked at the heat in his gaze. "Okay," she said, trying to remember what they'd been talking about. He was doing something to her brain, scrambling her thoughts. *I bet he's murder on cell phones*, she thought, and then dragged her attention back to what he was saying.

"My partner and I were there because a woman called and told us that Bradley was going to be there," Zack said, speaking very clearly as if he thought she was slightly backward. "That is all she said. 'Bradley's going to be at Harvey's Diner on Second at one.' Now, could that have been your sister?"

Lucy pulled back a little so she could think. "My sister would love to see Bradley arrested and shot, but even she wouldn't call and tell you he was going to be there if there wasn't any reason for you to arrest him. Trust me, Tina does not think that Bradley is involved in a crime. And neither do I. And neither do you. You're just annoyed because your instincts failed you."

"No," Zack said. "Somebody shot at you this afternoon. Remember when I grabbed you by the alley?"

"Vividly."

He leaned forward suddenly and touched the cut on her cheek, and she jerked back. "How did you get that?"

"A car hit a stone...."

Zack shook his head. "Somebody shot at you and missed and the bullet kicked back a piece of the brick wall. I saw it hit you. That's why I dragged you into the alley."

"Oh." Lucy digested the information. "So you thought you were saving my life while I thought you were mugging me."

"I didn't *think* I was saving your life, I..."

"And then I beat you up. I'm really sorry."

Zack closed his eyes and then looked at Lucy again. "Listen to me carefully. Somebody is trying to kill you."

She glared at him. "Listen to *me* carefully. Nobody is trying to kill me, and if you looked at this logically, you would see that."

"Wait a minute."

"There are two people standing against the wall. One of these people is a mild-mannered high-school teacher whose students all adore her. The other is a condescending police officer who grabs innocent women and drags them into alleys and who has probably alienated everyone in the greater Riverbend area. Now, which of these two people is most likely to be shot at?"

"You," Zack said. "My instincts tell me you."

"Your instincts stink," Lucy said and blinked. "I'm sorry. I'm usually not rude. I've had a bad day."

"That's all right," Zack said. "People are rude to me all the time."

He shoved his notebook back in his jacket and stood. "Listen, we'll argue about this later. Right now, I'm going to look around the outside of your house. You stay inside."

Lucy stood, too. "I beg your pardon?"

"Inside. You. And the dogs." Zack looked down at Heisenberg. "Stay. All of you."

Lucy put her hands on her hips and glared at him. "Who do you think you are?"

"Me?" Zack said on his way out. "I'm the guy who saved your life, so you owe me. Stay put."

He glanced back and grinned at her as he went out the door. Lucy said, "Listen, you, you didn't..." and then he was gone.

"Who does he think he is?" she asked the dogs. "He just comes in here, out of the blue, and tells me somebody's been shooting at me, and orders me around. Just what I needed. Somebody else ordering me around."

Only she hadn't let him. She'd fought back.

And it really felt good.

"I think I'm on to something with this independence thing," she told the dogs. "I really enjoyed arguing with him."

Of course, it hadn't had much effect on him. He'd just glared at her and charged on ahead. And he hadn't been all that mad, anyway. A minute after the glare, he'd been grinning at her again. She pictured him again, those bright blue eyes heating her and that crazy grin scrambling her thoughts, and she had to remind herself that she was mad at him. "This is my problem," she told the dogs. "I'm too easygoing. I should be mad at him. I should want to *kill* him." She stopped on the last thought.

He'd said somebody was trying to kill her.

Who would want to kill her? That was ridiculous. That was something that happened on TV. A car backfired and kicked up a stone. People did not go around shooting guns in downtown Riverbend.

He must be wrong.

Wrong, but gorgeous.

She pictured him again, much against her better judgment. That grin, that swagger, those blue, blue eyes that connected with hers with such impact on her breathing. "The thing is," she told the dogs, "even though I know he's a policeman, he doesn't look like a policeman. He looks like a very, very sexy bad guy."

She heard a noise in the vestibule and looked up to see Zack leaning in the doorway, and she blushed so hard she almost passed out.

"You talk to the dogs," he said.

"Well, of course I talk to the dogs." Lucy prayed he hadn't heard what she'd said. "It's not like I talk to plants or anything nonsentient."

"What I was going to ask was why you have such expensive locks on this place. You must have dropped a small fortune on the front doors alone, and from what I can see from the front, the windows are locked, too."

"Oh, they are," Lucy said, eager for a change of subject. "Even the attic windows. Did they really cost a lot?"

"So they weren't your idea." Zack looked satisfied. Smug, even. "Bradley ordered them, right?"

"No. It was my sister."

His satisfaction disappeared. "Your sister was afraid you'd be robbed?"

"No, my sister hates my ex-husband. She did it to annoy him. She said it was to keep him from taking anything out of the house that I might possibly be able to strip him of in the divorce. My sister plays hardball in divorce court."

"I bet she does," Zack said, taking out his notebook again. "And when was this?"

"Oh, she had them put on as soon as I told her about...the blonde. I mean, within the hour, the locksmith was here with a crew. That was about two weeks ago." Lucy thought back. "The end of January."

Zack went out to the vestibule. "Do you have burglar alarms?" he called back to her.

"No." Lucy followed him. "Look at this place. Does it look like it needs a burglar alarm?"

Zack glanced around the high-ceilinged hall. "It's not bad. It'll be nice when it's fixed up. So, for protection, you've got the locks and the dogs." He looked down at the three dogs who had followed them to the vestibule and were now sitting in a row, watching him.

"Don't make fun of my dogs," Lucy said.

"I'm not making fun of your dogs. Dogs are a good deterrent for thieves. They make noise. Thieves hate noise. Killers aren't crazy about it, but they'll cope."

Lucy folded her arms. "Nobody is trying to kill me."

Zack spread his arms wide. "Look. Humor me, okay? Just in case somebody really is trying to get you?"

"Who would want to get me?"

He cocked his head at her. "Well, ex-husbands have been known to go after the wives who locked them out of their houses."

"Bradley didn't want this house. He signed the divorce papers without a fight. He didn't want the house or me." Lucy stopped. "Sorry about that last part. I'm not really that pathetic, it's just that—"

"You're not pathetic at all." Zack flashed his grin at her. "Bradley, however, must be an idiot."

"Thank you," Lucy said.

"You're welcome," Zack said. "Now stay inside."

ZACK WALKED AROUND the house, checking the windows and the back door. The basement door was in the back near the neighbor's alley on the right, an old-fashioned, sloping wood door that had two metal bars across it, both with locks. The locks, like every other one he'd seen on the house, were very new, very efficient, and very expensive. Sister Tina either hated Bradley a whole lot or really worried about Lucy.

And possibly she had a reason to be worried. Zack frowned at the scratches on the basement-door lock. He was peering into the lock with his penlight when someone screamed at him, startling him so much that he dropped the light as he spun around.

"I've called the police so you might as well run off like all those other young punks," she screeched. "Go on. Go on!"

"Damn it, lady, you scared the hell out of me!"

The gray and wizened woman on the back porch of the next house was hunched over the rail in a nothing-colored coat three sizes too big for her. Her clawlike hands waved at him while the pleats of skin on her face worked soundlessly for the moment in indignation. Then her voice came back.

"Get out," she screeched. "Smart-mouthed good-for-nothing!"

"Excuse me, ma'am," Zack said, gritting his teeth. "I was startled. I'm a police officer."

"Well, if you are, the world's in worse trouble than I thought, and I thought it was in the toilet." She stared at him viciously, and Zack wondered briefly about the evil eye. If such a thing was possible, this hag could deliver.

"Hello, Mrs. Dover," Lucy called out from the back door. "It's all right. He's with the police."

"I knew this neighborhood was finished when you moved in," Mrs. Dover shouted back. "Torturing my cat. Bringing those vicious dogs in. Coming and going at all hours."

"Lovely day, isn't it?" Lucy came out onto the porch and looked down at Zack.

"Torturing her cat?" Zack asked and Lucy shook her head.

"Phoebe hasn't been the same since the Porters moved in," Mrs. Dover said. "I've called the humane society, but they won't do anything. Oh, no."

"Usually the sun doesn't come out much in February," Lucy said brightly to no one in particular. "We're very lucky today."

"And now this trash." She gestured at Zack. "Does your husband know you're entertaining hoodlums?"

"Actually, I'm divorced now, Mrs. Dover. And Detective Warren really isn't a hoodlum. I made the same mistake, too, but he's really very nice." She looked at Zack. "I think it's your jaw and the five o'clock shadow. I know you can't do anything about your jaw, but you would look much more reassuring if you'd shave. And get a haircut. Really."

"Thank you," Zack said.

A patrol car pulled up in front.

"Maybe he's the police." Mrs. Dover climbed down her back porch steps while she kept an eye cocked on Zack. "Maybe. But I bet he's on the Most Wanted list. Ha! We'll know soon." She nodded and hobbled down her driveway to the street to meet the uniforms.

"Great," Zack said. "This makes the second time today somebody's called the cops on me."

"Well, as I was saying, I think your image needs work. I realize you're probably undercover—"

"No, I'm not."

"Oh. Sorry."

"Forget it." Zack started for the street. Then he screamed in pain.

A large dirty yellow cat had leaped on his leg, burying her claws deeply into his calf through his jeans. Zack kicked out, and the cat dropped away while Mrs. Dover screeched at him from the street.

"Meet Phoebe," Lucy said.

"Damn!" Zack nursed his shin. "What's wrong with that animal?"

"I think she's psychotic. I hate her because she uses my car for a litter box so I have to keep the windows rolled up all the time, even in the summer. And because all three of my dogs are terrified of her."

"Her, who?" Zack glared at Mrs. Dover's back as she gestured wildly to the police in the street. "The woman or the cat?"

"Both," Lucy said. "Do you want some iodine?"

"No," Zack said, as a young patrolman approached him. "I want to shoot that damn cat."

"Sir?" the patrolman began. "This lady has a complaint."

Zack looked at him closely. "How old are you? Twelve?"

The young patrolman stiffened. "Sir…"

Zack got out his badge again. "I'm sorry. I'm having a bad day. I'm investigating an attempt on this woman's life." He nodded toward Lucy.

"You are not," Lucy said. "They shot at you, not me."

"Shut up." Zack looked at the patrolman. "Do you ever get tired of defending the public?"

"All the time," the patrolman said. "I'll just have to call this in, sir…" he began, looking at Zack's ID, and then he, too, screamed.

"Shoot the cat," Zack said. "It's assaulted two officers and resisted arrest. Do it."

Mrs. Dover hissed at him, scooped up Phoebe, and disappeared into her house.

"Is this some kind of a joke?" the patrolman asked, nursing his shin.

"No. Tragically, no. Go ahead and call that in." Zack looked up at Lucy as the patrolman made his way back to the car. "What does it mean when everyone you see is younger than you are?"

"It means you're getting old. There's a new teacher at my school. She asked me yesterday what it was like in the old days when I first started teaching."

"Did you deck her?"

"No." Lucy stuck out her chin. "But I may when I go back in to school tomorrow. I've gotten a lot meaner today."

Zack laughed. She looked so funny, neat and round with all that crazy dead black hair haloing her face, calmly announcing that she was a lot meaner today. What a sweetheart.

Dumb as a rock, but sweet.

"You're not going back to school tomorrow," he told her. "You're moving in with your sister until I figure out what's going on."

Lucy frowned. "How long will that take? Especially if you're going to figure it out by instinct. I don't have that much sick leave. I don't think anybody does."

She wasn't that sweet. Zack glared at her, and she blinked.

"Sorry," Lucy said. "I don't know what's gotten into me today."

"Forget sick leave," Zack said. "How much dead leave do you have? I'm not kidding here. You could be in danger."

"I think—"

"Don't. Trust me on this one. I know what I'm doing. Somebody's been trying to pick your locks."

"What?"

Zack pointed his finger to the back door behind her. "There are scratches on your back-door lock, and there's a piece of metal broken off inside this basement-door lock. Somebody's been trying to get in here."

Lucy swallowed. "Bradley?"

"Well, that would be my best guess. He may just be trying to get his golf clubs back. But then again..." He shrugged. "Somebody shot at you on the street today."

"At you," Lucy said, but her voice held a lot less conviction.

"Just stay with your sister for a while. She's got room, right?"

"Oh, she's got room. But I'm not going. She can't take the dogs, and I'm not leaving them." Lucy stuck her chin in the air. "Besides, I don't believe this."

Zack lost his temper and stomped up the back porch steps. He grabbed her arm and pulled her around to face the door as he pointed at the lock. "See those scratches?" His face was so close to hers they were almost nose-to-nose. "Those were made by a pointed metal tool. Somebody was trying to break in."

Lucy blinked at his closeness. "Well, they didn't get in, did they? So I must be pretty safe."

"Only because they're trying to be subtle for some reason. Sooner or later, they're just going to smash a window and climb in. Lord knows why they haven't already. I advise you to move to your sister's."

"No," Lucy said.

Zack let go of her arm and closed his eyes and counted to ten. Then he looked down at her with all the patience he could muster.

She looked up at him, wide-eyed and trusting.

Oh, hell. If somebody did hit her, it'd be his fault for not taking care of her.

He forced himself to speak calmly. "Look, just do me one favor. Stay inside tonight. I'll call you when I find out more tomorrow, okay? And I'll have the patrol car keep an eye on you. Just until we can get a handle on your Bradley and see what he's up to."

Lucy opened her mouth to speak, and he overrode her again. "Just for tonight and tomorrow. That's not much to ask. Please."

"I'd have to leave, anyway," Lucy said. "I'm a teacher. Even if I wasn't going in to school tomorrow, I'd have to take in lesson plans."

Zack looked again into Lucy's huge brown eyes and thought again about how much she needed a keeper.

Not him, of course.

Still...

"I will take them in. Now, about this sick-leave thing. How long have you been teaching?"

"Twelve years."

"And how many sick days have you taken?"

"None."

"That's what I figured. So how many do you have saved up?"

"One hundred and thirty-eight," Lucy said.

"So if you use a couple, you could still develop a major disease and have everything covered, right?"

"Right," Lucy said, "but that's not the point. The point is, I'm not sick."

Why was it he finally found an honest citizen only when it worked against him? "Look. Think of this guy who's trying to kill you as a life-threatening illness. I do."

"I really think—"

"I told you, don't think. Just do what I tell you. If it will help, I'll shave and put on a suit and come back and tell you to stay inside. I'll do whatever it takes. Because I really do think you're in danger." He gestured to the basement door. "These are all good locks. Take advantage of them. Stay inside and I'll call you tomorrow."

"Well..." Her pointed face was so confused under all that dead black hair that suddenly Zack's annoyance faded and he felt protective again. She seemed so helpless, so soft and round and absolutely clueless about reality.

"Please," he said. "Just for tonight."

"All right." Lucy swallowed at his earnestness. "But I still think you're wrong. Anyway, if you give me a couple of minutes, I'll print out the lesson plans. This is very nice of you. Thank you, Detective Warren."

"Zack." He grinned at her in relief. "Detective Warren is for people who haven't hit me with a purse."

Lucy smiled back uncertainly. "Zack." She hesitated. "I'm Lucy." Then she turned and went back inside.

Cute. A little snippy but very cute. Even with the hair. Very, very cute. And she thought he was sexy.

Maybe he could convince her that he really had saved her life, and she'd be grateful.

He tried to picture Lucy, naked and grateful, but all he could see was Lucy, blinking at him, surrounded by dogs.

That could be a bad sign. He was losing his ability to fantasize.

Maturity.

Death.

"Sir?"

Zack turned back to the patrolman who had joined him again.

"You're cleared," the patrolman said. "What's going on here, anyway?"

"I'm not sure," Zack said. "I need you to question the neighbor."

"The old lady?"

"Yeah. I don't think she's going to talk to me."

"I don't think so, either. She wanted me to shoot you. So what do you want me to ask her?"

"She said she'd seen somebody hanging around here, possibly trying to break in. And the locks have been tampered with." Zack frowned back at the house. "Find out what she saw, and when she saw it, and get it to me as fast as you can, okay?"

"You got it. Anything else?"

"Yeah. Keep a close eye on this place for the next couple of days. I think she might really have trouble."

"With neighbors like she's got, that's no big deduction," the patrolman said.

"You should see her sister," Zack said.

"I ALMOST INVITED HIM back in," Lucy told the dogs when Zack had driven away with the lesson plans. "That would have been stupid." She pulled back the lace curtain at the front window and looked out at the empty street. "He was just so different, you know? I just didn't want him to go. So much for my new life. I make these big plans to be independent, and then I cling to the first man I meet an hour after my divorce. Still, you should have been there when he told the other policeman to shoot Phoebe. You would have loved it."

She dropped the curtain and turned to the living room.

Her room.

Her house.

She remembered the first time she'd seen it. She'd passed it one day when she'd taken a wrong turn near the university. A big old cream brick house on a hill with a porch and a cracked old driveway and big beautiful beveled-glass windows.

And a For Sale sign in front.

And she'd wanted that house with a passion that she'd never in her life felt for a man. A big, safe, *warm* house she could fill with dogs and books and comfortable things. Beautiful things. A house with a big kitchen where she could make cookies and bread and soup. A house with a huge fenced-in backyard where Einstein could run. And maybe another dog. Or two. She didn't want Einstein to be an only child.

A house. A house instead of her cold, tiny little apartment where Einstein took up half the floor space, and the oven didn't work right, and she never felt safe. A house.

Her house.

After that, for three months, even after she started seeing Bradley, she'd drive by the house and long for it hopelessly, the way some women long for movie stars. She knew it would never be hers but it was the dream of her heart. And then one day she'd been with Bradley and they'd driven by, and she'd said, "Slow down so I can see my house," and he'd asked her what she meant, and she'd told him. And he'd said, "If we were married, we could buy that house. Will you marry me?"

And she'd said, "Yes."

What she hadn't realized at the time was that she was saying "Yes" to the house, not to Bradley.

"Maybe it wasn't a mistake," she told the dogs as she moved back into the room. "At least we have the house."

It sounded cynical. And selfish. Tina would be pleased.

Einstein barked at her.

"I know," Lucy told him. "I should pull myself together and stop talking to dogs. Well, you're the only ones who listen to me without telling me what to do. Especially Tina, lately…"

Tina. Telling her to get rid of Bradley. Actually, packing up all his stuff in a box might be another small step toward independence. She wouldn't throw it out on the lawn, of course, but she could store it neatly in the basement. That would make the house seem more like it was hers alone.

Alone.

With Zack gone, she suddenly felt alone, as if something warm was missing.

She wasn't sure she wanted to be alone. Especially if Zack was right about the shooting and the scratches… Except of course, he wasn't right because it was ridiculous that anyone would be threatening her, and besides there was probably a perfectly good explanation for those scratches.… And if there wasn't, what was he doing leaving her alone? He should be there, protecting her. Obviously he didn't think she was in danger, or he wouldn't have left her alone.

Alone.

Of course, she wasn't alone. She had the dogs.

And besides, there were some kinds of alone that were good. In fact, wonderful. For example, the without-Bradley kind of alone was heaven. No more chill in the air, no more one-right-way-to-do-things, no more long silences and emptiness. Just her and the dogs and the fireplace. Warm.

And alone.

"Enough of this daydreaming stuff," Lucy told the dogs, suddenly straightening. "We have work to do. Let's get rid of Bradley."

Lucy packed up everything of Bradley's that she could find in the house, surprised to find it filled three boxes, not one. "There was more to Bradley than I thought," she told the dogs. Most of the stuff was papers and books. His clothes were already gone; Tina had thrown them all out the front door while the locksmiths were changing the locks. By the time Bradley had come back that night, his entire wardrobe was on the front lawn.

Mrs. Dover had enjoyed it immensely.

He hadn't argued much. He'd knocked on the door and called her name, and then Tina had opened it and threatened him, and he'd gone away.

Not much of a fighter, Bradley.

Not much of a lover, either.

Or maybe that was just with her. Maybe he was better with the blonde.

The blonde. Lucy tensed as she remembered the shock she'd felt when she'd come home to find the blonde standing in the middle of the living room. Her living room. Saying that she and Bradley had been together in the house. Her house. Her bedroom. How could she have been so stupid, not to even have had a clue? How could Bradley do that to her?

He had just stood there with his mouth working like a fish, saying he could explain.

Except he never had.

He was a creep. Bringing that woman into her house. Her house. What a creep.

At least she was free of him now.

Her eyes fell on the boxes.

Or she soon would be.

She stood, gently displacing Einstein's head from her knee, and carried Bradley's boxes to the basement door. She set them down, opened the door, picked them up again, and threw them down the stairs, watching them turn and smash against the steps as they fell.

"Too bad there wasn't anything breakable," she told the dogs, and shut the door.

Then she went back into the living room and studied it. Beautiful. Bradley-less. Un-Bradleyed.

Almost.

His chair still sat in the middle of the room beside the love seat. It was ugly—a recliner upholstered in synthetic olive-green flecked with red. If Bradley had been born a piece of furniture, he would have looked like that chair. Practical, boring, and irritating. The fact that he'd loved it and wouldn't let the dogs on it only made it more Bradley-like. The dogs had been napping on it regularly since he'd gone, but it was still an annoyance.

"What do you think?" Lucy asked the dogs. "Getting rid of a perfectly good chair would be totally irresponsible, right?"

The dogs cocked their heads at her.

"Right. Just think how proud of us Tina will be." Lucy opened the basement door. Then she pushed the chair to the doorway, shooing Maxwell away just in time, and shoved the chair down the stairs. Halfway down, it hit the stair rail and broke through it, tumbling over the side of the steps to smash on the concrete below in a small cloud of dust.

"Independence Day," Lucy said, and slammed the door.

Four

→ ←

"So then she said, 'You mean that hood is following my sister?' and tried to take off after you," Anthony told Zack an hour later. They were back in the squad room, their feet propped up on their desks in the thin warmth of the dusty late-afternoon sunlight that filtered through the dirty windows. "I almost let her have you. I was hoping she'd rip that damn jacket off you and shred it. But then I remembered you were my partner, and I saved you."

"Thank you." Zack was stretched out in his desk chair, feeling every bruise that Lucy had given him that afternoon. "I gather she did finally talk to you?"

"Of course."

"There's no 'Of course' about it," Zack said. "Lucy told me about her sister. You're lucky you're still in one piece."

"We had coffee in the diner." Anthony stretched and put his hands behind his head. "She was no problem at all."

"You get the mean one, and she drinks coffee from your hand. I get the nice one, and she tries to beat the tar out of me. God, to have your luck."

"It's not luck. It's charm," Anthony said. "You don't have any."

Zack gave up. "So what does Tina Savage know about Bradley Porter?"

"That he's a womanizing, weak-kneed, slime-covered scum who made her sister cry, so he should be shot, strangled, drawn, quartered, and castrated. I don't think she likes him at all."

Zack scowled. "He made Lucy cry? I'm with her, then."

"But the problem is…"

"He's not our Bradley." Zack nodded. "I know. Lucy explained that. I'd hoped for a while there was a chance he might be, but she says it's no-go."

"I know," Anthony said. "But I floated the possibility by the sister anyway, just to see what she'd say."

"And?"

Anthony grinned. "Oh, she's in favor of it. The thought of Bradley in jail for bigamy, embezzlement and tax fraud perked her right up. She was completely cordial by the time she'd thought it through." Anthony shook his head. "This is a waste of time, Zack. Granted somebody shot at you today, that still doesn't necessarily tie Lucy Savage's Bradley Porter with our John Bradley."

Zack scowled. "He's not Lucy's Bradley. He's nobody's Bradley, the rat. And there's got to be a tie. Come on, Tony. We get a tip that John Bradley's going to be at the diner, and Bradley Porter asks Lucy to meet him there on the same day? That's too much of a coincidence."

"Maybe." Anthony leaned back. "I'm not convinced."

Zack stared at the ceiling while he thought. "So what have we got? We've got John Bradley somewhere in the city with a million and a half in embezzled government bonds. We've got Bradley Porter somewhere in the city with an unidentified blonde. We've got an unidentified female caller who tips us that John Bradley will be at the diner. We've got Bradley Porter's letter to Lucy telling her to meet him at the diner, or we will have as soon as she remembers what she did with it. And we've got somebody shooting at Lucy."

"Or you," Anthony put in. "Don't underestimate your unpopularity."

"Or me," Zack amended. "Hell of a coincidence, though, to get shot at when Lucy's right beside me. So what have we got?"

"We have nothing."

"The two Bradleys have got to be in it together," Zack said.

"I suppose it's remotely possible," Anthony said. "If Bradley Porter is keeping a blonde on the side, he could probably use a couple of government bonds. But it's hard to believe that John Bradley would steal the bonds in California and then come clear out here to share with Bradley Porter out of the goodness of his heart."

"Blackmail?"

"Let's not make this any more complicated than it already is. Here's a good question. Why would somebody try to shoot Lucy?"

"Bradley's mad at her about the divorce," Zack said.

"So he shoots at her on the street? I don't think so."

"Here's a better one. Why is somebody trying to break into Lucy's house?"

Anthony jerked his head up, suddenly interested. "Somebody's trying to break into her house?"

"There are scratches on her locks, and the next-door neighbor saw somebody sneaking around the house. Granted, the next-door neighbor is not totally wired, but even so, if she says she saw somebody, I bet she did."

"You interviewed the next-door neighbor?"

"No." Zack looked pained. "She won't talk to me. She thinks I'm a punk. I had the patrolman ask her."

"A punk. That's not so bad." Anthony grinned at him. "At least punks are young."

"Thank you."

"So you think somebody's trying to break in to get Lucy?" Anthony shook his head. "That doesn't make sense. There are a hundred easier ways to grab somebody than breaking into a house. Hell, you grabbed her on the street today." Anthony looked at Zack's lip. "Well, it might not be that easy. She does seem to have a fairly healthy sense of self-preservation."

Zack gave him a dirty look. "I was trying not to hurt her. If I'd wanted her, I'd have had her. Hell, anybody could have grabbed her."

"So they're breaking in for something else." Anthony leaned back in his chair. "Like to get a million and a half in government bonds that John Bradley gave to Bradley Porter who put them in the silverware drawer and then forgot to take with him when Lucy kicked him out? I don't think so."

"Wait a minute." Zack swung his chair around and planted his feet back on the floor. "He couldn't get in. Tina put locks on. She wouldn't let him in."

"So he just went meekly away and left a million and a half there? No," Anthony said. "I bow to no one in my respect for Tina Savage's temper, but I'd walk over her in a minute if it meant a million and a half. Particularly a million and a half that could put me away if somebody else found it. Like my ex-wife. No."

"Something's in that house, and the two Bradleys are involved." Zack drummed his fingers on the desk. "I've got to get her out of that house until we find it. Only the dummy won't go."

"Can't she stay with her sister for a while?"

"No. She won't go without Einstein and Heisenburg and Whosis. She won't budge at all." His scowl changed suddenly. "At least I hope she hasn't budged."

"Einstein?" Anthony said, but Zack ignored him to flip through his notebook until he found the page he wanted and then dialed the number he'd found.

"Lucy? This is Zack Warren." He listened for a moment. "I'm fine, thanks. I was just checking to make sure you hadn't gone out." He listened again, looking exasperated. "No, I don't trust you. Because you're a flake, that's why. Now, listen, did Bradley leave any papers behind? He did? Have you looked at them? Great. Did you find any official-looking certificates? No, I'm not patronizing you. Did you find any government bonds? A lot of them. About a hundred of fifty, to be exact. Oh."

He covered the receiver and spoke to Anthony. "She packed up all his stuff. No bonds."

"I gathered that," Anthony said. "Maybe he hid them. Did she check the cookie jar?"

Zack ignored him. "Lucy, do you have a safe anyplace in the house? Any place where you keep your valuables? No?" Zack sighed and tapped his fingers on the desk. "Listen. We're going to have to come over tomorrow and search your place. Yeah, sometime tomorrow. Now, listen to me. *Stay in that house and don't answer the door tonight.* And stay away from the doors and windows. Those lace curtains are a joke. When the lights are on, anybody can see in. Why? *Because I said so.* What do you mean, who do I think I am? I'm the guy who saved your life today. Yes, I did, damn it. What?" He listened to her again, frowning. "I told you, you did not beat me up. Thank you. *Now stay inside that house.* Good night."

He hung up and glared at the phone. "I don't know why I worry about that woman. She could *argue* any attacker to death."

"I thought you were never going to worry about anybody," Anthony said, trying to suppress his grin. "I thought responsibility meant death. And what's with you calling her 'Lucy'? The two of you are on a first-name basis already? What's going on?"

"She has a dog that does a dog joke." Zack rolled his eyes in disgust. "It's the most pathetic thing I've ever seen. She's all alone in that big house with three of the most un-vicious dogs that ever barked. She was married to a rat, and now somebody's taking potshots at her. *Somebody* has to look out for her."

Anthony began to laugh. "Zack, she split your lip and gave you what the doctor calls a minor concussion. He said you should be home in bed. You're talking about a woman who beat you up in an alley."

"She did not..."

"All right, all right. So what's the plan? To search the house tomorrow?" Anthony shook his head. "I hate to tell you this, but we've still got paperwork from Jerry this morning to finish. I can put it off for a little while, but not the whole morning. Isn't there some way we can short-circuit this search thing?"

"Yeah," Zack said. "We can go to interview Bradley Porter first and see if we can get him to spill everything he knows. Lucy told me he's a branch manager of a bank out in Gamble Hills. Nobody knows where he's staying right now, but he'll be at work tomorrow. We can start with him first." He stared at the ceiling again. "Actually, I'm really looking forward to meeting him."

Anthony narrowed his eyes. "Why?"

"I want to see what a rat like that looks like. You wouldn't believe what a sweetheart Lucy is."

"A sweetheart?" Anthony grinned. "She beat you up."

"She did not..." Zack closed his eyes and gave up. "Forget it. I'm sore. My head hurts. I need a hot bath and a beer. I cannot argue with you anymore. You win. She beat me up."

"When you can't fight, we're definitely finished for the day." Anthony stood. "Want some help getting down to your car, old man?"

"Drop dead," Zack said, and got up carefully, trying not to groan from his bruises.

BEFORE LUCY WENT UP to bed, she found the phone table on its side and the receiver thrown off its hook.

"Did you do this?" she said to Einstein as she righted the table, and he immediately turned and walked away. "Most nights I wouldn't care," she said to his swaying rear end. "But tonight I thought maybe I might actually get another call from him."

Einstein turned his head and looked at her over his shoulder.

"Right," Lucy said. "That is pathetic."

Then she put the phone back on the table and went up to bed.

LUCY GOT UP TO RUN at eight on Friday morning, but she stopped at the front door.

She wasn't supposed to go out. Every muscle in her body wanted to run, but she wasn't supposed to go out.

Zack Warren had forbidden it.

"I don't believe this," she told the dogs. "He just says 'Stay put,' and I stay put. And today was supposed to be the first day of the rest of my independence. If I had any backbone at all..."

On the other hand, he said he was coming by to search the house. She had to be home for that. It was her civic duty. Sort of.

Also, she didn't want to miss seeing him again.

She sighed and started to run up the stairs. Two steep flights. About a thousand trips up and down should do it.

But just for today. Tomorrow, she was going out to run like a rational human being, no matter what Zack Warren said.

"HE TOOK TWO WEEKS OFF?" Zack glared at the immaculate matron behind the mahogany manager's desk at Gamble Hills First National. She wore her dark hair styled like a helmet, and she glared back at him militarily through horn-rimmed glasses.

Zack scowled at her. "How can a bank manager take two weeks off?"

"He was getting a divorce." She jerked on the cuffs of her navy polyester suit jacket for emphasis. "He was very disturbed about it. The past two weeks, he couldn't concentrate at all. Mr. Porter was always very efficient, so it wasn't like him. Not at all. We all understood that he needed a little time off."

"We appreciate your help, Mrs. Elmore," Anthony said, trying to reduce the fallout from Zack's scowl. He was rewarded with a slight smile and a nod. "We have just a few more questions and we'll go. We know how busy you must be with Mr. Porter gone. Now, his last day was yesterday?"

"Day before yesterday." Mrs. Elmore lowered her voice. "Yesterday was the Divorce."

"Ah." Anthony smiled at her in sympathy. "This must make a lot of extra work for you."

The woman smoothed her jacket and smiled complacently. "I don't mind. It's the least I can do for the poor man."

"The poor man?" Zack said, thinking of Lucy.

Mrs. Elmore glared at him.

"Zack, why don't you go over there and interview somebody?" Anthony jerked his thumb toward the tellers.

"Fine." As Zack wandered off, he could hear Anthony saying, "That's terrible. Mr. Porter must have been very upset for the past couple of weeks. Did he say anything..."

"Hi."

Zack turned around to see a very young, very blonde teller smiling at him.

"Can I help you with anything?" Her smile deepened.

"Full service banking?" Zack said and grinned.

"Well, we try to please," she said, dimpling at him. "I'm Deborah."

"So tell me, Deborah." Zack leaned on the ledge across from her and smiled into her eyes. "What's it like to work for Mr. Porter?"

"It's boring," Deborah said. "And I don't talk about my employers."

Zack showed her his badge. "I'm one of the good guys, Deborah. Tell me about Mr. Porter."

"You don't look like a good guy." She smiled at him again.

"Mr. Porter, Deborah. Concentrate. Other than boring, what was he?"

She shrugged. "Nothing. He came in, worked hard, and went home."

"Ever make a pass at you?"

Deborah chortled. "Mr. Porter? Not a chance. He was so crazy about his wife, he didn't even know there were other women on earth."

Zack stopped smiling. "But he just got divorced."

"Oh, that was her idea." Deborah looked around and dropped her voice. "Long overdue, if you ask me. I mean, he would have bored me to death. I met her at the Christmas party. She was really nice. Quiet, but nice. Mr. Porter showed her off like she was something he owned, but he was crazy about her. You could see it. I mean, Evan Hatch just asked her to dance, and he was furious about it. He hasn't spoken to Evan since."

"Evan Hatch?"

Deborah jerked her head to her right and Zack stepped back to look at the teller two windows down. He was about five foot four, a hundred and twenty pounds, and bald.

Zack frowned at Deborah. "Porter was jealous of him?"

"He was jealous of everybody. I told you. He was crazy about her."

Zack tried again. "I thought I heard the divorce was because he'd had an affair."

"No way," Deborah said. "It was his wife and nobody else. And listen, he had his chances. I mean, have you ever seen him?"

Zack shook his head.

"Check out his picture. It's over there." Deborah nodded her head in the direction of the big glass doors. "He's really great looking. Believe me, a lot of women were interested." She cocked her head. "Not me. I like my men a little rougher, not as handsome, if you know what I mean." She smiled at Zack again.

"And I even shaved," Zack said.

"What?"

"Nothing. So aside from being boring, he was the perfect boss?"

"Well, he was a nitpicker." Deborah made a face. "But we got used to it. And then about two weeks ago, he really let up and stopped watching us all the time. It would have been really nice, except he was so grumpy. That's when Mrs. Elmore came around and told us about the divorce. She said we should be understanding."

Zack squinted back at Mrs. Elmore. "She doesn't look like the understanding type."

"She's not," Deborah said. "Unless it's Mr. Porter."

"Oh."

"The divorce may have depressed Mr. Porter, but it cheered Mrs. Elmore right up. When he comes back, he's not going to have a chance."

"Maybe I won't arrest him then." Zack gazed over his shoulder at Mrs. Elmore. "That could be punishment enough."

Deborah's mouth dropped open. "You're going to arrest him?"

"No." Zack turned back hastily. "That's a little police humor. Very little. Did you notice anything else different about Mr. Porter lately? Besides the grumpiness?"

"Nope. The grumpiness was it."

"Okay, listen. Here's my card." Zack handed it over. "If you think of anything else, call me, please."

"Anything?" Deborah batted her eyelashes at him.

"Anything about Mr. Porter. You should be ashamed of yourself, trying to pick up a cop on duty."

"Don't you ever get off duty?"

"No. I live for my work." Zack turned to see Anthony waiting patiently by the door. "Well, I've got to go, my driver is waiting. Thanks, Deborah. You were a great help."

"Anytime," Deborah said. "Really."

On his way out the door, Zack stopped by the gallery of employee portraits that Gamble Hills First National had assembled to give the customers a nice feeling of family as they parted from their money. Among the dozen or so faces, Deborah dimpled, and Mrs. Elmore grimaced and, at the very top like the Big Daddy of banking, Bradley Porter stared down and was not amused.

He was classically handsome—thick wavy blond hair, a straight Roman nose, a chiseled chin with a hint of a cleft, and the coldest grey eyes Zack had ever seen.

What the hell had Lucy been thinking of to marry this...this... *fish*?

"Zack?" Anthony called from just inside the door. "You ready?"

She needed a keeper. Not him, of course, but still...

"Zack?"

"Yeah." Zack followed him out to the car.

"Another blonde?" Anthony said when Zack got in the car beside him. "Is this a trend for you?"

"Blonde?"

"The teller."

"Deborah? No. Blondes are too dangerous. I'm only interested in brunettes. Like Mrs. Elmore. Drive and tell me all about her undying passion for Bradley Porter. And then tell me what motel she's been meeting him at so we can go get him."

Anthony put the car into gear and pulled out of the parking lot. "We can't go get him. He's in Kentucky."

"Kentucky?" Zack scowled at him as if it were his fault. "What the hell is he doing in Kentucky when we want him here?"

"Communing with nature to heal his tortured soul. Or something like that. He's brokenhearted. His wife, who is cold and unfeeling, did not understand him."

"He said that? The rat. Drive to Kentucky."

"I don't think so. We have reports to fill out. And we do not have any conclusive link between our Bradley and Lucy's Bradley."

"He's not Lucy's Bradley." Zack tapped his fingers on the window edge. "I tell you what. Let's search the house. We'll find the link. Trust me on this one. I've got…"

"Reports to fill out," Anthony said.

"Oh, hell," Zack said.

THE SHOWER FELT wonderful.

The hot water stung Lucy's body and made her skin tingle, which made her think of Zack, which made her tingle more.

It was ridiculous. He'd mugged her in an alley, then he'd argued with her in her living room, and now she couldn't stop thinking about him. It was particularly ridiculous to be looking forward to seeing him again. Of course, that was mostly because he was coming to search her house, and when he didn't find anything, then he'd have to admit that he was wrong and she was right, and that the only criminal thing Bradley had ever done was bring that blonde into her house.

Lucy tested herself for pain on the last thought. Did that hurt anymore? Maybe it never had. Maybe the emotion she'd felt was more repressed rage that Bradley had brought that woman into her house. She was going to have stop repressing her rage.

She definitely wasn't feeling any pain over Bradley's blonde anymore.

And she'd lost the feeling she'd had that the house had been contaminated. That really went when she threw Bradley's chair down the stairs. That had been a wonderful moment. For just a moment, she'd felt totally out of control.

Like Zack.

Zack. What did she see in him? The man was a patronizing maniac who thought he had a hot line to the universe. Trust his instincts. Ha, as Mrs. Dover would say.

Well, sort of ha.

Actually, she was willing to bet that he had great instincts for some things. In fact, she was willing to bet that he had better instincts than she'd ever had. She was willing to bet...

Lucy stuck her head directly under the water from the showerhead, trying to wash Zack out of her mind.

Think about something else. Think about anything else.

Well, there was exercise. Like running the stairs instead of the road because some maniac with incredible instincts...

Try again.

Running the stairs was terrific for your heart, but murder on your quadriceps. Lucy glanced down to look at hers only to stop, horrified, all thoughts of Zack gone, as she stared at the water as it swirled into the drain.

It was black. The blackest water she'd ever seen.

Which meant her hair wasn't anymore.

"Oh, no," she moaned and leaned her head against the shower wall.

It left a big black smudge when she stood straight again.

Five minutes later, her body wrapped in a full-length white terry-cloth robe and her head in a terry-cloth towel, Lucy stood in front of her bedroom mirror and prayed. Then she took a deep breath, pulled the towel off her head, and stared at her hair in the mirror.

It was a strange color, like very bad moss; a sort of intensely dull, dark grey-green that absorbed all the light and energy around it.

"My hair has turned into a black hole," she said to the mirror. "Complete absence of light." She looked down at the towel. It was covered with black smudges. "How long before this washes out of my hair? How long before I'm a horrible blonde again?"

As she stared at herself, a new and even more horrible possibility hit her.

How long before it *falls* out?

Einstein waddled into the bedroom and stopped to stare.

"Independence is not working out for me," Lucy told him.

"THE LAB REPORT IS IN," Zack said when he joined Anthony back in the squad room. "The brick wall did not help the bullet at all." He tossed the report to Anthony who was typing a report of his own. "As always, Patricia will be glad to hazard an unofficial guess if we ever find another .38 to match, but she says no way will we ever have anything to take to court based on the bullet from the wall."

Anthony shoved the report out of the way and went back to typing. "So we have nothing."

"Not exactly. We have Lucy." Zack sat on the edge of his desk. "And Lucy's house, which we're going to have to search now that we can't find Bradley the rat. I need to talk to Lucy again anyway."

"Is this an instinct?" Anthony hit the return carriage.

"Oh, yeah. Definitely. I have a real instinct about Lucy Savage."

"So now the only question is, What kind of instinct?" Anthony grinned while he typed.

"What? Oh, no. Not a chance. I can't even imagine her naked."

"What?" Anthony stopped typing and started to laugh. "I don't believe it. You were the one who once described Queen Elizabeth naked."

"That was in college."

"Yeah, but I've never forgotten it." Anthony shook his head. "So now you've lost the ability to imagine women naked? That's a bad sign, Zack."

"I haven't lost anything," Zack snapped. "And it's just with Lucy. It's her fault. She's just not that kind of woman."

"And Queen Elizabeth is? I don't think so. I think you're attracted to her. You respect her. This could be it. Love. Marriage." Anthony paused. "Maturity."

"Don't be juvenile. Did you try those phone numbers that Elmore gave you for Porter? The motel in Kentucky and the one for the place where he's been staying here in town?"

"Just a couple of minutes ago. He has a room in Kentucky, but he's not answering. The one here is a hotel in Overlook. The room is rented to a guy named John Beulah. And the phone is busy."

Zack frowned. "What would Bradley Porter be doing registered under an assumed name in a hotel in Overlook?"

"Saving money? It's definitely the lowest of the low-rent districts."

"Well, then, that's our next move." Zack stood. "Let's check out the hotel right away before whoever it is gets off the phone. I love Overlook. It always makes me feel like a real cop—paranoid."

"I have to finish this first." Anthony frowned as he typed. "It's almost done. Patience."

"And after the hotel, we can hit Lucy's place," Zack said. "I think we're making progress." He started to pace. "Could you hurry up? We've got things to do here. I want to get to Lucy's before lunch."

"Just a minute. Just one minute. Amuse yourself." Anthony's phone rang and he answered, "Taylor, Property Crimes." Then he looked grim, and said, "Right away," and hung up. "We have a gunshot victim. Female."

Zack's heart stopped for a moment. "Not Lucy. Tell me I didn't leave her alone for some creep to—"

"Not Lucy. Not unless she went blonde again and checked into a hotel in Overlook."

Zack shook his head, relieved. "No. Not a chance. The dogs wouldn't like Overlook." Then he stopped. "Overlook? It can't be."

Anthony nodded. "Same room number as our rat Bradley. After I called, the desk clerk went up to check and found her unconscious, still clutching the phone. He called the rescue squad, and she's on her way to Emergency now."

"I'll be damned. He's shacked up with the blonde in the slums, and then he shoots her and leaves for Kentucky? This makes no sense. Wait. How did they know this was our problem?"

"Because they found your name and phone number on a paper in her purse. Detective Warren. Property Crimes. And you'll love this part..."

"Come on, come on."

"Shot with a .38."

Zack smacked his hand on the desk. "She's our phone tip. John Bradley found out, shot at us on the street, and then went back and shot her. So where is Bradley Porter in this? This makes no sense, but at least it's a connection between Bradley Porter and crime. Let's go."

"What about Lucy? Aren't you going to call her?"

"And tell her what?" Zack grabbed his jacket. "She'll keep. Let's go."

"What did you do, hypnotize this woman?" Anthony said, but he picked up his jacket and followed him out the door.

IT WAS EARLY AFTERNOON when Lucy's phone finally rang.

"Hello?" she answered, trying to sound nonchalant.

"You didn't call me last night," Tina said. "I got your message on the machine and called you back, but all I got was a busy signal. What happened?"

"I forgot," Lucy said, trying not to feel disappointed. She curled up in her blue overstuffed chair. "And the busy signal was Einstein. He knocked the phone table over."

"Why you don't have everything bolted to the floor in that place is beyond me. If you must live with a herd of animals, you should be prepared. Anyway, tell me about the mugger. You really beat one up? That's terrific!"

"Well, sort of."

"You only 'sort of' beat him up?"

"No, it's only sort of terrific. I really beat him up. His lip looked awful. Of course, he keeps swearing that I didn't beat him up—"

"You talked to this creep? That means the police got him. Good!"

"Well, in a manner of speaking. I sent some policemen after him, but I didn't realize what had happened until he showed up at my door—"

"Who?" Tina asked, confused.

"Zack. He…"

"Who's Zack?"

"The guy in the alley," Lucy said, and Tina groaned.

"And now you're on a first-name basis with him and you won't press charges because he's told you about his horrible childhoood in reform school. Lucy, you are too damn nice!"

"Not exactly—"

"Forget it. I'm coming over, and we're going to the police and get this Zack character sent up the river for life. I know a cop now. That suit in the diner yesterday turned out to have a badge. You stay there. I'll call him and Benton."

Lucy sat up straighter and clutched the phone. "No, Tina—"

"Do you think the police will be able to find him?"

"Probably. He works for them."

There was a short silence. "What?" Tina said finally.

"He's a cop," Lucy said.

"You beat up a cop?"

"That depends on who you talk to. From my point of view, yes. From Zack's, no."

"Zack."

"Zack Warren. Detective Zachary Warren." Lucy relaxed into her chair again. "He has blue eyes. You remember. He was the black leather in the restaurant yesterday."

"Don't do this," Tina said.

"What?"

"We've got to talk. Meet me for lunch at the Maisonette."

"I can't. Zack told me not to leave."

"What? He just told you…"

"He thinks somebody's trying to kill me."

There was another silence.

"Stay there," Tina said finally. "I'm coming over with Chinese takeout, and you are going to tell me everything."

"All right," Lucy said. "But I better warn you. My hair is… different."

"Different," Tina said. "I can't wait."

"SHE'S UNCONSCIOUS." Zack slumped, defeated, in a plastic chair outside the hospital-room door. "Of course, she's unconscious. She's been bleeding into the carpet for hours. No ID. Nothing. This is making me crazy."

"You were already crazy." Anthony checked his watch. "Come on, we have things to do. The desk clerk just identified John Bradley as the man who used the room. We have to get a picture of Bradley Porter to him, too."

Zack stared into space. "Bradley. Rat Bradley. I wonder where he is now?"

"Well, not back at the hotel. Let's go check out the room. Forensics hasn't found anything so far, but maybe…"

"I really want to arrest him," Zack said. "Attempted murder is as good a reason as any."

"Better than most," Anthony agreed. "Now move. We need to get started on this. It's looking like it will take us the rest of the day and most of the night, as it is."

"Rat Bradley," Zack said, and Anthony gave up and pulled him to his feet and out the door.

TINA BROUGHT HER A baseball bat.

"Thank you." Lucy looked at it doubtfully. "You haven't signed me up for intramurals or anything, have you?"

"Of course not. It's for your protection."

Tina marched through the living room and dining room and into the kitchen, while Lucy trailed behind her with the bat. She dumped two bags of Chinese food on the kitchen table, and then took the bat from Lucy and propped it by the back door. "If anybody tries to break in here, you hit him with this. Hard."

"Tina, nobody is trying to kill me. That's Zack's fantasy, not reality."

"Tell me about it." Tina opened the first carton of food.

An hour later, she was still curious. "So he really thinks somebody was shooting at you?" she said as she polished off her Mu Shu pork.

"Yes. Isn't that the dumbest thing you've ever heard?"

Tina thought about it. "No. Not if there were marks on the locks, too. He's right. You stay inside."

Lucy shoved her plate away, exasperated. "What is it with you two? I don't even talk to my dogs the way you two talk to me."

"Well, you should," Tina glared at Einstein who was eyeing the Mu Shu pork carton. "They'd have better manners. So what's Zack like?"

"Erratic. Quick temper. Never still. Gorgeous blue eyes. Very short attention span. Not my type at all." She stopped and then added primly, "Although I have had some inappropritate thoughts about him. Very inappropriate. Not that I'll ever do anything about it. Still, the dogs like him." She pulled her plate back and scooped up some garlic chicken while she contemplated Zack. "He's sort of bossy, but I like him."

Tina grinned. "Imagine my surprise. I've changed my mind. I think you should do something about it."

"About what?"

"About this thing you have for Zack."

Lucy shook her head. "Not a chance. My hair alone would send any sane man screaming into the street."

Tina looked at Lucy's moss-colored hair. "Maybe if you wear a lot of forest green. Maybe he's a Tolkien fan."

"Maybe I'll kill myself," Lucy said.

"Don't be ridiculous," Tina said. "I brought Häagen-Dazs. Triple Brownie Overload."

"Maybe I'll live," Lucy said.

WHEN TINA FINALLY LEFT Lucy's house at eleven, Zack still hadn't called.

It was for the best, Lucy knew. After all, she'd just gotten divorced. After all, he was too much of a loose screw to ever be good for her.

After all, her hair looked like a bad carpet.

"Tomorrow is another day," she told the dogs. "And it's the first day of the rest of my independence. The heck with Zack Warren.

The heck with all men. It's easier to be independent without them anyway."

The dogs looked skeptical.

"Oh, forget it," Lucy said. "Let's go to bed."

"OF COURSE, IT WON'T GO into court," Anthony said at eight the next morning as he hung up the phone. "But Patricia and the lab send you their best wishes and the considered opinion that the bullet from the blonde is a match for the bullet that missed you."

"I think it's time we talked to Lucy." Zack picked up the phone and dialed. "I was going over there later today, anyway."

"That explains why you shaved two days in a row. We're all grateful."

Zack ignored him. "Come on, pick it up," he said into the phone. "I told you not to answer the *door*. It's okay to pick up the phone." But after the twelfth ring, his annoyance faded and turned to cold fear. "She's not answering."

Anthony grabbed his jacket. "Let's go. Looks like she opened the door, after all."

Five

Lucy tried to run off her anger in the cold Saturday-morning light. After all, it was a waste of time to be angry with a man because he didn't call or come over when he said he was going to. Men never did.

Especially men like Zack, who ran around one minute shouting, "Somebody's trying to kill you," and the next minute forgot you existed. If he was so worried about her being killed, why hadn't he called all day yesterday? Him and his instincts. As Mrs. Dover would say, Ha.

She turned to jog back down her street, and when she looked up at her own house, Zack was on the front porch.

Her first thought was that he was even more magnetic than she'd remembered him. He seemed, even from a distance, to be vibrating with energy.

Her second was that her hair was probably even stranger in the daylight than it was in artificial light.

Her third, when she got closer, was that he wasn't vibrating with energy, he was vibrating with anger. Well, the heck with him. So what if he was angry. So was she. He hadn't called. He'd just left her there like a potted plant, and he hadn't called. Who did he think he was? Who the *heck* did he think he was?

Yeah.

He came to meet her as she walked up the steps, and he looked wonderful—tall, dark, and enraged.

"You shaved." She was still breathless from running. "And your lip looks much better. You look much more reliable."

"Reliable? Me? What about you?" Zack stabbed his finger at her. "I told you to stay put!"

"Listen." Lucy tried to keep an edge on her anger. It was hard because she really was glad to see him, and he really was gorgeous.

She put her hands on her hips and concentrated. "Listen, you. You told me it was for one night and then you'd call. You didn't call. Which isn't surprising because you're a man, and men never call, but still, in this situation, you would think..."

"I've been out of my mind with worry about you," Zack said through his teeth. "I had you pictured dead in a pool of blood in front of the fireplace. And now you show up alive, and I want to kill you myself."

"And anyway, who do you think you are, saying 'Stay put' like I'm some...I don't know...trained dog, or something."

"I thought you were *dead.*" Zack grabbed her arm. "I thought somebody had grabbed you. I thought I was going to have to raise your damn dogs...."

"Why would you have to raise my dogs? I just needed exercise." Lucy tried to tug away from him. "I ran two miles. Big deal. Let go of me."

"My partner is next door right now, calling for help to look for your body." Zack tightened his grip. "I'm so damn mad at you.... Just...*get in that house.*"

"*Now wait just a minute!*" Lucy began, but then she stopped, distracted by the streak of yellow that blurred past her feet. "Look out, Phoebe's loose again."

In an instant, the cat had raced across the lawn and dived into the window of Lucy's car.

"No!" Lucy jerked free from Zack. "That's it. That's the last straw." She started across the lawn to the car, and Zack grabbed her sweatshirt and yanked her to the cold ground, falling on her as he rolled them both down the hill into Mrs. Dover's driveway.

They landed with a thud, Lucy on the bottom, and all the breath went out of her lungs as Zack fell on top of her. "Hey," she said, but all that came out was a whisper.

He was covering her with his body, one hand braced over her head, listening for something. He looked exactly the same as he had the day he'd flung her into the alley—the same anvil jaw, only clean-shaven now, cocked away from her at the same angle while he tensed against her.

Just like in the alley.

Lucy stopped trying to shove him off and clutched at his arms. "Zack? Was somebody shooting at you again?"

He looked down at her, focused and sharp. "I thought you said you always rolled your car windows up. Because of Phoebe."

"I do..." Lucy began and stopped, distracted by the realization of how warm he was on top of her. "Uh, Zack..."

"They're down now. Phoebe jumped in."

"Big deal." Lucy tried to shift his weight off her without enjoying it. "Maybe I forgot. You're squashing me. Get off."

"They were up when I left day before yesterday. And you haven't been in the car since, right?"

Zack was almost nose-to-nose with her, his electric blue eyes staring down into her brown ones, his hand cradling her face, the weight of his body stretched warmly along the whole length of hers, and she lost the thread of her argument in the heat she was feeling everywhere. It was so unfair. He was gorgeous, he was on top of her, and he was asking her questions about a cat. She might have to kill herself, after all.

"Zack." She pushed gently at him. "Nothing is happening here. There are no gunshots. Get off me."

She stopped when her eyes connected with his. She could feel him relax against her as his attention shifted from the car to her.

"I wouldn't exactly say nothing is happening." Zack smiled down at her.

"Well, nobody's trying to kill me," Lucy said, trying to sound reasonably calm. "Get off."

"So you're telling me I overreacted." The warmth in his eyes went to her bones, and she swallowed hard.

"I know." Lucy tried to keep her tone cool while she melted under him. "You couldn't help yourself. It was an instinct. I forgive you. Now, get off me."

He raised himself up on one elbow and flicked one of her curls with his finger. "You know, in this light, your hair looks sort of...green."

"*Get off me now!*" she said, and Mrs. Dover came onto her front porch and screamed, "*Perverts!*" at them, and Phoebe raced across

Zack's back using every claw she had for traction, and Zack yelled in pain.

And the car blew up.

"Zack!" Lucy threw her arms around him and pulled him down to her, and Mrs. Dover screamed again and fell backward into her house, and Phoebe hit high C and disappeared under the porch.

After a moment of silence, Zack raised his shoulders off Lucy and gazed cautiously over the hill at her burning car.

"Nice little bomb," he said reflectively. "Very neat."

Lucy eased the top of her body up, too, still under him, and watched the flames, horrified. He looked down at her, and when she turned back they were nose-to-nose.

"You okay?"

"Zack," Lucy said. "Somebody's trying to kill me."

"You know," Zack said, "I had an instinct about that."

HALF AN HOUR LATER, Anthony sat in an overstuffed armchair between Lucy and Zack, feeling like a tennis ref.

"Okay," Zack said from where he stood in front of the fireplace. "One more time. How long were you gone?"

Lucy leaned back against the love seat. "I told you. I just ran two miles. Fifteen, maybe twenty minutes. I didn't check the clock when I left."

"That's not enough time." Anthony said. "In broad daylight, with a delayed fuse? And no one saw him? Face it, Zack. It doesn't matter when she ran. He must have set this up last night." He turned back to Lucy. "Do you remember if the windows were up or down when you left to run?"

"Zack already asked me that. I didn't pay any attention. I didn't even notice the windows when I came back until Phoebe jumped inside the car." She stopped again. "That was such a nice car. It's totaled, right?"

Zack smacked his hand on the mantel from exasperation. "Lucy, you dummy, this was a bomb, not a rear-end collision!"

Lucy looked back at him, just as exasperated. "Well, it's totally destroyed, right? Which means it's totaled, right? What are you so

mad at me for? And don't call me a dummy, either, you...you..."
She blinked.

"Listen, lady..." Zack began, stabbing his finger at her.

"Okay, children, that's enough," Anthony said. "Fight on your own time. We've got a serious problem here."

"I'm sorry," Lucy said to him. "I'm usually not this rude. It's just Zack. He brings out the worst in me."

"That's good to know," Zack said. "I'd hate to think this was your best."

"I beg your pardon," Lucy said.

"Zack, shut up." Anthony turned to Lucy and smiled. It was a great smile, his sure-you-can-trust-me smile, and Lucy smiled back.

Zack glowered at both of them.

"Now look, Lucy," Anthony went on. "I know Zack didn't call you, and that was wrong." Zack started to say something, and Anthony shot him a warning glance that was pure venom. Zack shut up, and Anthony returned to his persuasion. "That won't happen again. I promise. The important thing is that now that we know for sure that somebody is trying to hurt you, we have to get serious about this. What we'd like to do—with your permission, of course—is put you in a hotel...."

"No," Lucy said.

"I told you so." Zack looked at Lucy. "You're either going to a hotel or to your sister's and that's that. No arguments. Get your stuff."

"No," Lucy said.

"I'll look after the dogs," Zack said. "Get your stuff."

"You won't remember," Lucy said.

"Of course, I'll remember. Get your stuff."

"Like you remembered to call me? No."

"Lucy!" Zack loomed over her.

"Forget it. I'm not leaving my dogs." She turned to Anthony. "How long would I be in this hotel? Two days? A week? A month?"

"I don't know," he said. "I think we can solve this within the week, but I can't promise you."

Lucy shook her head. "I can't leave them. They wouldn't understand. And what if this man decides to get me by burning the house down? They trust me to take care of them. I'm not stupid. I know I'm in danger, and I'm scared, but I'm not leaving them."

"Then we'll have to put somebody here with you," Anthony said.

"No," Zack said.

"Fine," Lucy said.

"We're shorthanded." Anthony stood. "I think I can get Sergeant Eliot—"

"Are you crazy?" Zack said. "Eliot is sixty-four, legally blind, and waiting for retirement. Lucy would have to protect him."

"Your other choice is Matthews," Anthony said. "And we'll have the patrol cars keep an eye—"

"Who's Matthews?" Zack asked.

"The tall blond one you keep calling Junior," Anthony said. "Stop doing that, by the way. It annoys him. Anyway, he's young, strong, and he's got 20/20 vision. Happy?"

"No." Zack searched for a good reason why. "He's young. He's new. He doesn't know…"

"Great," Anthony said, a savage edge creeping into his voice. "You want somebody not too old, not too young, who knows. That leaves us with a middle-aged cop with experience. The only one of those available is you. Are you volunteering?"

Zack looked first at Lucy and then at Anthony, and said, "Yes. Watch her while I go get my stuff. And by the way, I am *not* middle-aged."

"What?" Lucy said.

"You're kidding," Anthony said. "I thought you were hot on the trail of Bradley the embezzler."

"I think the trail's here. When I get back, we're going to search this place."

"I thought you needed a warrant for that," Lucy said.

"Not if the home owner gives us permission." Anthony tried to signal Zack to shut up, with no success. Zack ignored him.

"And you're going to give us permission because I just saved your life," Zack said.

"You did not…" Lucy began. "Oh. I guess you did."

"Right. Remember that." Zack turned back to Anthony. "I'll be back in half an hour. Watch her every minute so she doesn't leave again. She has no survival instincts."

When Zack was gone, Anthony smiled at Lucy. "He means well. He just has no tact."

Lucy bit her lip. "I'm not stupid. I just didn't believe him when he said somebody was trying to kill me."

"That's all right. I didn't, either. It's the most annoying thing I know about Zack. He makes these stupid assumptions, and then he turns out to be right. Fortunately, he's also a great guy. You just have to get used to him."

"Oh, I could get used to him," Lucy said. Anthony heard a note of wistful enthusiasm in her voice and sank back down into the big soft chair again as she went on. "I just don't know why he's always grabbing me and yelling at me. I'm a very calm, logical, unemotional person. It really isn't necessary."

Anthony nodded. "He worries about you."

Lucy blinked and Anthony sat back and thought, *I wonder if Zack has noticed that she blinks every time she thinks of something she can't say aloud. I bet he has.*

I bet he's noticed just about everything about her.

"He didn't even call yesterday," Lucy went on. "He forgot me. He put me in this house, and then he forgot me."

Anthony shook his head. "No, he didn't. We had some problems yesterday. Big ones. A woman was shot." He watched her closely as she flinched at the news.

"That's awful."

"It was. It's the only time I've ever seen Zack look worried."

"Why?"

"He thought it was you."

"Oh." Lucy blinked again.

Bingo. She was a darling, and she liked Zack. If Zack moved in with her for a month, he'd be a goner, and Anthony could stop worrying about him. It was perfect, although he might have to start hiding evidence to keep Zack there for that long.

Now all he had to do was convince Lucy.

"You know, Zack really needs to solve this case," Anthony said. "He's been depressed lately, even thinking about quitting the force.

If he could just relax a little, it would do him a world of good. Moving in with you for a while may be just the thing he needs. A calm, secure environment to grow up in."

Lucy grinned. "You make him sound like a foster child."

"That's pretty much the way I think of him. And by the way, I know he's obnoxious, but please don't hit him again. He's still got a concussion from the last time."

"He does?" Lucy said, appalled. "He told me he wasn't hurt."

"Well, he thinks he's Superman. Take care of him."

Lucy looked at him suspiciously on his last remark, but he smiled back at her, as artless and open as the sun, and finally, she smiled, too.

"All right," she said.

Anthony's smile widened.

All right.

ZACK DUMPED HIS BAG on the quilt-covered spool bed in the attic bedroom. The ceiling was slung low and canted under the eaves, the wallpaper was scattered with tiny yellow flowers, and the little windows at the end of the room were patterned with diamond panes. "This is a great room," he told Lucy, who'd followed him up the stairs. "If you had any sense, you'd be sleeping up here."

Lucy took an extra blanket from the closet and draped it over the end of the bed. "I know. I wanted to put our bedroom up here, but Bradley said the one downstairs was bigger."

Zack felt the same spurt of annoyance he was beginning to feel every time Lucy mentioned Bradley in the same breath with herself. "Why'd you listen to him?"

"Well, it was going to be his bedroom, too," Lucy said, and Zack felt really annoyed.

He opened a drawer, unzipped his bag, and upended it into the drawer to unpack it. "Bradley is an idiot."

Lucy shrugged. "Not really. It is warmer downstairs. You have to leave the door to the stairs open at night or this place gets really cold."

Zack stopped trying to shove everything into the drawer. "How do you know?"

"I started sleeping up here in October. Bradley and I...had a disagreement."

"Good for you." Zack felt much better, and then he felt like a fool for feeling much better. Aside from that flash of lust he'd given in to in the driveway, he had no interest in this woman besides a passing sense of responsibility. All he had to do was find out what was in her damn house, get rid of it, and possibly arrest her ex-husband for attempted murder. Then he'd never have to see her again.

Lucy brushed against his arm as she moved beside him to spread his shirts evenly into the drawer. She smelled faintly of flowers and warmth.

Never seeing her again suddenly didn't have much appeal.

He left the drawer open and stepped away from her. "Let's start searching this place. Where's the best place to start?"

"I threw all of Bradley's stuff into the basement," Lucy said, shoving the drawer closed. "You probably want that first."

"Threw? Literally?"

"I stood at the top of the stairs and pitched it. It felt wonderful."

Zack grinned at her suddenly, and Lucy looked startled. "I thought you were mad at me."

"Naw. I just thought you were dead, and it threw me for a minute."

"A minute?" Lucy said. "That's all?"

"Well, then you showed up and the car exploded. I haven't had much time to dwell on things lately." Zack took her shoulders and turned her toward the stairs. "C'mon. Let's go to the basement, so I can solve this case, and you can get rid of me."

LUCY FELT GUILTY WHEN Zack whistled at the wreckage at the bottom of the stairs.

"I'll pick it up." She started past him, and he grabbed her arm.

"Look out. The stair rail's gone."

"I know. The chair fell through it."

"The chair?"

"The chair I shoved down here." Lucy peered cautiously over the broken rail. "See? It sort of rolled to the right, back there."

"You threw a chair down these stairs?"

"I felt like it. Are we going down there or not?"

"Stay close to the wall, behind me." Zack went down the stairs. "Don't fall over the edge, or I'll be picking splinters out of you for a week."

Lucy put her hands on her hips and glared at him. "You know, I'm not helpless."

Zack ignored her. He dragged the smashed cartons into the middle of the basement and shoved the chair upright. "Nice chair."

"No, it's not." Lucy followed him down the stairs cautiously. "It's ugly."

"That's just the upholstery. Cover that up and it's a good chair."

"It's too big."

"It's a man's chair." Zack deepened his voice. "A manly chair for a manly man."

"It was Bradley's."

Zack shrugged. "Okay, so it's not that great. Are these all the boxes?"

"Just those three. And there's nothing in them. I packed them up so I know. Just papers and junk."

"Papers? I love papers. Do these papers have numbers on them?" Zack sat down on the floor next to the first box and pried at the layers of tape that sealed it. "Did you seal these for life? There must be twenty pounds of tape here."

"I was a little enthusiastic." Lucy turned back to the stairs. "Let me get a knife."

"Good. Get me a beer while you're at it."

Lucy stopped halfway up the stairs. "I don't have any beer."

"Yes, you do. It's in your refrigerator. I put it there myself. Can you cook Mexican?"

"I suppose," Lucy said coldly. "Why?"

"I got some stuff when I picked up the beer on the way here. Nachos, olives, cheese, that kind of stuff." Zack continued to poke at the box while he spoke, missing Lucy's frown. "I figured you could cook. You look like the type. Could I have that knife, please?"

Right between your ribs, Lucy thought and blinked. Then she turned and went upstairs to get him his knife and beer.

Two hours later, they'd looked at every piece of paper and book in Bradley's boxes and hadn't found a clue.

"Half of this stuff is years old." Zack sat on the floor by the stairs and stared at the mess. "Doesn't he ever throw anything out?"

"I guess not." Lucy threw the last of the papers back in the box. "It's kind of sad, isn't it? All his personal papers are business papers."

Zack frowned at her. "Don't start feeling sorry for him. He's a rat."

"Well, he wasn't always a rat."

"Oh, yeah. What was he?" Zack leaned back against the stairs and watched her. "What do you know about him? Where did he come from?"

Lucy sat down on one of the boxes. "I don't know much. He's from a little town in Pennsylvania called Beulah Ridge. It's on the high-school yearbook in that box there beside you. His parents are both dead, and he hasn't been back in years. We had a very small wedding, and Bradley didn't invite more than two or three people, and he said none of them would be able to make it. It was just my parents and Tina and some friends from school."

"Who did he send wedding invitations to?"

Lucy frowned, trying to remember. "I think a couple of friends from high school. Not family. And anyway, he was right. Nobody showed up that he invited. It was sad, really, but he didn't seem to mind. Anyway, after the wedding, we just settled in here. He worked at the bank, and I taught school, and Maxwell and Heisenberg moved in. And then the blonde showed up, and he moved out, and we got divorced, and you mugged me in an alley." She shrugged. "It's never going to make a Movie of the Week, but that was my life."

Zack snorted. "Bradley is a rat."

"Oh, not entirely. He was really very nice to me for most of our marriage."

Zack looked at her skeptically. "Then why did you move upstairs in October?"

"He snored."

"Right." Zack turned back to the boxes to pull the yearbook out again.

"Why doesn't anybody ever believe that?" Lucy asked.

"Because no man in his right mind would let you out of his bed for that." Zack flipped through the book. "Is this his high-school yearbook?"

"Yes," Lucy said faintly.

"John Bradley the embezzler taught high school in California," Zack said absently, as he flipped to the senior portrait section. "High-school phys ed. That was his downfall."

"What do you mean, 'downfall'?"

"He seduced a cheerleader." Zack ran his finger down the page. "Knocked her up."

Lucy's head jerked up. "That's awful! He should be in jail."

"I think so, too." His finger stopped on one picture. "Of course, I also want him there for embezzlement. But he paid in his own way."

"He must have lost his job. School administrators can be really good at ignoring anything ugly, but in this case..."

"Oh, yeah, he lost his job. But the best part is, the girl's family was really powerful. A bunch of very big guys with very big bank accounts and very big shotguns. They probably could have killed him and gotten away with it, except there was Bianca with a baby on the way, so they did the next best thing. They got him a job in a bank and made him marry her."

Lucy winced. "How awful for her. That's barbaric."

Zack snorted. "More than you know. I've talked to Bianca on the phone, and she is not a pleasant person. I almost felt sorry for John Bradley. I personally would have told Daddy to go ahead and shoot me rather than spend a week with her, let alone six years, but then Bradley and I are different."

"You certainly are." Lucy blushed when Zack looked up. "I mean, I can't imagine you seducing a teenager."

"Well, I tried hard enough when I was a teenager. I just never had much luck. My technique needed work." He turned back to stare at the picture in the yearbook.

It doesn't anymore, Lucy thought. Then she mentally shook herself. The moon must be full or something. Maybe she was ovulating, although she usually didn't get this crazy. As a matter of fact, she'd never been this crazy. Maybe she'd just reached that mid-thirties plateau where a woman's sexual desire was supposed to peak. Just her luck, she was peaking and here came Zack.

Of course, the real problem wasn't that he turned her on. The real problem was that she liked being with him. She felt good around him. Happy. Warm.

Really warm.

Hot.

Okay, the other part of the real problem was that he turned her on.

"He doesn't look like a crook," Zack said suddenly.

"Who?"

"Porter. Your ex."

Zack shoved the yearbook in front of her, his finger pointing to a picture on a senior gallery page. "He looks like an amoeba."

"They all do. They're so young." Lucy looked down at her ex-husband, frozen forever at eighteen. He was as classically good-looking back then as he was now, but he was also as stiff and dull, too. "Poor Bradley."

"Stop feeling sorry for him." Zack took the yearbook back and leafed through it again. "He's implicated in a major crime."

"He is?"

"Yeah. He got a hotel room in Overlook. A woman was found shot there today. We don't have any proof that he did it, but we'd like to talk to him."

"You think Bradley shot somebody?" Lucy shook her head. "No. He's not violent."

"How do you know he's not violent? He's a rat, possibly an embezzler, and definitely a seducer of blondes. You found one in your living room, remember?"

"Not a chance." Lucy's voice was firm. "A rat, maybe, but not a seducer of blondes. The blonde must have seduced him. Bradley just wasn't that interested in sex."

Zack flipped back a page in the yearbook. "Bradley is an idiot."

"Of course, maybe it was just me."

"It wasn't you."

Lucy started at the warmth in his voice, but his attention was suddenly riveted to the yearbook. "I'll be damned," he said. "I will be damned."

"What?"

He shoved the book in front of her and pointed to a picture near the bottom of the page. The boy in the picture was good-looking in a sly way.

"I've seen that smile on kids before," Lucy said. "I bet he was a cheat."

"No kidding. Look at the name." He pointed again and Lucy read the legend underneath.

Most Likely To Succeed
John Talbot Bradley

Six

"They went to high school together." Zack's voice was thick with triumph. "Both of them named Bradley could be a coincidence. Both of them involved with banks could be a coincidence. You in the restaurant yesterday at the same time as the phone tip? Not likely, but could be a coincidence. But now this..." He took the book back from her and gazed in satisfaction at the picture. "This is not a coincidence."

"No," Lucy said. "It's not. I don't understand any of this, but it's not."

Zack looked up from the book at the sadness in her voice. "Hey. This doesn't have anything to do with you."

Lucy bit her lip. "I just feel stupid. I never saw any of this in him, and I was married to him for eight months. I feel so stupid."

"You're not stupid." Zack flipped the book closed and stood, holding out his hand. "Come on. Let's shove the rest of this stuff under the stairs and go up and call Tony. Then we can have dinner. What are you making, anyway?"

He grinned down at her, and she forgot Bradley for a minute and just basked in his nearness. Then she took his hand and let him pull her to her feet. "I'm not making dinner." She dusted off the seat of her jeans. "You are." She smiled up at him then, glad to have him so close. It was hard to stay depressed when he was so close.

"I don't know how to cook." He sounded distracted as he stared down at her.

"What's wrong?"

Zack shook his head. "That's some smile you've got there when you let it go all the way. I hadn't seen it before. You should smile like that more often." He turned her around and started her up the stairs, pushing her in front of him, and then stopped after the first step.

"What now?" Lucy looked back over her shoulder.

"Nice jeans," he said, looking at her rear end. "Tight, though."

Lucy felt herself go cold. She went up another step and turned around. "What did you say?"

He let his eyes drift up to meet hers. "I just hadn't thought of you as the tight-jeans type."

"Neither did Bradley." Lucy felt suddenly remote. "Is this a problem?"

Zack frowned at her. "What are you talking about? What problem? I'm leering at your rear end. Slap me if you want to, but don't look at me like that."

"Oh." Lucy blinked.

Zack's frown dissolved. "I get it. Bradley didn't like you in jeans."

"Bradley liked me in suits. He hated jeans."

"Bradley is an idiot. But then we already knew that. As far as I'm concerned, you should be wearing jeans all the time. Enough about you. I'm hungry. Move it." He started up the stairs. "Now, as I was saying, I don't cook."

"You do now." Lucy turned back and speeded up to keep him off her heels, relief making her buoyant. "I'm teaching you."

"Whatever happened to women who like to cook for men every day?" Zack asked as she opened the door to the kitchen at the top of the stairs.

"There were never any women who liked to cook for men every day. There were only women who cooked for survival and pretended to like it. And now there are men who cook for survival. Like you. Think of this as survivalist training. Very macho."

"I don't think so," Zack said, but he followed her through the door into the kitchen.

AN HOUR LATER, ZACK was feeling pretty good.

"I'm really great at this," he announced as they sat on the floor in front of the fireplace, their plates on their laps and their backs against the rose-flowered love seat.

"Zack, they're nachos." Lucy protected hers from Einstein. "They're very good, but they're just nachos."

"Yeah, but I made them. I think I have an instinct for this."

"I'm just grateful you chose Mexican instead of French." Lucy eyed the mound of food on her plate. "We'd be up to our hips in coq au vin."

"We'll do that tomorrow night," Zack said, and Lucy said, "No, we won't. Do you like chili?"

"Yeah, but that comes in a can. I want to chop something." He grinned at her, and she felt her heart lurch sideways.

Oh, boy, she thought, but all she said was, "You can make chili from scratch. And you get to chop the onions. You'll like it."

"Great." Zack scooped up another nacho with pride. "Forget it," he said to Maxwell who was doing his best impression of a starving dog. "It's all mine."

Lucy laughed. "Anthony was right. You are like a little kid. Who's fed you up to now? Your mom?"

"Nope. Mostly, I eat out. Sometimes I open a can or nuke something, but not too often. Canned stuff tastes terrible, and the frozen stuff is worse."

"And you're how old? This is just amazing."

"Hey, I'm alive and healthy. I'm doing okay." Zack scooped another nacho. "What were you discussing me with Tony for, anyway?"

"He said you have a concussion." Lucy looked apologetic. "I feel awful about that."

Zack met her eyes. "You still made me cook."

"Well, I didn't feel that awful. Besides, you liked it."

"It's the principle of the thing." Zack ate another nacho. "What else did Tony tell you?"

Lucy blinked. "I don't remember."

"Oh, yes, you do, Blinky. Come on. Give."

"I thought he was very nice," Lucy said primly, her chin in the air.

Zack shook his head. "You stay away from him. You're not his type."

Lucy's chin dropped. "That's not what I meant. And what do you mean, I'm not his type?"

"He's into plastic Yuppies. You know, suits and running shoes and briefcases and car phones." Zack shuddered at the thought and started on another nacho.

"And what's your type?" Lucy asked, and then mentally kicked herself. That's all she needed was for him to start thinking she was interested.

"I don't have a type," Zack said. "I'm an equal-opportunity lover."

"How very broad-minded of you," Lucy said, and fed a nacho to Einstein on the sly.

"Speaking of types, how did you end up with Bradley?"

"Well, I had decided to get married because of the second law of thermonuclear dynamics." Lucy kept her voice brisk to keep herself from getting emotional. "And about that time, he picked me up in the library at the university. I considered it a sign."

"It wasn't." Zack picked up another nacho, gazed at it proudly, and then ate it.

"I thought I was going to end up a crazy old lady living with my dog."

"Dogs," Zack corrected.

"I only had Einstein then. Maxwell and Heisenberg showed up after we moved in. Well, actually, I found Maxwell down on Fourteenth Street across from the Music Hall, but it was the same principle." Lucy looked over at Zack. He was staring into the fire so she slipped Heisenberg a nacho. Maxwell noticed and quietly padded around the love seat to her side.

"So you got married to keep from being a crazy old lady?" Zack shook his head. "It would never have happened, but I guess I can see your point. What I still don't understand is, why Bradley?"

"He was there. It seemed right." She shrugged and slipped Maxwell a nacho.

"It was wrong," Zack said sternly, and then he looked from his empty plate to hers. "Do you want the rest of your nachos?"

Lucy passed her plate over, and the dogs followed silently to sit in front of Zack.

"Listen, I just fed you guys a whole bowl full of dog food, so I know you're not starving. Cut it out." They sat and stared and he said, "Okay, one each. *One.* That's all."

Lucy watched him feeding her dogs nachos and felt a wave of heat roll over her. She was one sick puppy. She'd been having hot flashes ever since she'd first seen him in the restaurant, and now he was turning her on by being nice to her dogs. She'd been divorced two days, and already she was lusting after a hyperkinetic dog feeder.

The phone rang, startling her, but Zack reached over and snagged the receiver off the piecrust table before she could get up and answer it.

"Hello?" He looked puzzled. "They hung up," he said, doing the same. "Who would hang up if a man answered?"

"Well, not Tina," Lucy said. "She'd give you the third degree. Not my parents, they wouldn't notice. Not my friends, they'd want all the dirt about you."

"How about Bradley?"

"Bradley doesn't call here."

"Ever?"

"I've only talked to him once since the blonde. He called the same day, but I was still pretty upset then, so I told him I never wanted to hear from him again. And he asked me to please not tell Tina he'd called, and I was so disgusted, I hung up. Oh, and there was one other time. I saw him at the lawyer's the day we signed the papers. He said hello. And he sent me the note. That's it."

Zack frowned. "That's weird. What's wrong with him?"

"Nothing. He's happy with his blonde."

"When I find Bradley," Zack said, "I hope he resists arrest."

"You can't arrest Bradley. You don't know that he's done anything wrong." Lucy stood and picked up Zack's plate from the floor.

"Oh, yes, I do," Zack said. "Even if he didn't shoot the blonde, he's a rat. And I, for one, am going to make sure he's sorry." Then he popped the last of the nachos into his mouth, got up, and followed Lucy out to the kitchen.

Anthony came over to see the yearbook, and they searched the downstairs until eleven that night and found nothing except Bradley's note to Lucy, asking her to lunch.

"He doesn't sound too damn apologetic," Zack said. "Listen to this. 'Please meet me at the diner on Second Street, so that I can explain to you why you've acted hastily.' And you were going to meet him?" He narrowed his gaze at her. "You must still be hung up on him."

"Of course not," Lucy said. "I don't want him back. I just want to understand what happened. And anyway, that's just Bradley's way. He'd never admit that he was wrong. Just the fact that he wrote and asked me to meet him is amazing. Bradley never asked for anything in his life. He always assumed people would do what he wanted, and usually they did. He was very...authoritative." Lucy took back the note and read it again. "Poor Bradley. He must have been really upset. He even wrote, 'Please.'"

"I don't like Bradley," Zack said.

"Actually, neither do I," Lucy said.

"Good. Hold that thought," Zack said.

WHEN ANTHONY LEFT AND Lucy went upstairs to take her shower, Zack enjoyed the fire, the dogs, and one last beer. *This is nice,* he thought, stretching his legs in front of the fire. *This is comfortable. This is...*

He stopped in the middle of a sip of beer.

This was a lot like what Anthony had been talking about in the diner the other day.

He put the bottle down to consider. Anthony had offered him two impossibilities as protection for Lucy, knowing he'd reject them and volunteer.

He'd been set up.

"I'll kill him," he said to the dogs, and Heisenberg flopped over on his back.

Well, it was no problem. He'd just call Anthony tomorrow and tell him to send over a replacement. Zack picked up his beer to drain it. Not Eliot, of course. He was too old and too slow.

And not Junior, either, because...

Zack stopped again, the bottle halfway to his mouth. There was nothing wrong with Junior. He was young and strong and quick, and he would do a terrific job of protecting Lucy.

Right here in her house.

In fact, Junior could be sitting right where Zack was by tomorrow night. All Zack had to do was call Anthony.

Hell.

He got up and stomped to the kitchen to throw his bottle in the recycling box, whistling to the dogs as he went, and two of them went trotting past him as he opened the back door.

Maxwell and Einstein. Zack looked around for Heisenberg, and then remembered. "Oh, for crying out loud, dead dog," he said, and heard the thump as Heisenberg rolled over and the click of his toenails on the hardwood floor.

"Thank you for joining us," Zack said and closed the door behind him.

WHEN HE CLIMBED THE stairs later, he met Lucy at the top, wrapped in a floor-length white terry-cloth robe big enough to cover a couch. Her hair was in loose, damp, greenish ringlets, and she looked vaguely like a cover on a science-fiction book he'd once read.

"I was going down to let the dogs out." She stepped back from the top of the stairs.

"I already did. All present and accounted for."

The three dogs had padded up the stairs by that time and sat watching them quietly. "Bed," Lucy said, and Heisenberg swerved into her bedroom while Einstein and Maxwell went up another flight to Zack's room. "Oh, I forgot." She hesitated. "They sleep on your bed."

"No," Zack said. "Maxwell, maybe, but Einstein, no. There won't be room for me."

"It's a big bed," Lucy said, but she called Einstein back down and held her bedroom door for him. "I did buy beds for all of them. They just didn't like them. They'd rather sleep with me."

They're no dummies, Zack thought.

"I put clean towels out for you," Lucy went on. "In the bathroom. Do you need anything else?"

You, Zack thought. She looked like a bulky mummy in her robe, and her hair was green, and he wanted her. It was crazy. He needed a shower. A cold one. "Thanks," he said. "Good night."

"Good night."

He turned toward the bathroom door, and then decided he'd been too abrupt, but when he turned back, her bedroom door was closing and she was gone.

Good. Because the last thing he needed was to get involved with Lucy Savage and her three dogs.

Even though all his instincts were for it.

He shook his head and went to take a cold shower.

THE NEXT MORNING, Zack took Lucy to the hospital.

"That's her," Lucy whispered, looking at the woman's pale face under the stringy blond hair. "That's the woman who was with Bradley."

Zack put his arm around her and led her away from the bed, alarmed at how white she was, almost as pale as the woman in the hospital bed.

"Are you okay?"

"Bradley did this? Bradley couldn't have done this." Lucy looked back at the bed. "I know it's the same woman, but he couldn't have..." She shook her head, too upset to finish.

"Hey." Zack took her through the door, away from the silence and the whiteness of the room. He found a bench for her in the hall and sat beside her, keeping his arm around her while she bit her lip.

"Somebody violent did that. Bradley's not violent," Lucy said finally. "I don't think Bradley has emotions."

Zack tightened his arm around her. "That's the kind who usually break, honey. The ones who yell all the time blow off steam. The ones who don't, well, when they blow, it's an explosion. And this was a gunshot. It's easy to shoot a gun. Too easy. One bang, and it's over, and you don't even have to get close."

Lucy shook her head. "It's like everything I knew has turned out to be a lie. I can't even trust my own judgment anymore. Look how wrong I've been. And I can't even talk to him to find out why this happened. I've been totally wrong, and I'll never know why. This could all happen to me again because I'll never know why."

Zack watched her bite her lip again, and the sight of her even white teeth cutting into her soft bottom lip disoriented him for a moment. What kind of fool could Bradley have been to risk losing

Lucy to be with that blonde? Hell, how could he have wanted to be with anybody but Lucy at all?

Lucy leaned back against the wall suddenly, pulling his arm with her. "How could I be so blind? How could I have been so stupid?"

"Hey." She looked so confused and betrayed that Zack was stung. He pulled her close and cuddled her to him, wrapping his arms around her as if to shield her from Bradley and anyone else who might hurt her. "Look, honey. A lot of people do things that the people who know them say are impossible." He closed his eyes, savoring her soft warmth and feeling slightly guilty about it. "It happens all the time. All we have to do is keep you safe until we catch him. You can talk to him then, if you want. But it won't always feel like this. It'll be okay."

"I feel safer with you after three days than I did with Bradley after eight months," Lucy said into his shoulder. "I'm so dumb."

"Oh, I don't know." Zack tightened his hold on her. "I'd say that's pretty smart of you."

ZACK TOOK LUCY OUT for Sunday brunch so neither of them would have to cook, and by the time they'd finished, she'd relaxed again. She was still quiet, but the terrible tension he'd felt in her while he held her was gone, and for Zack, for a while, that was enough. Anything was better than watching Lucy suffer.

He really wanted to kill Bradley.

"Now we search the upstairs," he told her when they got home. "All your secrets will soon be mine."

"I don't have any secrets," Lucy said.

"Well, then you should get some," Zack said, and they looked at each other for a moment, and then both looked away.

The first room they searched on the second floor was Lucy's—a big sunny room almost filled with a huge Victorian bed covered with an equally huge crazy quilt.

"I made the quilt," Lucy said. "It's just tied, not quilted, which is why it's kind of lumpy, but that's okay because that way I could put more layers of fill in it." She smiled at Zack. "It's really warm. I love it. It's the best thing I've ever done."

Her smile made Zack's mouth go dry. He hadn't seen it often

enough to get used to it, and the thought made him both sad and angry. She should be smiling all the time. If she were his, he'd make damn sure she was smiling all the time.

Of course she wasn't his, and he didn't want her to be his because he was too young to settle down, and anyway, he couldn't visualize her naked, which he was pretty sure meant she was like a sister to him, but still…

She should be smiling all the time.

"Zack?"

"I really like the quilt. Let's look at your closet."

Her closet had two racks in it. One side was full of soft pastel flowered dresses. The other was full of severe tailored suits in navy and black and dark brown, all with their price tags still attached.

"You schizophrenic?" Zack asked.

"No," Lucy said. "I bought the dresses. Bradley bought the suits."

"Then Bradley should have worn the suits. Why did you stay with this guy?"

"He wasn't a bad person…" Lucy began, but she stopped when Zack rolled his eyes. "I know. The blonde. But that isn't the Bradley Porter I knew. He was good to me. He loved me. He just wasn't…fun. And he didn't approve of me, really. He wanted to, but he didn't. None of that is enough grounds for divorce. He's not a bad person. He's just…lonely. I couldn't leave him. He was so lonely."

"Which would explain the blonde," Zack said and then kicked himself as Lucy winced. "Sorry."

"No, I asked for that one," she said. "What next?"

They tapped the walls, and turned the drawers upside down, and looked under the rug and found nothing. By late afternoon, they'd turned both the second and third floors as upside down as Lucy's drawers and found exactly the same thing—nothing.

"You don't even have any junk," Zack complained as they finished the last room on the third floor. "What's wrong with you?"

"I've only lived here nine months," Lucy protested. "It takes time to accumulate good junk."

"You've had time to accumulate three dogs." Zack stepped over

Maxwell, who was staring into space again. "If you could do that, you could accumulate a little junk."

"You don't accumulate dogs." Lucy patted Maxwell, who didn't seem to notice. "You meet them, and you both know that you belong together. And even if you know that that's dumb, and you don't need a dog, and you can't handle the responsibility, and you don't even want a dog anyway, there it is and you have to go with it. It was meant to be."

Zack stopped in his tracks. "Why does this sound like some dumb women's magazine description of the perfect relationship?"

Lucy's head jerked up from Maxwell to him. "Listen, the best relationships of my life have been with dogs. And they aren't dumb at all. Einstein never brought a blonde into my house, and Maxwell never stood me up in a restaurant, and Heisenberg never grabbed me in an alley."

"Hey," Zack said. "How did I get into this?"

"Sorry," Lucy said.

ANTHONY CAME BY THE house late in the afternoon. He stood in the middle of Lucy's soft, flowered living room and said, "This is a wonderful room. It feels good just to be here." He smiled down at Lucy. "It's like you."

Lucy beamed back. "That's the nicest thing you could have said to me." She stood on tiptoe and kissed him on the cheek, and he put his arm around her.

"Hey," Zack said. "Let's be professional here."

"You want to be professional?" Anthony raised an eyebrow. "Get a haircut."

"Very funny. What are you doing here?"

Anthony let go of Lucy and sat down in one of the overstuffed armchairs. "I went in to catch up on the reports this afternoon and found a message from the lab. You know the bomb that blew up Lucy's car?"

"I'll never forget it." Zack sat on the arm of the loveseat and pulled Lucy down onto the cushions beside him.

Anthony leaned back in his chair. "It wasn't much of a bomb to begin with, according to the lab, although granted it did a nice job on the car. But the really interesting part is that, besides the extremely long timer that not only gave you time to notice the cat, knock Lucy into the driveway, and then have a long conversation with her—"

"Get to the point."

"It also had a hell of a big alarm clock taped to it with a lot of sinister-looking wires. None of which had anything to do with the mechanism that caused the explosion."

"Oh, hell," Zack said.

"I don't understand," Lucy said.

Anthony turned to her. "If you had looked in your car, you would have seen a big package about the size of a shoe box with a clock taped to it and a lot of wires. What would you have done?"

"I'd have thought it was a bomb and run like crazy," Lucy said. "I still don't get it."

"He's trying to tell you that you were right," Zack said, disgusted. "Nobody's trying to kill you. They're just trying to scare you out of the house. You would have called us, the bomb squad would have confirmed that it was a real bomb. And we would have moved you out of the house for safekeeping, so the house would have been empty. Except that you wouldn't leave the dogs."

Lucy looked back and forth between them, incredulous. "My car blew up. This guy blew up my car to scare me out of my house?"

"Well, he didn't know about the dogs," Anthony said. "Without the dogs, it would have worked."

"He could have killed me!"

"No," Zack said. "The timer on that sucker was almost five minutes. If the package was as big as Tony says, you'd have been long gone before it went off. This nut was just trying to scare you." He met Anthony's eyes. "Which means..."

"...there's something in this house," Anthony finished.

"No, there isn't," Lucy said. "We've looked. We've looked everywhere."

Anthony shook his head to stop her. "That's not all. Your report from the patrolman came in. And not only has Mrs. Dover been complaining about prowlers around this house for two weeks, she also phoned in another complaint last night. If she's really seeing somebody, he's still around."

"You know, I wanted to move out of my apartment because I never felt safe there," Lucy said. "I moved here because it felt so safe." She looked around her at the bright, warm room. "I don't feel so safe anymore."

"Are you crazy?" Zack said. "You've got me for a bodyguard and you don't feel safe? What's wrong with you? First no junk, and now this."

"No junk?" Anthony said.

"Cleanest house I've ever searched," Zack said. "No junk."

"That's un-American," Anthony said.

"So what happens when I go back to school tomorrow?" Lucy said.

"We keep somebody in the house," Anthony said.

"You're not going back to school," Zack said.

Lucy and Anthony both frowned at him.

"Don't look at me like that," he told Anthony. "Suppose this guy grabs her and forces her to let him in the house? Suppose he decides to take a hostage? Suppose…"

"Suppose you stop scaring Lucy," Anthony said. "He's not going to grab her."

"We don't know that. We've got one attempted-murder charge that could turn into murder at any time. We've got a million and a half that's floating around somewhere. And we've got the guy who's mixed up with both, who also makes bombs and shoots guns. You want to tell me again about how we should dress Lucy up and send her off to the one place where everybody knows she's going to be?"

Anthony considered Zack for a moment. "All right. If it's all right with Lucy."

"All right," Lucy said after a moment and went upstairs to phone her principal.

"What are you doing?" Anthony asked when she was gone, and for once Zack was serious when he answered.

"I'm scared for her. You should have seen her at the hospital. She was absolutely rocked. I just want to keep her safe until we get this guy. We've got to pretty soon. We're close. I just want to keep her safe."

"There's something else," Anthony said. "I spent most of the afternoon on the phone to Beulah Ridge, Pennsylvania, trying to catch people while they were home. I talked to a couple of people who knew both Bradleys."

"And?"

"And John Bradley was the school's golden boy until he got caught one too many times stealing and cheating. The strange thing was, even while people were talking about how bad he was, there was admiration in their voices. And they said, every one of them, that the one person who stuck by John Bradley through thick and thin, no matter what he did, was—"

"Let me guess."

"Right. Lucy's Bradley." He held up a hand when Zack opened his mouth. "Sorry. Bradley Porter. Seems like there wasn't much to Bradley Porter except for straight A's and the cleanest locker in the school. All the excitement he had, he got from hanging around with John Bradley. Hero worship."

"That was twenty years ago."

"Bradley Porter invited him to his wedding."

Zack straightened so quickly that he almost fell off the love seat. "What?"

"Bianca Bergman Bradley found the invitation and set out about two weeks ago to track him here. The Bergmans called this morning. They haven't heard from her since Thursday. Her description matched the shooting victim. We told them about her, and they're on their way now."

Zack sat down on the loveseat, totally confused. "The blonde in the hospital can't be Bianca Bradley. She's Bradley Porter's girlfriend. Lucy ID'd her."

"Maybe she's both."

"How?" Zack almost snarled the question. "How could she be? She was in California until two weeks ago."

Anthony ignored him. "You know, if John Bradley came here to hide with Bradley Porter, a lot of things that didn't fit suddenly make sense. John Bradley embezzles the money in California and escapes from the cops, his homicidal in-laws, and his shrew of a wife. That part I could understand. But then I could never figure out why he'd come here to Riverbend. Let's face it, we're not the Paris of the Midwest. But if he's got an old friend here who has always done anything he wanted, that part falls into place, too. He calls Bradley Porter. Bradley gets him a room in Overlook using the name of their old home town as an alias."

"What about the bonds?" Zack said.

"John Bradley hands over the bonds to Bradley Porter for safe-keeping. After all, he'd have to be a fool to keep them in Overlook. Those people will kill you for your socks, let alone a million and a half. Then Bianca shows up and calls you to put the pressure on him, and he shoots her."

"Right. How did she get my number?"

"She called the station and asked who was handling the Bradley case. They'd give her either you or me."

Zack leaned back against the loveseat, scowling. "So how did Lucy get involved? Because Bradley Porter hid the bonds in this house?" He shook his head. "We really combed this place. Unless he took up the floorboards, the bonds aren't here."

"Well, something is." Anthony stood to go. "It's possible that Bradley Porter doesn't even know about it. The desk clerk never saw him, so he may still be just an innocent bystander, helping out an old high-school friend."

Zack shook his head. "Bradley Porter is involved. I know it."

Anthony checked his watch and started for the door. "Well, just in case, you take care of Lucy. And don't assume because she sits there and blinks that she's okay."

"Oh, you picked up on the blink, too, did you?" Zack followed him to the door. "You're spending too much time with her. And what's this about telling her about the concussion? What else did you tell her?"

"Nothing important. I'm going home to salvage what's left of my Sunday. Give my love to Lucy."

"No," Zack said, and Anthony laughed as he went out the door.

"THERE'S JUST SOMETHING about it that just doesn't make sense," Lucy told Zack later while she watched him chop onions at the big old porcelain sink in her kitchen. "This whole master-criminal thing. Especially this thing with you and Bradley pitting your wits against each other. Bradley never pitted a wit in his life."

"Maybe he just hid that side of himself from you." Zack picked up the cutting board and moved to the old white stove next to Lucy, where a cast-iron pan full of hamburger was simmering. He dumped the onions into the pan with the hamburger. "Face it, you weren't close."

"We weren't," Lucy agreed. "Bradley's a very...closed person, I guess. I thought he would relax after we were married, but he didn't. And after a while, I didn't try very hard to open him up. I had the house and the dogs, and that was enough." She picked up a wooden spoon and stirred the hamburger to keep it from sticking. "I should have tried harder."

"Why?" Zack took the spoon from her. "He's a rat who possibly tried to murder his girlfriend. That's like Mrs. Bluebeard saying 'I just didn't give enough.'"

"I suppose." Lucy felt herself growing depressed again. She opened a blue enameled cupboard door, took down the chili powder, and handed it to him. Then she changed the subject. "Wait until Anthony hears you can cook."

"Forget Anthony," Zack said.

THEY ATE DINNER IN THE dining room in the soft amber light of the stained-glass lamp over Lucy's big oak dining-room table. They talked about his family and hers and about their jobs, moving in front of the fire to the love seat with their coffee when dinner was done. The hours passed, and they lost all track of time, sitting and laughing in the firelight. The only interruptions were two phone calls, both hang-ups that made Zack uneasy. He didn't discuss them with Lucy, and he made a conscious effort not to talk about either one of the Bradleys or the case, and he watched while all the tension drained out of her, and she smiled and laughed with him.

Maybe when this was all over, maybe then he could call her. Maybe they could go out, or just stay in and laugh.

Maybe when this mess was out of the way, and she was over Bradley, they could make love.

Maybe even fall in love.

It was a terrible thought because it appealed to him so much.

Falling in love meant commitment. Commitment meant marriage. Marriage meant responsibility and adulthood, which led to loss of instincts and old age and death. Or at least children.

Einstein poked his cold, wet nose at Zack's hand.

And dogs.

He looked around him, at the big old warm house, and the three dogs that were draped comfortably over his legs and snuggled next to Lucy, and most of all he looked at Lucy.

He'd be a fool to fall for her. She was a forever kind of woman, and his idea of forever was a three-day weekend.

Lucy looked up and caught him staring at her.

"Zack?" Her eyes were huge in the firelight, and her lips were soft and full, and without thinking, helpless with wanting her, he bent and kissed her.

Seven

Lucy's lips parted a little, and then she kissed him, too, moving gently against his mouth, leaning into him so slightly that he sensed rather than felt her and went dizzy at the sensation.

And he wanted to pull her close more than he'd ever wanted anything. She was soft and warm and the best place he'd ever been, but he had to get away. If he didn't get away, he'd do something stupid like make love to her, and then when he'd leave—and he would because he always left—she'd be unhappy. He'd be worse for her than Bradley had been.

The thought of hurting her cooled him down considerably.

"Sorry." He drew back. "I'm really sorry. Very unprofessional of me. I'm really sorry. Really."

Lucy looked lost.

"Uh, excuse me." He gently tipped Maxwell and Heisenberg off his legs and got up. "I better check in with Tony. I'll use the upstairs phone."

"Oh." Lucy bit her lip. "This late? It must be after ten."

Zack checked his watch as he edged away. "Twelve, actually. But he won't care." Then he escaped to use the phone while Lucy sat with the dogs and hugged herself in front of the fire.

"GET ME OUT OF HERE," Zack said when Anthony answered the phone on the sixth ring. He stood in the hall, stretching the phone cord to peer nervously over the banister into the faint glow cast by the fireplace below.

"Zack?" Anthony mumbled, half asleep. "Are you in trouble? Where are you?"

"Lucy's. Get me a replacement. Now." Zack thought for a moment. "Just not Junior."

"What are you talking about? It's the middle of the night."

"It is not." Zack dropped into a chair on the landing. "It isn't even one yet. Wake up."

"I am awake. But I'm not coming to get you just because you've decided you don't like the company."

"That's not the problem." Zack pressed his hand to his forehead. "I'm crazy about the company. I'm having immoral thoughts about the company. At any moment, I'm going to start making my move on the company, and then I will be in trouble. Get me out of here before I do something to make this permanent."

"Go take a cold shower," Anthony said. "Better yet, grow up. Learn to control your baser instincts."

Zack looked over the banister again to make sure that Lucy hadn't come within earshot. "Listen," he said, lowering his voice. "She runs around in this white thing that's big enough to roof Riverfront Stadium, and she still drives me crazy. A cold shower is not going to do it."

"She has green hair, too," Anthony said. "I meant to ask, did she do that on purpose?"

"Will you please concentrate?" Zack took a deep breath. "I'm serious here. I'm too young to be married. Married is for old guys."

"Married? Zack, you've only been there two days. Get a grip. You're hysterical."

"Listen to me. Lucy is not the kind of woman who plays around. Lucy is the kind of woman who gets married. And I want her, but I don't want to get married. And I don't want to hurt her."

"Good. I don't want you to hurt her, either. I like her."

"Forget it. You'd be worse for her than I am."

"Zack..."

"If you really like her, you'll get me out of here. Think what a lousy husband I'd make."

"Zack..."

"Tony, get me some backup and get me out of here, or I will end up the stepfather of three dogs."

"Worse things could happen."

"Get me out of here," Zack said.

"No," Anthony said and hung up.

"Hey!" Zack said to the dead phone, so loud that the dogs came up the stairs to see what was wrong, their toenails clicking like castanets.

"Zack?" Lucy called up from the living room.

"Nothing," Zack called back. "It's nothing." He looked down at the dogs. "If you have any loyalty to your mother, you will bite me if I get within two feet of her."

Einstein leaned against his leg, Maxwell stared into space, and Heisenberg rolled over on his back.

"You guys have got to get a new routine." He left them, calling back, "Dead dog," when Heisenberg refused to roll over. "I'm going to take a shower. I'll see you in the morning," he yelled down to Lucy, and then all but ran for the bathroom.

"Zack?" she called after him, but he slammed the bathroom door behind him to shut her out.

And in the morning, I'm gone, he thought. *Because if I don't leave in the morning, I will never leave, and I'll end up remodeling this house, and telling Heisenberg "Dead dog" twenty times a day, and making love with Lucy until I die.*

He stopped, nailed by the thought.

"Cold water," he said, and stripped off his clothes.

WELL, THAT'S THAT, Lucy thought, settling back in front of the fire. He kissed her once and then he ran up the stairs to get away from her.

She couldn't possibly be that bad a kisser.

It must be that she wasn't his type. He probably went for really exciting women. Women who wore black lace and had long, thick, blond hair.

As opposed to, say, dry, fuzzy, curly, green hair.

Could hair as bad as hers send a man running up a flight of stairs?

"It's not the hair," she told the dogs who had padded down to rejoin her when Zack shut them out of the bathroom. "It's me. I'm dull and unemotional. I should have jumped him when he kissed me, but did I? No. I was too polite."

She let her head fall back against the love seat.

"Maybe this is all just fallout from the car blowing up," she told the dogs. "You know, that 'You're never more alive than when you're on the edge of death' thing people are always talking about. Except, even with the car bomb and everything else, I still find it hard to believe somebody's trying to kill me. Which would seem to mean it's not the edge of death that's getting me into trouble here. It's the edge of Zack."

She considered what Tina had said. "Be irresponsible." She should just go right up those stairs and climb into bed with him and seduce him until he was witless.

Except she wasn't sure how.

She thought about it for a while, trying to figure out how black lace nightgowns and champagne and all the other classic stuff would fit with Zack's cheerful eroticism. Zack would probably prefer somebody who just crawled into his bed naked.

She couldn't do that.

And then there was her hair.

Forget it.

She sighed and called the dogs to go upstairs to bed.

AFTER A NIGHT OF frustrating fantasies about a fully-clothed Lucy, Zack came downstairs planning to tell Lucy he was leaving right after breakfast. Then the phone rang, and he answered it, and the caller hung up.

"I don't like that," he told Lucy as she came down the stairs. "That makes me nervous."

"Everything makes you nervous." Lucy moved past him to the kitchen. "You are a walking exposed nerve."

"Hey, I can be calm." Zack followed her to the kitchen, wanting to be with her. "I'm steady."

"Well, I've got to admit I'm amazed you've stayed in one place this long. I thought you'd be out the door by now."

Zack froze in the doorway. "Oh? Why?"

Lucy opened the refrigerator and took out an egg carton and the milk. "I thought you'd get bored. I had no idea you had this much staying power. And I want you to know, I appreciate it." She nudged the refrigerator door shut with her hip and smiled at him.

"I'm not really scared. But I appreciate it anyway. What do you want to make for breakfast? Eggs or French toast?"

Zack looked into her calm, open, trusting face. She needed him. "Eggs. We can have leftover chili for lunch."

THE PROBLEM WAS, there wasn't anything for him to do all day but look at Lucy and fantasize. He still couldn't see her naked, but it almost didn't matter.

Anthony was out checking prowler reports for Lucy's neighborhood, calling Pennsylvania again, and running credit-card checks to see if either one of the Bradleys was dumb enough to use his Visa card while he was on the lam. Even Junior was probably arresting jaywalkers. Only he was stuck baby-sitting three dogs and a marrying kind of woman he couldn't imagine naked.

He needed to do something with his hands. Fast. Before he put them all over her.

"You know, this kitchen tile is really ugly," he said, kicking at the gray speckled stuff as Lucy put the breakfast dishes away. "I wonder what's underneath it?"

"I don't know," Lucy said. "It's on my list of things to— Hey!"

As she spoke, the floor had slipped under her feet and she fell against the cupboard. When she turned, Zack was holding the edge of her kitchen floor in one hand, waist high, like a bedsheet.

"I don't believe this. The idiots put tile squares over sheet flooring. What dummies." He looked under it to see what was left on the floor and missed Lucy's glare.

"Zack, put my floor down," she said, but he didn't hear her.

"Come on," he said, dropping it finally. "Water got under here and the whole thing's loose. Let's move the table and chairs out of here and peel this up. There's wood under there!"

"Of course, there's wood under there," Lucy began, but he was already pulling the table toward the door.

"Pick up your end. We're going to have to turn it sideways."

Lucy sighed and obeyed. She was going to have to do the floor anyway sooner or later, and at least it kept him out of trouble.

And with her.

He might even kiss her again, and if he did, she was going to pounce this time. No more shrinking violet.

As long as he made the first move.

"Okay, tilt it to the right," Zack said, and Lucy obediently tilted the table.

Maybe if she wore her old tight jeans. He seemed impressed with them that day on the basement stairs.

Would that be fair?

Did she care?

"Come on," Zack said, and she followed him with the table through the door into the dining room.

"Listen," she said as they put the table down, "if we're going to do messy stuff, I'm changing into my jeans."

ANTHONY CALLED, AND ZACK took it in the living room, sinking into one of the oversoft chairs and moving his arm so Maxwell could climb into his lap.

"Glad you called. I want a phone tap," Zack said. "Somebody is calling and hanging up every time I answer."

"Sounds like a jealous ex-husband. You may want to watch your back. Mrs. Dover reported another prowler. If it's Bradley Porter, and he's the one running around with the .38, he uses it."

"Just so he doesn't use it on Lucy. She insists that he's not violent, by the way." Zack idly scratched Maxwell's ears. "Anything new on the car bomb?"

"I've got the final report here. Very neat. Plastic explosive, timer set on a five-minute delay, controlled damage. Professional job. And our Bradley—John Bradley—was in the Navy. Very tidy."

"If this case is so tidy, why are we still so lost?"

"Speak for yourself," Anthony said. "I'm pursuing the investigation with my usual cold, clean logic. What are you doing?"

"Ripping up Lucy's kitchen floor."

"With your teeth? Well, at least you're calmer than you were last night. What happened, anyway?"

Lucy came down the stairs and walked by wearing her jeans. She smiled at Zack before she went into the kitchen.

He had a sudden vision of her naked.

"Oh, *hell.*"

"What?"

"You know that fantasizing problem I was having?"

"Is this the 'Lucy naked' part?"

"Right. Well, I'm not having that problem anymore."

"Oh."

"I'm having other problems."

"Try a cold shower."

"There's not enough water in Riverbend." Zack stood, dumping Maxwell off his lap, and craned his neck to try to see through the dining room into the kitchen. "I'm relying on self-control and maturity."

"I'd be worried," Anthony said, "but I know Lucy can defend herself. How's your lip?"

"Great. I have to go now. You wouldn't believe how tight this woman's jeans are."

"Zack?" Anthony's voice was suddenly serious. "You know, it's not a great idea to seduce a woman you're protecting. All kidding aside, do you want me to send Matthews over?"

"Who?"

"Junior."

"I will shoot him on sight," Zack said and hung up so he could follow Lucy into the kitchen.

BY EIGHT THAT NIGHT, the phone tap was on, the floor had come up with a minimum of effort and a maximum of mess, and Lucy had shown Zack how to make roast beef with dry onion-soup mix for dinner.

"This is amazing," he said, after the floor was in the backyard, and they were in the dining room eating. "All I did was pour some water and that powder stuff on the meat and throw it in the oven, and three hours later, we eat. Do you have any idea what chefs get paid in this town?"

Lucy tried not to grin. "I don't think the Maisonette uses onion-soup mix. I think they chop more than we do."

"Absolutely amazing," Zack said, and Lucy laughed. "What?" he said.

"You just make everything so much fun. Even boring things like cooking and taking out the kitchen floor. You're excited about everything."

"Not everything. Just about some things." Zack watched her for a moment, her face warm and happy in the soft light. She was so calm, there was so much peace wherever Lucy was, that lately, whenever he looked at her, he felt like he was home. It was a dangerous feeling. If she could do that after only three days, where would he be in a week?

"Zack?" she said, and he said, "Tell me about yourself."

Her eyes widened in surprise. "Me? There's nothing to tell."

"Sure, there is. I already know you're a great teacher." He gestured at his plate with his fork. "And I know you're a great cook. And I know you have the sister from hell."

"No, she's not. She's just had bad luck with men."

"Three times? No offense, but that temper of hers must have had something to do with three divorces."

Lucy shook her head. "It wasn't like that. She used to be a lot nicer than me, although she was always really practical. The first time she got married, she thought she was getting married for money. Well, she didn't just think so, she did. Morgan was very rich. And he was a lot older than she was, too."

"A lot?"

"Forty years. She was nineteen."

"That's a lot."

"Yes, but then she fell in love with him. Our parents weren't...well...*warm* people. I mean, they took very good care of us, but there wasn't a lot of hugging. When we were kids, like in grade school, Tina and I used to talk about what it would be like when we got married, and we both swore we were going to marry men who hugged a lot, like the men in the movies. But then when we got older..." Lucy sighed. "Well, I still believed in that, and I think Tina wanted to, but then Morgan proposed. He was crazy about Tina, and Tina was just tired of not having any money, and she wanted to go to art school. Morgan promised to put her through, so she said yes. I tried to talk her out of it, but she said it was stupid to wait for love, and that Morgan was very sweet, and

she was going to do it. I cried all the way through the wedding because I thought she'd made a terrible mistake."

"So what happened?"

Lucy's face softened into a smile as she remembered. "He was
wonderful to her. It wasn't just the money. He thought all her paintings were beautiful, he thought she was beautiful, and he told her
so. He hugged her all the time, praised her all the time..." Lucy's
smiled turned rueful. "Six months after they were married, I apologized to her for trying to stop her. By then, she was crazy about
him. They were so happy together, people even stopped saying
she'd married him for his money."

"So what happened?" Zack repeated.

"Nothing for four years. They were waiting until Tina graduated,
and then they were going to go around the world for a year seeing
every art museum they could find for Tina, and..." Lucy stopped
again. "Tina was so excited. She told me that she was going off the
Pill for the trip because they were ready to start a family. She was
thrilled."

Zack winced. "Why do I have a bad feeling about this next part?"

"He died," Lucy said. "The week after she graduated, he had a
heart attack and died. And Tina was devastated. She was in mourn-
ing for almost two years. She wouldn't do anything but paint and
listen to music. Morgan had a huge record collection, and she used
to listen to it because she said it was like he was there."

Zack shook his head. "That doesn't sound like the Tina I saw in
the diner."

"The Tina you saw in the diner has had two husbands since
then." Lucy picked up her fork again. "One slept with her best
friend and one hit her. Don't criticize Tina. She's a survivor. I
should be more like her."

"No, you shouldn't," Zack said, alarmed. "You're fine the way
you are."

Lucy looked thoughtful for a moment. "You know, that may be
part of the reason I went ahead and married Bradley. I mean, marrying without passion worked for Tina. She got it all anyway. And
I didn't seem to be having much luck finding a hugger."

"So you didn't feel passionate about Bradley? What a shame. Pass the potatoes."

"I don't think I'm a passionate person." Lucy carefully avoided looking at Zack as she handed him the vegetable dish.

"Oh, you meet the right guy, and you'll be surprised," Zack said. "You got any plans for dessert?"

THEY SPENT THE REST of the evening scrubbing the old glue off the kitchen floor. At ten, they quit to take a beer-and-pretzel break, and the phone rang. Zack followed Lucy and waited while she picked it up. "It's Tina," she told him, and he took the pretzels and the beer over to build a fire with the dogs.

"So how's life with the cop?" Tina asked.

Lucy curled up in an armchair, draping the phone cord over the arm. "Difficult. But nobody's tried to kill me lately, so I'm not complaining."

"Hell, yes. It's been over twenty-four hours since anything's exploded in your vicinity. By the way, I'm buying you a new car for your birthday. What do you want?"

"Nothing. My insurance will cover it."

"There must be some kind of car that's bomb-proof."

"Forget the car. Get me something that's Zack-proof." Lucy dropped her voice and kept a wary eye on Zack across the room in front of the fire.

"Is he being difficult? Shall I have somebody beat him up?"

"No. If I need that, I'll do it. He's just driving me crazy."

"How?"

"Well, he's ripped up my kitchen floor, for starters."

"Why? He thought Bradley was under there?"

"No. I think he got bored, but he's afraid to leave for fear I'll get killed."

"So he ripped up the kitchen floor."

"Well, it keeps him off the streets. He's also cooking."

"He cooks? He didn't seem the type."

"I'm teaching him. We're starting with the basics. Nachos and chili."

"Lucy, what's going on?"

"I'm crazy about him." Lucy's voice sank to a whisper. "I've had more lustful thoughts in the past three days than in the entire rest of my life. Somebody blew up my car, and all I can think about is ripping off his clothes. I've never had so much fun, and I've never been so turned on, and he doesn't seem to notice."

"Jump him," Tina said.

"I don't know how. Ideas. I need ideas."

"Take off your clothes and crawl into bed with him. I know it's not subtle, but he looked like the elemental type in the restaurant. If you get too subtle, he may not catch on."

Lucy clutched the phone. "I can't do that. What if he says no, and there I am, naked? I'll die."

"He won't say no, but who cares if he does? Do it. Hell, guys go through this every time they make a move on a woman, and none of them has died yet. In many cases, that is, of course, unfortunate, but rejection is definitely not lethal. Go get him."

"I can't." Lucy shot another glance at Zack. "He kissed me last night, but then he stopped. Do you think it was my hair?"

"No. I think you should get your hair fixed, but I definitely do not think it was your hair."

"Maybe I'll make an appointment to get my hair done and then..."

"Lucy. You're just using this hair thing to hide behind. When you are ready to be that new independent woman you kept babbling about in the diner, you'll seduce him with your hair the way it is."

"Maybe. But maybe the hair makes a difference. Maybe that's why he kissed me and stopped."

"Maybe he was being a gentleman," Tina said doubtfully.

"Zack?"

"Maybe not. I'll stop by tomorrow night and check him out— No, I won't. I've got theater tickets."

Lucy breathed again. "Good. I don't need you helping. You'll hurt him."

"I'll stop by Wednesday night. If you haven't made your move by then, we'll work something out."

"Tina, really —"

"You have forty-eight hours. Do it. Just don't get hung up on him. I think this lust thing you're developing is very healthy, but Zack is not husband material. Just use him to get over Bradley, and then I'll introduce you to somebody nice and quiet and rich." A doorbell chimed in the background on Tina's end of the line. "Oh, hell. I've got to go. Bye."

"Tina, I don't think so…" Lucy began, but Tina had already hung up.

"Lucy?" Zack called from over by the fire. "Is everything all right?"

"Tina says hi," Lucy said and went to join him.

"THIS IS THE LIFE." Zack sat on the floor leaning back against the love seat. "Great food, great fire, great company." He looked over at the three dogs lined up expectantly beside him. "Don't look at me. Your mom's got the pretzels."

"Forget it," Lucy said to them from where she had curled up on the love seat. "Pretzels are bad for your figures."

The dogs lapsed into their favorite activities. Einstein put his head between his paws and watched the food, Maxwell sat and stared into space, and Heisenberg rolled over onto his back.

"Einstein, Heisenberg, and Maxwell," Zack said. "Is there a pattern to these names? Obviously, Einstein even I can figure out. He looks just like the old guy. But why Heisenberg and Maxwell?"

"They're both famous physicists. Heisenberg was because Einstein was suspicious of him, and I thought he was uncertain about whether he wanted to stay. I was wrong about the second part, but the rest of it fit."

"I don't get it."

"Werner Heisenberg said the universe was an uncertain place, with no real rules. He drove Albert Einstein crazy because Einstein wanted to believe that the universe was completely understandable. So when this poor little dog showed up at the front door and Einstein growled, and the next day the dog was gone but he came back again in the evening, I just thought, well, Einstein is suspicious of him and he's uncertain about staying, so…"

"You named him Heisenberg," Zack finished for her. "What part were you wrong about?"

"Heisenberg wasn't uncertain," Lucy said grimly.

"What?"

"Heisenberg was gone every morning for three days in a row. Bradley would tell me that he'd let him out and he'd just disappear, which I thought was strange because the backyard is fenced, but then Heisenberg is a small dog, so I thought maybe he'd found a hole. So I looked, but I couldn't find one. And then I got up early one morning and glanced out the front window and saw Bradley putting Heisenberg in the car. So I went out on the front porch and asked him what he was doing."

Lucy clenched her jaw, and Zack saw the old anger seep back into her eyes.

"I hate Bradley," he said.

Lucy swallowed and went on. "He didn't say anything, but while he was standing there, Heisenberg jumped out of the car and came trotting back into the house. Bradley just stood there, sort of annoyed. I wanted to *kill* him. I should have known right then that everything was over, but..."

"But?" Zack prompted.

"Well, we were married. That's serious. You don't go to court and say, 'I want a divorce because my husband tried to lose my dog.' And after all, he could have taken him to the pound, and then Heisenberg would have died."

Zack shook his head, disgusted. "No, he wouldn't have. If Heisenberg hadn't come back one night, what would you have done?"

"Called the pound." Lucy stared into the fire. "Bradley wasn't so dumb."

Her voice was lost, and Zack wanted to hit somebody. Preferably Bradley. "Yes, he was," he said. "He lost you. That was extremely dumb."

"Oh." Lucy blinked. "Thank you."

"You're welcome." Their eyes met for a moment, and then he looked away, searching for a diversion. Any diversion. No matter how lame. "Hey. Stop hogging the pretzels."

She passed him the pretzels, and he tried to remember the part about not getting involved.

"What I need to know," he said finally, dragging his mind back to the investigation, "is the kind of guy Bradley is. You seem really sure he's not a criminal."

Lucy picked up her cue. "It's hard to believe. He has no imagination. He's essentially a good man, but he's boring. If he was a criminal, at least he'd be interesting."

How boring? Zack wondered. *Was he boring in bed?*

"Actually," Lucy went on, "we were both boring. We were the most boring couple in Riverbend."

Zack gave in. "In bed, too?"

"I beg your pardon," Lucy said.

"It's a legitimate question," Zack said, trying to convince himself. "After all, he may have seduced and shot a blonde."

"No, he didn't. I told you, the blonde seduced him, which was more than I was ever able to do." Lucy blushed, but plunged on anyway. "Bradley approached sex the same way he approached everything else. He did it correctly, and then he forgot about it."

"Correctly?" Zack almost spilled his beer. "There's a correct way to have sex? Where am I when these rules get passed out?"

Lucy shrugged. "All right, efficiently then. I didn't like it. I mean, he was doing all the right things, but..."

"He was all the wrong guy," Zack finished for her, his voice thick with disgust. "You need a keeper. How could you have married this creep?"

Lucy glared at him. "Oh, let's talk about some of your ex-girlfriends. I bet there's a million stories in your Naked City."

Zack glared back. "Didn't you notice the sex was lousy before you got married?" He took a swig of beer to hide his annoyance.

"We didn't have sex before we got married. Bradley respected me."

Zack choked on his beer.

"No, he did." Lucy frowned. "That's what I can't figure out. I mean, Bradley wasn't exciting, but I was sure he respected me. I'd still swear that he loved me. Not passionately, of course, but... well...firmly. He sort of took me for granted, but he always wanted me around. He was very upset when I moved upstairs to the attic after he tried to kidnap Heisenberg."

"I bet he was." Zack stopped, putting himself in Bradley's place, a Bradley used to having Lucy warm and loving in his bed and then suddenly losing her. "I bet he was upset. Why didn't he move upstairs, too? I'd have been up those stairs like a shot."

There was a short silence, and then Lucy said, "Bradley wasn't you."

"Guess not." Zack shifted uncomfortably. "Want some more pretzels?"

A FEW MINUTES LATER, Zack took the dogs out for their last run, made sure the doors were all locked, and then stopped by the fire to say good-night.

"I'm sorry we had to talk about Bradley," he told Lucy, his face all shadows, backlit by the fire as he stared down at her on the love seat. "I know it upsets you."

"It doesn't upset me. Thinking somebody was trying to kill me upset me. Talking about Bradley hardly qualifies."

"Good." Zack hesitated.

Lucy waited, holding her breath, and then he said, "Good night," and went upstairs.

"Good night," she said and turned her eyes back to the fire.

FIFTEEN MINUTES LATER, Zack stretched out in Lucy's old bed in the attic and stared out the little diamond-paned windows.

He could just go down there and say, "So, Lucy..."

So Lucy what?

So Lucy, you want to take off your clothes and have incorrect sex with me?

Very smooth, he jeered at himself. *Just forget it. There is nothing you can say to her that will interest her. Go to sleep.*

But when he closed his eyes, he could see her. And just as he'd feared earlier, he wasn't having any trouble at all thinking about her naked.

And she didn't look anything like Queen Elizabeth.

"Oh, hell." He sat up in bed. *Think about something else. Something depressing.*

Fast.

Okay. The Orioles. Game seven of the '79 World Series.

The game appeared before him in vivid, depressing detail. And there on third base was Lucy. Naked.

"Oh, *hell*," he said, and fell back against the pillows.

HER FACE IN THE bathroom mirror was pale under her mass of green curls. Wrapped in her terry-cloth robe, Lucy stared at her hair in despair, and then suddenly leaned to look closer.

Her hair wasn't just plain green anymore. Part of it seemed lighter, so that her hair looked mottled in places. And part of it was a lot shorter, too. She ran her fingers through her hair and some of it broke off when she tugged.

She looked a lot like Einstein had after he'd rolled in chewing gum and she'd had to cut it out of his fur.

Except he hadn't been several shades of green.

Lucy leaned her head against the bathroom mirror. This was the absolute nadir. She would never again look this bad as long as she lived.

So, of course, tonight Zack was upstairs inspiring in her the most toe-curling fantasies of her entire life. Not that it mattered. Because she wasn't ever going to do anything about it anyway.

Was she?

Lucy stared at herself, lost for a moment.

Of course, she wasn't. Why was she thinking about it?

Because she wanted him so much she'd die if she didn't have him. She felt hot just thinking about him, the heat starting low and spreading as she thought about his hands, and his mouth, and his body rolling hard against hers, and the heat in his blue, blue eyes, and his mind-numbing, heart-stopping grin.

No.

She turned out the light and left the bathroom, depressed beyond reason. By the time she climbed into bed, she was almost in tears.

It was impossible. If she went up there to Zack right now, and crawled into bed with him like Tina had said, he'd look at her and say, "No." He'd be sweet about it, but he'd still say, "No."

But maybe he wouldn't. Maybe he'd just say, "Are you sure about this, Lucy?" and she'd say, "Yes," and he'd draw her down next to him and touch her and make love to her....

Her whole body tensed at the thought of his hands and his mouth, of Zack's warmth everywhere, of Zack pressing her so close to him that she was seared by his heat. She let her mind go, feeling the way he'd touch her, remembering his kiss in the firelight, the weight of him against her in the alley, on top of her in the driveway, knowing he'd be electric and vital and safe at the same time. She began to breathe more deeply, and her fingernails dug into the sheets as she imagined him first hard against her, and then hard inside her, and she shut her eyes so tightly that she saw stars, trying to feel Zack making love to her.

And then, finally, when she couldn't stand it anymore, she gave in to it and sat up in bed, wrapping her arms around herself. She didn't care anymore about her hair or her robe, or anything. And her mind was as clear as her body was racked.

I say I want to be independent, and then I lie down here too terrified to go after what I want.

Independence means going after what I want.

And I want Zack.

She slid out of bed, crazy with need for him, and walked with a pounding heart toward the attic stairs.

Eight

Zack sat up in bed and turned on the light when he heard her on the stairs, so his shoulders were naked in the lamplight when Lucy saw him. He stood out in sharp relief against the yellow-flowered wallpaper, the definition of his muscles a hard contrast to the softness of the flowers behind him and the quilt rumpled over him. His dark hair was tousled and his eyes heavy-lidded, and Lucy stopped, frozen both by how beautiful he was and by how much she wanted him. Her need choked her, pressed on her so heavily that she couldn't breathe, and she leaned in the doorway and breathed him in instead of air.

"Lucy?" he said, and she found herself floating toward him, drawn by the energy he radiated, feeling at once both suffused with desire and liquid with heat.

She sank onto the bed beside him, trying to find the right words, any words, but there was so much heat in her that she couldn't speak. She pushed herself through layers of air with only Zack's warmth to guide her to him, so that she was almost surprised when her lips touched his. It was like finding him underwater or in the dark, she'd had to penetrate so much to get to him.

She moved her lips softly against his, feeling the heat there, and then tasted him cautiously with her tongue while he sat, stunned. He was nectar and ambrosia and everything she'd read about; forbidden fruit and lotos, too. She kissed him again, this time falling against him with her lips parted, her tongue slipping inside his mouth to the hot sweetness there, and now, suddenly, he was kissing her back, his hands moving to pull her hard against him, the pressure of his body filling her with such heat and need that she clawed at his shoulders and bit his lip. Then he rolled with her until she was pinned under him, straining against his weight, and he pulled her robe from her shoulders, biting kisses down her neck while his hands pulled her frantically to him again, flesh to flesh, and she cried out first at the heat in him, and then, gratefully, at the sweet roughness of his mouth on her swollen breast.

Zack touched her the way she'd fantasized, with the same intensity that he lived every minute. His mouth and hands were everywhere, hot on her skin, now light, now rough, until she writhed against him and forgot to feel anything but need and heat and touched him with a hunger that she'd never conceived possible before. He tormented her with his tongue and fingers until she moaned from the frustration and the pleasure. He devoured her with his eyes, his hands, his mouth, intense and focused on her, all laughter gone as he concentrated the entire force of everything he was on loving her.

And when he slid his fingers inside her, she cried out, opening her eyes suddenly to see him staring at her, his eyes electric with desire for her. "God, you're beautiful," he said. "I can't believe how beautiful you are. I can't believe how hot you are."

His whole body was tense, rigid with control as he moved against her, and she moved against him, too, relishing his hardness against her softness. Her tongue traced his muscles, and he shuddered under her touch and forced her mouth up to his, crushing her lips against his while he stroked inside her mouth with his tongue. Lucy writhed under the twin tortures of his hands and his mouth, needing him so much now that she finally broke away from his kiss and sobbed aloud.

"Now," she said wildly, pulling his hips to her. "Now. I want you inside me, now," and he kissed her again, swift and hard, and then moved away from her.

"No," she said, and he ran his hand up her body to caress her breast again. "Wait," he said. "Just for a minute. I promise you."

She saw him roll over to sit on the edge of the bed, and she reached for him, dragging her fingernails down his back, luxuriating in the shudder it drew from him. She'd never felt so powerful in all her life or so alive, every cell in her body swollen with desire. Then Zack turned back again and pulled her to him and kissed her, rolling so she was beneath him. Lucy arched her hips to his, and then he slid slowly inside her, and she lost her mind.

She arched up once, sharply, galvanized by the shock of him so hard inside her, bringing sweet relief and tormenting pleasure at the same time, and then she began to surge against him, over and over, again and again, out of control as he moved against her, inside her, over and over, again and again, holding her so tightly that she felt both safe and destroyed at the same time, the tormenting rhythm of him in her driving her beyond pleasure into ecstasy. She wrapped her legs around him, trying to bring him closer, to hold him forever so that the feeling would never stop, and he laced his fingers in her hair and pulled her head back to face him as he rocked inside her.

"You're amazing," he breathed and kissed her, biting her lip, licking his tongue into her mouth as he rolled over, pulling her on top of him, holding her to him as he rocked up into her, and she felt suffocated by the sweet pressure inside her, her blood screaming and hot and swelling in her veins until she exploded in his arms, locked there while her orgasm surged into her fingertips and sent her mind into oblivion.

Then she lay gasping, feeling the pounding of her blood in her temples and in her swollen fingers, and the hot hard core of her diffusing into warmth and joy. He still moved against her, and as she eased back into reality, she was caught and warmed in the ebb and flow of him in her, and then she felt him tense hard in her arms and moan into her hair, and then they were both quiet, clinging to each other.

"I didn't know," Lucy said finally, when her heart had stopped pounding, her voice muffled against his chest. "I didn't know there was this."

"That makes two of us," Zack whispered, and his arms tightened around her. "Wait." He eased himself out of her, and she made a small sound of protest. "I know," he said softly, and then he turned away again to get rid of the condom. He pulled the sheet up over her where she lay tumbled on the bed, and then slid in beside her, pulling the comforter over both of them. "Next time," he said, his voice soft with exhaustion, "we'll go slower. We got a little crazed there. I wanted you so much, but I wasn't expecting you, and then when I got you, I wasn't expecting you to be like this." He kissed her and laughed softly into her hair. "I thought you were a good girl."

"I am." Lucy fought the sex-drugged sleep she was falling into. "You corrupted me. I thought I was going to die if I didn't have you. I couldn't have waited any longer."

"Thank God, you didn't. I was so nuts I was having fantasies about making love to you on third base."

"What?" Lucy said, losing her fight to stay awake.

"Go to sleep," he said and kissed her again before he fell asleep himself, his cheek pressed against her hair.

Zack, Lucy thought as she, too, sank into sleep. *This feels so good. I had no idea.*

WHEN ZACK WOKE UP the next morning, he was alone, bathed in the honeyed glow of the sunlight bouncing off the yellow walls. For a moment, he wondered if he'd dreamed the whole thing, but then he knew it had to be real. He could never have fantasized that calm, sensible Lucy could make love like that.

It must have been real.

Which meant he was in a lot more trouble than he'd realized. This was the first time his reality had ever been better than his fantasy. He'd found the perfect woman living in a great house with three dumb dogs. The smartest thing to do would be to run.

The smell of bacon frying wafted up to him. Breakfast. He had a sudden picture of Lucy in the kitchen, talking to the dogs. The same sunlight that was warming him would be filtering through the front windows, making shadow patterns through the lace curtains. The paper would be on the front porch, and the dogs would be ready for a morning run in the backyard.

It was all calm and quiet and regular and routine, everything he'd never wanted; and now he wanted it and Lucy, too, but most of all just Lucy, blinking at him, and telling him he wasn't logical, and rolling hot in his arms.

It was what he wanted forever.

What do you know? he thought, amazed, and, trusting his instincts as he had all his life, he surrendered without a qualm. *So this is it. I never thought it would happen, but this is it. Responsibility. Adulthood. Dogs.*

Lucy.

LUCY WAS STANDING AT the counter, blotting bacon on paper towels and trying to get her thoughts in order, when Zack walked up behind her and put his arms around her, pulling her close. She melted into him, instantly flooded with warmth and happiness, tipping her head back so that he could bend down and kiss her. Then she turned around in his arms so she could snuggle closer to him.

"No regrets?" he whispered into her hair.

"Of course not." She tilted her face up to smile at him. "You are a wonderful lover."

He smiled down at her. "I'd be a wonderful husband, too."

Her smile vanished. "What?"

"I think we should get married."

Lucy went cold with panic.

Married? After five days? She hadn't even been divorced three weeks.

Married? With her instincts for men? With her amazing ineptitude at understanding people?

Married? With all her talk about independence and freedom and...

Married?

"No." Lucy pulled away.

"Wait a minute." Zack pulled her back. "The 'No' was bad enough. Don't stop touching me, too."

Lucy relaxed against him again, but not with the same melting openness as earlier. "I'm sorry. You surprised me. Thank you very much for asking. That was very gentlemanly."

Zack scowled at her. "No, it wasn't. That was for me. I like it here. I want to stay."

"So stay. I like having you here. I just don't want to get married again."

Zack's scowl deepened. "What 'again'? This would be like a first time. You've never married me before. I'm not like Bradley."

Lucy smiled up at him. "That's for sure." His scowl disappeared, and then she added, "But I'm still not marrying you. It would be to-tally illogical. I've only known you five days."

"Five incredible days," Zack prompted. "Six, counting today. Admit it. Your life is a lot more exciting since I showed up." His eyes slid away from hers. "Is that pan supposed to be smoking?"

"I don't think you can take credit for the car blowing up." Lucy drew away from him to rescue the bacon.

"Well, there have been other exciting moments. I can think of several from last night alone. Hey, don't touch that. You'll burn yourself." He took the pan from her. "Ouch!"

"Run cold water over it." Lucy took the pan back and turned on the water.

"How come I'm always trying to take care of you, and you end up taking care of me?" Zack stuck his hand under the water.

Lucy began to fork the bacon out of the pan onto paper towels. "I think it's mostly mutual. I bet if we really analyzed it, it would come out about equal."

Zack stopped buttering. "You think?"

"Yep. Omelet's in the microwave."

Zack opened the door and peered inside. "We've got to get mar-ried. I love living like this." Lucy looked at him, exasperated. "What?"

"Nothing," she said. "Sit down and eat your omelet."

THE MARRIAGE QUESTION put a damper on breakfast. They'd moved from loving warmth to polite chill in the space of five seconds, and there were no signs of a warming trend.

The rest of the morning went downhill from there.

"I'm going back in to school next Monday," Lucy said after breakfast.

"No, you're not." Zack studied the kitchen floor. "I think this gunk will come up if we keep soaking it with soap and water. You got another bucket?"

"Zack, listen to me." She waited until his eyes drifted up from the floor, and then she spoke slowly and distinctly. "I cannot stay in-side this house forever. I have to go back to work."

"No."

"Listen, you," Lucy exploded. "You can say no all you want. I'm going back to work next Monday and there's nothing you can do about it. You have the rest of this week to get used to the idea, and you'd better do it because on Monday, I am out of here."

"Not a good idea," Zack said, and Lucy gave a smothered scream of exasperation and stalked out of the kitchen.

"Women are so emotional," Zack said to the dogs. "What do you think about this floor?"

AT TEN, ANTHONY dropped by, and Zack forgot the floor.

"Bradley Porter's using his credit cards," he told Zack when he answered the door. He walked into the living room and smiled when Lucy came into the room through the dining-room archway. "Hello, Luce," he said and Lucy went to him and hugged him.

"What is this?" Zack said. "Unhand that woman."

Anthony turned back to him, one arm still around Lucy. "So, you coming with me? We have to move on this. There's a patrol car out in front to watch the place while we're gone. Lucy will be fine."

"Oh, no, you don't," Lucy said, pulling away from Anthony. "I've been here since Thursday. I'm going stir-crazy. At least take me with you."

"Not a chance." Zack grabbed his jacket. "Bradley's been shooting people. I'm not taking you into that."

"Which Bradley, yours or mine?"

Zack shrugged into his jacket. "You don't have a Bradley. Remember that. Come on, Tony."

Lucy put her hands on her hips and glared at him. "Don't you think you should narrow down who you're chasing before you go charging off like this?"

"We'll argue about it when I get back." Zack started for the front door, and Anthony kissed Lucy on the cheek. Zack backtracked, grabbed his arm, and pushed him toward the door. "Why don't you cook dinner for a change?" he said to Lucy on his way out.

Lucy leaned against the back of one of her overstuffed chairs, defeated. "I'll order a pizza," she said, and Zack stopped and said, "No, you won't. I haven't gone through all of this to get you wasted by a pizza deliveryman." He followed Anthony out the front door, and Lucy felt like killing him.

"Maybe Phoebe will get him again," she told the dogs, and then the door opened again.

"I almost forgot," Zack said, and grabbed her and kissed her, bending her back over the chair in his enthusiasm. She clutched at him to keep from falling, and then relaxed into his kiss, relieved that he was kissing her again and reveling in his heat. "I will definitely be back," he said to her and kissed her again, pulled her back upright and left.

"Oh, good," she said, but he was already gone.

By noon, the silence had gotten to Lucy.

She'd made a big pot of vegetable soup, and talked to the dogs, and turned on the radio, but the silence was still there, even though there was enough racket for anybody.

There was nobody talking to her.

It had never bothered her before. But now, after days of Zack's constant rambling, it made the house seem empty.

"It's not like he's not coming back," she told the dogs. "Actually, I don't think it's him at all. I think it's just that I haven't been out of this house for days. I need to get out."

She caught sight of herself in the mirror over the fireplace. Her hair was even shaggier than before. She looked awful.

"I could go out and get my hair fixed." Even as she said the words, she knew she would. It was too awful not to. And how many people got killed in beauty parlors, anyway?

The dogs looked skeptical.

"This is so ridiculous," she told them. "People blowing up my car and shooting at me. This makes no sense. I'm going out."

Lucy was careful. She called a cab to pick her up three houses down so that the patrol car out front and any miscellaneous killers lurking around wouldn't know she was gone. She felt guilty about the patrol car, but she was tired of arguing with policemen. Granted, Zack was probably the worst of the bunch, but she was fairly sure that the one in the patrol car wouldn't be any more understanding.

And she left a note for Zack, so if he came home early he wouldn't panic. "Dear Zack," she wrote. "I can't stand the thought of you waking up to see my hair like this anymore so I'm getting it fixed. And I'll get something for dinner, too. Don't go to bed without me. Lucy." Then she stuck it on the mantel where anyone coming into the room would see it.

She just hoped that anyone was Zack. If it was Anthony she was going to be embarrassed.

LUCY ASKED THE CABBIE to recommend a good beautician, and he dropped her at a dingy strip mall paneled in peeling redwood and rusted chrome. It had a bar, a convenience store, a drugstore, a secondhand clothing shop, and a beauty parlor. The basics.

The beauty parlor was Thelma and Lou's.

It was dim inside the pink-and-orange salon, so it took her eyes a moment to adjust to the light and to the young amazon who walked forward to meet her.

"Hiya," the girl said and cracked her gum, and Lucy's eyes swept up, startled, to her hair.

It was purple, shaved at the sides, and gelled until it stood straight up. Since the girl must have been close to six foot before the hair, the effect was riveting. So riveting that the nose ring and the skull tattoo on her chest were hardly noticeable.

"Are you Thelma or Lou?" Lucy asked, unable to take her eyes off all that purple hair.

"I'm Chantel." The girl stared at Lucy's hair, fascinated. "Thelma and Lou are in Florida. Like, permanently. What can I do for ya? As if I didn't know already. Jeez."

Her own eyes still fixed on Chantel's hair, Lucy said, "I have a hair problem."

"No kidding." Chantel cracked her gum again. "I've never seen anything like it in my life."

They had to look like Harpo Marx meets the Bride of Frankenstein on a bad color TV. Lucy started to laugh.

"Well, at least you still got your sense of humor," Chantel said. "So, you want me to fix you or not?"

"I don't know. Do you have any experience fixing this kind of mistake?" Lucy touched her hair and it crackled under her fingertips.

"I don't have any experience at all. I just got out of beauty school yesterday." Chantel cracked her gum and smiled cheerfully. "If you don't want to take a chance, it's okay. I mean, somebody obviously did a number on you once. Why take a chance again?"

Chantel's smile was as open and honest as a child's, which Lucy knew was no reason for her to put her already ravaged head into her hands.

Or maybe it was.

"Somebody did do a number on me," Lucy agreed. "I ended up with the most awful bleach job you've ever seen. And then I tried to fix it with shampoo-in color, but that didn't work."

Chantel looked at her hair again and nodded. "That explains the green."

Lucy took a deep breath. "Can you fix this?"

Chantel looked cautious. "I can try. You sure you don't want to try one of those big places downtown?"

Lucy hesitated. "Yes. Yes, I'm definitely sure. What are we going to do first?"

Chantel's eyes narrowed, and she became all business. "Condition. We're gonna megacondition that mess and hope it doesn't fall out from relief."

Lucy swallowed. "And then?"

"A cut. Real short to cover up the breakage. And some color. I suppose you want brown or something."

"Brown." Lucy looked up at Chantel's purple hair and swallowed again. "No, not brown. That's not me. I'm the spontaneous, independent type."

Chantel cracked her gum. "Oh, yeah. I could tell that right off."

THE HOTEL ROOM WAS generic: bad paintings, worn green carpeting, tan flowered bedspread, and beige curtains at the sliding-glass doors.

Unfortunately, it was also clean. One of the Bradleys had checked out four hours earlier.

"The desk clerk recognized John Bradley's picture but not Bradley Porter's. So John Bradley was here using Porter's credit cards." Anthony surveyed the spotless hotel room. "Bradley Porter was probably never here. This makes no sense. This should be such a simple case. We have Porter's credit-card numbers. We have his house. We have his ex-wife."

Zack started guiltily.

"So why don't we have him?" Anthony went on, tactfully ignoring him. "Why hasn't anyone seen him? If he's innocent, why can't the Kentucky cops find him? If he's guilty, why did he give John Bradley his credit cards? I don't get this."

"We're not going to find anything here," Zack said. "It's got to be the house. Although I'm telling you, there are no government bonds there. I even took up the kitchen floor, which is the only floor that's not plain hardwood. If something's there, it's small." He folded his arms and sat down on the chipped edge of the desk. "You know, Bradley Porter's a banker. He wouldn't keep bonds in his house. Not for more than a night, anyway. What do you think?"

"A safe-deposit box," Anthony said. "I thought of that. I asked at Gamble Hills. No dice. He doesn't have one."

"There are other banks."

"Almost a hundred. Talk about hopeless. There's no guarantee he's using his name. And we'll need some specifics to get a warrant. Any other ideas?"

"Find the key and work from there. Which means, back to Lucy's."

Anthony looked around the room again and gave up. "Fine. Let's go back and look again. This place has been wiped so clean, we'll never find anything here anyway."

"Let me call Lucy first." Zack picked up the phone on the desk beside him and dialed. "We may need groceries."

"Groceries?" Anthony looked confused. "You do groceries now?"

"Hey, I've changed. I've matured."

"What do groceries have to do with maturing?" Anthony asked and then stopped when he saw Zack's face change. "What's wrong?"

"She's not answering." Zack let it ring a few more times before he slammed the phone down. "If she's out running again, I'm going to kill her. Let's go."

"She wouldn't be that dumb," Anthony began and then stopped when he realized the alternative. "Then again, she might," he said, and they both ran for the elevator.

THREE HOURS LATER, Lucy paid off her cab and climbed the steps to her house. Just as she was fishing for her key in her purse, a young patrolman came to the door and looked her up and down, smiling in appreciation.

"Can I help you?" he said.

"Yes," Lucy said. "We've met. Your name is Matthews, but Zack calls you Junior, and this is my house. Let me in. What is this, anyway?"

Matthews stepped back immediately to let her in. "Boy, are we glad to see you. We were about ready to drag the river."

An older patrolman was on the phone, but he stopped and squinted when he saw Lucy. "Didn't you use to be blond?"

"Don't remind me," Lucy said. "Do I know you?"

"Forget it. We're done. She's here," the older man said into the phone and hung up. "I'm Falk. You sent us after Warren a couple days ago, remember?"

"Oh." Lucy winced. "I'm sorry about that. What's going on here?"

Falk grinned. "Warren couldn't find you. It upset him. So we only got most of the force looking for your body."

"Oh, no," Lucy wailed. "I left a note. Why doesn't he read notes?"

"Go get Warren," Falk said to Matthews. "Let's put him out of his misery."

ZACK WHISTLED TO BRING the dogs in and headed through the kitchen to the living room, trying not to think the worst. She could be anywhere. Except with Tina, who was making plans to have Riverbend dismantled brick by brick until she found her sister. Or at her parents, who were annoyed because he had bothered them without any concrete reason.

Or here.

He walked into the dining room with Einstein on his heels and found Junior practically drooling over a strange redhead. She was cute, Zack thought absently, her head haloed in short, bright, coppery curls, but she wasn't Lucy, and Lucy was all he wanted right now.

Then she turned, and it was Lucy.

"Where in the *hell* have you been?" He surged toward her, relief supercharging his anger.

"I left a note." Lucy glared at him. "And I told you before, you can't just put me down someplace and tell me to stay. Why did you cause all this fuss?"

"Why did *I* cause all this fuss?" Zack threw up his hands, speechless for a moment. "Well, to begin with, there wasn't any note. None. Trust me. We have been over this place inch by inch. Looking for your body, bloodstains, anything. There was no note."

"Well, I left one." Lucy folded her arms in front of her. "You know, Zack, you've got to stop overreacting like this."

"Overreacting? Overreacting?" He stepped in front of her until they were nose-to-nose. "Lucy, *somebody could be trying to kill you.*"

She stepped back. "No. That's not..."

"Then who blew up your car? *Heisenberg?*"

"There's no need to be insulting," Lucy said, and Anthony walked in.

"She's not..." Anthony began and stopped. "Lucy?" He squinted his eyes at her. "Is that you?"

"Well, of course, it's me," Lucy said.

Anthony let out a healthy sigh of relief. "Sorry, the hair threw me. You look great, by the way." He looked from her to Zack and back again and grinned. "So I guess this means we can assume you weren't kidnapped?"

"Of course, I wasn't kidnapped," Lucy said and Zack said, "There's no 'of course' about it, damn it."

Falk shook his head and turned to go. "I already called off the search," he said on his way out. "Come on, Junior."

Matthews scowled at him but went.

Anthony turned back to Lucy. "We're all going to go now. Glad to see you safe, Lucy. Don't ever do that again. Zack, we'll try that search tomorrow."

He kissed Lucy on the cheek and walked out the door, visibly relieved.

"We need to talk," Zack snarled, and Lucy threw her purse on the table and went into the kitchen.

I CAN'T BELIEVE THIS, Lucy thought as she banged the soup pot on the stove. *I get my hair done, and he calls out the army. Honestly.*

She flipped the burner on under the pot and turned to see Zack standing in the doorway, scowling at her.

"I was careful," she said, tossing her potholders onto the counter. "I called a cab. I made sure I wasn't followed. I didn't go anyplace I'd ever been before. I left a note. I was careful."

Zack jabbed a finger at her. "I told you not to leave. You gave the patrol car the slip on purpose. I was worried. Worried, hell. I was frantic."

"Zack, I can't spend the rest of my life in this house because you worry," Lucy said, but she felt awful. He was looking at her like she'd come back from the dead, and there was a muscle twitching along his jaw. "I know you think this is serious. But you can't keep me locked in this house forever..."

He ran his fingers through his hair in frustration. "It's not forever, Luce. Just until I figure this out."

"Well, what if you don't?" Lucy folded her arms, determined to stand her ground. "Whether you like it or not, I'm going back to school on Monday. Are you going to frisk all my seniors? Pat down the custodians?"

"I'll figure it out." Zack rubbed his hand across the back of his head. "I will figure this out. I just can't get hold of this one, for some reason. It just doesn't make sense. My instincts just aren't kicking in."

"I can't live my life waiting for permission from your instincts." Lucy turned and lifted the lid on the soup pot to stir it.

"No, but you can stop taking such dumb chances," Zack flared. "You went out today for no good reason...."

"I went out for an excellent reason." Lucy slapped the lid down hard on the pot and turned to face him. "I'm an independent woman, and I wanted to go out. And my hair was driving me crazy."

"You went out because of your hair?" Zack's voice rose again, incredulous. "That's what this is all about? Your damn hair?"

"Listen, if you'd been walking around under my hair, you'd have broken, too," Lucy snapped. "You don't know what it was like. I mean, everybody who saw me just stopped, amazed..."

"It wasn't that bad, once you got used to it," Zack said, taken aback by her fervor.

"Oh, that's a real testimonial, Zack. That makes me feel so much better...."

"Will you take it easy?"

"Take it easy?" Lucy gritted her teeth, her anger fueled by her guilt at making him worry. "Take it easy? You know how awful it was. How many times when you were in bed with me last night did you look at me and think, 'God, she has awful hair'?"

"Never," Zack said flatly. "Not once. Are you kidding?"

"No, I'm not kidding." Lucy's anger surged. "Don't you care what I look like? What is this? Once the lights are out, I'm just like any of your other women? We're all alike in the dark, is that it?"

"Lucy," Zack said through clenched teeth. "Shut up." He took a deep breath. "You are absolutely unlike any woman I have ever met, thank God, and I don't care what color your hair is, and if you ever scare me again like you did today, I will walk out of your life forever because I can't take that kind of fear." He shook his head and turned away from her to stare into the dining room. "You were right about us getting married. Dumb idea. I'm not ready for it."

"Well, that's what I thought," Lucy said, but she felt herself go empty inside.

Zack turned back to face her. "I knew it would be like this. I told Tony it would be like this. You start caring for people, and your instincts go. Hell, your brains go. I don't mind being scared for myself. I'm scared for myself all the time. That's just part of being a cop." He took a deep breath. "But the way I felt about you today...no. I was so damn scared I couldn't think. I am never...*never* going to feel like that about anybody ever again."

They both stood still for a moment, silenced by the emotion between them, and then Lucy turned back to the stove, unable to cope
with the pain in his eyes.

"I'm sorry. But I think you're overreacting." She picked up the
lid again and began to stir the soup. "You and Anthony both told
me that this man is only trying to scare me out of the house. Nobody thinks I'm in danger anymore. Not even you."

"I'm overreacting."

"Yes."

"Fine." He turned and left the room, and fifteen minutes later he
came down with his bag packed.

Lucy felt her breath go when she saw him, but she made herself
sound calm. "Leaving?"

"This isn't going to work, Lucy," he said. "I'm too emotional
about this to be doing you any good. And you're probably right. I
probably overreacted. If you want somebody here with you for a
while, I'll call Matthews."

Lucy swallowed. "Junior."

"I don't think he likes being called Junior." Zack seemed
dimmed, as if a current had been switched off inside him. "You
want me to call him?"

"No." Lucy drew a deep breath. "Thank you for staying with
me."

"Oh, the pleasure was mine." Zack smiled tightly. "I've already
called a patrol car to watch this place. A different one. The first guy
is still pretty upset with you. And Tony will call you tomorrow."

"Fine," Lucy said, and he nodded and was gone.

LUCY WALKED INTO THE living room and sank down on the love
seat. "What happened?" she asked Einstein when he padded over.
"He wanted to marry me this morning, and now he's gone?" The
ache in her chest swelled into her throat, and she bit her lip to keep
from crying. "Boy, this has been a bad month. Good thing I'm independent now."

The lump in her throat grew until she thought she'd choke, and
she concentrated on not crying.

After all, nobody had died.

It was just the emptiness inside her that made her feel like somebody had.

"WHAT THE HELL ARE YOU doing here?" Anthony asked Zack when he came in the squad room.

Zack sank heavily into his chair. "Lucy doesn't need a bodyguard. We all know nobody's trying to kill her. There's a patrol car out in front. She's okay."

Anthony narrowed his eyes. "We knew all this yesterday. You stayed last night."

"Well, that was a mistake." Zack began to sort the mound of paperwork on his desk.

"But, Lucy—"

Zack looked up. "Forget it. You tried. It didn't work out."

Anthony looked as innocent as he possibly could. "I didn't..."

"Forget it."

Anthony shrugged. "All right. It's probably just as well. We got an interesting conversation between Lucy and her sister on the phone tap."

"Not interested," Zack said.

"Okay," Anthony said, "how about this? Mrs. Dover called again."

Zack felt himself freeze and kicked himself for it. "Maybe she's just lonely."

"I'm starting to wonder myself." Anthony leaned back in his chair, watching Zack. "She saw prowlers again last night and this afternoon. She's starting to see them everywhere."

Zack squelched the beat of fear he felt. "She's a crazy old lady with nobody to talk to except cops."

Anthony was still watching him closely. "We still haven't found what's in Lucy's house."

"Fine," Zack flared. "You go over and move in with her. I'm not going back there."

"She looked beautiful today," Anthony said. "I like her hair red."

"Shut up, Tony."

"Maybe I will drop by later, to check on her, make sure she's all right."

Zack swiveled his chair away, cranked a report form into the typewriter, and began to pound on the keys.

"Maybe I'll have dinner with her."

Zack hit the return carriage with enough force to send it across the room.

"Just a thought," Anthony said and went back to his own report.

LATE THAT EVENING, Lucy went into the bathroom and startled herself pleasurably in the mirror with her new red hair. Then she took a long, hot bath and thought about Zack.

He'd rocked her earlier with that marriage thing. Zack, of all people, planning commitment. It was like Madonna becoming a nun. Interesting but not likely to last. Especially since he seemed to be basing his decision on sex and food. He hadn't even told her he loved her. Not that she expected it. Although something along those lines usually turned up in a marriage proposal.

And then he'd walked out. Because she'd scared him.

Well, he scared her, too. He scared her because she felt so lost without him. And so lonely. It was as if the world was Technicolor with Zack and black-and-white without him. She felt colder and paler and smaller without him, shriveling without his warmth.

Well, all that was immaterial now. He was gone. It was over.

She climbed out of the tub and wrapped herself in her big terry-cloth robe and headed for the bedroom. Inside the door, she flipped on the light and walked toward the bed, only to stop about a yard from it.

It didn't look right.

She frowned at it, trying to figure out what was wrong. Nothing. Her bed, her quilt, her embroidered pillows. She put her hands on her hips and studied it again.

Maybe the problem was that Zack wasn't in it. Maybe this was an honest-to-God instinct kicking in.

Or maybe not.

She was still debating the problem when Heisenberg came trotting in and launched himself at the bed. Without thinking, Lucy swung out her arm and knocked him away before he could land on the quilt, and Heisenberg hit the floor and yipped and cowered away from her.

"I'm sorry, baby." Lucy scooped him up even as he shied away again. "I'm so sorry. I don't know..." She caressed him as she looked back over her shoulder at the bed. "No. I don't know what this is, but we're talking to Zack."

The relief she felt was so overwhelming that she almost ran for the phone.

Nine

➤ ◄

Zack's doubts had begun the moment he'd walked out Lucy's door, and Anthony hadn't helped any at all with his needling. He knew he'd had a good reason for walking. His feelings for Lucy were screwing up his life. But she was also the best thing that had ever happened to him, and he was growing increasingly more miserable without her every moment. He'd been dumb. So had she. They were both dumb, but they'd never have any dumb children now because he'd walked out instead of staying to fight.

Or talk.

He'd been at his apartment for several hours, staring at four empty walls and a moth-eaten couch, wondering why he'd never fixed the place up better and kicking himself for leaving a place that was perfect, when the phone rang. If it was Anthony trying to make him feel guilty again, he was going to pay.

Zack picked up the phone and snarled, "What?" into it.

"There's something wrong with my bed," Lucy said.

"Lucy?"

"There's something wrong with my bed. I know it's stupid, but I'm scared."

Zack sat down on the couch, his heart hammering. "What's wrong? What happened?"

"I don't know. I was going to bed but it just didn't seem right. And then Heisenberg tried to jump on it, and I hit him."

Zack's hand tightened on the receiver. "You hit a dog?"

"I know. I feel terrible. My hand just shot out.... I don't know."

"Instinct," Zack said. "You stay away from that bed. I'll be right over."

FIFTEEN MINUTES LATER, Lucy followed Zack up the stairs, still clutching Heisenberg. The relief she'd felt on seeing him had been overwhelming, and for the first time she really began to doubt that there was something wrong in the bedroom. Maybe she'd just done this to get back upstairs with him.

Would she hit a dog to get great sex?

Of course not.

Not if she was in her right mind.

Maybe Zack had made her insane.

If anybody could do it, he could.

Zack stopped at the bedroom door, and Lucy almost bumped into him. "Stand here in the doorway," he said. "Now what's wrong?"

She peered in through the doorway and looked around the room. "Nothing. I'm sorry. There's nothing."

Zack shook his head. "No. If you hit Heisenberg, there's something. Take your time. What is it?"

Lucy surveyed the room again. Nothing. It was exactly as she'd left it. "I'm sorry. There's nothing." Then her eyes went back to the bed, and she frowned.

"What?" Zack said. "It's the bed, isn't it?"

"I don't know." She shrugged. "It looks the same. It's just..." She stopped and then she shook her head. "Forget it."

Zack turned to the phone on the hall landing table. "I'm calling the bomb squad."

"No!" Lucy stepped between him and the phone. "Riverbend P.D. already thinks I'm a flake. You are not calling the bomb squad because I've got a funny feeling about my bed."

Zack jabbed a finger at her. "Hey, don't knock funny feelings. They've saved my life more times than..."

"Yours, not mine," Lucy said.

"Yours once," Zack reminded her. "But okay. We'll compromise."

"You? Compromise? I don't believe it."

"Get a safety pin and a ball of string. And put the dogs in the kitchen." Zack stepped cautiously into the bedroom. "You sure you don't know what bothers you in here?"

"Zack, get out of there," Lucy said with an edge of panic in her voice.

He looked back, interested. "That's a good healthy instinct you've got there, lady. Go get the stuff."

TEN MINUTES LATER, the dogs were shut in the kitchen, and the end of the string was safety-pinned to a corner of Lucy's quilt.

"Everything okay downstairs?" Zack asked Lucy when he met her outside her bedroom.

"Yes. Except I hope you didn't tell Anthony to call. Einstein knocked over the phone again. That's the second time tonight."

"Forget the phone." Zack took a deep breath. "Here's the deal. Chances are, if it's a bomb, it needs some kind of pressure to set it off. Like you getting into bed, for example. So, if we pull the quilt off, we should be able to see if there's anything wrong with bedding underneath. That quilt is so lumpy they could hide damn near anything under there, but the sheets are flat. If there is something there, we call the bomb squad. You with me?"

Lucy nodded. "I'm going to feel really stupid when there's nothing under that quilt."

"You'd feel even stupider if you got into bed and there was." Zack went cold at the thought. "Thank you for calling me."

"Thank you for coming over," Lucy said. "I'm scared."

"Good. Stay scared." Zack looked at the bed again and then closed the door part way as a shield. "Stay behind me."

When she moved back, he pulled firmly on the quilt and yanked it off the bed.

The bed blew up before the quilt hit the floor.

Dust whooshed out the partly opened door, and Lucy sat down on the floor, her legs suddenly giving out from under her.

"So much for the it-won't-explode-without-pressure theory." Zack slammed the door. "Call 911. Where's your fire extinguisher?"

The phone rang.

"The closet." Lucy pointed at the next door and then ran to call the fire department.

THE PHONE RANG AGAIN as she got downstairs, and she grabbed it to tell whoever it was to get off the line so she could call for help.

"Get out of the house," a voice rasped on the other end. "There's a bomb."

"What?" she whispered.

"Get out of the house now. There's a bomb. It's going to go off. Get out."

"It already did." Lucy's voice returned with her anger. "You creep, it already did. Who are you?"

But the caller had already hung up.

Lucy yelled for Zack as she dialed 911.

THE FIRE DEPARTMENT left when all the random embers in the bed were dead. The bomb squad left after a detailed search of the house for other explosives, making several pointed remarks to Zack about amateurs messing with things they didn't understand. Most of them stopped to say goodbye to Lucy on their way out, having met her when her car had exploded. It was almost a party.

And Anthony came by to see the mess for himself.

"Well, this is interesting," he said, looking at the wreckage of Lucy's bed, and Zack said, "More than you think. Lucy got a phone call warning her about the bomb. After it went off."

Anthony leaned in the doorway, considering. "He was cutting it awfully fine. The bomb went at around eleven-thirty. A lot of people are in bed by eleven-thirty." He looked at Zack. "He could have killed her."

Zack leaned on the doorframe opposite him and shook his head. "That was Einstein's fault. He knocked the phone off the hook. The guy had probably been calling in a cold sweat for hours."

"What are you talking about?" Lucy said.

"This is the same deal as the car bomb," Zack said to her. "Nobody's trying to kill you. The bomb squad said this one was more like a big firecracker. A big firecracker with a hair trigger, but still. It wasn't meant to hurt you. There's no point in warning you if he wanted to kill you."

Lucy's jaw dropped. "But I could have died!" she said finally. "I almost got into that bed! I don't care if it was a firecracker. Firecrackers kill people. That was a real explosion in my bed!"

"Well, if there was a fake one, his plan wouldn't work," Anthony pointed out. "He's still trying to scare you out of the house, Luce. The first bomb should have been enough. Remember? We tried to get you to go to a hotel, but you wouldn't go."

"So he had to really scare you out this time," Zack said. "Only the son of a bitch almost killed you. I really hate Bradley. He's dumb and he's dangerous."

"You think Bradley's doing this?" Lucy shook her head. "No. He knows if he just calls and asks, I'll give him his stuff back. Everything he owns that he left here is in those three boxes. And he can get in any time he asks. Bradley is not doing this."

"It's not in those boxes," Anthony said. "I've been through them. Zack's been through them."

"Wait a minute," Lucy said, ignoring him. "This really makes no sense. He had to get in here to plant the bomb, right?"

"Right," Zack said. "Which door did you leave unlocked this afternoon?"

"None of them," Lucy said, outraged. "But that's not the point. If he broke in here to plant the bomb, why didn't he just take what he wanted then?"

"Because he doesn't know where it is," Zack said. "It's lost somewhere in here."

"Oh, come on," Lucy said. "We've been searching this place for days. What could we have missed?"

"I know what I'd like to find," Anthony said.

"The safe-deposit box key," Zack said, nodding, and turned back to Lucy. "If the bonds are in a box, and the key is here, John Bradley can't leave town. He's shot Bianca, the Bergmans are on their way, looking for blood…"

"Actually, they're here," Anthony said.

"…and he can't get out of town until he gets those bonds."

Lucy frowned at him. "What safe-deposit box? We didn't have a safe-deposit box."

"We deduced a safe-deposit box," Zack said. "Just like in the movies."

"The only thing that John Bradley wants to do is get out of town," Anthony told her. "And the only thing that would stop him would be if he didn't have the bonds."

"And the only reason he wouldn't have them would be if somebody stole them, or he gave them to somebody for safekeeping," Zack said.

"Bradley," Lucy said. "He'd never steal, but the safe-deposit box sounds like him. He's very careful."

"But he doesn't have a box at Gamble Hills," Anthony said. "Now if we had a key, we could find the bank, and get a warrant, and open the box...."

"Bradley doesn't have a key chain," Lucy said. "He said it spoiled the line of his suit when he put a chain with a lot of keys on it in his pocket. He uses key fobs, one for each key. And then he keeps them in different pockets. He's very organized."

Anthony looked at Zack. "He lost the key. Here. Someplace here."

"Listen," Zack said. "Trust me. I've looked. I took up the couch cushions, I..."

"His chair," Lucy said.

"What?"

"His chair. If he sat in his chair, the key could have fallen out of his back pocket and into the chair. It slopes. The back of the seat is lower than the front. Every time I sit in it, my knees are up high and I have to lean forward."

"I remember," Zack said. "The first time I was here. You were sitting in it, all folded up." He started for the stairs. "Come on. It's in the basement."

THE CHAIR WAS EVEN MORE forlorn-looking than Lucy remembered. Falling through the stair rail hadn't done a thing for it.

Zack started by pulling the seat cushion off and handing it to Lucy, who poked and prodded at it. "There's no seam or anything here that's open." She tossed it down. "It's just a cushion."

Zack and Anthony had the chair upside down by then.

"Nothing," Anthony said.

"The hell with this." Zack took out his pocketknife and slashed the burlap fabric covering the chair bottom. They both peered inside it.

"Nothing," Anthony said.

"Turn it right side up again." Lucy knelt down in front of it when it was upright again. "When you sit in this chair, you tilt back, so anything that falls out of a pocket would go into the crease between the back cushion and the seat cushion."

"I already checked," Zack said. "I shoved my fingers clear to the back."

Lucy shook her head. "But every time somebody sits down in this thing, it jerks forward and then flops back. Anything that fell in the crease two weeks ago could be anywhere in this chair by now. Give me your knife."

Zack handed it over. Lucy moved around to the back of the chair, slashed at the upholstery, and peeled it up. She pulled out the foam and the wadding and exposed the coils at the bottom of the back.

"If it's anywhere, it'll be here." She crouched until her chin was almost on the ground, peering into the coils, and then reached her hand inside.

"Lucy," Zack said. "I really did…"

His voice trailed off as Lucy pulled out a small key with a square black head, stamped with a number.

"How did you know?" Anthony said.

"Logic," Lucy said.

"I'll be damned," Zack said.

AFTER HE LOCKED THE DOOR behind Anthony, Zack went back upstairs to find Lucy in her bedroom doorway, staring at the wreckage.

The windows were gone, replaced temporarily with boards, and the plaster ceiling sagged, and the hole in the middle of the bed had left it only a charred frame.

Lucy bit her lip. "I don't care if it wasn't a big bomb. It did a lot of damage. There wouldn't have been much left of me."

Zack put his arm around her. "You've got great instincts, kid, but we shouldn't be here now. Close the door and come on upstairs."

"My quilt." Lucy looked down at the torn and stained mess on the floor.

Zack tried to be helpful. "It has to stay where it is for now. The lab people will be back tomorrow to look at it. But maybe after that we can fix it." He looked down at it doubtfully. "Or something."

Lucy tilted her head to look at it. "Is that the way it was on the bed?"

"I suppose. I pulled it straight off. Why?"

"It's sideways. The square from the Confederate uniform goes at the top. I always put it at the top. Now it's over here. That's what I noticed, that the quilt wasn't right."

"Good for you." Zack tightened his arm around her and pulled her away from the door. "Come on. We're not supposed to be here."

He closed the door and put the tape back across it, and they turned toward the stairs. Then from inside the room, there came a loud cracking noise and a massive thud.

Lucy stopped cold. "Was that another bomb?"

"No." Zack opened the door to the attic stairs. "That was your ceiling. Falling. Don't go back in there, okay?"

Lucy swallowed. "I don't think I'm ever going to feel safe again."

Zack felt a surge of anger. Lucy loved this house and now some creep was making it a hell for her.

Then she turned to him, and he forced himself to grin. "Well, I can guarantee that if you go upstairs and get into bed with me, you won't be safe. I guarantee that you'll be attacked immediately. All my instincts say so."

Her eyes widened, and he held his breath.

"I thought we were finished," Lucy said. "I thought you left."

"I thought so, too." Zack stuck his hands in the back pockets of his jeans. "I can still go if you want. My instincts could be wrong, for once."

Lucy shook her head slowly. "Your instincts are never wrong."

"Good." Zack breathed deeply again and jerked his thumb at the stairs. "Get moving." She smiled at him suddenly, and he went dizzy just looking at her. "You know, I really like your hair," he said, trying to keep his voice light.

"Thank you," Lucy said, and went up the stairs.

"You didn't call Junior, did you?" Zack asked, and followed her.

ZACK WOKE UP THE NEXT morning, shifting against Lucy, feeling her warm weight as both a memory and a promise.

Thank God, he was back with her. Now all he had to do was figure out a way to stay with her. But he was going to have to be subtle. Take it slow. Think it through.

Then he looked down at Lucy, waking slowly, flushed and warm from sleep.

He'd think it through later.

Lucy yawned. He bent to kiss her, and she said, "Ouch."

"What?"

"Whisker burn." Lucy rubbed her cheek.

"I know, I know." Zack started to roll out of bed. "I'll shave."

"No!" Lucy caught at his arm and pulled him back. "Don't shave." She snuggled up next to him. "I like it."

"I thought on the porch the other day you said…"

"Well, I like waking up with you like this," Lucy amended. "You'll have to shave later to go to work, but I like it now. It reminds me of the first time I saw you."

Zack wrapped his arms around her and pulled her on top of him so he could see her better. "So it's all right in bed, huh?"

"Mm-hmm." Lucy balanced her chin on her folded hands and smiled sleepily into his eyes. "It helps with one of my new fantasies."

"Yeah?" Zack shifted a little to center her on top of him for maximum pleasure. "What new fantasy is that?"

Lucy grinned, the sleepiness in her smile melting into guile. "The one about the innocent schoolteacher and the vicious, uncivilized cop. Want to play?"

"Sure." Zack ran his hands up her back. "Who do you want to be?"

"I, of course, will be the innocent schoolteacher." Lucy batted her eyes at him.

"Which makes me the cop. All right, you have the right to remain naked."

Lucy laughed.

"Innocent schoolteacher, huh?" Zack watched her eyes close as he moved his hands over her. "This isn't going to work."

"Why not?" Lucy popped her eyes open.

"You're not that good an actress." Zack rolled and pinned her beneath him.

"Well, I *used* to be an innocent schoolteacher," Lucy said, and then he took her mouth, and she drowned in the heat there. *Thank goodness, I'm not anymore,* she thought, and then she thought of nothing but Zack.

THE DAY DRIFTED BY, a mix of unpleasant reminders like the forensics unit showing up to take Lucy's bedroom apart, and mindless pleasures like laughing over lunch and playing with the dogs in the backyard. Everything was back to normal between them except that they were being very careful not to discuss anything controversial, like marriage.

By the time dinner was over, Lucy still didn't know what she wanted in the future, but she knew what she wanted in the immediate present. She wanted Zack.

She leaned against the dining-room table and watched him as he sat on the floor and talked to the dogs.

And wanted him.

It was a new feeling for her, this helpless love and lust and longing that grew while she watched him. She'd never felt more out of control and had never enjoyed a feeling more.

She just wasn't sure what to do about it.

Zack looked up at her and caught her watching him, and she blinked.

"Say it," Zack said.

"What?"

"Say it." He grinned at her from the floor, Maxwell in his lap. "I've been meaning to mention that to you. You're about as transparent as window glass."

"What are you talking about?"

"Every time you start to say something you think you shouldn't say, you stop and blink."

"You're kidding," Lucy said, wide-eyed.

"Nope. Every damn time. Anthony noticed it, too."

Lucy felt herself blush. "Well, that's humiliating."

"No, it's not." Zack's smile washed over her, and she stopped blushing. "We thought it was cute. Anyway, the point is, you don't have to do that with me. There's nothing that you can't say to me. Just say it."

Lucy opened her mouth and shut it again.

"Say it." Zack tipped Maxwell off his lap and stood. He stepped toward her and put his face close to hers and his hands on each side of her on the table, trapping her there. "Nothing you can say will shock me. Just spit it out, honey."

"Make love to me here," Lucy said suddenly, as if she had to get the words out fast. "On the dining-room table. Right now."

"What?"

"Now," Lucy said. "I want you now. On the table."

"I was wrong," Zack said. "I'm shocked."

"Well," Lucy began, and then he put his hands on her waist and boosted her up onto the table.

"And delighted. Did I mention 'delighted'?" He moved himself between her knees, parting her legs as he moved closer to her, pulling her skirt up as he moved his hands up her thighs. "Don't you ever blink again. I might have missed this." Then he kissed her, and she fell into his heat, moving her hands across his shoulders to the back of his neck, tangling her fingers in his hair as he pulled her hips hard against him and licked his tongue into her mouth. She wrapped her legs around him, and he moved against her once and then stopped.

"Lucy."

"Don't stop," she said into his neck. "You feel so good."

"Oh, you do, too. Believe me, stopping is not what I want." He laced his fingers in her hair and pulled her head back to look into her eyes. "But I forgot. The condoms are upstairs. So you have a choice. You can sit down here and think hot thoughts while I set the land-speed record for a round trip on two flights of stairs, or you can set one with me and we can make it a one-way sprint. Your choice."

Lucy licked her lips. "Can we do it on the table some other time?"

"Often," Zack said fervently. "Whenever you want. I swear."

"One-way trip." Lucy slid off the table and down Zack at the same time. "Don't dawdle."

She kissed him hard and then raced into the living room, heading for the stairs while he recovered from the rush her slide had given him.

"You know, I used to think you were an old-fashioned girl," Zack called after her. "Thank God I was wrong." Then, having given her a healthy head start, he started running, too.

WHEN ANTHONY RANG the doorbell the next day, Zack answered then left Anthony to close the front door while he went back to Lucy in the living room.

"Absolutely not," he said to her. "No way."

Lucy sat down on the arm of one of the overstuffed chairs and visibly gathered her patience.

"What is it now?" Anthony asked, keeping an eye on Heisenberg, who had rolled over onto his back. "Lucy getting stir-crazy again?"

"She wants to paint the kitchen floor." Zack ran his fingers through his hair in exasperation. "Can you imagine? A great hardwood floor, and she wants to paint it."

"It's water-stained!" Lucy wailed. "It's all blotchy! It looks ugly, and if we painted it…"

"No," Zack said. "It looks just like my grandma's floor. You let it be. We'll just varnish it, and it'll look great."

"I don't think so…" Lucy began, but Zack's mind had already leaped to another subject.

"Have we got anything to eat? I'm starving. Nachos, that's what I need. Have we got nachos?" He turned toward the kitchen.

Anthony watched him, dumbfounded, and then turned to Lucy. "What have you done with Zack's brain?"

Lucy stood to follow Zack. "What brain? I don't think he has one. I think he's just one giant exposed nerve-ending. I swear sometimes at night, I can hear his neurons snapping like popcorn."

"Why does he give a damn about your kitchen floor?"

"Well, he sort of discovered it a couple of days ago, and I think he bonded with it. And now I'm not going to be able to paint it because it would break his heart, and it's *blotchy*."

Anthony looked at her closely for the first time since he'd walked in the room. She was wearing one of Zack's shirts with the top three buttons unbuttoned and tight jeans with the cuffs rolled up. Her hair was a halo of rumpled auburn curls, there was color in her cheeks from arguing with Zack, and she stood resolutely with her hands on her hips and her feet planted firmly apart, glaring at the kitchen and presumably at Zack inside it.

She looked positive and confident and alive and glowing. And pretty damn sexy.

Zack stuck his head out the kitchen door. "I found the nachos. Am I cooking for one, two, or three?"

"You're *cooking*?" Anthony said.

Zack looked at him in mild surprise. "Well, I have to eat."

"Three," Lucy said. "And remember, if the cheese explodes in the microwave..."

"I'll clean it up. Big deal." Heisenberg barked and Zack looked down. "Dead dog," he said, and went back into the kitchen, and Heisenberg rolled over, quivering with pleasure, and trotted into the kitchen, too.

"This is eerie," Anthony said. "It's like the Night of the Living Yuppies."

"Watch your mouth," Lucy said. "We never Yup."

"You know those old science-fiction movies where the mad scientist puts a steel cap on a human being and another steel cap on a chimpanzee and pulls a switch, and their brains scramble?" Anthony looked toward the kitchen. "That's what this reminds me of."

"Are you calling me a chimpanzee?" Lucy demanded.

"No, that would be Zack," Anthony said. "What's going on here?"

"What are you talking about?" Lucy blushed. "There's nothing going on here."

Anthony grinned at her. Lucy was hooked. Now all he had to do was make sure of Zack.

Zack called him into the kitchen for a beer.

"I found the bank," Anthony told him, lounging against the

counter to watch him cook. "We should have the warrant by to-morrow. You coming with me?"

"Oh, yeah." Zack sprinkled cheese over a plate of nachos with a practiced hand. "I want to see inside that box."

"Patrol car out in front for Lucy again?"

"Yeah. And I think her sister's coming over, too. We met yester-day for the first time." Zack shook his head. "That wasn't pretty. Another good reason for me to leave."

Anthony snagged a nacho chip from the bag on the counter and crunched it. "You know, Zack, if we find the bonds, you'll be gone permanently. We'll spread this all over the papers. Whichever of the Bradleys is trying to break in here will give up. Lucy won't need protection anymore."

"No, but she'll need me." Zack slid the nacho plate into the mi-crowave and punched the button. "I'm not going anywhere."

"I like Lucy—" Anthony began.

"I do, too, and I saw her first. Stay away from her."

Anthony tried again. "As I was saying, I like Lucy, and I don't want to see her get hurt."

"I don't, either," Zack said, exasperated. "That's why I moved in here, remember?"

"I'm not talking about the Bradleys." Anthony picked up another nacho, and Zack moved the bag away from him. "I'm talking about you. You worry me. I don't want you to hurt her."

"Why would I hurt Lucy?" Zack frowned at him. "What are you talking about?"

Anthony abandoned subtlety. "I'm talking about your inten-tions, you fool. Are you planning on living here forever?"

"Yes. And to answer your next question, I already proposed. She said no."

Anthony dropped his nacho. "You proposed?"

"But she'll give in. She just needs time." Zack leaned against the counter and folded his arms. "Hell, she just got divorced a week ago."

Anthony bent to pick up the dropped chip, but Heisnenberg was already there. He straightened. "Let me get this right. You asked Lucy to marry you?"

Zack looked unconcerned. "It may take a couple of months, but she'll say yes."

"You want to get married? You?"

"Only to Lucy." The microwave dinged and Zack took out the nachos. "We need salsa with these." He handed the plate to Anthony. "Be careful. It's hot." He began to rummage through the refrigerator, looking for salsa.

Anthony stood in disbelief as the plate seared his fingers. "This is eerie."

"No." Zack found the salsa and more beer. "This is Lucy. She has this effect on me. I like it." He slammed the refrigerator door and headed for the dining room.

"Well, I'll be damned," Anthony said and followed him.

TINA SHOWED THE NEXT morning on the dot of nine, striding into Lucy's empty kitchen as if she owned it.

"Your baby-sitter's here," she announced. "That coffee smells wonderful. I can't believe that I'm up at this ungodly hour. Only for you."

"Go upstairs and go back to bed," Lucy suggested, turning from the counter to hug her sister.

"No. Just give me some coffee. Where's the kitchen table?" Tina stepped back from Lucy as Zack came in from the dining room with the three dogs. "Oh, look, you hired a shepherd."

"You know, you remind me of somebody," Zack said.

"Spare me." Tina looked down at her feet. Maxwell had draped himself over her suede pumps. "Get off my feet, you little rat."

"Got it," Zack said. "Cruella deVil. If she doesn't scare you, no evil thing will."

"I see you're dating the cultural elite," Tina said to Lucy.

"Stop it, both of you," Lucy said. "It's too early for this."

"I'll put the boys in the backyard on my way out," Zack said as he put on his jacket. "Anthony's out front. Gotta go." He kissed Lucy on the cheek. "Don't forget the dogs. It's cold out." He passed Tina on his way out. "Great seeing you again."

When Zack and the dogs had gone, Tina said, "Don't forget the dogs? You? Who is he kidding? Exactly what is going on here?"

"Nothing."

A grin crept over Lucy's face, and Tina pounced. "Tell me everything."

"No." The coffee stopped dripping into the pot, and Lucy poured two mugs and handed Tina one. "I'm happy, and I'm being careful. You don't need to worry."

Tina leaned against the counter and sipped from her mug as she considered what Lucy had said. "What do you mean, careful?"

Lucy shrugged. "I know how bad my instincts are for men. I'm not counting on Zack sticking around. I'm staying independent." The toaster popped and she put two more slices of bread on a plate that already held four. "Strawberry or grape jam?"

"Strawberry. Where's your table?"

"We're refinishing the floor. Zack's idea. Come on, we can eat in the dining room."

Tina followed her in and sat down. "Lucy, you're not paying attention here. You don't have to worry about Zack sticking around. He's moved in. He's adopted your dogs. I think he's planning on being around for the next sixty years. In fact, I think you'd better prepare yourself to turn down a proposal."

Lucy slid into the chair across from her and reached for the jam. "He already proposed. But that was just heat-of-the-moment stuff."

"Men will say anything in bed," Tina agreed, and sipped her coffee.

"Oh, we weren't in bed. We were here. Having breakfast." She bit into her toast, enjoying the crunch.

Tina choked on her coffee. "Breakfast? He proposed in the clear light of day? In the morning?"

"Yep. Even before I fed him."

"It wouldn't have been the food, anyway. You don't cook that well." Tina sat back and marshalled her thoughts. "You're going to have to face it. He's serious."

Lucy tried to shrug it off. "Probably. But I don't know if I am."

Tina started to say something and then blinked instead.

"I don't believe it," Lucy said. "You do it, too."

"Do what?"

"You blink when you think of something you can't say. Zack says I do it all the time. And now you're doing it, too."

"I am? We do?" Tina was nonplused. "You're joking."

"Nope. What was it you were going to say?"

"Nothing."

"Something about Zack."

"No." Tina stopped and blinked again. "I don't believe it. I could feel it coming, and I couldn't stop it. That is one habit I am definitely breaking."

"What were you going to say?"

"Just that if you think you're not serious about Zack, you're deluding yourself." She looked again into Lucy's glowing face. "I give up. He's not the guy I would have picked for you, but he's obviously the guy you've picked for you."

Lucy looked prim. "Don't be ridiculous. I just got divorced. It would be foolish to talk about getting married again so soon. Really foolish."

"Illogical." Tina buttered a piece of toast and bit into it.

"Right."

Tina licked the butter off her fingers. "Don't put me in pink for the wedding. I hate pink."

ZACK AND ANTHONY stood in the dry metal-lined basement of the Third National Bank of Riverbend and stared into a dry, metal-lined safe-deposit box, the contents of which they had just inventoried. It did not have one hundred and fifty ten-thousand-dollar government bonds in it.

It had one hundred and thirty-two.

"He spent a hundred and eighty thousand dollars in less than a year?" Zack shook his head. "This guy needs a budget."

"Running from the police and homicidal in-laws is not cheap," Anthony said. "I think it's time to alert the media and get this guy off Lucy's tail."

"Hell, yes."

But when they got back to the station, there was a new report.

Bradley Porter—or somebody—was using his credit cards again.

In an Overlook motel.

OVERLOOK WAS A MISERABLE part of town, bleak and gray. As Zack got out of the car, an old hamburger wrapper blew down the street in front of the motel, startling a dirty mongrel who skipped away, limping, and a metal sign creaked and banged over a derelict gas station. The only signs that humanity had ever been there were the two cars parked in front of the motel, and the overflowing trash cans outside the burger place next to it.

There were no people.

"You take me to the best places," Zack said to Anthony, as they went into the motel lobby.

Anthony ignored him.

Fifteen minutes later, they were back on the street again. John Bradley had stayed there and then checked out. There were other people in his room now. In fact, there had been several other people in the room since.

Bradley Porter had never been there.

"This is nuts. This makes no sense," Zack said. "What is he, the Invisible Man?"

"Zack..."

"We know he's in this with John Bradley. So why doesn't anybody ever see him?"

"Zack..."

"If this guy really is in Kentucky all this time..."

"*Zack!*"

"What?"

"You've got to stop obsessing about Bradley Porter," Anthony said. "Get back to the case. It is entirely possible that he's not really that involved, that he was just doing a few favors for an old friend and got in over his head."

Zack set his jaw. "Porter's involved. Let's ask the people in that burger joint. They had to eat. Maybe they went there."

Anthony stared at the cracked plastic restaurant sign with distaste. "If they did, they were desperate."

"Exactly," Zack said.

Five minutes later, Zack was back outside with a greasy burger and a great feeling of annoyance. The counter girl had never seen

Bradley Porter, but she'd recognized the picture of John Bradley immediately.

"Are you sure you haven't seen this man?" Zack had pressed her, showing her Bradley Porter's picture again.

"Positive. He's hot. Him, I'd remember."

Great. He was hot. Great.

Zack had picked up his burger and stalked out, leaving Anthony to question her about John Bradley. Now out on the street, he unwrapped the burger. It didn't look like food. It didn't smell like food. And he didn't want to know what it tasted like. He went to put it in the trash and noticed the mongrel he'd seen earlier, sitting by the can. It was a middle-size dog, dirty gray-brown and mangy, but it had huge eyes that looked up at him.

And at his burger.

"This is your lucky day, mutt." He broke the sandwich in half and then in fourths so it wouldn't choke trying to swallow the whole thing at once.

He put a quarter of the sandwich down, expecting the dog to lunge for it. The dog looked at the sandwich and then at him with huge, pleading eyes.

"Go on." Zack nodded. "Go on. Eat it."

The dog moved cautiously toward the sandwich and then grabbed it and wolfed it down.

"Easy." Zack put the second quarter down. "Easy. You're going to choke, and I don't do the Heimlich maneuver on dogs."

The dog wolfed that section down, too.

When Zack reached down with the third quarter, the dog took it directly from his hand. Gently.

"You were somebody's dog once, weren't you?" Zack crouched down across from him, watching the third section disappear. He held out the last section and the dog took it, as gently as before. Zack wadded up the paper while the dog chewed and tossed it in the trash can. It immediately blew out again and tumbled down the street, startling the dog into skipping back a few paces.

"Rough life, huh?" Zack said, and the dog came back, cautiously, to stand only an arm's reach away.

Zack reached out and scratched him carefully behind the ears.

The dog closed its eyes in ecstasy.

"Don't get used to this," Zack said, and then he heard Anthony behind him say, "You talk to dogs?"

"Of course, I talk to dogs." Zack straightened quickly and scared the dog back another couple of steps with his movement. "It's not like I talk to plants or anything non-sentient."

Anthony cocked an eyebrow at him. "Non-sentient?"

Zack winced. "Sorry. Lucy's rubbing off on me."

"Well, if your conversation's finished, we've got things to do."

"Right." Zack got in the car, deliberately not looking at the dog. It was just a dog. Big deal.

Anthony started the engine, and Zack turned to the door to get his seat belt.

And there was the dog, sitting exactly where he'd left him. Staring at him.

Oh, hell.

"Wait a minute," he said, and Anthony stopped.

"What?"

Zack opened the car door. "You coming?" he said to the dog.

"You're kidding," Anthony said.

The dog just sat there, looking at him.

"Well, come on," Zack said, and the dog stood and walked slowly toward the car.

"Get in," Zack said. "We don't have all day." And the dog climbed in carefully, favoring its back leg, and curled up at Zack's feet.

"I don't believe this," Anthony said.

"Just drive to Lucy's." When Anthony didn't move, Zack glared at him. "Listen, I have no choice. If I left this dog, she'd never speak to me again."

"She'd never know."

"You don't know Lucy." Zack suddenly grinned down at the dog, and it thumped its tail. "Besides, this is a great dog."

Anthony stared at the dog and Zack with equal incredulity. Then he started the car and drove to Lucy's.

Ten

When Zack and Anthony came in the back door, Lucy was startled. She dropped a spoon back into the cake batter she was stirring and wiped her hands on a dish towel. "You're back early. What happened? What's wrong?"

Tina appeared in the doorway from the dining room and made a face when she saw Zack.

"Nothing," Zack said, his hands in his pockets. "We found the money. But we found something else, too." He steped to one side.

Behind him was the most pathetic-looking dog Lucy had ever seen.

"You poor baby." She sank to her knees on the bare wood floor and held out her hand.

The dog limped over to her instantly, and Lucy began to scratch it gently behind the ears, trying not to cry.

Zack had brought her a dog. Nobody in her life had ever brought her a dog. They rolled their eyes when they found out she had three, and they acted as if she were crazy, and they made jokes about her zoo. But Zack had brought her a dog. A wonderful dog that obviously needed her. And him.

She looked up at him. "Where did you find him? He must be starving. Tina, get me the biscuits. The poor baby. Where did he come from?"

Zack snagged the biscuit box off the counter and crouched down beside her. "Actually, he's full of hamburger. He was in Overlook, but he's a nice dog."

"He's a beautiful dog," Lucy crooned as Zack fed him a biscuit.

"That's the ugliest dog I've ever seen," Tina said from the doorway.

Anthony met her eyes. "Thank God. I was starting to feel guilty, because I wouldn't have touched it with a cattle prod."

Zack and Lucy ignored them.

"All he needs is a bath and some food," Zack said. "I'll give him a bath tonight. We'll take him to the vet tomorrow if that limp doesn't go away."

"He's precious," Lucy said, and the dog sighed and lay down beside her with his head on her knee.

"And he's not that much bigger than Heisenberg and Maxwell," Zack said. "He won't be much trouble."

"He won't be any trouble," Lucy said. "But he's going to be a lot bigger than Heisenburg and Maxwell. Look at his feet."

The dog had feet as big as saucers.

"He's only half-grown," Lucy said. "That's probably why whoever had him dumped him in Overlook. He wasn't a puppy anymore, so they didn't want him." She scratched the dog behind the ears again. "I think people like that should be shot."

"Well, he's ours now," Zack said, trying not to sound pleased. "Just what we needed, another dog."

"We have room," Lucy said.

Tina and Anthony exchanged glances.

"We'll have to think of a name," Zack said, and Lucy said, "You get to name this one."

"Okay," Zack said, and patted the dog's hip. "Pete."

"Pete?" Lucy stopped scratching. "Pete?"

"I had a dog named Pete when I was a kid," Zack said defensively. "It's a real dog's name. Not like...well, some I could mention."

"I didn't know you'd had a dog." Lucy smiled at him suddenly. "Okay, Pete it is." She scratched the dog behind the ears again. "Hey, Pete."

Pete drifted off to sleep, his head on Lucy's knee.

"I COULD HAVE FIXED YOU up with somebody rich who'd bring you diamonds," Tina said. Zack and Anthony were gone again, the dogs had been introduced to their new brother with a minimum of snarling, and Lucy was stirring her cake batter again. "But you want a guy who's never going to make six figures and who brings you flea-bitten dogs."

"Yes," Lucy said.

"You're hopeless," Tina said.

WHEN ZACK CAME HOME at six, he walked Tina out to her car.

"There's something I've been wanting to ask you from the beginning," Zack said as she got in her sleek red two-seater.

Tina looked at him impatiently.

"Why did you put those locks on Lucy's house?"

Tina shrugged and started the car. "I didn't want Bradley taking anything out. It was her house."

"Bull," Zack said. "I don't believe it."

Tina started to say something nasty and then stopped and cut the engine. "Get in the car."

Zack went around to the passenger side and got in, sinking down into the butter-soft black leather seat.

"Give," he said.

Tina took a deep breath and turned to face him. "I'm afraid of Bradley."

"What?" Whatever Zack had been expecting, it wasn't this. "I didn't think you were afraid of anything."

"I'm not afraid for me." Tina drew back, annoyed. "I'm afraid for Lucy."

"What did he do?" Zack said, murder in his voice.

"Nothing," Tina snapped back. "If he'd ever done anything, I'd have had him arrested and executed. This is why I didn't want to say anything. He never did anything. Get out of the car."

"No," Zack slouched lower in the seat from stubbornness. "You don't have to prove anything to me. If all you've got is a feeling about him, that's fine. Just tell me. I need to know."

Tina frowned at him.

"I need everything I can get on this," Zack said. "I'm afraid for her, too."

"It's hard to explain." Tina stared across the steering wheel at the empty street. "It was the way he looked at her. Like she was the most precious woman in the world and he owned her. It used to scare the hell out of me." She turned to face Zack. "He hated me. But it wasn't because of what I said or did. It was because Lucy loved me. He hated that. He wanted her all to himself. And he hated the dogs, too. Anything that Lucy loved, he was jealous of. He scared the hell out of me."

Zack tried to stay calm. "Did he ever lose his temper? Hit her?"

Tina flushed, and Zack remembered too late that she'd been married to a man who had. Before he could apologize and get himself in deeper, Tina went on.

"No. He treated her like...a queen. He didn't know her, not the real Lucy." She stopped and then tried again. "When you first meet Lucy, she's very quiet and polite because she's shy."

"The first time I met her, she beat me up in an alley."

Tina smiled suddenly and Zack was amazed. It was Lucy's smile, and Tina was an entirely different person with it. "Well, then you know the real Lucy." Tina's smile faded. "Bradley didn't. He thought he was marrying this...I don't know, this quiet, proper, wife kind of person. I think she tried to tell him that she wasn't, but he didn't want to see anything that wasn't what he wanted. And he was awful when she wasn't what he wanted. She told me that he wouldn't speak to her when she was wearing jeans. He just pretended that she wasn't there if she wasn't wearing what he wanted."

Zack clenched his jaw. "I really hate Bradley."

Tina nodded. "I know. It's the only thing you and I have in common."

"Why did she stay with him?"

"She's not a quitter. And he wasn't beating her or cheating on her or even yelling at her. He never yelled. So she just moved upstairs and they lived this very polite fiction. I honestly think Bradley may have preferred it that way. Making love to Lucy was probably too emotional for him."

"Bradley is an idiot."

"No," Tina said. "Bradley is scary as hell, but he's not an idiot. That's another reason why I hated him so much. I didn't think he would ever be dumb enough to do something that would make Lucy divorce him."

"Ah," Zack said. "I begin to see the light."

Tina clenched the steering wheel as she remembered. "When

Lucy called me, crying, that day, I wanted to kill Bradley, but I was also really grateful. Because he'd finally done something wrong. I bribed a locksmith to get there in minutes because I knew he'd be back, and I was afraid she'd let him in and listen to him." She turned to look Zack in the eye. "Lucy is very fair. I'm not."

"Good for you," Zack said, looking at Tina with unqualified approval. "You know, I like you."

"It won't last," Tina said. "I'm a bitch. Ask Bradley. You should have heard the things I threatened that man with when he showed up at the door. I think I seriously told him I'd have him killed. Not just as a figure of speech. The real thing. I threw everything I had at him, shrieking."

Zack's smile broadened. "I really like you. Thank God you were there."

"He's not going to just go away, you know." Tina looked very sober. "He's not going to give up. He's almost...obsessed with her. This government bond thing may be keeping him busy right now, but he'll be back for her."

Zack spread his hands. "Hey, I'm here. I'm not leaving her."

"Well, that's another thing." Tina darted a glance at him. "He's going to be furious about you. I'd watch your back very carefully if I were you. Bradley's too proper to ever do anything actually illegal in the normal course of things. But if he lost his temper for once, I think he could be homicidal. And the person he'd kill would not be Lucy."

"I'll remember that." Zack grinned at her. "I didn't know you cared."

Tina shook her head. "I'm not joking."

"Listen, people try to kill me all the time. It never happens. I'm Superman."

Tina rolled her eyes to the heavens. "Oh, terrific. Listen, I don't give a damn who you are. Right now, you're the only thing standing between my sister and that...that..."

"Rat," Zack supplied.

"No," Tina said. "That homicidal loon who wants her back. You be careful. We need you."

"Relax. I'll be careful." Zack hesitated, and then plunged on.

"Listen, as long as we're being honest here, I should probably warn you. You're not going to like this, but I'm going to marry your sister. She hasn't said yes, but she will."

Tina sighed. "I know. I'm past that. You're not my choice, but you're Lucy's. She won't admit it yet, but you are."

Zack relaxed. "Well, that's a load off my mind. I want you on my side. You'd make one bitch of an enemy."

"And don't you forget it," Tina said, narrowing her eyes. "If you ever hurt my sister, I'll cut your liver out. Now get out of my car. I've got things to do."

Zack opened his car door and then, on an impulse, leaned over and kissed her on the cheek. "You're not that tough," he said and then slid out of the car before she could retaliate.

"WHAT IN THE WORLD were you talking to Tina about?" Lucy asked when he found her in the kitchen, pulling cupcakes out of the oven.

"I was asking for your hand in marriage." Zack opened the refrigerator. "She said sure. What's for dinner?"

Lucy froze, the cupcake pan in one gloved hand. "She said sure?"

"She knows quality when she sees it. We've got steak? When did we get steak?"

Lucy put the pan down and slid another unbaked one in the oven. "Tina brought it," she said, easing the oven door shut. "And her cook made stuffed potatoes, too."

"You know, I like your sister a lot." Zack took the steaks out and started opening cupboards, looking for a pan.

Lucy's mouth dropped open. "You do? You really like Tina?"

"Oh, yeah. She's great."

Lucy looked at him closely to see if he was being sarcastic.

He wasn't.

"What kind of pan do you cook steaks in?" he asked, his head in one of the bottom cupboards.

Lucy gave up and went to find the broiler.

ON FRIDAY MORNING, Anthony came by with bad news. He stood in the living room and watched Zack mediate a truce among the dogs, and then he dropped his bomb.

"We've made the paper, but we're not on the front page. Another plant closing, more graft at city hall, and storm warnings for a major snowfall headed this way, but not us. We're on page two. The guy at the paper said he could have done better it we'd actually caught somebody, but just the bonds alone weren't very interesting."

Zack stood and left the dogs to stare suspiciously at each other. "Oh, come on, we've had two bombs here."

Anthony shook his head. "I tried that. Both already reported. Yesterday's news."

"Hell, *they* made the front page."

"Yes, well, if there'd been a bomb in the box, this would have, too."

Zack sank down onto a chair arm. "So all we can hope for is that John Bradley will read the paper all the way through. Great." He looked up at Anthony. "We're screwed."

"Possibly," Anthony said. "Maybe John Bradley reads his papers cover to cover. But just in case he doesn't, do not take your eyes off Lucy."

"I never do," Zack said.

ON SUNDAY EVENING, they put the dogs out in the backyard and sanded the kitchen floor. Zack had sent Anthony out for varnish, and he'd brought back three gallons and a spray can.

"What do we need spray varnish for?" Lucy asked.

"Touch-ups," Zack said. "Whatever can go wrong, will go wrong. Be prepared."

Lucy looked over at him and felt her breath catch, the way it always did lately when she looked at him. He was on his knees, scraping at the last stubborn spot of glue before they began to varnish, giving it the considerable force of all his attention. His shirttail was out of his jeans, and his hair was rumpled, and his eyebrows were drawn together as he concentrated. He looked solid and electric and safe and exciting and like everything she'd ever wanted, and she felt her breath go again, just watching him.

She slumped back against the cabinets and tried to breathe normally as she looked at him. Even now, semirelaxed, he looked like a coiled spring. She ached to touch him, to feel all that electricity under her fingertips. There was so much energy in Zack, it flowed into her, too. And some of her calm went into him. Maybe he was right. Maybe they should get married. Because she knew for sure that after only two weeks, she never wanted to be with anyone else. Ever.

How could she ever want anybody else but him?

She thought of all the times in the past few days that they'd laughed and argued and talked to the dogs, and even just sat side by side together in front of the fire, warm and happy from just being together. And then she thought of how they'd made love together in the past week, how hard his body was under her hands, how sweet his skin tasted under her tongue, and her heart began to beat faster. She closed her eyes and thought about loving him there on the floor, pulling his shirt from his shoulders and running her tongue down his body, tasting him everywhere. *I can't believe I want him this much,* she thought. *I want all of him, all the time, everywhere.*

I was never like this before.

It must be Zack.

He looked up then and caught her staring at him. "What?"

Lucy blinked.

"I told you to cut that out." Zack pointed the scraper at her. "What?"

Lucy hesitated, torn between her usual reserve and surging lust. Zack opened his mouth again and she cut him off. "Wait a minute. I'm trying to think how to say this."

Zack frowned and rolled off his knees to sit with his back against the stove. "Don't think. This is me. This is us. Just say it."

"Okay." Lucy swallowed. "Okay. Well. Okay. It's like this." She opened her mouth to speak and then shut it again. It was such an inappropriate thought. Saying it out loud was out of the question.

She blinked again.

"*What?*" Zack said, exasperated.

"I want you," Lucy said. "I want you...in my mouth." She blushed. "I want you hard in my mouth."

Zack closed his eyes for a second. When he opened them, he said, "You know, you've got to quit taking me from zero to eighty in two seconds without a warning, or I'm going to have a stroke." He tossed the scraper over his shoulder and rolled back onto his knees to crawl across the floor to her. "Come here."

Lucy met him halfway, and he pulled her to him. She arched up into him to feel the pressure of his chest on her breasts as he pushed her down onto the stripped wood floor and she ran her hands up his sides under his shirt to feel the hardness of his body. And when he kissed her, his mouth warm and open against hers, she wrapped her legs around him and pulled him tightly to her.

And the phone rang.

"Oh, hell." Zack pulled back from her, breathing deeply from her kiss.

"Ignore it," Lucy said breathlessly and pulled him back down to her, licking her tongue in his ear as she unbuttoned his shirt.

Zack said, "Right," and kissed her again, stroking his tongue into her mouth as he moved his hands over her. He ripped open the snap on her jeans and slid the zipper down, sliding his hand down into her jeans as he kissed her harder. Lucy rocked with the charge that surged through her, arching her hips up to meet his hand and biting him on the lip.

And the phone rang again.

"I want you so much," she said, her eyes locked on his. "All the time."

"Lucy," he said and fell into her to kiss her again, pulling her up hard against him.

She pushed up at him, tilting her hips so that he rolled onto his back and she was balanced above him. He ran his hands up her sides under her big work-shirt and then back down to pull her hips tighter against his.

And the phone rang again.

She leaned forward onto him to shove her jeans off, laughing as her fingers tangled with his on the waistband as he helped her strip them down over her hips, stopping to kiss him again.

And the phone rang again.

"Oh, *hell*." Zack stopped as his hands gripped her hips. He glared in the direction of the living room. "If that's Anthony, he's not going to quit." He rolled and tipped her off him gently and kissed her.

And the phone rang again.

Zack sat up. "I'm going to kill him. Then I'm going to leave the phone off the hook."

"Hurry," Lucy whispered, and Zack kissed her again, hotly, once quickly and then again, slowly.

"Count on it," he said when he came up for air.

The phone rang again.

Zack snarled in the direction of the phone and then stood, stopping to look at Lucy for a moment as she lay sprawled half out of her jeans on the floor. "You stay here, just like that," he said finally. "You stay hot, too. I don't want to find those jeans on when I get back here."

And the phone rang again.

"*Damn* it!" Zack said and went to answer it.

Lucy pushed her jeans all the way off and walked through the dining room to stand in the archway to the living room in her shirt and underpants. Zack turned as he got to the phone, and she held up her jeans and dropped them on the floor. "Ta-da."

"More," Zack said. "Take it all off." He picked up the phone in the middle of the next ring and said, *"What?"* and then he swore and hung up as she walked toward him. "I don't know who that is who keeps hanging up—" he began as he turned back toward her.

And then one of the front windows behind them exploded, and Zack yanked Lucy off her feet and onto the floor with him.

"Stay down!" he yelled, and another window shattered, and he rolled with her to a corner near the windows but away from the shattered glass.

"What is this?" Lucy screamed back, clutching him. "What's going on?"

And then there was silence.

"Are you okay?" Zack was holding her so tightly that she couldn't breathe. "Are you all right? Tell me you're all right. Say something."

"Yes," Lucy whispered, and his grasp on her loosened. "Those were gunshots, weren't they? Somebody's shooting at us."

Zack let her go. "Just stay down and stay *here*. Don't move." He spoke quietly as he drew away from her, but Lucy could hear the excitement in his voice. She reached out and hooked her fingers in the waistband of his jeans and yanked on it hard. His knees slid out from under him sideways on the hardwood floor and he fell, half on his hip, in front of her.

"Hey, cut it out," he whispered, annoyed. "There's glass all over..."

"What do you think you're doing?" Lucy whispered back. "Where do you think you're going? Somebody out there has a *gun*. Somebody out there is *shooting* at us."

"I know." Zack flashed his grin at her as he tried to pull her fingers off his jeans. "Isn't it great? Let go of my pants."

"What do you mean, isn't it great? Are you *crazy?*"

"Listen," he whispered, as he peeled her fingers one by one from his jeans. "I'd almost given up hope of ever finding this guy. Now that he's here, I think I should say, 'Hi.' Or something. Now shut up and stay down and *stay put*. There's glass all over the place and you're half naked."

"No," Lucy's voice rose with fear for him. "He's *shooting* at you, for heaven's sake. You stay put. I'm calling 911."

She leaned forward to crawl across the floor to the phone table, and Zack blocked her. "No!"

"Why not?" Lucy snapped, and the third window exploded, showering the phone table with glass.

"That's why," Zack said, pushing her back against the wall. "And also because by now your neighbors will have made the call for you. Mrs. Dover alone has probably called the Army, the Navy and the Marines." He let her go and started to move away again. "Now stay put. I've got things to do."

"Like getting shot at?" Lucy hung onto his arm. "No. Just wait for the police."

Zack yanked his arm away from her. "Lucy, I *am* the police. It's my job to get shot at. Get used to it."

"Get used to it?" Lucy sat stunned while Zack began to inch his way toward the dining room again.

"Can we talk about this later?" he said, as he crawled toward the kitchen. "While you're yapping at me, Bradley is getting away. Stay there."

"You're a Property Crimes cop, for heaven's sake," Lucy hissed after him. "You're supposed to be chasing burglars and embezzlers. How many crooked embezzlers shoot people?"

Zack had pulled his jacket from the dining-room table. While she watched, he took his gun from the inside pocket and checked the clip. "More than you'd think." He snapped the clip back in, and then, before she could reach him again, he was gone into the kitchen, and she heard the back door open and close softly. It was then that she suddenly felt the cold, not only on the outside from the February wind that blew the lace curtains away from her shattered windows, but deep inside, too, and it was the cold inside that made her shudder while she waited for him to come back.

It was very quiet for a while—quiet enough that Lucy could hear sirens in the distance. Gunshots anyplace would bring the police, but gunshots at her place would bring everybody in southern Ohio. It was getting to be like the O.K. Corral. With bombs.

Then she heard the shots.

There were three of them, one right after the other, and then silence.

The silence was worse.

Zack woudn't shoot first, she knew. Which meant that Bradley had. And once he had fired at Zack, Zack would shoot back. Except he hadn't.

It was really cold now where she was sitting. The February air was icy, but she hardly felt the wind on her body. The cold that was eating at her would have been the same in August, if she'd been the same place, hearing those shots, and wondering if Zack was bleeding someplace.

Or dead.

She was very calm, she realized. That was good. Amazing, but good. It was amazing how calm you could be when you didn't know whether or not you'd lost everything that mattered to you.

She heard cars pull up, sirens screaming, and red lights swinging through her living room, and she still sat frozen in the corner of her living room, shivering in the dim light from kitchen, waiting for Zack. She heard voices, but not his, and the dogs barking from the safety of the backyard, and slamming car doors and running feet.

But not Zack.

And I was afraid of commitment, she thought. *I was afraid of getting married and getting hurt again.*

What could hurt more than this?

Well, there's one thing for sure. If there was ever a litmus test for love, this has got to be it. If he comes back, I'll tell him....

If he comes back...

She heard the shouts outside, and then more car doors slamming, and then, after about fifteen frozen, tortured minutes, somebody cautiously kicked the rest of the glass out of the bottom of the middle window and climbed through.

He was too tall to be Zack.

"Lucy?" Anthony peered into the dimness. "Are you all right?"

"He's dead, isn't he?" Lucy's voice came out funny, strained and scratchy.

"Zack? No, he's fine. He's mad, but he's fine. Are you all right?" He came over to her and crouched down beside her.

"Don't lie to me," she whispered.

"I'm not," Anthony said gently. "I wouldn't. He got shot at but not hit. He's got nine lives, didn't he tell you? He's Superman." He put his arm around her and urged her up. "Come on. Let's get you out of this glass. It's cold in here."

She stood, shivering from fear and cold, and he looked down at her long pale legs in gloom.

"Barefoot all the way up, huh?" he said, and picked her up.

She buried her head in the hollow of his neck and he carried her into the kitchen, kicking the door shut behind him to get her some kind of warmth. Then he put her down and took his coat off and wrapped her in it while she clung to him.

"I don't know what I'd do if anything happened to him," Lucy whispered. "I just didn't realize it until now."

Anthony held her until she stopped shaking. "I can't tell you nothing's ever going to happen to him," he said into her hair. "Zack tends to attract trouble. But he's not stupid, regardless of what he looks like, and he's not reckless, and he likes life a lot." He tilted her head up with his finger so she could look in his eyes. "He likes it a lot more, now that you're around. He'll be more careful because of you now."

Lucy swallowed, and the back door opened, and Zack came in and stopped. "Very nice. My best friend and my babe. Unhand that woman, you rat. I'm out there getting my butt shot off...."

"Shut up, Zack," Anthony said, letting go of her. "Getting-shot jokes are not funny right now."

Zack took one look at Lucy's pale face and shut up, moving toward her so fast that Anthony stepped back to get out of his way. "I'm fine," he said as he wrapped his arms around her. "The guy has no aim at all. Never even got close." He hugged her so tightly she couldn't breathe. "I am fine."

"I know," Lucy said, muffled against his chest. "But it was bad there for minute. Does this happen to you a lot?"

"Hardly ever." Zack put his cheek against her hair. "And even then, crooked accountants are lousy shots. Most of them are pretty nearsighted, too. And of course, I move with superhuman speed."

"Of course," Lucy said, finally looking up at him. Her color was coming back slowly and both Anthony and Zack relaxed. She tried to glare at Zack, but it was weak because she was still so worn-out from the cold and the fear, and he held her close while she buried her face in his coat again. "Listen, you big dummy," she said finally, pulling back from him a little. "If you ever do that again, *I'm* going to shoot you."

Zack tried to look annoyed. "Hey. It's my *job*. It's what puts nachos on the table. Not to mention into your dogs."

"My dogs don't need nachos that much," Lucy began, and Anthony interrupted them.

"Well, since things are back to normal here, I'll just take my coat and go back out front. You should probably go on upstairs and take the dogs with you, Luce. We'll be downstairs for quite a while digging bullets out of your wallpaper. We've got people coming to board up your windows for the night, too, although if I were you, I'd call your sister and have her put in bulletproof glass for you."

"My windows!" Lucy pulled away from Zack. "That glass was almost a hundred years old. It was *beveled!*"

"Sorry about that. My coat?" Anthony held out his hand, and Lucy took it off and gave it to him, still fuming about her glass.

"Nice legs," Anthony said, grinning at Zack, who moved in front of her.

"You can go now," Zack said. "Some friend."

The back door opened again and Matthews came in, followed by the four dogs.

"Don't let them into the living room, there's glass all over." Lucy moved around Zack to stop them, while Matthews watched her with great appreciation.

"Okay, that's it," Zack said. "Excuse us." He pushed Lucy into the dining room and picked up her jeans. "Get dressed. And you, sit," he said to the dogs who obediently sat down in a row, Pete a beat behind the rest. Then he picked Lucy up and carried her through the living room to the bottom of the stairs, crunching glass as he went. "Go," he said, putting her on the bottom step. "And don't come down again until you're wearing shoes."

"The dogs," she said, but there were more people coming through the front windows, so she turned and ran upstairs while Zack watched, scowling.

Then he went back to the dining room and carried the dogs to the stairs, one by one, while Lucy stood at the top and called to them, shutting them in the attic so they wouldn't go back down. Maxwell, Heisenburg, and Pete enjoyed the trip, but Einstein weighed about eighty pounds and was not happy about being carried. Several people in the forensics unit applauded when Zack finally got him to the stairs.

Lucy called to Einstein and then grinned down at Zack, and he forgot to be mad. "It's a good thing you're cute," he told her, still scowling for effect.

Then he turned back to the mess in the living room.

"Somebody doesn't like you much," one of the technicians said. "Three .38s, right through the front windows."

"I don't like him much, either," Zack said. "The difference is, I'm the good guy and I'm going to win."

ANTHONY STOOD WITH Zack in the wreckage of the living room when everyone else had left.

"This doesn't make sense," Zack said. "We could have been

killed. This wasn't a scare thing. This guy wanted us dead. Or at least me dead. He may not have seen Lucy stripping in the dining room. It was dark in there and he was looking through lace curtains. He was shooting at me."

Anthony turned to him, interested. "Lucy was stripping?"

"Yeah. This guy is one hell of a chaperon." Zack scowled. "This was not John Bradley. This was Bradley Porter. Whether John Bradley read about the bonds or not, this was Bradley Porter."

Anthony shook his head. "You've got Bradley Porter on the brain. This is our same guy, trying to scare Lucy out. I'm going to lean on the paper on this one. The bonds, two bombs, and all Lucy's windows gone should be newsworthy enough for the front page."

"It won't matter. It was Bradley Porter," Zack said. "I'll make sure Lucy doesn't go to work tomorrow, just in case. But it was Bradley Porter."

IT WAS ALMOST TWO before Zack crawled into bed beside Lucy, shoving Maxwell and Heisenburg aside and waking her from an uneasy sleep.

"Move," he said. "I'm freezing."

Lucy, still foggy with sleep, rolled against him, wrapping her warmth around him, and the three smaller dogs settled against his back and across his feet. When he put his arm around her, he could feel Einstein radiating heat against her back.

"You okay?" Lucy asked groggily.

"As long as I don't try to move. It's a little crowded in here." He put his cheek against her hair and held her close. "I'm sorry I scared you, honey."

"Me, too," Lucy said sleepily. "Don't do it again. Although I guess it makes us even."

"How's that?"

"I scared you last Saturday, you scared me today. We're even."

"No, we're not. You took ten years off my life to have your hair done. I went after a dangerous criminal. We'll never be even."

"Oh, have it your own way." Lucy shifted a little against him. "Have you got enough room?"

Maxwell put his cold nose against Zack's neck and made him shudder. "We've got to get a bigger bed." Zack shoved the dog down away from his neck. "Or maybe we could get the kids their own room. What do you think?"

Lucy put her cheek against his chest and held him tightly. "You know, for a while, I thought I'd never have you like this again. And I decided then, if I got you back, I'd make every minute with you count."

Zack lost his breath, both because of her warmth and because of the ache in her voice. "Every minute, huh? You planning on a lot of these minutes?"

"Every one I can get." Lucy began to kiss her way down his neck.

The dogs spent the rest of the night on the floor.

THEIR FIRST MONDAY argument started at six-thirty in the bathroom when Zack realized Lucy was still planning on going to work.

"Somebody just shot out your windows," he said, his mouth full of toothpaste while he watched her towel her hair dry. "You could have been killed."

"Well, in that case, it makes sense that I go to work." Lucy spread the towel neatly over the shower rod to dry. "Why stick around someplace where somebody shoots at you?"

She tried to move past him, but he caught at the back of her robe, stopping her.

"Luce, it's too dangerous—"

She shook her head. "I'm going to school. That's final. Whoever wants in here doesn't want me, he wants the key, and the paper's going to print the story on the safe-deposit box today now that the windows have been shot out. It's over."

"But the shots last night—"

Lucy got away from him by slipping out of her robe and walking out of the bathroom naked.

"Hey," he called after her. "I was saying something important." He dropped the robe, rinsed the toothpaste out of his mouth, and hung up his toothbrush next to Lucy's. *Remember to propose again today*, he thought. *Find a new approach.* Then he followed her into her bedroom.

She was wearing pink cotton underwear, and as he walked in, she pulled a fuzzy pink sweater over her head.

"If you think you're going to win all the arguments from now on just by being naked," Zack told her, "you're probably right."

Lucy pulled her sweater the rest of the way down and laughed, her face lit from inside with love for him.

"At least let me meet you here after school," he said.

"Thank you. I'd like that." She turned and bent to pick up her skirt from the bed.

"How long do you have for lunch?" Zack asked, enjoying the view. "We could..."

"Half an hour and no, we couldn't." Lucy turned back to him. "I get off at three-thirty. Can you wait that long?" She bent over again to step into her skirt.

"Just exactly that long. I'll have to speed coming home." He reached for her as she zipped up her skirt, and she came into his arms, soft and warm and laughing again, and he held her close and thought, *We can't let go of this. Whatever happens, we've got to keep this.*

"I'M RUNNING LATE," Zack said half an hour later as he let the dogs out for their morning run. He was wearing a tailored shirt and a tie, and Lucy marvelled again at what an adult he looked like when he was well dressed.

"What?" Zack said. "You're staring at me. What?"

She leaned back against the sink and surveyed him carefully. "I was admiring you. You look very...adult. Sophisticated. Mature. It's a good look for you."

Zack scowled. "Don't say 'mature.'"

"I like the tie. It turns me on."

"A tie turns you on?" Zack shook his head. "You are sick."

"Well, I'll try to control myself." Lucy turned back to the sink.

Zack turned her around and bent her back in his arms. "Never control yourself." He kissed her long and hard, and Lucy leaned into him, drowning in the heat from his mouth on hers. When he finally let her go, he grabbed his keys and his jacket and then pulled her to him again. "We have a date at three-thirty, babe," he said. "Don't dress." Then he kissed her quickly and went out the door.

Maybe I'll propose this afternoon, Lucy thought. *At about four-thirty.*

The doorbell chimed while she was spreading jam on her toast.

Zack wouldn't ring the front door chime, so it had to be Anthony. She went to let him in.

The man on the porch was tall, dark, and well dressed, and she'd never seen him before in her life. Lucy watched him for a moment through the stained glass in the front door and then turned away. It was rude to leave him standing there, but it was the smart thing to do.

She went back into the kitchen and listened tensely as the doorbell chimed again. *Go away,* she thought, and tried to figure how she was going to get to her car with that man on the porch. He was probably only selling magazines or religion, but still…she wished that damn chime would stop…

The door chime stopped, and Lucy sighed in relief. She shoved her toast away, her appetite gone, and began to clean up the kitchen counter, picking up Zack's spray can of varnish last.

And then a black-gloved fist smashed through the glass on her back door and threw the dead bolt.

Eleven

Lucy screamed, and then he was in the kitchen, pointing a gun at her and kicking at the barking dogs that surrounded him.

"Don't move," he said, and she froze, the can of varnish in her hand.

"The key," he said. "All I want is the damn key." He was tall and tense and terrifying, and his eyes burned into hers, angry and desperate.

"It's too late," Lucy said, and her voice came out in a terrified whisper. "They found it. It was in the chair. They already opened the box."

"You're lying," he said through his teeth, and Lucy shook her head frantically.

"No, it's true. I can prove it. They counted what was in the box. There was $180,000 missing. The police have it all."

His jaw clenched, and she saw him clutch the gun tighter. "Then the police can give it back."

Lucy took a deep, deliberate breath, trying to stay calm. *Somebody help me,* she thought, and then she shoved the thought away and concentrated on saving herself. "You're better off just getting away."

"No." He kept the gun on her. "I can get the bonds. I've got you as a hostage. Where's the phone?"

Lucy tried to think around the terror that lapped at her brain. "That hostage stuff never works. Haven't you seen the movies? They surround the place and bring in negotiators. You'll never get out of here. Really, you're better off just getting away."

"We're not going to call all the police," he said and smiled at her. It was a chilling smile that never went near his eyes, and it made the next breath she drew sound like a sob. "We're going to call just one. Just the cop you've been screwing."

Lucy swallowed hard, too scared to be outraged. "What?"

"The dark-haired one. Call him and tell him to bring the bonds."

For just a second, the bottom dropped out of Lucy's mind, plunging her back to the night before, the darkness, and the shots, and the terror of losing Zack. "*No*," she said. "There is no way I will call him here so you can shoot him. *No*."

"You don't have any choice," he said.

"No." Lucy brought the spray can in front of her and hugged it to her chest, popping the lid off as she clutched it. "No. I won't."

"You don't have any choice," he said again. "Because I will shoot your dogs, one at a time, until you do."

He aimed the gun at Heisenberg, and Lucy screamed, "*No!*" and hurled herself at him, and the dogs screamed and leaped in response, so that when he fired the gun, the bullet missed Heisenberg and went harmlessly into the floor.

By then, Lucy was on top of him with the only weapon she had. And when he jerked his head up to her, raising the gun at the same time, she sprayed him full in the face with the varnish.

He stumbled backward, screaming and clawing at his eyes with his free hand, tripping backward over Einstein who had leaped behind him at the sound of the shot, propelled by Pete who didn't have the upbringing of the other three dogs and who went for his throat.

Lucy shoved past him in her scramble to get to the back door. She grabbed the baseball bat as she landed against the wall, and then, without thinking, while he tried to fight Pete off and clear his eyes, she swung the bat as hard as she could and connected solidly with the side of his head.

His head made a sound like a melon dropped from a great height, and he toppled over.

Lucy yelled for the dogs and flung open the back door, and when they were safely over him and out, she ran out after them and stumbled next door to Mrs. Dover's.

The old woman opened the door before Lucy could knock and stood there, scowling at her.

"I have to call the police," Lucy said, breathing hard, trying not to tremble. "A man just broke into my house and tried to kill me."

But Mrs. Dover had already swung the door open wider. "Get in here. I already called them. Gunshots. What's the world coming to?" She was saying all the words she always said, but there was no venom this time. She patted Lucy's arm awkwardly, frowning at her. "Is he still looking for you? Should we hide?"

Lucy's mouth dropped open. "I don't think so. I sprayed him with varnish and hit him with a baseball bat."

"Good for you," Mrs. Dover said, still scowling. "Want some tea?"

ZACK HAD JUST REACHED the door to the squad room when Matthews grabbed him. "Shots and screams at your place. It's Bradley. Falk's already there. I just waited to tell you. Go."

And Zack had gone, his heart frozen and his breath stolen.

Shots and screams.

His place.

And then he was there, and there was an ambulance, and he parked the car crazily against the curb and ran to find out how badly she was hurt.

That was when he saw her standing on Mrs. Dover's cement porch.

"I'm okay," she called to him, but he went to her anyway, holding her carefully to reassure himself that he hadn't lost her.

TWO HOURS LATER, THINGS were calmer, but Zack wasn't.

"What does he say?" Zack said, pacing back and forth through Lucy's living room.

"He doesn't say anything," Anthony said. He was stretched out in one of the overstuffed chairs, collapsed more from relief than from tiredness. "He's in surgery for a cracked skull. God knows what the varnish did to his eyes. Lucy really did a job on him. And more power to her. He's John Bradley, all right."

Zack stopped pacing. "We've got that for sure?"

Anthony nodded. "We've got it for sure. The Bergmans identified him. With great pleasure. I'll tell you, between Lucy and his in-laws, anything we do to him in court is going to be superfluous."

"We're still going to do it to him. What about the gun?"

"A .38. It's a match."

"So that's it?" Zack said.

"Well, we still need to talk to Bradley Porter," Anthony pointed out. "He has some explaining to do. But he didn't steal the bonds, and he didn't shoot Bianca. He's important, but not like this guy. The worst is over."

"Great," Zack said.

Anthony sighed and pushed himself out of the chair to stand in front of Zack. "I know what's bothering you. You weren't here for Lucy. But you couldn't have been here. He was waiting for you to leave so he could get her. You protected her as well as you could. And she's fine."

Zack hunched his shoulders. "Yeah, I know she's fine." He turned and walked away to drum his fingers on the mantel. "Tony, this whole thing *stinks.* Every instinct I've got says we screwed up."

"How?" Anthony demanded. "We've got John Bradley. We've got a bullet match, we've got him attacking Lucy, we've got him tied to the plastic explosive.… Hell, we've got everything but videotapes. He was trying to get Lucy to get the key. She got him first, thank God. It's over."

"No," Zack said stubbornly.

"Fine." Anthony shook his head. "I give up. You and your instincts stew. I'm leaving. I haven't had a full day off since I met Lucy, and I need one. I'm going back to do the report on this, and then I'm going home. If you need me, call." He turned to the door.

Lucy came in from the kitchen with two beers. "I know you're on duty—"

"Right." Zack took one of the cans.

"Thank you, Rambette, but no," Anthony said. "I'm just leaving, and regardless, I want all my reflexes sharp in case you attack."

"Don't laugh," Lucy said. "It was awful."

"I should have been here," Zack said and his voice cracked.

Lucy shook her head as she went to him. "It was awful, but I'm glad I did it. He tried to destroy my house. He tried to hurt my dogs. I'm glad I took care of it." She put her arms around him and looked up at him while he stared down at her miserably. "I wanted to be the one to handle it. That was important. I didn't know it until it was over, but it was."

"It's bad for my ego." Zack cradled her face with one hand while he pulled her closer. He brushed her cheek gently with his thumb and tried to grin, but he was tense still.

Anthony broke in. "Fortunately, as we all know, your ego has miraculous powers of recovery. And by the way, Lucy, I almost forgot. We got you something."

"We?" Lucy said, turning to him, and Zack said, "We who?"

"We everybody. Wait here." Anthony went out to the hall and brought back a long thin package. "It's from all of us—Falk, Matthews, Forensics. We all signed it."

Lucy stepped away from Zack and took the package. She opened one end and tipped out a brand-new baseball bat covered with scribbled signatures. "You're kidding! You all got this for me?"

Anthony grinned at her. "Actually, Forensics felt guilty about taking your bat as evidence, so I went out and got one about an hour ago. Everybody's signed it except Zack, and I'm sure he'll get to it later."

"Sure," Zack said.

Anthony studied him carefully. "You coming back to the station today?"

Zack nodded without looking at him. "In a minute."

"Well, I'm going now." Anthony put his arm around Lucy and kissed her on the cheek. "We're all very proud of you, kid. The only bad part is that we're not going to get anymore 911's from here. The boys are going to miss those trips."

"I'm not." Lucy leaned into him a little. "I just want my house fixed, and my life back to normal."

When Anthony was gone and Lucy had stashed the new bat in a place of honor by the back door, Zack leaned against the kitchen counter and said, "We need to talk."

"All right," Lucy said, her voice wary.

Zack folded his arms and tried to look calm. "Am I part of the 'back to normal'?"

Lucy started to blink and stopped herself. "Of course, you are," she said. "What are you talking about?"

"Well, look. I know you don't want to get married," Zack said, "but..."

"Well, actually," Lucy broke in, "I..."

They both stopped to let the other finish, and the door chime went.

"Wait a minute," she said. "It's probably one of your guys. Somebody probably forgot something."

He followed her to see, almost bumping into her in the vestibule when she stopped suddenly as she looked through the colored glass on the outside door.

She turned, and Zack, looking past her through the jeweled window, knew what she was going to say before the words were out.

"It's Bradley."

THE NEXT MOMENTS WERE jumbled for Lucy, trying to reassure Zack while not shutting out Bradley—a Bradley who looked so white and shaken and angry and so grateful to see her, all at the same time, that she felt sorry for him after all.

"Are you all right?" Bradley grabbed her by the upper arms and looked her over frantically. "I saw the police cars. Are you all right?"

"She's fine." Zack held out his hand to Bradley. "I'm Detective Zachary Warren, Riverbend P.D. We'd like to ask you a few questions about John Bradley. Where have you been?"

"Detective Warren." Bradley looked at Zack's hand for a moment, and then he released Lucy so he could shake it. "I've been in Kentucky. I left a forwarding address with the bank." He put his arm around Lucy. "Thank you very much for helping my wife."

"Ex-wife," Zack said, his teeth clenched.

Bradley looked down at Lucy. "Thank God, you're safe." He gave her shoulders a squeeze. "I think it's time we talked."

"I do, too." Lucy stood rigid inside his arm, keeping an inch of space between them by sheer force. "I think we should have talked about this a long time ago. Why didn't you call?"

"Tina told me not to," Bradley said. His arm dropped away, and Lucy relaxed a little. "And you were being unreasonable. You threw my clothes out on the lawn. You threw my chair down to the basement." He stopped as if he realized he was sounding petulant and then smiled down at her, tightly, forgiving. "But I understand. You were upset. I think we should talk now."

"I don't," Zack said, almost spitting the words out. "I think *we* should talk now."

"Zack," Lucy said to him, willing him to understand. "I need to know what happened. Then I can pick up and go on."

Zack glared at her. "Lucy, I'm a cop. He has information about a crime. I need to take him in for questioning."

"I know," Lucy said. "But I'm his ex-wife. I need a few answers myself. Give us just a little time. Please."

Zack clenched his jaw. "Swell. Let's all go in and talk."

Bradley's grip tightened on Lucy's shoulder. "There's no need for you to stay. This is between Lucy and me."

"Just half an hour alone." Lucy pleaded with him with her eyes.

Zack hesitated and then said, "All right."

Lucy stepped back so that he wouldn't kiss her. She didn't want Bradley putting up any more walls. She wanted to know what had happened, and how that blonde had come into her life and blown it into pieces just like the other Bradley's bomb had blown up her house.

And when she knew that, she'd have a new life, one with Zack this time, full of laughter and promise.

But first she needed to know what had happened.

Zack looked back at Bradley one more time. "All right. I'll wait outside. You have half an hour."

And then he was gone, out the front door.

Lucy took a deep breath. "Come on," she said to Bradley. "I'll make you a cup of tea. Two sugars."

ZACK SAT IN HIS CAR in front of Lucy's house and seethed.

Something was wrong. It wasn't jealousy. Okay, he was jealous as hell, but that wasn't it. He knew Lucy wasn't going back to Bradley. He knew she'd stay with him. At least, he was pretty sure she would. Hell, they'd adopted a dog together.

Think, he told himself. What was wrong with Bradley? He'd felt uneasy before he'd met Bradley, but afterward, he'd been crazy with suspicion. So it was something Bradley had said. Or done. And all he had to do was go through everything word by word, movement by movement, until he figured it out.

Fast.

LUCY WAS UNEASY.

There was something really wrong with Bradley. He kept looking at her like she was some precious treasure he'd lost and found, and, worse, he kept talking that way, too, in spite of everything she'd said.

"It's good to be home." Bradley surveyed the kitchen. "Where's the table? What happened to the floor?"

"It...came up." Lucy took a mug from the shelf and filled it with water, trying to think of how to get the answers she needed. Two weeks with Zack had taught her the futility of subtlety, so she put the mug of water in the microwave for his tea, punched the button, and then turned to face him. "Bradley, what's been going on?"

He frowned at her, annoyed by her directness. "It's very simple, really. An old friend of mine from high school came into town and asked for help."

"John Bradley."

"We called him J.B. in high school."

"He was an embezzler," Lucy said.

Bradley suddenly grew remote. "Unfortunately, I didn't know he'd broken the law. All I did was help an old friend."

"How?"

He frowned at her. "I arranged a hotel room for him."

"In Overlook?"

Bradley's frown deepened. "He didn't have much money. I offered to lend him some, but he refused. J.B. was always very proud."

"He had money," Lucy said, folding her arms. "He had almost a million and a half in government bonds."

"He didn't tell me that." Bradley was visibly angry with her now, annoyed that his statement had been questioned, and Lucy fought the coldness that his anger always drenched her in.

He couldn't do that anymore. Zack was going to keep her warm forever.

"You knew," she said calmly. "You put them in a safe deposit box."

"Once he told me he had them, of course, I did." Bradley was rigid with anger now. "It was the only prudent thing to do. I can't understand how you could even question that."

"I'm not questioning it," Lucy said. "I'm amazed by it. Where did you think he'd gotten that many bonds? K Mart?"

"Really, Lucy—" Bradley began, and she interrupted him, fueled as much by his anger as by hers.

"So how does the blonde figure into this?" Lucy said, glaring at him. "You know, his wife. The one you…"

"So that's it." Bradley's anger disappeared. "You're still upset about that."

"Well, *of course*, I'm still upset about that. I—"

"She lied."

Lucy stopped, dumbfounded. "What?"

"She lied," Bradley said. "She wanted to force me to tell her where J.B. was, so she said if I didn't, she'd tell you that ridiculous story, that we'd been…together. I told her not to bother. I told her you'd never believe her." Bradley's eyes were suddenly hurt and accusing. "And you believed her."

"Bradley, she described my bedroom," Lucy said, trying to keep her temper. "And you didn't say one word. Not one."

"I told you I could explain. You wouldn't listen."

"I listened," Lucy said. "You didn't explain. You said you would, and then you just stood there."

The microwave beeped, and Lucy took the mug out and plopped a tea bag in it before she shoved it at Bradley. Water slopped over the edge.

Bradley took the cup and watched the water drip off it. "A wife who loves and trusts her husband believes him without an explanation," he said, not looking at her at all.

"Not in this century," Lucy said, and when he didn't say anything, she went on. "So you never had an affair at all. And I've gone through all this pain and all this soul-searching for nothing."

"You should have trusted me. You know how much I love you."
He looked up at her. "I was going to tell you the day of the divorce.
Bianca said she'd meet me at the diner if I brought J.B. and then
she'd explain it all to you. But she didn't come. We watched from
across the street, but she didn't come. It seemed like no matter how
hard I tried, things just got worse. I thought for sure if she'd
come..." He stopped, and Lucy felt almost sorry for him, he
sounded so trapped and frustrated. Then his voice changed. "And
then we saw you with that man. J.B. said he was from the police."
He frowned at her, cold and remote again. "You were with another
man."

"He was asking me questions about your friend," Lucy said.
"About J.B. Bianca had telephoned him that J.B. would be there."

"She was a terrible woman," Bradley said. "She wanted the
bonds, and she thought she could get them if J.B. was arrested." He
put his tea down on the counter untouched and leaned forward to
take her hand, speaking to her earnestly but without warmth, as if
she were an important depositor at the bank. "But it doesn't matter
now. What matters is that we're back together again. From now on,
you'll trust me. We'll be fine."

"No," Lucy said gently. "We're divorced."

Bradley tightened his grip on her hand. "We'll get married
again."

"No," Lucy said, not gently, and tried to pull her hand away.
"We won't."

Bradley gripped her hand even harder, and she winced. "I know
you've been upset with me. But it's over now. It's just us. They're
both gone, J.B. and the policeman. I'm back, Lucy. And I've missed
you so much."

Lucy heard the determination in his voice and opened her mouth
to tell him firmly to get lost. Then she looked in his eyes and saw
something she hadn't expected to see.

Passion. Not sexual passion, but a blinding, possessive, obsessive
passion for her, all the same.

She closed her mouth and blinked instead.

ZACK WENT OVER THE conversation for the millionth time. "Thank
you very much for helping my wife." Zack glowered at that mem-

ory. Claiming her as his wife and then bitching at her for throwing his stuff on the lawn and in the basement. He was lucky she hadn't thrown it in the river. Zack pictured Bradley's face when he'd seen his clothes all over the lawn. It was petty, but it helped.

It couldn't have been pretty seeing his chair smashed at the bottom of the basement stairs, either....

Zack froze.

When had Bradley seen his chair at the bottom of the basement stairs? Lucy had done that after the locks were on.

He hadn't been in Kentucky.

He'd been in the house.

He'd helped John Bradley set the bomb.

And now he was in there alone with Lucy.

Zack started to get out of the car so he could kick down Lucy's front door, but then he stopped.

"He was crazy about her," Deborah had said. "He could be very jealous," Lucy had said. "He wasn't really sane when it came to Lucy," Tina had said.

Zack closed the car door quietly and walked around to the back of the house.

"I CAN'T, BRADLEY," Lucy said, trying to sound calm. "I'm sorry. I can't go back to you. It's over." She tried again to disentangle her hand from his, but he held on tight.

"This is because of that detective, isn't it?" Bradley clenched his lips until there was a white line around his mouth. "You even dyed your hair for him—"

"I really dyed my hair for me," Lucy temporized while she tried to think of something soothing to say, but Bradley plunged on, not listening.

"—so he wouldn't have to wake up in the morning and see you with brown hair."

"Green," Lucy said automatically and then raised her eyes to his face, startled.

"I loved you with brown hair," Bradley said.

"You read my note," Lucy said around the icy lump that suddenly filled her throat. "You read it, and you took it."

Bradley stepped closer, and she took a step back, bumping into the counter. "You don't need to change for me."

"You were here," Lucy said. "You helped that man put a bomb in my bed."

Bradley shook his head. "It wasn't supposed to hurt you. J.B. was going to call you and warn you about the bomb so you'd be scared and leave. But the phone was busy."

"That bomb had a hair-trigger fuse," Lucy said, her voice shaky with fear and anger. "Anything would have set it off. It could have killed me."

"I wouldn't have let him hurt you." Bradley blocked her against the counter. "I love you."

"No," Lucy said, trying to push him away. "No, you don't. You don't even know who I am."

"I know who you are." Bradley's jaw clenched so that he could hardly speak. "You're my wife." He shoved her arms away from him and pulled her to him before she could protest, and then he kissed her with as much passion as he could.

It was horrible.

BRADLEY HAD TO HAVE gotten in somehow.

Zack prowled around the outside of the house, trying to think how Bradley could have breached the security of Tina's locks. They were all fine. He'd tried every one, and now he was back at the basement doors. He yanked on the locks again, but they held.

"This makes no sense," he said aloud, and then out of the corner of his eye he saw a flash of yellow fur.

He spun on his heel, startling Phoebe, who stopped practically in mid-leap. "Back off, you furry little bitch," Zack snarled. "I'm not in the mood."

Phoebe snarled back at him and leaped away.

Oh, good. He was up against insane house cats now. Lucy took care of armed men, and he repelled flea-bitten unhinged…

He stopped in mid-thought.

Unhinged.

He reached down for the door and, this time, instead of tugging at the center of the bars, he tugged on the hinges to the left.

Nothing.

But when he pulled on the hinges to the right, they lifted away, the double doors fused together with Tina's locks, swinging up smoothly on the left-hand hinges.

Bingo. Zack started down the stairs.

So did Phoebe.

LUCY DUCKED AWAY, shoving hard to break Bradley's hold. "No. *Stop it.*"

"It's that policeman, isn't it?" Bradley's face was wooden, but he let go of her.

Lucy backed into the corner of the kitchen nearest the door, giving herself an escape route. "No, Bradley, it's you. You let that man in here to bomb this house and try to kill me. You knew he was dangerous. He shot his wife. You knew that."

Bradley stepped forward to reach for her again, and Lucy stepped back, grabbing the back-door knob, and then they both froze, trapped by the scream of a cat in the basement.

"That's Phoebe." Lucy moved toward the basement door. "How did she get in the basement?"

"I know," Bradley said, and when she turned he was holding a gun.

"Bradley?" Her voice came in a squeak.

"Get away from the door," he said calmly. "There's a prowler down there."

Lucy edged away from the door, praying Bradley wasn't the type to hold a grudge. How rude had she been?

How out of touch was he?

He moved slowly toward the basement door, like an avalanche gathering speed. Just before he opened the door, he stopped and looked at her. "You stay here. We still need to talk."

"Right," Lucy said, bobbing her head frantically. "You bet."

STIFLING HIS SCREAM WHEN Phoebe went for his leg had been one of the hardest things Zack had ever done, but he'd managed it, smacking her away with his fist and provoking a scream from her that could have peeled paint. She ran back up the stairs to the outside, and he froze for a moment until he was sure no one had heard.

He was on the first step up the stairs to the kitchen when Bradley opened the door and pointed the gun at him.

"Back." Bradley let the basement door swing closed behind him, and then he walked carefully down the stairs until he was halfway to the bottom.

"Where's Lucy?" Zack asked, backing away. "Is she…"

"Forget Lucy," Bradley said coldly. "Lucy is my wife. She's staying with me."

Zack tried to think. Present tense was a good sign. Maybe he'd sent her out for milk. Maybe she wasn't bleeding to death on the kitchen floor.

He hadn't heard any shots.

"I'm going to have to kill you." Bradley sounded as if he wasn't positive that killing Zack was a good idea, but he was willing to chance it.

"Hey," Zack said, wishing Anthony was there. "I think we should talk about this. You're not a bad guy. I'm not a bad guy. We've got a lot in common. How about you put down the gun, and we discuss the situation?"

If possible, Bradley grew colder. "Evidently we do have a lot in common. You've been sleeping with my wife." He pointed the gun at Zack's midsection.

This was not good. "Your wife? Lucy? Not at all." Zack shook his head. "Nope. Just protecting her. Trust me."

"I'm not a fool. I read the note she left for you that day. And I can tell from the way she looked at you in the hall." Bradley raised the gun higher. "I'm going to kill you."

"Bad idea," Zack said quickly. "Murder is always a bad idea, but killing a cop? No." He shook his head. "Don't do it. The hassle is enormous."

"It's not murder," Bradley said after a moment. "It's self-defense. I heard an intruder in the basement and shot him. It's self-defense."

"Well, actually, Brad, it's not," Zack said, trying to sound calm and friendly. "Self-defense only works if the intruder is actually approaching you in a threatening manner. Just offing somebody in your basement doesn't count." Bradley appeared to hesitate, and Zack took heart and moved on. "Now, obviously you were duped by John Bradley, so there's no need..."

"No." Bradley looked into Zack's eyes. "You're not stupid. You know about the windows."

"The ones John Bradley shot out," Zack said helpfully.

"You know it was me."

Terrific. Shut up, Bradley.

"You knew it was me all along. That part of this was always between us." Bradley smiled as he said it. "You knew. I kept calling to see if you were here, and you always were. So I told J.B. to call you for me, and I stood in the front yard, and when you picked up the phone, I shot at you."

"You almost shot Lucy that night," Zack said, and Bradley's smile disappeared.

"I would *never* hurt Lucy. When I shot at you on the street that day and almost hit her, I was terrified. I was trying to hit you, not her. I won't miss this time."

This was bad. Bradley raised the gun another inch and Zack stared down its barrel. A .45. Again, a .45. They'd be scraping him off the house next door. He had to get out of Property Crimes. It was too damn dangerous. Then he looked past the gun into Bradley's angry eyes and made a discovery that scared the hell out of him.

Bradley wasn't nuts. He was just mad as hell. At him. Because he'd slept with Lucy. And Zack knew exactly how that anger felt because it was one of the reasons Zack didn't like Bradley much, either.

If I thought he'd slept with her while she was seeing me, Zack thought, *I'd be furious, too. Imagine if I'd been married to her. Imagine if she obviously wanted him more than me.*

I'd want to kill him.

Which meant that unless he came up with something fast, he was going to die.

"You know, Bradley," Zack said suddenly, "if you shoot me, you'll never get Lucy back. If we sit down and work this out, you could get off with probation, a suspended sentence. Once Lucy finds out the blonde was lying, she'll understand why you did it. Unless you shoot me. I'm a cop, Bradley. They'll throw away the key. And you'll never get to explain to Lucy."

"I already explained it." Bradley dropped the gun slightly. "She doesn't care. She wants you. As long as you're alive..."

He began to sight down the barrel again, and Zack gave up.

"Put the gun down, Bradley."

Lucy's voice cut through the silence, and they both froze. Zack stared past Bradley to the stairs where she'd appeared, a few steps above him, her brand-new autographed baseball bat balanced above her shoulder.

"Lucy?" Bradley turned slightly, just enough to see her from the corner of his eye. Not enough to give Zack room to move.

"Put it down, Bradley," she said. "This won't help things. If you shoot him, you'll only be in more trouble. Put it down."

"Lucy, you don't understand. Go back upstairs." Bradley turned back to Zack.

"Go, honey," Zack said, and Bradley's face went red with anger.

"*No, Bradley*," Lucy said. "Listen to me. I have a baseball bat here, and I will hit you with it if you don't drop your gun." She said it very calmly, as if it were the most sensible thing in the world instead of the most ridiculous, but Zack could see the bat tremble in her hands, and he felt a chill of fear for her like nothing he had ever felt for himself.

Bradley turned back to her, and Zack had a nightmare vision of him suddenly swinging the gun around to her.

"Go away, Lucy," Zack said, and Bradley turned back to him, furious.

"Drop it, Bradley," Lucy said, and Bradley twitched his eyes back to her and then back to Zack.

"Don't be ridiculous, Lucy." Bradley's voice began to shake with impatience. "You won't hit me with a baseball bat. The whole idea is ludicrous. You are not a violent person."

"Oh, I can be." Lucy swallowed hard. "I cracked your friend's skull with a bat this morning. It made the most awful sound, Bradley. Like a bad melon. I don't want to hit you, Bradley, and I know you don't want to shoot Zack. Just put the gun down. Please."

"Oh, I want to shoot Zack." Bradley took careful aim at Zack. "I really do. And you won't hit me, not even to save him. You can't. You're not capable of violence. I know you. You're my wife, and I know you better than you know yourself." He began to squint his eyes, ready to pull the trigger.

Zack gave up hope and looked at Lucy because he wanted her to be the last thing he saw before he died.

"Well, the thing is, Bradley, I've changed," Lucy said.

And then she swung the bat solidly into the back of his head.

His head jerked forward, and he flung his arms wide as he fell through the broken rail to the floor, jerking on the trigger of the .45 in reflex action, narrowly missing Zack, who had gone in low the moment that Lucy had moved. Bradley fell hard and then staggered to his feet, and Zack was there, putting him down with one punch that had a lot of pent-up frustration behind it.

Lucy sat down hard on the stairs, clutching her bat and staring at them both in amazement.

Zack picked up the gun and held it on a dazed Bradley. "I enjoyed that," he said as he nursed his left hand. "Call 911."

"I already did," Lucy said. "Before I came down here. I opened the front door so they'd come in when they got here." Even as she spoke, she heard cautious footsteps above. "Are you all right?"

"Yes," Zack said. "I think I broke my hand, but it was worth it. I've been wanting to punch him out for two weeks. By the way, thanks for saving my life."

"If I saved it, does that mean I get to keep it?" Lucy asked, but there were people coming down the steps, and he didn't hear her. She sat on the stairs and watched it all, sad for Bradley and relieved at the same time.

WHEN EVERYONE HAD GONE, Zack went to find her to tell her that Tina was coming to stay with her while he went downtown, to tell her that she really was safe now, to tell her…

He found her still on the steps, and sat beside her, trying to figure out how to tell her the most important part.

"He really thought he loved me," Lucy said. "Before this John Bradley mess, I mean. I still feel terrible about that. He thought he loved me, but I only loved the house and then you. It's almost my fault that this happened."

Zack scowled at her. "No, it isn't. That's dumb. Obviously..." Then he stopped, his scowl vanishing. "Back up a minute. You said you loved me."

"I know. Do you think I could talk Tina into getting Bradley a lawyer?"

"Not in a million years. Forget them for a minute." He took a deep breath. "I think we should get married. I know you think it's too soon, but you're wrong."

Lucy started to say something but he stopped her. "Now just listen for a minute. There are a lot of good reasons why we should get married. For example, the dogs need a father."

"Zack—" Lucy began.

"Hell, they're *boys*. They need a male around."

"Zack—" Lucy began again.

"Okay, okay. Here's a good one." Zack put his arm around her because it felt so good to have her close. For a moment, looking down into her big brown eyes disoriented him, and then he remembered what he was doing. "Where was I? Oh, right. We're bound to make a go of it because people always work harder on their second marriages, so you'll give it everything you've got. And not only that, but you'll be comparing me to Bradley, and Lord knows I'm a step up, so you'll think I'm terrific, which will make me happy. There's no way we can fail."

Lucy tried again. "I think—"

"Okay, how about this. We're great in bed together. There's a sure-fire guarantee for marriage—great sex."

Lucy frowned at him. "That's a terrible reason to get married. I think—"

Zack gave up. "Okay, forget the reasons. I love you. I'm crazy about you. I even understood why Bradley wanted to kill me, because if I'd been him, I'd have wanted to kill me, too. I want to spend the rest of my days plotting with the dogs to kill that damn cat next door, and the rest of my nights making love to you. Actually, I wouldn't mind spending a fair part of the days making love to you, too, but that's not logical."

"I don't believe in logic," Lucy said. "I believe in love. Especially with someone who is spontaneous, irresponsible, and inappropriate." She surveyed him critically. "That's you."

The relief that flooded through Zack was as intense as his amazement.

"What? When did all this happen?"

"Last night when Bradley shot out the windows and almost killed you," Lucy said. "I thought you were dead, and it was the worst thing I could imagine." She stopped, chilled at the thought and at how close he'd come again that afternoon, and then she went on. "And then you were all right, and that's when I decided to marry you."

"You did? Last night?" Zack glared at her. "Why didn't you mention it before now? I've been tying myself in knots trying to figure out a way to get you to say yes."

"Evidently," Lucy said. "'The dogs need a father'? That's pathetic."

"I was desperate," Zack said. "I can't believe this. You really are going to marry me? Not that you have any choice. I'm moving in anyway."

"Yes, I will marry you," Lucy said, and Zack said, "Damn right, you will," and kissed her, holding her tight, until she broke the kiss, laughing and gasping for air, and then he buried his face in her coppery curls, almost paralyzed with gratitude that everything was finally all right.

"So you're going to marry a cop," Tina said later, when Zack was gone with Anthony, and they were alone. "They have the highest divorce rate next to dentists, you know."

"Don't be so logical," Lucy said.

Tina blinked.

Lucy laughed.

Charlie
All Night

For Valerie Taylor,
who has the eye of an editor and the
heart of a reader, and for Brenna Todd,
whose big hair is exceeded only by her big heart,
because they got me through this book.

One

Allie McGuffey knew a yuppie bar was a lousy place to find a hero, but she was desperate, so she had to make do with what she had on hand.

Unfortunately, what she had on hand was pretty pathetic.

She shoved her horn-rimmed glasses back up the bridge of her nose with one finger and peered at the row of stools at the bar. Businessman. Businessman. Empty seat. Businessman. Businesswoman. Empty seat. Empty seat. Thug. Businessman.

She swallowed the lump that had been in her throat for the past fifteen minutes. Okay, fine, if that's what she had to work with, she'd work with it. But it was going to have to be the thug, because she was never going to have a relationship with a suit again as long as she lived. Even a relationship that was only going to last five minutes.

And he really wasn't a thug. Allie tried to drum up some enthusiasm before she made her move. His dark blond hair was shaggy over his collar, and his brown leather jacket had seen better days, and his jeans were authentic grunge, but he was big and clean and most important of all, he made a nice contrast to all the charcoal suits that looked like Mark. And what Allie wanted more than anything right then was a not-Mark.

She knew she was behaving like an idiot, but given the bomb that had just exploded in her face, the fact that she was not sitting in a trance was a step in the right direction.

It had not been a good day.

Allie had hit the radio-station doors that afternoon at her usual clip, banging them open like saloon doors. If they ever locked those doors, she was going to seriously hurt herself, but they never did since everyone had to be buzzed in from the street level four floors below. So she'd gone charging through as usual, happy to be there. As usual, what seemed like forty people converged on her.

Allie beamed as they pounced, loving the feeling that WBBB couldn't run without her, that without her there would be dead air and dust. This was who she was, Allie-the-producer, Allie-the-brains-behind-The-Mark-King-Show, Allie-the-savior. She knew she was probably a little whacked to depend on a radio station for her identity, but compared to all the other psychological problems running loose at the station, she was in relatively good mental health, so she didn't dwell on it.

At first it was just Karen, the receptionist, who called out "Allie!," but that alerted Lisa, her former student intern, who popped out of the hall looking miserable and said, "Allie, I—" and who was promptly pushed aside by Albert the financial manager, who said, "Allie, the ratings—" and who was overrun by Marcia, the two-to-six-time-slot barracuda, who said, "Allie, I heard—" and who was shouldered aside by Mark, Allie's ex-lover and present boss, who said, "I need to see you in your office. Now."

Allie pushed her glasses back up her nose so she could see him better. The silence that settled over the reception area was a tribute to how bizarrely Mark was behaving. Usually, he made his presence known through talking too loudly, dropping names and laughing heartily in the wrong places. Allie had once felt sorry for him, but she didn't now, having been dumped as his lover two months ago when he decided he'd look better standing next to Lisa than he did with her. He was right, of course, but it still hurt to look at him now. He stood in the entrance to the hallway, quietly superior, and it was such a change that everybody shut up and she followed him to her office without question.

Once inside, he closed the door behind her, went around to her desk chair and sat.

Allie fought back a snarl. All right, she wasn't territorial, but this was her office, no matter how tiny and cluttered, and her desk, and that was her desk chair, and he was making her a visitor in her own domain. So she scowled at him and said, "What is this?"

Mark crossed his arms and leaned back in her chair, which tilted so that he was almost horizontal to her vertical, and then he said,

"There's no good way to tell you this, Allie, so I'll just say it. I know it's going to be hard, but I also know you're an adult and you realize that things change. People grow. Change is good." He let his head fall back and addressed the ceiling as he began to wax philosophic. While Allie waited for him to get to the point, assuming he had one, she considered how amazingly good-looking he was, and how mad she was at him, and how much she wanted him back.

This was the great mystery of her life. He was an insecure twit. So why had she fallen for him and why was she still hung up on him? Why did she miss going to dinner with him and lying in bed with him, all the while listening to him talk about himself? Of course, that had been research for the show, but still… As he droned on and she automatically began to edit his speech for broadcast purposes, the possibility dawned on her that what she'd fallen for was the edited Mark King she'd created on the radio, not the real Mark King who sat in front of her now, boring her to tears. And that what she was most mad about was that she'd created him, and then he'd taken her work to another woman.

Mark was still waxing. "So that's why—"

Allie cut in, more exasperated with herself than with Mark. "Look, I've got things to do here, so if you'll just cut to the chase, I'll get back to keeping you a hit." Okay, that was below the belt, but he'd started the fight by sitting in her chair, the louse. Not to mention dumping her for a younger woman.

Mark sat up straight and put his palms flat on her desk. "All right, here it is. You're not going to be working on my show anymore."

The room spun. Allie dropped into the remaining chair in the room and said, "What?"

"I've sensed a certain hostility since our breakup, and it's affecting my performance. So Bill and I have decided it's best to put Lisa in your place since you've trained her. That way, the show won't suffer at all."

Allie sat stunned.

Mark smiled at her and spread his hands, fait accompli. "Lisa is producing the show, starting now. It'll be better for all of us."

"All of us who?" She took a deep breath. "Not all of us me. You have the drive-time show. I'm the drive-time producer. Unless I get the slot while you and Lisa move someplace cozy, this is not better for me."

"Well, of course I'm not moving." Mark sat up straighter in the chair. "I'm the talent."

He was the talent? Then what was she?

"And you're not fired or anything like that. We do appreciate what you've done," he went on, and Allie jerked her head up, anger finally evicting her panic.

"Of course I'm not fired. Why would I be fired? This makes no sense."

He plowed on through her anger. "And Bill's going to give you another show to produce. I made sure of that."

Good old Mark. Taking care of her. What a pal. She stood up, refraining from killing him where he sat only by Herculean effort. "Well, gee, Mark, thanks for the support and good luck in the future. Now get out of my chair."

He stood, doing what she'd said as if by instinct. After two years of doing everything she said, it was probably a hard habit to break. He moved toward the door, brimming with patronizing goodwill. "Look, why don't we go out for a drink? Just to show there are no hard feelings."

She wanted to scream at him, *Of course, there are hard feelings, you jerk. If I could, I'd beat you senseless with one right now.* But she was too adult for that, and too rattled, so she lied instead. Mark might have kicked her in the teeth, but she still had her incisors.

"Sorry, I've already got a date. In fact, I have to go now. Maybe some other time." She ducked out into the hall in front of him, trying not to cry. That would be a real mistake because she never cried. If she did, people would probably assume somebody had died. And then she'd have to tell them that, tragically, Mark still lived.

Mark followed her, so she speeded up.

Karen yelled "Allie" again as she went past the receptionist's counter, and this time shoved an envelope at her. "Bill—"

Allie took the envelope without slowing down, flashing the best smile she could under the circumstances, and bolted for the elevator with Mark still in pursuit.

Then Karen called out to him, too, and stopped him, and Allie caught the elevator and escaped to the street.

She'd been fired. She still had a job, but her career was gone with Mark. Allie stuck her chin out and tried to fake defiance—well, big deal, she'd just build another great show—but it was no good. She'd spent two years making Mark's show a hit, taking surveys, researching topics, devising contests, doing everything she knew to showcase Mark's strengths. She'd majored in Mark King, and now he'd expelled her.

For a moment, outside the restaurant across from the station, Allie felt a moment of pure fear. What if she couldn't do it again? What if Mark was right and he was the talent? What if she really was a loser? Nobody coming to her for help, nobody relying on her.

No. She'd find a way back. She gritted her teeth and went into the restaurant.

The hallway divided the restaurant from the bar, a sort of DMZ that separated the eating yuppies from the drinking yuppies. Allie stopped there and opened the envelope Karen had thrust at her. She found the kind of note the station owner was famous for: short, tactless and to the point:

> I'm taking you off Mark's show and giving you to Charles Tenniel, the man taking over for Waldo Hancock. Meet him tomorrow, Tuesday, five o'clock, my office.
> Bill

Weird Waldo had the 10:00 to 2:00 a.m. spot. She'd just been demoted from producing the radio equivalent of *Oprah* to the radio equivalent of an infomercial.

She shoved the note back into the envelope and looked around the hallway. Her roommate Joe who was supposed to meet her wasn't there to comfort her. The hell with it. She was going home.

She turned around to go back into the street, but outside the door was Mark, greeting people who greeted him back as if he were a celebrity. Which, of course, he was.

And he was going to come into the bar and find her alone after her big talk about a date because Joe was late again. Not that Joe would have been very impressive as a date, but he would have been more impressive than no date at all.

So she went into the bar to find a date, and there were all those suits and the thug. She couldn't face another suit, and at least the thug looked like a change of pace, so she went over to the thug and said, "Hi!" as vivaciously as she could. She wasn't vivacious by nature, so she sounded as if she'd been sucking helium, but he turned and looked at her anyway.

Allie didn't know what she'd been expecting. Maybe some fantasy guy who was even better-looking than Mark, which, in all fairness to Mark, would be impossible, but this guy wasn't even in the running. He had the kind of face that the big, good-natured kids in the back of high-school English classes always have, slightly dopey and comfortable.

He looked nice. That was about it, but after Mark, it was pretty good.

Allie plopped her bag down on the bar. "So! You meeting someone?" she asked, still on helium, and looked over her shoulder to check on the Mark situation. All she had to do was keep the thug in conversation until Mark walked in, saw she was with him and left.

Mark didn't like competition.

"So, are you?" Allie smiled like a telemarketer. "Meeting someone?" She sat down beside him, praying Mark wouldn't come in.

And he said, "No. What are you doing?"

SHORTLY BEFORE Allie picked him up, Charlie had been contemplating his future. It looked complicated and possibly dangerous, so his best plan was to lay low, not make waves, do the job and get out. Investigating the source of an incriminating anonymous letter to a radio station in Tuttle, Ohio, couldn't be that hard. The station wasn't that big. Hell, the *town* wasn't that big. His biggest problem was going to be pretending to be a disc jockey, and how hard could that be? If his brother had done it stoned, he could certainly do it straight. And he'd made it clear to everybody concerned that he was only around for six weeks, tops. He had things to do, he'd told them, places he had to be in November.

He hadn't decided yet exactly what place he had to be in November, but he was positive it was somewhere uncomplicated and re-mote. Especially remote from his father who had taken to asking weird favors lately. Like "Check into this radio station for my old friend Bill..." This was what came of going home for his father's birthday. From now on, he'd just send a card. And as soon as he was done, he was out of here and someplace else. Someplace where he could do something simple for a while, like raise pigs. No, too complicated. He'd raise carrots. You didn't have to feed carrots.

He'd stopped thinking when somebody had squeaked, "Hi!"

Charlie had blinked at her, mildly surprised. She didn't look like the vivacious pick-up-a-guy-in-a-bar type. Her sharp brown eyes gleamed behind huge, round, horn-rimmed glasses, and her glossy gold-brown hair swung in a tangled Dutch-boy bob. There was nothing wrong with her nose or mouth, either; good standard-issue all-American-woman features. She just seemed sort of scrubbed to be trolling for guys. The long flowered skirt and oversize vest weren't right for a pickup, either. She looked like a nice, clean kid. Well, she was no kid. Early thirties easy.

She raised her eyebrows so high they disappeared under her bangs and batted her eyelashes. "So! You meeting someone?" She looked over her shoulder and flopped her bag down on the bar. It looked as if it was made from very old blue flowered carpet. Charlie had never seen anything quite like it so he poked his finger into it. It was fuzzy.

"Are you?" She smiled at him again, a sort of strained, too-many-teeth, trying-too-hard smile. "Meeting someone?" She sat on the stool beside him.

"No." Charlie looked at her with interest. "What are you doing?"

"Picking you up?"

Charlie shook his head. "I don't think so. What are you really do-ing?"

The artificial smile morphed into a genuine scowl, and her perky voice dropped an octave. "I don't believe this. Can't you even pre-tend on the hope you'll get lucky?"

"I never pretend. I'm the natural, open type." Charlie considered moving away from her and then rejected the idea. If he left her, he'd never find out what she was up to. And besides, when she'd scowled at him, her voice had gone husky. She had a great low voice. He smiled down at her, trying to make her talk again. "Why don't you just give me the drift, and then we can take it from there."

She lowered her head a little and stared at him over the rims of her glasses. "Look, the drift will take too long, and besides, it makes me look pathetic. All I ask is that you pretend to be having a drink with me." He must have looked skeptical because she added, "I swear that's it."

Right. Charlie had been wandering through the world long enough to know that wouldn't be it, that there would be complications. There were always complications, which was why Charlie had spent his thirty-four years learning to be light on his feet and fast out the door.

On the other hand, she wasn't part of his current problem so there weren't likely to be long-term complications. He had a free evening before he had to go poking around in other people's business, so he might as well poke around in hers for a while. At the very least, he'd get to listen to her talk. He shrugged. "Hell, it's worth one drink just to find out what happens next." He motioned to the bartender.

"I'm quite sure he won't come over here." She looked back over her shoulder again.

The bartender came and Charlie said, "The lady would like..." He turned back to her.

"The lady would like to pay for her own amaretto and cream, Max." She took a couple of bills out of her carpet bag and handed them to the bartender as she looked over her shoulder again.

"You got it, Allie," the bartender said and moved away.

"Amaretto and cream?" Charlie frowned. "That's disgusting."

"At least the cream part is good for me." She turned back to him. "Well, it should be skim milk, but bars never have skim milk."

"That's true." Charlie drew back a little. "You know, you have the weirdest pickup line in North America."

"Pickup line?" She swiveled on the stool and faced him. Her eyes sparked at him and her cheeks glowed rosy with outrage. Outrage looked very good on her. "This isn't a pickup line. The pickup line was before, the one that didn't work." She swiveled again to keep lookout. "Oh, great." She swiveled to face him again. "There he is. Okay, here's the deal. We're together. Try to look like you haven't just insulted me."

"I didn't insult you. I made an observation."

"Well, stop." She looked back over her shoulder again. "Oh, no." She closed her eyes. Charlie saw her lips moving and leaned closer to hear her, but she wasn't talking to him. "He's going to go by. I'm sure he's going to go by. I'm sure..."

A male-model type stopped on the other side of her. "Allie! There you are. I—"

She jerked as if she'd been shot. "Mark! What a surprise. To see you. Again. So soon." She looked at Charlie and said, very softly, "Oh, hell."

Then she stuck her chin out and turned to smile at Mark.

She was doing pretty good, Charlie thought. Good smile. Pretty lame answer, but the smile and the chin would probably make up for it. He looked at the guy. Tall, dark and handsome, if you liked really pretty men. Very expensive suit. Toothpaste grin. And the jerk was smiling that grin at her as if he knew she was in agony. Charlie shook his head at the situation and finished his drink. Good thing he wasn't involved in this one. It was a mess.

"Let me buy you a drink, Al. It's the least I can do." Mark the jerk motioned for the bartender.

Max wandered back and put Allie's amaretto in front of her.

"No, no." Allie's mouth went lipless with stress. "I have one. Thanks, Max."

"Amaretto and cream." Mark laughed. "Good old Allie." He sat down beside her at the bar and patted her on the back.

"Grrrrr." It was a very faint low growl, locked behind her teeth, almost indiscernible in the babble of the bar, but Charlie heard it because she'd turned to him as she made it. "I'm sorry about this," Allie whispered to him.

Charlie leaned forward and whispered in her ear, "Try not to look like a wounded basset hound."

Allie flashed Mark a brilliant smile over her shoulder.

"I didn't realize the two of you were together." Mark paused for an introduction.

Allie kept on smiling like a half-wit, so Charlie took pity on her and extended his hand past her nose. "Charlie Tenniel."

Allie started, but Mark took his hand with enthusiasm, gripping it in a he-man clasp. Charlie let his hand go limp. Mark smirked.

What an idiot, Charlie thought.

Mark was positively jovial. "Well, this is a coincidence. I'm Mark King. You've inherited my producer, you lucky dog. I've taught her everything there is to know about radio. You're in good hands."

Allie made that low growling sound in her throat again, and Charlie blinked at them both and then let Mark babble on about his own many successes, ignoring him for heavier thoughts. So much for diverting himself with Allie. Allie worked at the station with Mark the jerk. They were probably both in trouble up to their necks.

Allie certainly looked as if she was in trouble. She turned bleak, questioning eyes on him. "Is this true?" she whispered. "You're my new DJ?" He nodded at her and she closed her eyes. "We were just discussing that," she lied as she turned back to Mark.

Charlie picked up her glass of cream and handed it to her. "Here you go, boss. Glad to meet you, Mark. This the place everybody at the station hangs out?"

"Pretty much. Convenient. Right across the street, you know." Mark smiled broadly while he sized Charlie up with obvious confidence. "Have you two known each other long?"

Allie put down her newly empty glass. "Oh, it seems like it."

Charlie brought his mind back to the problem at hand. "Don't chug cream like that." He took the empty glass from her. "This isn't skim milk, you know. This is the real thing, the hard stuff. Max, another amaretto and cream for the lady. In fact, just bring over the bottle and drive in the cow."

"A comedian." Allie nodded her head. "Five guys sitting at a bar, and I pick the comedian."

"What?" Mark leaned closer to catch what she was saying.

"She thinks I'm funny." Charlie put his arm around Allie and gave her an affectionate squeeze. She was a lot softer than he was prepared for, so he left his arm where it was for a while. "Funny is the basis for any good relationship."

"Maybe that's what was wrong with us, huh, Allie?" Mark looked soulfully at her.

What a goof.

"You two were once..." Charlie wiggled his eyebrows at Allie. "You never told me that."

"It never came up." Allie glared at him from the curve of his arm.

"You're a lucky man, Tenniel." Mark was still trying to recapture Allie's attention, but she missed his meaningful looks because she was busy glaring at Charlie.

Charlie beamed at them both, enjoying the situation. "That's what everybody keeps telling me. Actually, it's not luck, it's skill."

Mark tried again. "So how did you two meet?"

"In a bar," Charlie said. "She picked me up."

"Allie did?" Mark looked astounded.

"She begged me to buy her a drink."

"Allie did?"

Charlie nodded. "Happens to me all the time. Animal magnetism."

"Oh, a joke." Mark looked relieved. "How did you two really meet?"

"I picked him up." Allie took a deep breath. "The truth is..."

Charlie pulled her tighter, momentarily shutting down her lungs. "The truth is, she sat down next to me, and I looked at her and thought, 'This is a good-looking woman,' and we started to talk, and we've been together ever since."

Allie jerked her head up and stared at him. Then she smiled, and Charlie smiled back by reflex, caught by the intelligence in her eyes and the warmth in her wide, soft mouth. She leaned toward him, and he bent to hear what she said.

She was almost nose to nose with him. "You are a good person. I forgive you for insulting me." She patted his sleeve and then disengaged herself from his arm.

Charlie missed her warmth. "I didn't insult you."

"How long have you two known each other?" Mark asked.

"Eternity," Charlie said.

"But it seems like only a few short minutes." Allie glared at him again and then she leaned back, her attention caught by something over Charlie's shoulder. She signaled someone away, and Charlie turned just in time to get the impression that someone was doing a fade from the doorway into the hall.

So, Allie had a secret. Life just got more interesting all the time. And of course that meant that he was going to have to stick with her until he discovered her secret. He'd been hired to find all the secrets at the station. It was his job. It was his duty. He looked at Allie, her hair shining like old brass in the warm light of the bar.

It was his pleasure.

"So, where's Lisa tonight?" Allie leaned on the bar in an attempt at languid unconcern. "What a shame she's not with you. We could all have dinner together."

Careful, Allie, Charlie thought.

"Lisa's at the station." Mark frowned. "You're right. It is a shame. This would be a great chance to meet Charlie."

"There'll be other chances." Charlie finished his drink. "I'm not going anyplace. Except to the top of the ratings."

Mark decided that was a joke, too. "Heh, heh, heh."

Mark had a laugh like an asthmatic horse, and Charlie wondered if that was why Allie had left him. Listening to that laugh would certainly be reason enough for anybody to leave him. Which brought an ugly thought. He'd have to be very careful because if Mark was any indication of his radio competition, he *would* go to the top of the ratings. That would be bad. One of the basic tenets of undercover investigation was not becoming a household word.

"Well!" Allie slid off the stool. "We've got to be getting in to dinner. Wonderful seeing you again, Mark."

Mark leaned forward to kiss her goodbye, and she tripped backward to get away from him.

Charlie caught her. "Falling for me all over again, huh?" He tightened his arm around her automatically. Allie was soft and round against his shoulder, and she smelled like flowers. He was in no hurry to let go. "Try to restrain yourself," he told her. "We're in public."

She looked into his eyes and swallowed hard. "It's your animal magnetism. I'm restrained now. You can let go."

"I don't think so," he said, and kissed her.

He'd only meant to kiss her quickly and let her go, mostly to annoy Mark and, all right, because she had a great mouth. But she clutched at him in surprise and fell into his arms so the kiss was a lot more than he'd planned, a lot more warmth and softness and weight, and her mouth was cool and sweet from the cream. He was a little dizzy by the time he remembered where he was and came up for air.

"What are you doing?" Allie sounded more breathless than annoyed when she pulled away from him.

"Making my move. Come back here." Charlie reached for her, and she stepped back.

Mark looked disgruntled. "Well, really, Allie, you're in public."

"That's lust." Charlie smiled at him happily. "She can't keep her lips off me." Allie took another step back, and Charlie stood up to follow her. "Well, it looks like we're moving on," he told Mark. "Tell Lisa we said hi."

When they were in the hallway, Allie shook her head. "Who are you really? Satan? I'm being punished, right?"

"I'm Charlie Tenniel." He held out his hand. "I work with that stuffed shirt you used to date. I assume all you did was date. I'd hate to think that any woman I'd kissed in a bar actually went to bed with somebody like that."

She looked down at his hand and sighed. Then she took it and shook it once and dropped it. "I'm Alice McGuffey, your producer at WBBB. It was nice meeting you, and thank you very much for helping me with Mark, but I have to go now. We can talk again tomorrow at the station."

She turned to go into the restaurant, and Charlie stepped around her to block her. The last thing he wanted now was to get dumped. There were too many things Allie could tell him about the station. He could probably get the information from other people, but other people didn't have Allie's voice. Or Allie's mouth. "Where are you going?"

"To dinner." Allie gestured to the dining room. "With my dinner date. The only perfect man I know."

"Ah." Charlie nodded at her encouragingly. "Your father. We should meet so he can see the kind of guy you're working with."

"No."

"No, he shouldn't see?"

"No, he's not my father."

"No?" Charlie thought faster. "Gee, I've never met a perfect man." He tried to look wistful. "I've always wanted a role model."

Allie looked at him with disapproval, but he smiled at her and finally she gave up. "Okay, I owe you. You want to eat dinner with Joe and me? If you can't, it's perfectly all right."

"Thank you." Charlie held the door to the restaurant open. "I can't wait to meet Joe, the perfect man."

"Terrific," Allie said.

Charlie followed her into the restaurant, a big room with too much mahogany and not enough light. Allie looked around the dimness and then smiled when a man across the room stood up and waved at her.

Charlie narrowed his eyes a little. This guy might actually be the perfect man. He was tall, even taller than Charlie's six-two, and classically handsome without being obnoxious about it. His jaw was strong, his blond hair gleamed, his blue eyes were warm and the smile he had for Allie was real and loving.

"Your brother?" Charlie asked, and Allie said, "No," and walked away from him. He followed her, trying to find something about Joe that wasn't perfect and feeling vaguely annoyed.

Allie introduced them at the table. "Joe, this is Charlie Tenniel, the new ten-to-two DJ. I'm producing his show."

"I heard. Karen called." Joe shot Allie a look that appeared to be sympathy, but Allie had already turned back to Charlie. "Charlie, this is Joe Ericson, my roommate. He's the station's accountant."

She sounded like a well-behaved child, but she didn't look like one. Charlie began to wonder what Allie was like when she wasn't behaving well in public. *No.* That sort of thought would add those complications he'd been avoiding.

"Charlie Tenniel." Joe's smile was open and admiring as he held out his hand. "Are you the one they call Ten Tenniel?"

Ouch. He hated lying, but it was better than "No, that's my brother, the drug-dealing DJ." He shook his head. "Call me Charlie."

Joe kept going. "I've heard about you. I've got a friend down in Lawrenceville who was very upset when you disappeared. I'm looking forward to hearing you myself now."

His smile was genuine, and Charlie liked him.

"Who in Lawrenceville?" Allie had already seated herself and picked up the menu. "I'm starving."

Joe sat down next to her. "Rona. Remember? From that seminar we took?"

Charlie took the chair across from her so he could watch her.

"Right. You kept in touch with Rona?" Allie ran her finger down the menu list. "Pasta."

"I keep in touch with everybody." Joe tapped Allie's menu. "Not pasta. I'll do pasta tomorrow night. Get something here that's a pain in the butt to make. You like pasta, Charlie?"

Charlie started. Joe and Allie were so in sync in their conversation, he was a little surprised to be suddenly included. "Yep."

"Come to dinner tomorrow night."

Charlie beamed his best smile at him. "Thanks." Another contact at the station. First Allie, then Mark, now Joe. And he'd only been in town a couple of hours. God, he was good.

Allie glared at Joe.

Joe mock-glared back. "Don't look at me like that. I want to get to know Ten Tenniel."

"Charlie," Charlie said. "Just call me Charlie."

ALLIE WASN'T SURE how she felt about Charlie. He'd done a nice job of saving her from Mark, but he'd laughed the whole time he was doing it, which made her feel like a dweeb. Of course, he had a point: panic was not a good look for her. *Don't do that again,* she told herself and turned back to the problem at hand.

She now had to work with a guy who'd kissed her in a bar. This was not a good way to start a professional relationship, especially since he was quite a good kisser. It would be hard to say no if he ever suggested they try that again, and of course she'd have to say no because sleeping with the talent was not a good idea. Look what had happened with Mark. No, forget about Mark. Socializing with Charlie was not a good idea, which was why she'd tried to look quelling when he suggested he eat with Joe and her, but Charlie didn't quell easily. In fact, Charlie didn't quell at all.

He did seem taken aback when he saw Joe for the first time. Allie considered her roommate as she sat beside him. Part of Joe's impact came from the fact that he was such a good man, so everything he was sort of infused his face, and his face was perfect, so people just felt good just looking at him. She felt good just looking at him now. She'd talk this whole job mess out with him later, and everything would make sense.

But Joe did have his faults. Food, for instance.

He'd picked up his menu and was studying it as if there'd be a quiz at the end of the meal, which actually there would be. He'd ask, "Too much oregano. And where was the basil? Obvious seasoning. Sure sign of a clumsy chef. What about the asparagus?" He could go for days on just a side dish. But for right now, all he did was gesture at the menu and ask, "What do you think?"

Allie prepared for the usual battle. She was still nauseated from the stress of the afternoon, so a large slab of dead animal did not appeal. But she had to eat or she'd pass out, and she had to choose something that Joe hated to make, or he'd be insulted. "Manicotti," she decided. "The last time you made that, you bitched about stuffing all that pasta."

"Not manicotti. Mine's better than here. Get a steak."

"I don't want a steak. I want pasta."

"Well, don't come home tomorrow and say, 'Pasta? We just *had* pasta.'"

Charlie looked from one to the other. "You guys been together long?"

Allie laughed at the annoyance in his voice. "You sound just like Mark."

"Yeah, and speaking of Mark, what was that?" Joe frowned at her. "You and Mark having a drink together after he fired you?"

"Yeah." Charlie frowned at her, too. "What was that? I was there, and I didn't understand it."

Allie slumped back in her chair, her lousy day returning in full force. "That was my worst nightmare. That's why I picked up Charlie. I didn't want Mark to think I still...you know."

"We know." Joe looked at Charlie. "She's usually not this wimpy. In fact, she's usually very confident. It's just Mark that makes her act like she's twelve again."

Charlie nodded. "You should have been at the bar. She was practically incoherent."

"I was not." Allie stuck out her chin and tried to look strong and defiant, and Charlie snorted. She gave up then and dropped her head into her hands. "Oh, hell."

Joe patted her head. "There, there. You have me."

"Oh, good," Allie said without raising her head. "That's a comfort."

"Now order," Joe said. "And don't screw up."

Allie finally got Joe to agree that she could have the chicken fettuccini since he wanted a taste of it himself. Chickens weren't really dead animals, she reasoned, ready to contemplate anything except her future. They were more like protein with feathers. Joe and Charlie ordered prime rib, and Joe gave the waitress lavish instructions on their side dishes, which she copied down word for word, having served him before. When the waitress was gone, Joe remembered that he hadn't designed Allie's vegetables, and Allie argued that she wanted hers plain, and he said that was no way to live, and they were off on one of their usual arguments with lots of laughing, when Charlie interrupted.

"So, how long *have* you known each other?"

"Four years," Joe said. "Ever since she came to the station."

Allie relaxed and smiled at Joe. "I was new in town and didn't have a place to live, and he was at the station picking up the books, and his roommate had just moved out, so he said I could borrow the spare bedroom until I found a place."

Joe grinned. "And then she came home with me, and we talked and laughed until two in the morning, and I said, 'Don't find another place,' and we've been together ever since."

Charlie looked from Joe to Allie, and he didn't look happy. Allie stopped smiling, wondering what she'd said that was wrong, not really caring as long as it wasn't another major trauma to deal with. Then Charlie said, "I don't get this. If Joe is the perfect man, why did you ever get mixed up with that clown, Mark?"

Joe blinked at him. "I'm the perfect man?"

"That's what Allie says."

Joe raised his eyebrows at her. "I'm flattered."

Allied tensed. "Well, almost." She shot a look at Charlie, prepared to jettison him permanently if he said the wrong thing.

Joe looked at Charlie. "I'm gay."

Charlie relaxed and beamed at him in what looked like relief. He picked up a bread stick. "Good for you, but that doesn't justify Mark. There must be other men in this town almost as perfect as you who like girls."

Allie blinked at him. She had obviously missed something there, but since it wasn't homophobia, she didn't care what was going on in Charlie's brain. It was a male brain. It was probably incomprehensible, anyway. Look at Mark.

Joe sat back. "I've got to admit, I wasn't happy about Mark, either." He turned to Allie. "Why did you pick him?"

"I didn't." Allie tried to look unconcerned. "He picked me. I don't know why."

"I don't, either," Joe said. "You're not his type."

"What is his type?" Charlie asked.

"Lisa." Allie stuck out her chin in defiant unconcern, but unfortunately, she stuck her lower lip out farther.

"Don't pout." Joe bit into a bread stick.

"You owe Lisa, whoever she is," Charlie told her. "She saved you from a man worse than death. You say thank you very much the next time you see her."

"Which should be any minute now." Joe pointed his bread stick behind Charlie. "That's them by the door."

Allie looked up in time to see Mark wave and take Lisa's hand and tow her toward them through the crowd.

The day from hell would never end. Well, she'd asked for it.

Charlie evidently thought so, too. "It's a shame Lisa's not with you," he mimicked. "We could all have dinner together."

"I know." Allie pushed her glasses back up the bridge of her nose and steeled herself for the mess to come. "I know. If I'd behaved like an adult, I wouldn't have picked up Charlie in a bar and lied to Mark. I deserve this."

"Nobody deserves this." Joe handed her a bread stick. "Eat. I'm with you. We can take them."

"Hell, yes." Charlie relented and patted her hand. "The odds are in our favor."

"You in this, too? Good." Joe handed him a bread stick, too. "We can always use another foot soldier in the fight against yuppie scum dweebs."

"That bad?"

"Lisa! Mark!" Joe stood up. "I was just telling Charlie all about you."

Someday, Allie told herself, *I'll look back on this and laugh.*

But not yet.

Two

——◆——

Allie sat numbly while Mark beamed at all of them. "Isn't this terrific. Can we join you?" He pulled out a chair for Lisa without waiting for an answer, and Lisa sat, giving Allie a cautious look under her lashes.

She had beautiful lashes. Actually, Lisa had beautiful everything. No wonder Mark had wanted her instead. There was no point in hating younger, more attractive women just because they existed. You had to wait until they did something to you to hate them. And Lisa hadn't fired her, Mark had.

Allie gave up and smiled at her. "Hi, Lisa. Congratulations on your promotion."

Lisa leaned forward, caution gone, her words tumbling out in her happiness. "It's so exciting, Allie. I can't thank you enough. Mark told me it was your decision—"

Allie's eyebrows almost hit the ceiling. "Oh?"

Lisa stopped. "It wasn't?"

Allie looked at Mark as if he were fish bait. "I'm really looking forward to working with Charlie," she lied. "Have you met Charlie yet, Lisa? Charlie Tenniel, Lisa Mitchell."

Charlie smiled at her and took her hand. "Nice to meet you."

Lisa smiled back, using her lashes on Charlie this time. "Welcome to the station. You're going to *love* working with Allie. She's—"

"So." Mark broke into the conversation loudly, and Lisa jerked her hand back. "Where are you staying, Charlie?"

Charlie leaned back a little. "I just got into town today."

Mark narrowed his eyes at Allie. "You haven't found him a place to live? That's not like you. You organize everybody."

What's your problem? Allie thought. *Jealousy? Good.* "He's staying with us," she said, and Joe choked on his drink.

"What's wrong with you?" Mark asked him.

"Nothing." Joe smiled blandly. "Nothing."

Mark frowned again at Allie. "You've only got two bedrooms."

"Yes, I know." It wouldn't hurt Mark to think she was sleeping with Charlie. She looked at Charlie over the top of her glasses. Actually, it wouldn't hurt her to think she was sleeping with Charlie. Bulky, friendly Charlie in shirtsleeves made a nice contrast to trim, tense Mark in a suit. In fact, the more she saw Mark next to Charlie, the less she missed having him around. Sleeping with Charlie might be the logical cure for her lingering case of Mark. Sort of like using penicillin to wipe out a bad bug that wouldn't go away.

The analogy was certainly apt anyway.

Allie's logic kicked into gear. She wasn't infatuated with Charlie the way she'd been with Mark. With Charlie, she could have an intelligent, well-planned one-night stand. Then her last sexual memory would be Charlie, not Mark, and she could get on with her life. The more she thought about it, the better she liked it. As long as Charlie didn't get hung up on her, it would be perfect. And even in her short acquaintance with him, it was fairly evident that commitment was not his byword.

Mark looked from Charlie to Allie to Joe, evidently reading Allie's mind. "So who is he sleeping with?"

"Me." Allie held up her hand like a polite child, her plan now in place. "Joe gets him tomorrow."

"Very funny," Mark said.

"Not so funny for me," Joe said. "I have to wait twenty-four hours."

"I don't think that's funny," Mark said.

"Neither does Joe," Charlie said, and Allie laughed, delighted he was part of them.

Lisa had been following the exchange, frowning as her head bobbed back and forth. "I don't get it."

"It's just a joke, Lisa." Mark put his arm around her. "Not a very funny one."

Charlie shook his head. "You have no sense of humor, Mark. That's why your relationship with Allie didn't work, remember?"

Mark decided to take offense, something, Allie reflected, that any sane man would have taken much sooner. "I don't know what Allie is doing with someone like you," Mark told Charlie. "You're not her type. Of course, I don't know what she's doing with *him*, either." He jerked his head at Joe.

Allie did not take insults to any of her friends well, but especially not to Joe. *"Look..."*

"I'm great in the kitchen," Joe said. "She loves my cooking."

"And I'm great in the bedroom," Charlie said. "She loves my body. Between the two of us, Allie has it all."

Allie glared at them both. "Actually—"

Mark snorted. "Allie doesn't like sex."

Allie swung on Mark. "Well, *actually*—"

Charlie smiled at Mark. "No, she just didn't like it with you."

"She didn't like your linguini, either," Joe pointed out. "She said it was rubbery."

Charlie frowned at Joe. "That's funny. She said the same thing about his—"

"Oh, *great*," Allie said.

"Don't be childish." Mark stood up, almost knocking over the waitress who'd come with their salads. "Obviously, we've intruded, and you don't want us. Come on, Lisa."

They watched him stalk across the room, Lisa trailing behind, throwing them curious looks over her shoulder.

"Feel free to discuss my sex life at any time in public," Allie told the two of them when the waitress had gone. "Don't mind me."

"We won't," Charlie said around a mouthful of salad.

"I almost feel sorry for Lisa," Joe said.

Allie picked up her fork and stabbed at her lettuce, shoving thoughts of sleeping with Charlie out of her mind to consider Lisa. She ate for a couple of minutes, looking at the situation from all sides. "I guess I do feel sorry for her," she said finally. "This isn't her fault."

"She ended up with your boyfriend and your job," Joe reminded her. "She has some responsibility there."

"Nope." Allie's voice grew firmer as she grew surer. "This is Mark. Mark wanted me out and her in. And he got it. I just don't know why."

Joe shook his head at her. "It's obvious. Mark's jealous of you."

"That makes no sense." Allie waved her fork at him to end the discussion.

"Yeah, it does." Joe pointed his own fork at her. "Everybody at the station knows that Mark's success is because of you. He likes to think it's because of him."

Charlie stabbed another chunk of lettuce. "So, if he shoves Allie out and puts Lisa the newbie in, everyone will know that his success is—"

"His success," Joe finished. "Except that's not going to happen."

"Why not?" Charlie shoved his empty salad bowl aside and reached for another bread stick.

"You eat like you're starving," Allie told him, amazed at the speed with which he'd destroyed his salad. "Don't they feed you back home?"

"You should talk." He pointed to her own half-empty bowl. "I've seen locusts move through vegetation slower." He turned back to Joe. "Why not?"

Joe scooped up a forkful of his salad. "Because the only reason Mark is a success is because Allie plans out every second of his show. She even has his ad-libs on cue cards. You have to see it to believe it."

Charlie raised an eyebrow at Allie. "How do you manage that?"

Allie shrugged. "There are only a dozen or so expressions that are really useful, anyway. I just pick the card that worked best. And he isn't that bad. In almost two years, he's never misread a cue card. Could we talk about something else?"

"Oh, that's talent, reading cue cards," Charlie agreed. "You were with him for two years?"

"Professionally." Allie squirmed a little in her chair. "The other thing only lasted about six months."

"Six terrible months," Joe added. "Thank God for Lisa, or I'd have had to kill him just to set you free. And you're right, Al, I do feel sorry for her. She's going to pay."

Charlie looked around the table for something else to eat. "Why? What did she do now?"

"Nothing." Joe grinned at him over his salad bowl. "Do you remember the flack Deborah Norville got when she replaced Jane Pauley?"

"Yeah." Charlie fished a pepper strip out of Allie's bowl, narrowly avoiding her fork.

"Well, that's going to be nothing compared to what happens when the station finds out Allie got screwed. Lisa is not going to have an easy time of it."

Allie was afraid for a moment that Joe might have a point. She didn't mind Lisa failing to keep Mark's ratings up, but she didn't want her to fail because everyone turned on her. She stared at her plate, not seeing the food. She didn't need this. She needed all her energy to revive her career.

Which now depended on Charlie.

She stole another look at him over her glasses and began to really think about Charlie and the new show for the first time. Things weren't nearly as bad as they'd seemed earlier. Charlie had potential. After all, he was intelligent. Verbal. Even occasionally funny. She could make him a star. All she had to do was study him, design a format that fit him and plug him into it. He and his mouth could take it from there, while she goosed the publicity along.

She could have him a household word by Christmas. Three months easy, and she'd be back on top.

She waited until the waitress had brought their dinners, and then she began her pitch. "You're really verbal," she told him, batting her eyelashes at him. "I like that in a man. Especially in a man whose show I'm producing."

Charlie stopped, his fork in midair, and eyed her cautiously. "What's that supposed to mean?"

Allie smiled at him, hearty and encouraging. "I'm going to make you a star, Charlie."

"The hell you are." Charlie went back to his dinner.

Allie pulled back a little and exchanged glances with Joe, who shrugged. Okay, so he'd have to be convinced. No problem. She returned to Charlie and her career. "Look, I know your show was a sort of cult hit in Lawrenceville and you like to do things your way, but you're starting all over here in a bad time slot. And radio is not exactly a secure career, as you well know. I can—"

Charlie pointed his fork at her. "No, you can't. Bill should have told you. I'm temporary. I'm going to be here five or six weeks, tops, probably not that long. I've got places I have to be by November. And this guy whose show I'm covering, Waldo, right?" Allie nodded. "Well, Waldo's coming back."

Allie frowned at him and even Joe blinked. "Waldo's not coming back," he told Charlie. "He's in San Diego with his sister. Resting comfortably at last report."

Charlie shrugged. "Must be for a visit. Bill knows I'm just temporary."

"Now what's Bill up to?" Joe asked Allie, and she shook her head, clearly as mystified as he was.

Charlie's eyes went from one to the other. "He's not coming back?"

"Waldo shot the console his last night on the air," Allie told him. "He said it was talking to him and wouldn't shut up."

"Maybe he just needs a nice vacation," Charlie suggested.

"Maybe he needs to be away from stereo equipment," Joe said. "He's not coming back."

"So that means," Allie began, ready to make her pitch.

"So that means you're going to be breaking in another guy in about six weeks," Charlie told her. "Do not bother making me a hit. I'm temporary."

He returned to his dinner and began to quiz Joe on Tuttle, and Allie sat back and regrouped. The problem wasn't that he refused to help her make him famous. She could do that without him. She'd made Mark a success without any appreciable input from him.

The problem was that he wasn't going to be around long enough for her to rebuild her career.

Unless she hit the ground running a lot faster than she'd intended.

Allie gave it a minute's thought. All right, she could do that.

And in the meantime, the news made the penicillin project a lot more possible. If he was only going to be around a few weeks, she could have a one-night fling with him without any consequences. She wasn't used to having flings actually, but she was thirty-six. Her flinging years weren't going to last forever. She had every intention of getting married and having children some day, and then flings would be out of the question. This might be it.

She looked at the situation from all sides. There didn't seem to be any serious obstacles, aside from Charlie himself.

"All right," she said and began to eat her dinner.

Charlie stopped eating and looked at Joe. "Why do I have a bad feeling about her giving in so easily?"

"Because you're a student of human nature," Joe told him.

Allie ignored them both to put her plan into action as soon as they were finished eating. "Let's take Charlie on a tour of the city on our way home. He should see Tuttle a little before he goes on the air tomorrow night. It'll give him something to talk about." *And I can find out what he's interested in and plan a program on it.*

"The tour sounds great." Charlie picked up his check. "But you don't need to put me up. I've got a room at a motel. Thanks for the offer, though."

Not good. She needed to get to know him fast if she was going to get the show moving right away. And then there was the Fling Plan. It was going to be hard enough for her to seduce him in her own apartment. A motel room would be impossible. Allie smiled at him. "I think you should stay with us. You told Mark you were."

Charlie shrugged. "Who cares?"

"Mark won't be mad if you're not staying with us." Allie batted her eyes at him again. It wasn't one of her better skills, but she was desperate.

Charlie leaned close until they were almost nose to nose. "You know, I haven't known you very long, Alice McGuffey, but I can tell you're up to something."

"As I said, a student of human nature." Joe leaned back in his chair to watch.

"Joe will make waffles for breakfast if we ask him nicely." Allie grabbed Charlie's hand again so he couldn't escape. His hand was broad and warm, and she was beginning to feel absolutely cheerful about seducing him. "We can talk about the station tonight. Where's your suitcase? At the motel?"

"Just a duffel bag. It's in my car." Charlie frowned at her. "I still think you're up to something."

Allie tried to look innocent and guileless while she cast around for a selling point. "Joe puts pecans in the waffles."

"I'm probably going to regret this." Charlie looked at Joe. "What do you think?"

Joe shook his head. "I'm staying out of this. Although we do have a couch, and I do put pecans in the waffles." He looked at Allie. "On the other hand, I do think she's up to something."

"They better be great waffles," Charlie said.

"They'll be unforgettable," Allie promised.

CHARLIE WASN'T USED to struggling with his conscience, but then his life wasn't usually this complex. His conscience said, stay away, lie low, don't get involved with these nice people. But he never listened to his conscience, anyway.

He was going to do it, he realized as they got up to go. He was going to move in with Allie and Joe and pump them for background on the station, all the news and rumor that only friends would repeat to friends. It would be low and slimy of him, but it was a great opportunity, and he'd been around long enough to know that great opportunities in life were few and far between.

Just keep your hands off Allie, he told himself sternly. It was one thing to use her for information; it was another thing entirely to use her for.... He glanced down at her, and she smiled, and he remembered how warm she'd been in his arms. Just thinking about her was a bad idea.

Waffles and gossip, yes. Allie, absolutely no.

He excused himself and went to find a phone to cancel his motel reservation. *Remember,* he told himself. *Be virtuous.*

It would be a nice change for him.

"WHAT ARE YOU UP TO?" Joe asked Allie when Charlie had gone.

Allie shoved her chair in, squaring her shoulders. "I'm going to seduce him." It sounded pretty stupid when she said it out loud.

"What?"

"I have a plan. He'll be like penicillin." Joe looked at her as if she were nuts, so she elaborated, warming to her topic as she explained.

"Mark's just a bad habit, like a virus. All I need is an antidote. I'll sleep with Charlie, and then I'll be over Mark."

Joe put his head in his hands. "Even for you, this is a dumb idea."

"Why?" Allie blinked down at him. "It's worked great so far. I don't mind about Mark much at all when I'm around Charlie."

"And what are you going to do to get over Charlie?"

"I won't need to get over Charlie. From now on, I'm concentrating on my career. Charlie is just a fling."

Joe looked at her as if she were demented. "Except you're not the kind of woman who has flings. And you're already concentrating too much on your career. That's how you ended up with Mark, because he was *convenient*. And I don't think Charlie is the kind of guy you forget."

"Well, I'm thirty-six," Allie said, exasperated. "If I don't start having flings now, I never will. And I'm tired of getting all wrapped up in a guy and then trying to cope when he's gone. I want a nice, simple, short, purely sexual one-night stand, and then I can forget about Mark. And Charlie's out of here in six weeks, he said so. This is perfect."

Joe spoke very slowly to her. "This. Is. A. Dumb. Idea."

"Listen." Allie fought back the anger that suddenly threatened her voice. "I know how dumb I am. I know Mark is worthless. I knew it when I was with him, but I kept making excuses. And now I'm stuck in this stupid thing where I want to be with him, and I don't even know why. Haven't you ever wanted somebody you knew wasn't worth it?"

"Yes," Joe said. "I imagine almost everybody has."

"Well, all I'm trying to do is get over it." Allie stuck out her chin. "Is that so bad?"

"No." Joe stood up and the sympathy in his eyes almost laid her low. "No, of course not. But Charlie is...well...I don't think I'd mess with Charlie." He looked over her shoulder. "He looks like the kind of guy who makes an impression."

"Not on me." Allie turned and saw Charlie walking toward them. He looked wonderful: big and broad and solid and fun. But not permanent. She could take him or leave him. Or take him *and* leave him. No problem.

Charlie came back to the table and smiled at them. "Let's go. You can tell me all about the station. Leave nothing out, no matter how disgusting. I'm braced for anything."

"Good," Allie said.

THEY GAVE CHARLIE a quick tour of old Tuttle in the late-September dusk. The town unfolded before him like a set of sepia-toned postcards: a white filigree bandstand in the park, a narrow Main Street mercifully free of aluminum storefronts, and a city hall that looked like a glowering, gargoyled sandstone castle.

"Historic preservationists, bless them," Joe told him. "They fight tooth and nail to keep old Tuttle pure. Of course, over on the other side, new Tuttle is a symphony of aluminum siding, but who cares?"

"But even the preservationists can't save city hall," Allie said.

"They're going to tear down that building?" Charlie craned his neck to look back at the ornate structure. He wasn't a historic-building nut, but tearing down something that magnificently outrageous seemed a waste.

Joe shrugged. "I think they're just going to abandon it. Too hard to heat or something. They've got a new building all planned. There's a model of it in the basement of the old building. It's awful." Joe turned a corner and a few minutes later it was dark.

"What happened?"

"East Tuttle, better known as Eastown." Allie pointed out the window. "See? Streetlights out, but nobody fixes them. This is not a Good Section of Town."

"In defense of the city department, they try." Joe slowed to let a weaving pedestrian cross. "The vandalism around here is pretty frequent."

"Not that frequent," Allie said. "These people get taken for a ride."

Charlie looked around at the peeling paint and broken steps and a derelict corner grocery store, and tried to make it fit with what he'd seen of Tuttle before. "A lot of drugs down here?"

Allie shrugged. "Probably, but I hear the best place to score is right by the old bandstand in the park."

Charlie started to laugh. "So much for Tuttle, the perfect small town."

Allie sighed. "It used to be sort of like that. A lot of mom-and-pop businesses run by people who called you by name. Most of them are gone now, run out by the chains." She peered out the window at another corner store left standing empty. "You know, I don't think there are any independent groceries left in the whole city."

"That's a shame," Charlie said absently. Tuttle was not a hotbed of crime. What the hell could be going on at a radio station in a town like this to make a man like Bill Bonner lose his cool and his father send him in as an amateur detective?

Something here didn't make sense. And since his father and Bill were involved, two men notorious for getting their own way no matter what the cost, Charlie was especially wary. They were up to something.

He sat silently while Joe drove and talked and eventually they came to a slightly better part of town full of old frame houses with big front porches, and Charlie smiled in spite of himself. Tuttle was a nice little town, the kind of town he'd always liked when he'd driven through one on his way to someplace else. He avoided stopping in any town like this one on the grounds that if he really liked it, he'd stay, and then he'd take a permanent job. And if things went the way they usually did, he'd get promoted, and then he'd be in charge, and pretty soon he'd be his father.

No town was worth that.

Then Joe turned again, and in a few minutes they were in a more modern neighborhood, passing a mall.

"Tuttle has a mall?" Charlie asked, amazed.

"There's a lot more to Tuttle than meets the eye," Allie said, and Charlie wondered exactly how much more there was, how much of it Allie knew, and how long it would take him to get it out of her.

IT WAS LATE when they got back to the apartment. They'd picked up Charlie's car at the restaurant and he'd followed them home, parking behind Joe on a side street away from the blare of the traffic. He joined them, and Joe gestured to a three-story white brick house. "This is us. Three apartments. We've got the second floor."

The house was simple but elegant in its proportions, and Charlie felt good just looking at it. "Very nice," he said and followed them up the wide stone steps and into the cream-walled hallway.

It was a great house. A comfortable house.

That made him uneasy. Getting too comfortable would be bad because he was leaving in November. Maybe he'd be better off in a really ugly motel.

"Come on up, Charlie," Allie called to him from the stairway, and her voice was husky, and he began to climb the steps to her without thinking about it.

ALLIE SHOWED HIM around the apartment: a big cream and peach living room with two couches and lots of lamps and bookcases, a white kitchen big enough for a full-size oak table and a mass of cooking gear, a large sea-green bathroom about the size of the bedroom in Charlie's last apartment with an old claw-foot tub about the size of his old bed, and two large bedrooms, one in gray and red for Joe, and one in peach and white for Allie. It confirmed all Charlie's suspicions that Joe and Allie were wonderful, warm, generous people who shouldn't be allowed out without a keeper.

"This is great," Charlie said when they were back in the living room. "But you people are nuts."

Allie flopped down on one of the overstuffed couches. "Why?"

"I'm a complete stranger and you just invited me into your apartment and showed me everything you own." Charlie shook his head at both of them. "You're asking to be ripped off."

"Nope. We know Bill." Joe headed back to the kitchen. "Want something to drink?"

"Iced tea, please," Allie called after him, and Charlie sat down across from her.

"What does Bill have to do with it?"

Allie snuggled down into the couch cushions, and Charlie let his mind wander for a moment. Allie was as well-upholstered as the couch. A comfortable woman. The kind of woman without angles or sharp bones or—

"Bill owns the station," Allie said. "And nothing or nobody gets in the station that Bill doesn't know everything about. If he hired you, he's seen your baby pictures."

Since Bill was Charlie's father's college roommate, this was truer than Allie knew, but Charlie was still not convinced. "You're telling me it's impossible for Bill to have hired a creep? Then how did he get Mark?"

Allie grinned. "You're biased. Mark's not so bad. He's a little insecure, and he's ambitious for his show, but who wouldn't be?"

"Me," Charlie said.

Joe came back in the room bracketing three iced-tea glasses in his hands. "You're not ambitious?" he asked as Charlie took one.

"Nope. I'm just here to have a good time." Charlie leaned back and sipped his tea. It was full and rich, sun tea laced with just enough lemon and sugar. He settled more comfortably into the couch. "And it's a good thing I'm not ambitious since I'm on from 10:00 to 2:00 a.m."

Allie smiled at him brightly. It was a smile he was learning to associate with Positive Career Talk. "The time could be a lot better," she told him. "But don't worry. I'm going to make you a star."

"No, you are not." Charlie narrowed his eyes at her. The only thing that was going to save him was that he was on late enough that nobody would notice how inept he was. All he needed was Allie drawing attention to him as he stuck a microphone in his eye or something, and then questions would be asked. "Don't you even think about holding up a cue card for me. I told you. I don't want to be a star."

Joe snorted. "You don't have any choice. If Allie wants you famous, you're going to be famous."

"Forget it," Charlie told Allie. "Wipe the thought from your mind."

"We can talk about it later," Allie said smoothly. "Now, tomorrow night's your first show and I thought—"

"Don't." Charlie scowled at her. "Thinking is bad for a woman. Tell me about the other people at the station. I already know about Mark and Lisa."

Allie sat silent with her tea, obviously regrouping, so Joe chimed in. "Bill owns the station and theoretically runs it as general manager."

"Theoretically?"

Joe exchanged a glance with Allie. "His wife, Beattie, decided about six months ago that she wanted a career. Bill gives Beattie anything she wants, so she's pretty much running the place now."

Charlie quirked an eyebrow at Joe. This was news Bill hadn't shared. "Is that good?"

"I think so," Joe said. "She fired Weird Waldo."

"He thought Martians were invading the station through the consoles," Allie said. "He kept announcing during his show that they were getting closer. It was actually kind of interesting if you suspended logical thought. Beattie wanted him gone, but Bill said he was just being colorful."

"And then he shot the console," Charlie said.

"Yep, just last week. Blew the whole thing away." Allie sighed. "At least we gained a new console. And lost Waldo, thanks to Beattie."

"Wouldn't even Bill have fired him at that point?" Charlie asked, incredulous.

"Bill's ability to ignore anything unpleasant is legendary," Joe told him.

"Great." Charlie drank more of his iced tea. If Bill could ignore somebody shooting up a broadcasting booth, the one anonymous letter that had made him call for help must have been a beauty. He brought his attention back to Joe. "What else should I know?"

They talked on into the night, Joe and Allie filling him in on the rest of the station personnel, like Albert the anal-retentive business manager who recited ad prices in his sleep, and Marcia the ambitious afternoon DJ who was breathing down Mark's neck for the prime-time slot, and Karen the receptionist who knew all the gossip not fit to print, and Harry the Howler who was on right before Charlie.

"Harry howls from six to ten," Allie told Charlie. "He likes to think he's wild and crazy, but he's really sweet with the volume turned up. His real area of expertise is cars, so if you ever have problems with yours, ask Harry."

"And then there's me."

Allie nodded. "Yep. Harry's audience usually starts to fade about nine, nine-thirty, and then we had Weird Waldo."

Charlie tried not to show his relief. "So, at the moment, my show has a listening audience of about..."

Allie grinned at him. "Oh, six or seven, tops. And they're all listening because they're concerned about the Martians, and they're waiting for the update."

Charlie started to laugh. "Oh, God. This is going to be awful."

"Then at two o'clock, there's Grady."

"Tell me Grady's normal."

"Well..." Allie stopped, obviously searching for the words to describe Grady. "Grady is sweet. He talks about things like the life force and crystal power and personal auras, and then he plays classical guitar music and Gregorian chants and other..." She stopped. "I can't describe Grady. His show is very soothing, and he has his own small but fanatically loyal following." She shrugged. "I like him. Grady's a good person."

"If he has only a small following, why is he still on the air?"

"Because he's Grady Bonner. Someday, all this will be his."

"The son and heir? Then why is he on the graveyard shift?"

"Because his following is small. Bill gave Grady two to six to keep him off the streets."

Charlie took a deep breath. "So I'm sandwiched in between Howling Harry and Grady 'I Have Lived In Other Times' Bonner?"

"That's about it."

It couldn't be better. No one would ever hear him. He started to grin. "I'm in big trouble."

"No, you're not." Allie leaned forward. "From ten to two, you have a lot of freedom. This is so all the really knee-jerk conservatives go to bed early so they can get up with the chickens, which means your audience, once you build one, will be open to new things. As long as you don't do anything that upsets Bill, you can say anything you want. We can do this, Charlie. We—"

"No, we can't." Charlie hated to ruin her plans, she looked so cute trying to sell them to him, but he was not going to be a success.

"I don't want to be famous. I just want a nice little radio show for a few weeks. That's all."

Allie shoved her glasses back up her nose. "But, Charlie—"

"No," Charlie said firmly.

Joe stood up. "I'd love to stay and watch this, but I have to go to work in the morning. Good night, all."

He disappeared into the bathroom, and Charlie leaned back on the couch.

"I think we should talk about this," Allie said.

"I don't," Charlie said, but Allie did anyway, explaining all the good things that would come his way if he just put himself in her hands.

She was a good persuader, and under any other circumstances he might have listened just because she talked such a good fight, but he was only temporary. He wasn't staying. He wasn't going to be a success.

He wouldn't mind being in her hands, though.

He jerked his mind away from the thought when Joe came out of the bathroom in his robe.

"Bathroom's all yours. Good night." Joe looked at Allie and shook his head, and then he went into his bedroom and closed the door.

Charlie frowned at Allie. She'd abandoned her argument about his career and was now looking at him as if she was sizing him up. He had the damnedest feeling she was going to try a new attack. It wasn't a reassuring feeling. "Why did Joe shake his head?"

"What?" Allie stood up and moved to stand beside him, smiling brightly. "Never mind. My bedroom, as you know, is on the left. Want to see it again?"

"Come here, McGuffey." He pulled her down beside him, trapping her hand in his. "What are you up to? Tell me everything, now. I can take it."

"I was going to tell you, anyway." She sat stiff and straight. "I just wanted to be in my nightgown to do it."

"Your nightgown." Charlie clamped down on his evil thoughts and patted her hand. "Well, I'm sorry I'm going to miss that. Why your nightgown?"

She sighed. "Joe thinks this is a bad idea."

"Joe's no dummy. If he thinks it is, it probably is."

"I think so, too. Forget it." She stood up, and he caught her hand.

"Oh, no, you don't. Just in case you change your mind, I need to be prepared. Are we going to go Vaseline Mark's car windows? Put Tabasco in Lisa's diaphragm?"

Allie sat down again next to him. "All right. I have a favor to ask."

Charlie tried to look encouraging. "Shoot." Allie looked so uncomfortable, he was ready for anything.

She took a deep breath. "I want you to sleep with me."

CHARLIE DIDN'T SAY anything, and she stole a glance at him.

He looked stunned.

She should have know it wouldn't work. She wasn't the seductress type. She flopped back against the couch, defeated. "I know it's dumb, but I had this plan. I thought maybe if I slept with somebody else, I'd get over Mark permanently. Sort of like getting right back on the horse after you've been thrown."

Charlie made a sound like a strangled laugh.

"What did you say?"

"I whinnied."

Allie fought back a smile. "You laughed. Okay, go ahead. I just…" The words were too dumb to say out loud, so she shut up and shrugged instead.

Charlie leaned back beside her. "Why don't you tell me about it?"

Allie hesitated and then gave in. "Well, it's hard to explain without sounding stupid. Everybody at the station thinks Mark is God. We were working together, making the show a hit, and when we started dating, it just felt right, I guess." She wrinkled her nose as she thought. "And he was really good to me." She turned her head to look Charlie in the eye, trying to make him understand. "I know he wasn't impressive today, but he really was good to me. I've never been that anxious to settle down, but I thought we'd be together forever, working on the show." She shook her head in disgust. "I was stupid. But it was still hard to give up. And I still miss it." She stopped and frowned. "But you know, I think I miss the relationship more than I miss him."

Charlie shook his head. "Everybody at the station thinks he's God? They must be morons."

"Not all of them. Just me."

Charlie frowned at her. "If you're going to feel sorry for yourself, get off my couch and go to your room."

Allie relaxed back into the couch. "You know, I'm a very good producer. I just can't handle my personal life."

Charlie snorted. "You and about twenty million other people."

She rolled her head sideways to look at him. "How do you do it?"

Charlie grinned at her. "Not very well. I have this commitment problem."

"You and about twenty million other guys." Allie grinned back. "Big deal. I bet once it's over for you, it's over. I bet you don't go on obsessing about it afterward."

"No. But then I've never loved anyone enough to obsess about it."

"Well, that's just my point." She sat up again. "I'm not sure I loved Mark. I didn't even *like* Mark much toward the end, which may be one of the reasons he dumped me. But I was used to being with him, working on the show, you know? I'm just...stuck in this stupid rut, and I need something to bounce me out of it."

Charlie looked confused but not condemning. "So, your plan was that we'd sleep together, and then what?"

"Then I'd be over Mark, and we'd go to work."

"A short-term arrangement." He sounded noncommittal, which wasn't encouraging.

Allie tried to get back to selling the idea. "Absolutely. A one-night stand. No strings. The last thing in the world I need right now is another relationship." The thought of trying to keep another man happy made her tired all by itself. "I'm just sick of feeling like I'm going to throw up every time I see Mark."

"You and about twenty million other people."

Allie laughed. "No, really." She tried to be serious. "He's a nice guy. Lots of people like him. His show is very popular. And he takes a nice publicity picture."

"Oh, that's important in radio."

Allie turned to look at him when she heard the scorn in his voice. "Oh? And what do you do in radio?"

Charlie tensed for a moment and then relaxed deeper into the couch. "Well, there used to be a really late show in Lawrenceville from two to six. After Two with Ten Tenniel." He grinned down at her and she grinned back because it was impossible not to. "Strange people call from two to six. I'm hoping the ten-to-two people are at least half as bizarre."

His voice was low but it kept his grin in it when he talked. That was one of things she liked best about him, although actually, there was a lot to like about Charlie. She leaned a little closer to him. "You like bizarre? Then you're going to love WBBB."

"I love bizarre. That's why I let you pick me up." He looked down at her, and she could have sworn she saw heat in his eyes. But then, what did she know about men?

Charlie stood up and pulled her off the couch. "Go to bed, Allie, so I can go to bed. You get the bathroom first." He patted her shoulder. "I'll help you with Mark tomorrow, *not* by sleeping with you, but now I've got to get some real sleep."

Well, that was that. Allie walked back to her bedroom door. She should have known it wouldn't work.

Rats.

Unless…

CHARLIE WATCHED her walk toward her bedroom and tried to feel virtuous for turning her down. He did feel virtuous. He'd made a great sacrifice. There was nothing he wanted more than to be in Allie's hands.

In Allie's bed.

Oh, hell.

Feeling virtuous was a lousy trade for what he was giving up.

Allie stopped, and then turned back to him, a much too innocent look on her face. "How about a smaller favor?"

"Smaller than sex?"

"Yes." She drifted back to him, and he felt wary again.

"What?"

Allie took off her glasses and lifted her chin. "Kiss me. So I can concentrate this time. I missed it the last time. In the bar."

Charlie ran his fingers through his hair. All his instincts told him to run, but she was standing there with that great mouth, and he wanted it. "You really are something. You treat all the guys you meet like this?"

Allie shook her head, and he watched the light glint in her hair as it swung back and forth. "Nope. You just happened to hit me on a very unusual day."

"Lucky me." Charlie swallowed and surrendered. "Okay, pucker up, but this time, pay attention. I don't want to have to keep on doing this."

She nodded. "Right."

Allie lifted her face to his, and he bent and kissed her. He meant to make it brief, but the softness of her mouth moved against his and took his breath away. *I'm in big trouble here,* he thought, and then he stopped thinking.

He felt her hand on his cheek, and he closed his eyes. She was intoxicating, and he opened his mouth and teased her lips with his tongue until she opened to him and he could taste her. Her body moved against him, and he held her close, moving his hands up to her shoulders and then back down to the small of her back, pressing her hips close to his, soft against him.

When he finally broke the kiss, they were both breathless.

"Thank you," Allie said unsteadily as she stepped back. "That was very nice. Good night." She backed away into the bathroom and shut the door.

Charlie sat down on the couch and tried to remember where he was.

He was not going to get involved with Allie. He had a job to worry about. He was going to lay low. He was going to not make waves. He was going to do his job and get out. He was going to forget Allie and get some sleep.

He unbuttoned his shirt and went to find his bag. He didn't have pajamas, but with Allie flitting about making suggestions, he had to wear something. He found his sweatpants just as Allie came out of the bathroom in a long blue cotton nightgown. She looked very virginal.

"Here are your sheets and things," she said, putting them on the end of the couch. "Do you need anything else?"

Charlie clamped down on his wayward thoughts. "No. Thank you."

"Good night." She hesitated, and then she went into her room.

He took his sweatpants and his toothbrush into the bathroom. *Don't think about her,* he told himself. He got ready for bed, concentrating on not thinking about Allie, and then he went out to the couch and made his bed, concentrating on not thinking about Allie, and then he got into his bed, concentrating on not thinking about Allie.

It wasn't working.

ALLIE LAY in bed and thought about Charlie.

God, he was beautiful, standing there in the living room with his shirt unbuttoned. She'd never been turned on just looking at a man before, but he was so broad and beautiful. And dangerous.

If they were on TV instead of radio, she'd make him leave his shirt unbuttoned. Women would be clawing at the set.

And then there was his mouth. Kissing like that should be illegal. Or at least licensed.

She put her hands over her face and groaned. Sleeping with Charlie would not be penicillin. Sleeping with Charlie would be cocaine. Of all the stupid ideas she'd had in her life, this was the stupidest.

Why didn't she ever listen to Joe?

She turned over onto her side, concentrating on not thinking about Charlie.

God, he looked good. And he kissed better.

She buried her head under the pillow and tried to think about her career.

CHARLIE ROLLED OVER on the couch. Sleeping with Allie would be wrong. She was emotionally vulnerable right now. By tomorrow, she'd be relieved he hadn't taken her up on her offer.

Of course, by tomorrow, he'd be insane with frustration.

It was that damn kiss. If she hadn't asked for the kiss, he wouldn't be thinking about how soft her mouth was, how soft she was all over...

He rolled over again, trying to think about the anonymous letter and how he didn't have a clue about what a disc jockey did and how tomorrow night he'd have to do it, concentrating on everything and anything but Allie.

She was probably asleep by now, anyway.

It was thinking about her mouth that was the worst.

ALLIE SAT UP in bed and put her arms around her knees.

Not thinking about Charlie wasn't working. She was breathless with not thinking about him. She wanted him. She physically itched for him. This wasn't the gauzy need she'd always assumed women felt for the men they lusted after. This was unpleasant and uncomfortable and would require full body contact to satiate.

And he'd already said no once.

Suppose she just strolled out there.

And then what? Took off her nightgown? Did the dance of the seven veils? That would never work. She was a lousy dancer. Production was her specialty, not seduction. Maybe if she made up some cue cards: "Yes, Allie, I'd love to sleep with you. Take off your clothes."

Right, that would work.

Besides, he was probably already asleep.

She put her head on her knees and moaned softly. She was never going to get to sleep.

CHARLIE SAT UP and put his head in his hands. He was never going to get to sleep. He wanted her so much now, he throbbed with it. How the hell had this happened?

What difference did it make?

He threw off the covers and stood up.

He'd just knock on her door. She was probably asleep. Then he'd go back to the couch and go to sleep.

Right.

He picked up his shaving kit and pulled out a strip of condoms, shoving them in the pocket of his sweats before he went to her door.

He knocked softly. "Allie?"

"Come in," she said.

She was sitting up in bed, her arms wrapped around her knees and her glossy brown hair tangled around her face. "I can't sleep," she said.

"Me, neither." He sat down beside her. "You and your one last kisses." He cradled her cheek in his hand. "Do you still want that one-night stand?"

"Yes," she breathed, and the heat flared in him.

"Thank God." He slid his arm around her. "Move over."

Three

➤ ◀

Charlie moved pretty fast for a big guy, shoving off his sweatpants and sliding her nightgown over her head while she drew a sharp breath at his touch. The heat flared in her when the shock of his skin touched hers, and he touched her everywhere. She clutched him to her, tipping her head back for his mouth as if the muscles in her neck had given way. His hands moved over her, stroking her back, her sides, sliding down to pull her close to the hardness of his hips, and all the while he tormented her mouth with his tongue. He was everywhere, and wherever he was, there was heat.

"Tell me what you want," he whispered against her mouth, and she clung to him and whispered back, "You."

He moved down her throat to the hollow between her neck and shoulder, making her squirm as he found the nerve there. He trailed more hot kisses down her shoulder until his mouth found her breast and she forgot who she was. He dallied there, sucking hard until she could feel the pull and tingle deep inside her. She moved against him convulsively, pressing him to her, and he moved his mouth to her other breast and made her moan again.

Allie drowned in the heat; waves of it washed over her as Charlie moved against her. Then his mouth found hers again and he was kissing her hard, his tongue thrusting into her mouth as he pulled her on top of him and pressed her head to his so that she couldn't escape his kiss. She stretched against him, drunk with desire, and he rolled over so she was under him again and moved his hand between them, lower this time.

His whisper tickled her ear and made her squirm. "You have a beautiful body, Allie. You were made for love." He slid his hand between her legs and she gasped and arched up to meet him.

"Don't ever stop touching me," she said thickly. Her skin prickled, and the pounding came stronger, in rhythm with his hand. "Don't ever, ever stop."

But he did, rolling away from her to reach for something on the floor. She heard foil tearing.

"Charlie?"

She struggled to sit up and then his mouth was on hers again, his hands on her hips, his body against hers. He pulled her under him and then he was sliding into her, and she felt her entire body clench and throb as he rocked into her, felt herself drawn into the pounding in her blood, in his blood, the pounding everywhere.

"Wait." She felt herself lurch out of control. "Wait. I can't…"

"Let go," he whispered in her ear. "Let go, Allie."

She clutched at him, and he stared down at her hotly, half in shadow, his eyes glittering as he thrust into her over and over again. *Who is he?* she thought. *I don't even* know *him. And he's inside me.*

Then he moaned and his head dropped to her shoulder, and she felt his grasp tighten on her as he slumped over her. She held him to her, rocking him a little, feeling warm and tingly and shaken and relieved and disappointed.

Charlie rolled off and pulled her close to him.

"I lost you along the way," he said, still breathless. "What did I do wrong?"

"Nothing." Allie settled against him, trying not to be annoyed. "That was incredible. You were wonderful." For a moment, it was like being with Mark again, and she sighed in resignation. Men were obviously not her strong suit.

Charlie held her until his breathing slowed, and then he propped himself up on one elbow and looked down at her, moving his hand up to cup her breast again. "You were with me there," he whispered. "I could feel it in you."

"I don't know." She tried to smile her usual supportive-lover smile at him, but she was distracted by his stroking thumb. "It doesn't matter."

He bent and kissed her cheek softly. "What part threw you off?" He moved his mouth to her breast. "Was it this?" He ran his tongue over her, and her body tightened at his touch.

"No." She moved against his mouth, her annoyance fading considerably. "No. It wasn't anything you did."

His hand moved down and stroked her gently. "This?"

"No," she breathed, and closed her eyes to concentrate on his touch.

"Allie?" He kissed her until she clung to him, dizzy again.

"I love it when you touch me." She moved under his hand as he stroked her.

"Good. I'll do it often." His fingers were stroking faster, and she found it hard to concentrate on his words. The pressure was everywhere, growing stronger, and she moved against the hard barrier of his body when she felt the itch start under her skin again.

"I won't let anything happen to you," he whispered, one arm tight around her. "Let go. I'm holding you."

Allie clung to him, drunk with the pressure, aching for release. The whole world was his hand against her, and the prickle in her blood, and she buried her face against his chest as she felt the pressure wind tighter, and she knew she was was going to explode if he didn't stop. Out of control.

"Oh, God." Allie tried to move away, but Charlie rolled and pinned her under him, thrusting his tongue in her ear, and she twisted at the shocking pleasure of it, crying out once as the pressure flared in her and her skin screamed, and then everything did explode, the heat arcing through her body as she gasped in his arms.

Charlie held her so tightly she had trouble breathing, but she clutched him to her anyway.

"Allie? Allie, love?"

She buried her face against his chest and tried to stop gasping, but the waves still lapped gently inside her, like little aftershocks.

"Allie?"

She clung to him, trying to find her voice, any coherent thought. "Oh, God, Charlie."

He held her tighter. "I thought you'd gone mute on me."

Allie took a long shuddering breath and then another until sanity returned. The heat and the release settled into her bones like a narcotic. She stretched against him, all her muscles aching, her skin sliding warm against his. "Oh." She drew another deep breath. "I may never talk again."

Charlie brushed her hair back from her face. "Can you sleep now?"

"Only if you don't touch me," she said, and he laughed and pulled her close, and she curled into him, and then they both fell asleep.

ALLIE WOKE UP when the sunlight flooded the room. She'd rolled away from Charlie in the night, but his hand was still on her waist, and she liked the weight and heat of it there. She lay very still and savored how good her body still felt, and only gradually did she become aware of Joe in the kitchen, banging pans.

As flings went, this one had been a beauty. No guilt, no fear, no emotion at all, really, except pleasure. Bless Charlie. And now she was going to make him a star. Life had done a one-hundred-and-eighty-degree turn on her overnight. She couldn't wait to get started again.

She stirred a little and felt Charlie's hand tighten on her waist in his sleep, and she moved her head on the pillow to look at him. His blond-brown hair was tousled and his eyelashes were like smudges on his cheeks, and he looked like a fallen angel.

It really was too bad they weren't doing TV.

She eased a little closer, and his arm gathered her to him until his cheek brushed against her hair.

"Morning," he said without opening his eyes. "How do you feel?"

Allie grinned against his chest. "Very smug, now that I know what all the shouting was about."

Charlie laughed softly. "You should know. You were the one doing the shouting."

Allie jerked her head back. "What?"

He smiled at her and kissed her forehead. "You scream when you come."

"I do not."

"The hell you don't." He gathered her back to him and sighed happily. "But it takes a lot of the guesswork out of making love to you, so I'm not complaining."

Allie thought about pushing him away and decided against it. "Very funny."

There was another crash from the kitchen.

Allie smiled again. "Joe's making breakfast. Aren't you hungry?"

"Yes." He kissed the top of her head. "But I've got to check out Tuttle in the daylight. So I'll just take a rain check, if that's okay with you."

"And miss Joe's waffles?"

"Hell, no. I'm eating waffles." Charlie rolled up on one arm and looked down at her. "I'm taking a rain check on you. Until tonight." He slid his hand under the sheet and cupped her breast, caressing her. "Same time, same place, same screams?"

He was gorgeous in the sunlight, and he had golden hands. She felt dizzy under them right now. But he was also her career. Mixing sex and business would be bad. Look what had happened with Mark.

"I thought we were a one-night stand." Her hand closed over his to stop his caress, but somehow she ended up pressing his hand against her, instead.

"We are." Charlie climbed over her to get out of bed, pulling the sheet down to kiss her breast on his way. "One night at a time."

She pulled the sheet back up and squinted myopically to watch him put on his sweatpants, admiring the muscles in his legs and his rear while she told herself she should stop now, that sleeping with Charlie was not a good idea, that he was leaving in November. Her brain told her to tell him she didn't want another night.

Her mouth flatly refused to say anything that stupid.

Something in her face must have tipped him off to her quandary because he stopped tying the string on his pants and grew serious. "You can always say no," he told her.

To you? The thought was so ludicrous, she laughed. "I'll try to remember that," she told him, and her spirits rose again. Enough of this chitchat. She had a career to resuscitate, and Charlie was a one-man rescue squad. She threw off the top quilt and got out of bed, fighting to keep the sheet wrapped around her, but it slipped as she yanked it free from the mattress.

Charlie approved. "The hell with the waffles." He reached for her, but she danced out of the way, blushing and covering herself with her hand and the corner of the sheet.

"Go eat." She flapped her free hand at him. "You need fuel for that body. You must be running on empty now."

"We get off at 2:00 a.m." He grinned while she grabbed her robe and tried to put it on without dropping the sheet. "We can be home by two-thirty. You don't want my side of the bed empty, do you?"

She tied her robe closed and stuck her chin out, taking control. "You don't have a side, and I'll be asleep by two thirty-five."

"Then you'll be awake by two thirty-six." Charlie grabbed the belt on her robe as she sidled past and caught her to him. He kissed her thoroughly, and then, while she was still reeling, he let her go and walked out of the room, whistling.

Hurry up, two thirty-six, she thought, and then she sat down on the edge of the bed again to get her thoughts back to her career, where they belonged.

"PECANS, right?" Charlie said to Joe who was pouring batter onto the griddle.

"Pecans." Joe closed the iron and turned to Charlie, his arms folded. "So, how did you sleep?"

Charlie sat down and tried to look innocent. "Am I going to get a lecture? Because she made the first move, I swear."

Joe rolled his eyes. "I know. She had a plan."

"Getting over Mark." Charlie nodded and poured some orange juice. "What a loser that guy is."

Joe leaned against the stove. "She has a tendency to pick losers. She has what might be described as a real genius for it."

Charlie winced. "Don't beat around the bush. Say what you mean."

"The only thing that's saved her is that her exes were lousy lovers. When they went, she wasn't missing much."

"I kind of got that impression last night."

"That's not all you got." Joe opened the iron and pried the waffles out onto a plate. "You don't exactly make love quietly." He put the plate in front of Charlie.

"That's Allie." Charlie was lavish with the syrup. "She's a screamer. Surprised the hell out of me."

"Allie's not the only one. You've got a nice deep moan yourself."

"Me?" Charlie stopped, surprised.

"The walls are thin here," Joe said charitably.

"I'm sorry we kept you up." Charlie took a bite of waffle. "You make a mean waffle. Do I get seconds?"

"Of the waffles, yes. Of Allie..." Joe shrugged. "That's my question. Was last night just an extremely vocal one-night stand or will you be back?"

Charlie stopped chewing. "Well, I was planning on coming back. We can go to a motel if we bother you. That's only fair."

"The noise isn't what bothers me." Joe sat down and started on his own waffles. "What I'm worried about is Allie. Are you going to hurt her? Because if you are, I'm against it."

Charlie stopped chewing, shocked. "I don't hurt people."

"What if Allie's in love with you?"

"She's not."

"She will be if you hang around." Joe pointed at him with a waffle-filled fork. "You're smart, you're funny, and you obviously know how to make her happy in bed."

Charlie thought about the job he'd come to do, and about how fast he'd be out of town when it was done. He sighed. "You're right. I have no serious intentions about Allie. I just like sleeping with her. So I'll do a fade." The thought was extremely unattractive, so he changed the subject. "You know, it's a shame you're gay. You're probably the perfect guy for her."

Joe grinned at him. "It's a shame you're not. You could be the perfect guy for me."

Charlie shook his head. "Probably not. I'm not the perfect guy for anybody."

"Good morning, all." Allie drifted into the kitchen and poured herself a glass of orange juice, smiling a lovely serene smile at both of them. All her tightness was gone. She looked confident and sexy, and they stared at the transformation.

Her smile faded as they stared. "Can I have waffles, too?" she asked Joe finally, and he blinked and then got up to make them for her.

"I've got to find my shoes and then we can make plans," she told Charlie. She smiled at him again, igniting him, and then she drifted back to her bedroom.

Charlie was halfway out of his chair to follow her before he realized it. "Oh, hell." He turned and looked at Joe. "You were right. I should have stayed on that damn couch."

"Maybe you'd better forget about doing the fade." Joe turned back to the waffle iron. "This could be a good thing. She looks invincible."

"She looks like…" Charlie stopped.

"She looks like she's had great sex," Joe said. "It's a new look for her. I'd pay money to see Mark's face when he sees her."

"Yeah? Well, what happens to that look when I stop sleeping with her?"

"Hey, I also saw the look on your face. What makes you think you can stop?"

Charlie put his fork down. Allie was absolutely not part of his plan. His plan was to do the job and get out.

And now there was Allie.

The look he gave Joe was pathetic.

Joe laughed.

WHEN SHE CAME BACK, Allie was wearing her day clothes: a plain, long, brown jersey dress and a man's brown and cream tweed jacket. She looked extremely round and soft, and Charlie reminded himself sternly that from now on, they had a working relationship only.

Then he watched her lick syrup off her fork and for the first time in his life, he envied silverware.

"We don't have to be at the station until four," she told him around bites of waffle.

"That's fine," Charlie replied. He needed some time alone to get his act together. "I want to wander around Tuttle on my own for a while. Get the feel of the place."

"Okay." Allie nodded at him. "I'll meet you in front of the station."

Joe left for an appointment, and Charlie and Allie talked about Tuttle and waffles and washed the dishes, and Charlie fought the feeling he was slipping into, that he'd always known her, that he always would. She was having a weird effect on him: she felt comfortable. Every internal alarm he had was screaming, but she smiled at him and he didn't care.

Out on the street, Allie twirled around on the sidewalk and her dress swirled out around her and she looked so happy, and she had such great legs, that Charlie abandoned all his qualms for the moment and just enjoyed the sunlight and Allie. If he wanted something to worry about, he didn't need to start with Allie; he had the anonymous letter and his first-ever radio show that night.

"Don't forget to meet me at four so I can introduce you to everybody before they leave at five," Allie said, and he promised and then escaped.

Stay away from that woman as much as you can, he warned himself. Then he thought about meeting her at four and grinned.

WBBB WAS ON THE fourth floor of a bank—"Bill's bank," Allie told him—and Charlie watched her smack open the double glass doors of the station as if she were attacking the place.

Instead of running for cover, the people inside converged on her like a last hope.

The dark-haired receptionist was the first to shriek at her as Allie blew past her with a "Hey, Karen."

"Wait, Allie, I need to talk to you," Karen said, but then the rest of the people began to come out of the narrow hall in front of them, one by one, like clowns out of a toy car.

Lisa darted out first. "Allie, can I have a minute? I need—"

"Allie!" A towheaded man the size of a small mountain lumbered toward her and slung his arm around her shoulder. "I need to talk to you. Alone."

A much smaller man in a too-tight tie with a too-tight face pushed between them. "Not now, Harry. Alice, the ratings—"

A steely-eyed brunette appeared behind him and shouldered

Jennifer Crusie

him aside. "Forget it, Albert. I just heard about this mess. I don't give a damn if Mark is dumb enough to dump you, *I'm* not."

Charlie watched Lisa wince, and then saw Allie pat her arm. "One at a time," Allie said, and Harry said, "Wait a minute," and Karen said, "Please, Allie," and Lisa said, "Oh, Allie, I need your help," and Albert said, "The *ratings*, Allie," and then from the hall someone said, "That's enough," and the whole room froze.

Charlie looked beyond the clump of people to the small, slender, older woman standing in the hallway.

"Nothing is changing," she said. "Alice is not leaving her position as Mark's producer."

"Well, actually, Beattie, I am." Allie reached out through the throng that surrounded her and grabbed Charlie by the bicep to drag him to her side. "This is Charlie Tenniel, our new DJ. I have some very exciting ideas for his program."

Charlie opened his mouth to object, but then Beattie spoke and it seemed like a bad idea to interrupt her.

"Bill did not discuss this with me first." The look in Beattie's eye said that Bill had paid dearly for this. "I was most disappointed in him."

"Well, I was, too," Allie said, and Charlie raised an eyebrow at her, surprised at her candor. Then his eyes went back to Beattie. Neat iron-gray hair, trim iron-gray suit, sharp iron-gray eyes. Not the kind of woman you lied to, Beattie. "But now I've met Charlie," Allie went on. "I think this is going to be interesting."

Beattie turned those gray eyes on Charlie, and he tried not to swallow. She surveyed him, starting at the top of his head and moving slowly to his feet before she started back up again. She made the return trip with a gleam in her eye.

Then she turned to Allie. "Oh. I see. Very well." She held out her hand to Charlie. "Very nice to meet you again, Charles. The last time we met, you were five, so I doubt you remember. How are your father and mother?"

Well, Mother is still insisting that Ten was framed when some undesirable planted all that coke on him, and Dad has lost his mind to the point of sending me here, but otherwise they're still golfing and drinking rum punch. "Just fine, Mrs. Bonner, thank you for asking."

Beattie's eyes narrowed for an instant, and Charlie reminded himself not to take Beattie Bonner for granted. She might be pushing seventy, but she was probably sharper than anyone else in the room, himself included.

Sharper than anyone, with the possible exception of Allie. When Charlie turned back to her, she was dispatching people with a warm efficiency that got them off her back without leaving them exasperated. She promised Marcia all the help she needed, Lisa a meeting as soon as she'd shown Charlie around, Harry a conference later that night before his show, Albert an analysis of the ratings by morning, and Karen the first minute she could spare. By the time she was finished, they were alone in the lobby except for Karen looking woebegone behind her desk, and Charlie had a new appreciation of how he'd ended up in Allie's bed the night before.

He also had a new apprehension for his immediate future. "Listen," he told her sternly. "I don't want to be famous."

"Of course not." She smiled up at him. "Let me show you the station."

Charlie followed her with foreboding, but the station itself was innocuous. Aside from the offices, the place was small, white, clean and uncluttered. One dedicated broadcast booth with a production room outside it, one combination broadcast and production room, one tape library, one room with the satellite feed, one conference/break room, and finally Allie's office.

Allie opened the door at the end of the hall of offices and gestured him in. "Welcome to my world."

"This is nice," Charlie said doubtfully as he looked around the tiny cubicle. Every square inch of three of the walls was covered with photos, handwritten notes, magazine articles, old scripts and anything else that Allie felt was valuable and that could be push-pinned up. It was like being inside a very messy desk drawer. The last wall was bookcases filled with reference books and loose-leaf binders and various treasures that Allie had stuffed there for some reason: a soapstone seal, a large rock, a ceramic goblet, a china doll, a bowl of shells. The center of the little room was crowded with an old teacher's desk, two thrift-store carved walnut chairs and a white filing cabinet with a stuffed owl on it. Charlie stared fascinated into the owl's eyes while Allie sat down behind her desk and began to search through the piles of papers.

If they ever made love in this office, he was going to throw his shirt over that owl so it wouldn't watch them. Not that there was room to lie down in here. They'd have to use the desk. Or against the wall… Charlie shook his head to clear it of the thought. He was definitely not going to be pressing Allie up against that wall—

"Your first appointment is with me to talk about how you're going to structure your four hours. Ah ha!" She held up her coffee cup, triumphant. "Also, you might want to start thinking about explaining your program ideas when we meet with Bill at five."

Charlie frowned at her, glad to bring his mind back to the problem at hand. "What's to explain?"

"He likes to preapprove the ideas." Allie looked dubiously into her cup and turned it upside down to shake it. Nothing fell out.

"He approves everything that goes out from this place?"

"Well, not Mark's stuff. Bill loves Mark." Allie got up and took a loose-leaf binder from her bookshelf. "Here's the WBBB handbook—Bill's personal philosophy of broadcasting. You're going to hate it."

Charlie took the book, opened it, read a page and sighed. Bill made Jesse Helms look liberal. "So Bill really does run the station? I thought maybe he'd be one of those distant owners who just drops by to read the profit sheet."

"He used to be."

Charlie looked up at the tone in Allie's voice. "But?"

Allie leaned back in her chair. "But then about six months ago, Beattie decided she wanted a job, so he gave her the run of the place. That upset the station manager and he quit. So Beattie took that job and now she really runs the station."

Charlie raised his eyebrows. "But you said last night she's not bad at it."

Allie nodded. "She's a fast learner, and she's not stupid in the slightest."

"And Bill just gave her the station." Charlie sat back. "Which parts aren't you mentioning?"

Allie bit her lip for a moment. Then she pushed her glasses up her nose and leaned forward. "Beattie doesn't particularly want to talk about this, so don't mention it. Last January, she was diagnosed with breast cancer. She had surgery and her doctor recommended some intensive chemo, and she was in pretty bad shape for a while. Then she started to get better, and in April, when she said she wanted to learn about radio..." Allie shrugged. "If Bill hadn't already owned a station, he'd have bought one for her."

"Well, it must beat chemo."

"She was done in July. And she's doing really well now, and good things have come of it."

"Such as?" Charlie prompted.

"Well, Grady has never been Bill's favorite son, but he stuck with his mom through the whole thing, taking her to chemo, cooking for her when she wouldn't eat, that kind of stuff. Bill hasn't called Grady a moron for months."

Charlie grinned. "I can see where that would be a step up."

"And Beattie's running the station just fine."

Charlie nodded as the pieces fell into place. Beattie had come in cold off the street and the station was still doing fine. Beattie had had some help. "It's doing fine because you showed her the ropes."

Allie shrugged. "I helped a little."

Charlie thought back to the scene in the hall. "Right. Why didn't you ask for the station manager's job?"

Allie looked horrified. "Business? Please, I'd rather die."

Well, he could sympathize with that. "Beattie would give you Mark's show back."

"I don't want Mark's show." Allie met his eyes. "I want Mark's time slot. The drive-time slot. That's where we're going to end up, Charlie."

"At 6:00 a.m.?" Charlie's voice broke in outrage. "In the morning a.m.? Are you nuts, woman?"

"You'll get used to it."

"No, I won't." Charlie leaned forward and spoke with great care. "Try to remember this. I am leaving in November. Do not make long-term plans for me."

Allie smiled at him. "All right."

Oh, Lord. He sighed at her. "Do you listen to a word I say?"

"Only the good stuff," Allie told him and he gave up and went back to the handbook.

ALLIE WATCHED CHARLIE open the binder and begin to read.

Now that they weren't naked, it was easier to make decisions about her future.

For one thing, she was definitely not going to be sharing her bed with him again. She was almost sure of that. She didn't need any more tension in her life. And after all, she barely knew him.

And sleeping with him would be bad professionally. It was wisest to break this off now, before she really started to care about him. Because she didn't care about him. She just wanted him. She wanted him right now on the floor of her office. Except there wasn't enough room. Maybe the desk—

No.

She looked at him, reading the stupid WBBB handbook, that lock of blond-brown hair falling over his forehead. The best thing she could do would be to stay away from him as much as possible. While he was on the air, there would be a glass wall between them, so that was safe enough. And maybe they could discuss the show through memos instead of face-to-face.

Face-to-face made her think of his mouth.

Definitely memos.

Charlie read something that was particularly inane and groaned.

"I told you it would be bad," Allie said unsympathetically. She had to get away from him. She had to do things that did not include fantasizing about being pressed against a wall while his hands—

She grabbed her coffee cup and stood up. "Listen, if you're happy here for a while, I promised to talk to some people. If you want coffee, the break room is down the hall, turn to the left, first door on the left. You can't miss it."

"Coffee is not going to make this garbage better," Charlie said.

"Be sure to mention that to Bill at the meeting at five," Allie said and made her escape.

ALLIE GOT COFFEE from the break room, smiling absently at Mark and Harry the Howler who were talking cars. She wasn't even mad at Mark anymore. Amazing what good sex and a new shot at a career could do for a woman's outlook. Mark looked at her strangely, so she ignored him. She had enough to do without worrying about Mark, especially since worrying about Mark was no longer her job. This was an incredibly cheering thought in a day that had been pretty cheerful to start with.

Buoyed beyond reason, she left the break room and went back to doing what she did best: keeping the station ticking. She picked up the ratings from Albert, promised Marcia they'd have a late lunch the next day to discuss her show and headed for the receptionist's counter.

"Hey, Karen," she said as she breezed into the lobby. She picked up a cookie from a plate on the counter and bit into it. "Where did the almond cookies come from?"

"Mrs. Winthrop brought them in for Grady again, but he said to leave them here for everybody." Karen looked around and then crooked a finger at her. "Come here for a minute."

Allie popped the rest of the cookie in her mouth and went behind the counter, mystified.

Karen picked up a basket covered with a baby quilt. "I'm in big trouble, Allie, and I don't know what to do."

Allie prayed there wasn't a baby in the basket. Some things were beyond even her ability to fix. Then she looked at the dark circles under Karen's eyes and felt ashamed. "You look awful," Allie said. "What's wrong?"

"I have to feed him every hour and I can't get to sleep in between. I've been doing it for two days now, and I'm afraid he's going to die." Karen started to cry, and Allie took the basket from her, expecting the worst.

It was almost that bad. Under the blanket, nestled in soft flannel, was a tiny black puppy, no bigger than two of Allie's fingers. "Oh, no." Allie shot an anguished look at Karen. "What happened?"

Karen's words came out in a rush. "Mopsy had her puppies, but there were too many, and he came last, and he can't suck or something, and she doesn't even seem to notice him." She gulped in some air. "And I've been trying to feed him every hour, but I'm not getting much down him, and I think he's going to die." Tears started in her eyes, and she sniffed them back. "And I'm so tired, Allie. I just can't think what to do."

Allie put the blanket back over the basket. "Is the formula in here?"

Karen nodded. "And the bottle and everything."

Allie patted her on the shoulder. "Go home at five and sleep. We'll take it from here."

Karen blinked. "I don't have permission to have him at the station. Bill doesn't know."

"Bill doesn't have to know. Charlie and I can handle it until two, and then Grady's in." Allie grinned at her. "And you know Grady and nature. He'll probably have this little guy sitting up and begging by morning."

Karen's tears moved from a trickle to a gush. "Are you sure? Will Charlie be mad? Oh, Allie, I—"

"Go home at five," Allie ordered. "Grady will pass the basket to you at eight, and I'll pick it up again tomorrow night at five. Charlie and Harry will be glad to help. They're good guys. We're covered. Go get some coffee to keep you going until you get off work, and leave everything else to me."

Karen mopped at her eyes and nodded. "His name's Samson. That's what I call him when I feed him. I wanted to give him a strong name, you know?"

"I know." Allie patted her again, back in control of the world. "We'll save him."

AFTER FIFTEEN MINUTES of trying to make sense of Bill's highly original take on broadcasting, Charlie gave up and went in search of the break room and coffee. Mark and Harry, the big tow-headed guy from the lobby, were deep in conversation about Mark's carburetor when he came in, and as far as Charlie was concerned, they could stay that way.

"Just came for coffee." He picked up a disposable cup and filled it at the coffeemaker. Then he turned back to the door.

"So, Charlie…" Mark was leaning back in his chair, smiling one of those man-to-man smiles.

"So, Mark." Charlie kept going.

"So you've moved in with Allie and Joe."

"Yep." Charlie was almost through the door.

"So how was it in the sack with our Allie last night?"

Charlie stopped. *Keep your mouth shut,* he told himself. *Get out of here.* He turned around. "What?"

Mark smiled his man-of-the-world smile. "You and Allie. How was she in the sack? Not what you're used to, I bet."

Don't make waves, Charlie told himself. He looked at Mark's smug face and thought about Allie and felt his temper spurt. He walked back and leaned over the table until he was almost nose-to-nose with Mark.

"Never...ever...make a derogatory comment about Alice again. Because if you do, I will wipe up this station with you."

Mark lost his smile for a minute, and Charlie turned back to the door.

"Tough guy."

Charlie kept going.

"Was she as lousy for you as she was for me?"

Charlie stopped. *Don't do it.* Then he turned around and walked back toward Mark.

Mark stood, caught his foot on the leg of his chair and fell over backward to the floor, taking the chair with him.

"I warned you not to do that," Charlie told him mildly. He looked at Harry. "Didn't I?"

"Yes," Harry said, nodding judiciously. "Yes, I'd have to say that you did." He didn't look particularly put out that Mark was on the floor.

Mark glared at Charlie from the floor. "It was just a joke."

Charlie frowned down at him. "Don't joke about Allie. It annoys me." He turned to leave and came face-to-face with Karen.

"Just came in for some coffee," she said brightly, waving her cup at him.

"Fine," Charlie said. "Step on Mark while you're getting it."

This will not do, he told himself on his way back to Allie. *This woman is screwing up your head. Keep away from her.*

Four

Charlie was still scowling when he got back to Allie's office. Threatening Mark had been stupid. He hated being stupid, although Lord knew he should be used to it by now.

"What's wrong?" Allie peered at him over a blanket-covered basket on her desk. "You look upset."

"Not me."

"You sure?"

Charlie tossed the handbook on the desk, feeling like a fool. "Well, Mark sort of fell over."

Allie froze. "Fell over?"

Charlie sat down and sipped his coffee. "He's not hurt. It wasn't that far to the floor."

Allie looked severe. "I suppose you had a reason."

Charlie shrugged. *He insulted you, and for some reason I lose my mind every time I think of you.* "I didn't like his looks."

"Right. What did he say about me?"

That was another problem with Allie. She was too damn sharp. "Don't be so conceited."

"He doesn't know you well enough to insult you. What did he say about me?"

"His very existence insults me. Can we get back to business?"

"I'll find out, anyway." Allie waited and then opened the folder in front of her. "Okay. Fine. We'll do business. Any questions so far?"

Charlie gave her the one that had been bugging him since the day before. "Yeah. How did an idiot like Mark get to be a star around here?"

Allie blinked at him. "He's not an idiot. He's a good broadcaster. His voice is clear and it makes people feel good. Plus he's great at

PR. He's good-looking, and his picture's been plastered all over the city on billboards. He pulls a pretty good female audience."

Charlie scowled harder, not sure why he cared. "So why isn't he on TV?"

"He's really shy." Allie's face softened, and Charlie got more annoyed. "I know he comes across as a conceited jerk, but he's really unsure of himself. He's never even thought about TV. All those cameras? He'd have a nervous breakdown."

"Shy." Charlie snorted.

"Hey, not everybody is as comfortable with himself as you are." Allie surveyed him. "You're exactly who you want to be, doing exactly what you want to do. That's pretty rare. Mark doesn't have your confidence, so he relies on his good looks to get him through, but he's still anxious. All the time."

Charlie focused on the part of her argument he liked the least. "He's not good-looking."

"Yes, he is. He looks like Richard Gere before he went gray."

"Mark's gray?"

"Richard's gray. Mark is still tall, dark and handsome, and women swoon."

Charlie slumped lower in his chair. "He's medium, dark and dweeby." He looked at her suspiciously. "Are you still swooning?"

Allie leaned back in her chair. "Nope. I've been cured. Thank you very much."

His spirits rose miraculously. "My pleasure, believe me."

Allie smiled at him, and Charlie felt himself slipping into lust. Oh, no. He yanked himself back.

"What's wrong?"

"Nothing." He shook his head. No more Allie. They would work together at the station where it would be almost impossible to make love—he shoved the desk thoughts firmly from his mind—but he was definitely finding another place to live. He'd take her to dinner tonight and let her down easy and then move to a motel. Good plan. He suppressed a sigh of relief at being back in control and returned to the problem of the station. "Who's on before me?"

"Harry the Howler. The big guy you met in the hall."

Mark's companion in the break room. "I think I just met him again. Calm sort of guy."

Allie nodded. "Exactly. That's what I keep telling him, but he insists on howling. Which is not your problem. In fact, I don't see that you have any problems." She beamed at him, the Positive Career Talk smile.

"I'm taking over for a paranoid gun-nut, and you think I have no problems."

"Of course not. After Waldo, *anybody* is a step up. And we've been at the bottom of the ratings for so long, you can only go up. Just remember, we're an easy-listening station, and you can't go wrong."

"Well, that's our first problem. I'm not an easy-listening kind of guy."

Allie looked exasperated. "You must have known we weren't hard rock when you signed on."

Charlie shook his head. "Bill told me I could play what I wanted"

"Which is?"

"Everything." Charlie leaned back and tried to sound as if he knew what he was doing. "I like it all. The way I figure it, I'll talk to people and they can call in and talk back and in between I play music I like."

Allie shrugged. "Well, Bill is a lot of things, but a liar he isn't. If he said you could do that here, you can do that here. You better go look at our library. I don't know how much of a variety we have."

"Well, I'll just have to give Bill a shopping list." Charlie shoved the handbook back across the desk to her. "I don't need this. As long as I don't do anything to give the FCC heart failure, I'll be okay."

"All right. Now, what do you need to get your show started?"

"Nothing." Charlie leaned back and spread his hands out to embrace the world, back in control again. "I can do it all."

"Great." Allie pulled the basket on her desk closer to her. "There's just one other little thing we have to do tonight." She reached under the blanket and pulled out a doll's baby bottle. "Samson needs to be fed every hour. We're going to have to cover this until two. Grady will do the rest. I've already called him, and he's fine with it."

"Samson?" Charlie said, totally confused.

"The station puppy." Allie pulled back the blanket and Charlie peered over the edge.

The tiny dark shape inside looked like an undersize chocolate Twinkie. "That's a puppy?"

"Well, he's small right now, but he's going to get a lot bigger." Allie tried to nudge the bottle into the puppy's mouth, but he made no movement to take it.

Another one of Allie's lost causes. First Mark, then Charlie's show, and now this puppy. Charlie squinted at the tiny scrap of protoplasm Allie insisted was a dog. "Are you sure it's not dead?"

He stepped back as Allie's eyes came up blazing. "This puppy is *not* going to die."

"All right." Charlie had some small experience with animals from the farms he'd worked on during his summer vacations, and all of it told him Samson was doomed, but he wasn't going to fight Allie on it. "Where's his mother?"

"He's the runt. Things didn't work out between them." Allie tipped the bottle so the formula ran into the puppy's mouth without him sucking, and his throat made weak swallowing movements. "See?" she said triumphantly. "He's going to be fine."

Charlie sat back and watched Allie work over the puppy, tickling its throat to get it to swallow. Well, if anyone could save an embryo dog, Allie could. He'd only known her twenty-four hours, but he already had a healthy respect for her determination.

"We may have to do this every half hour," Allie told him. "He's not getting enough this way. He's got to learn to suck."

So now he was a dog nurse, too. Well, he liked dogs. And if this was what Allie wanted... "All right."

Allie covered the basket again. "He's going to make it. I know he is."

At least when the dog died, he'd be there to comfort her.

Platonically.

CHARLIE SPENT the next two hours checking out the tape library and meeting Stewart, the night engineer. Stewart looked like a peeled egg and was not a ball of fire when it came to engineering, but he was something that Charlie found a lot more useful: a talker. After a half hour with Stewart, Charlie knew more about the station than Bill probably did. And the one incontrovertible fact he gleaned was that Allie was universally admired. Mark wasn't.

"Allie's good people," Stewart told him. "She gets things done. Mark is just a..."

"Yuppie scum dweeb?"

"That would cover it," Stewart agreed.

Cheered by the knowledge that not everyone at WBBB was certifiable, Charlie went back out into the city to find something to say about Tuttle on his first show. Nothing too controversial, he told himself. No waves.

ALLIE WAS STANDING in the lobby with her hands on her hips when he walked in an hour before his show. "Bill was looking for you earlier. You were supposed to meet him at five. Mark apologized for whatever it was he said. Bill says that you are never to strike another employee here again. Also, don't play liberal garbage on the air. Where have you been?"

Charlie grinned at her. She looked like an aggressive cocker spaniel, her hair swinging like a bright bell around her face, her eyes warm and challenging behind her glasses, which had slipped down her nose, as usual. He resisted the impulse to push them up for her. They weren't that close. They weren't ever going to be that close. "I missed you, too," he told her. "And I didn't hit Mark. He fell over. What do you know about the city building here?"

Allie turned and went down the hall to her office, and he trailed after her, trying not to admire the swing of her hips in her brown jersey dress.

"It's one of the oldest buildings in the city," she told him over her shoulder. "The marble is Italian. My mother and father were married there. The mayor wants to build a new one. That's about it. What do you want me to find out about it?"

"Nothing." He rubbed his hand over the back of his head and followed her into her office. "The tape library here isn't too bad. I can fake it for a while."

"Good." Allie looked at him. "Close the door and sit down."

"Why?" Charlie looked wary as he closed the door.

"I just need to talk to you for a minute." Allie swallowed nervously. "This is about us. I've been thinking all afternoon—"

Oh, Lord, he should have said something earlier before she started making plans for their future. "Listen, before you say anything, I think you're a terrific lady, but I'm not ready for a steady relationship, so if you're planning—"

"Great." Allie sank into her chair. "Don't think I didn't enjoy last night. I did. But I don't think it should happen again." She beamed up at him. "I'm so relieved you feel the same way."

"Well..." Charlie stopped, confused.

"Not that we can't still be friends," Allie went on. "And even roommates. I talked to Joe while you were in the bathroom this morning, and if you'd like to stay with us on the couch for the time you'll be here, it's all right."

"Oh, well..." Charlie nodded four or five times, his head wobbling a little as he tried to gather his thoughts. "Uh, sure. Good."

"Great." Allie picked up some papers from her desk, clearly eager to get back to work. "I'll tell Joe when I get home tonight."

"Good." Charlie stood up. "Well, I'm glad that's settled. Uh, I think I'll go watch Harry for a while."

Allie waved her hand at him as he left, already working on those papers. Efficient at all times, that was Allie.

It was really irritating of her.

Why don't I feel better about this? Charlie thought as he headed for the booth. This was what he wanted. She'd just taken care of it for him. Just the way she took care of everything. He shook his head at the acidity in the thought. This was probably just stupid male pride. He wanted to be the one to break things off. Oh, well. Her loss.

He walked off down the hall, wondering why he felt so empty if it was her loss.

INSIDE THE OFFICE, Allie threw the papers down on the desk beside Samson's basket, and sat back. She was really glad. Glad, glad, glad. At last she'd made a mature adult decision about a man, and now she could concentrate on the important stuff like making Charlie's show a hit.

Boy, was she glad.

Really.

CHARLIE WATCHED Harry through the window into the booth. He was talking animatedly into the mike, his hands moving up and down the console like a maniac's. Howlin' Harry.

Great. First he got kicked out of Allie's bed and now he was following an insane person.

When Harry stopped talking and leaned back, Charlie knocked on the window and Harry motioned him in.

"Nice job on Mark in the break room today." Harry grinned at him as he came in. "Look, Ma, no hands."

Charlie grinned back. It would be impossible not to grin at Harry. He radiated goodwill. "I should have known better," Charlie told him.

"Why? Mark didn't." Harry gestured to the console. "Anything you need to know about here?"

"Why don't you give me a fast refresher?" Charlie said, and Harry looked at him strangely and then explained how the noise level on the cassette and CD players were controlled by the red plastic sliding tabs on the console. Charlie did fine until Harry told him that if more than one slide was up at the same time, they'd all be heard, and then began to discuss the three thousand ways the slides could be combined for effect. "Great," Charlie said when Harry was finished and Charlie was lost. "I think I'll just stick with one at a time."

Harry shrugged. "Whatever."

"Can I sit in here and watch the rest of your show?" Charlie asked him, hoping that he'd learn by watching what he hadn't gotten by listening.

"Hey, you're welcome anytime," Harry told him and then went back to the mike to announce that Tuttle had just heard a Howlin' Harry triple play.

His howl was actually worse in the booth than it was on the radio.

AT NINE FIFTY-EIGHT, Allie took her seat at the production console and watched through the window as Charlie leaned on the wall of the booth and Harry hunched over the mike. Charlie's loose-limbed body relaxed against the white acoustic tile, and she followed the lines of his arms with her eyes, focusing finally on his long, large-knuckled fingers. He had big hands, but they were agile, she remembered. Lovely, long fingers.

She wrenched her mind back to the show. Fingers didn't count in radio. Just in bed. And from now on, they were just in radio, not in bed. Tonight was the first night of the rest of her career. If she was going to make Charlie a star—and she was—tonight was the night she studied him to see how he worked. Then she'd know how to shape the show, how to publicize it, how to make Charlie the Tuttle flavor of the month. She felt her heart beat faster and grinned at herself. She'd be back on top in no time. She turned her attention back to the booth, keeping her mind firmly off Charlie's body and strictly on his potential. For radio.

Harry was shrieking, "And that's it for tonight for all you wild and crazy Howlers out there. Next up is the new boy on the block, Chucklin' Charlie Tenniel. So here's one last Howler from Harry. *Harooooooo!*"

Harry moved the mike slide down and the disk slide up, and Allie heard the "The Monster Mash" come up on the speakers.

Chucklin' Charlie Tenniel? Poor Charlie. Well, she could fix that. She could fix everything as long as she kept her concentration. She was going to make him a star if it killed them both.

Harry talked to Charlie for a minute and then came out and joined her. "The news is punched up and ready," Harry told her, then frowned slightly. "I thought Bill said Charlie had a lot of experience."

"Yes." Allie checked the phone lines in front of her while she talked. The chances of anyone calling in were slim, but she was prepared to nurture anyone who did, even on the first night. "He had a couple of years with a Lawrenceville station."

"Sure doesn't act like it." Harry shrugged. "Oh, well, it's not like it's brain surgery. If I can do it, he can."

"Stop that." Allie looked up at him, exasperated. "You're very good. You'd be better if you stopped that damn howling, but you're still good. And, Harry, that Chucklin' Charlie thing has got to go. We're running a class program here."

"That I wouldn't know anything about. How does he want to be intro-ed?"

"Well, he hates Ten Tenniel for some reason, so that's out." Allie sat back. They needed a good title. A catch phrase. "Just Charlie is too bland. Charlie Late Night?"

Harry shook his head. "Sounds like Letterman."

"Okay, uh, Charlie At Night?"

Harry shook his head again. "Boring."

Allie cast around for more ideas. "Charlie Overnight? Charlie Midnight? Charlie All Night?"

"Last one's good," Harry said. "Kind of sexy. He's got that voice."

Allie tried not to look hopeful. "You think he's going to be good?"

"Hard to tell." Harry shifted on his feet. "Listen, Al, I was wondering…"

His voice trailed off and Allie was left with the unheard-of occurrence of a speechless Harry.

"Yes?" She nodded at him, trying to be encouraging.

Harry swallowed. "I know you don't have time to work on my show, but if you could give me a few tips, well, I'd really—"

"Stop howling," Allie said firmly. "You're a lovely, warm, intelligent man. Use it."

"Howling is my life."

Harry didn't appear to be joking. Allie sighed. "Let me think about this and get back to you tomorrow."

Harry grinned, lighting his whole face. "Thanks, Al, that's great." He looked over his shoulder at Charlie who was surveying his new domain with what looked like terror. "I'd stay on top of him tonight, if I were you. He looks like he's going to blow."

"Not Charlie," Allie said loyally, but she wasn't reassured by the look on her new star's face. "He'll be okay once he starts talking."

"That's usually when I screw up," Harry said.

When the news was over, they both watched as Charlie leaned over the console, pushing the mike slide up and the cassette slide down, and then spoke into the mike. His deep voice filled the production room for the first time.

"This is Charlie Tenniel for WBBB, and I never chuckle. I just play good music and talk to people. I only got into town yesterday, and a beautiful little town it is, but I've already got a few questions, especially about your new city building."

Allie looked at Harry and saw her own confusion reflected in his eyes.

"But mostly I just like it here. This is a great place to do a little late-night talking and play a little late-night rock and roll. I'm assuming this city does rock and roll? I thought so. This one is for my new hometown."

Cheap Trick came on with "I Want You To Want Me," and Allie grinned.

Now if he'd just give her some scope, she could move him from fun to fantastic. He had a great voice and a terrific personality, and wonderful hands—

Scratch that last part.

She pulled her mind back to the show. He was really good. Harry listened for a while and then left, giving Charlie a thumbs-up through the booth window as he went. Charlie nodded and then looked out at Allie.

"You're doing great," she said to him, doing her cheerleader imitation through the production mike. It was like being back with Mark, except this time she was telling the truth. "Your voice is terrific. No wonder you were a hit in Lawrenceville."

Charlie shook his head. The song ended, and he worked the slides and leaned into the mike again. "Like I said before, I never chuckle, but I don't mind having a few laughs now and then, for all the right reasons. One of those reasons seems to me to be this new city building His Honor the Mayor wants built."

Allie froze at the console. *No.* Not the mayor. Bill played poker with him every Thursday. This was not the way to build an audi-

ence, this was the way to build an enemy. An enemy they didn't
need, especially if it was the boss. She tried to shake her head at him
through the window, but he was oblivious, concentrating on the
mike.

"Now, I'm new in town," Charlie went on, "so maybe you can
call in and tell me I'm all wet here, but I was in your old city building today, and it's a beautiful place. Marble floors, frosted glass, lots
of wood paneling, and that's real wood paneling not that splintery
stuff they sell for two dollars and ninety-nine cents at the back of
the lumberyard. This is a building that was made with good mate-
rials, fine workmanship, and above all, pride. It's the kind of building that might inspire a politician who worked there to take the service part of being a public servant seriously. Now, if you laughed at
that, my friend, you're a cynic. Shame on you."

Allie clasped her hands in front of her and prayed, *Don't say anything dumb, Charlie. Please.*

"So where's the joke? Well, have you seen the model for the new
city building? Hey, take a trip downtown to the old building to the
planning office and have yourself a laugh. It looks like a one-story
parking garage with windows. Which might be pretty appropriate
for the politicians around here—a place to park and watch the
world go by. Of course, like I said, I'm new in town, so I don't really
know much about your politicians. Except that if they prefer this
new concrete bunker to their old marble palace, they have lousy
taste in architecture.

"If you think the old city building deserves another hundred
years, call in and let the city know why. And if you think the new
plan is better, well, call in and tell me I'm wrong. In the meantime,
this one's for the city building. Hang in there, old lady."

When she heard the beginning of Aretha Franklin's "Rescue
Me," Allie put her head in her hands and gave herself over to a moment of panic. Then reality claimed her. Bill never listened to the
show, and she was pretty sure the mayor didn't, either. The station
had been playing opera for the past week, and before that there had
been Waldo and the aliens. Charlie couldn't have more than four
people listening to him, and they were going to be mad he wasn't

discussing the Martian question. There was nothing to worry about.

Then the phone rang.

"WBBB, the Charlie Teniel show," Allie said.

The voice was an old man's, raspy and loud. "Yeah, let me talk to that disc jockey fellow."

"Certainly, sir. Can I tell him what you'd like to say?"

"No, damn it, I'm gonna do that."

"Uh, right. Sure." Allie hesitated, knowing she should find out what the caller wanted before turning him over to Charlie. On the other hand, he obviously wasn't going to tell her. And it would be a bad idea to alienate any callers. After all, this might be the only one Charlie got. And it would be a chance for her to find out how he handled himself with callers. "Could I have your name, please?"

"Eb Groats."

"You've got a caller," Allie told Charlie over the production mike. "A Mr. Eb Groats."

Charlie nodded and Allie punched up the call. Samson whimpered at her feet, and Allie stuck her head under the desk to see what was wrong. He actually seemed hungry, and she hurried to drip more formula into his mouth, giving all her attention to him until Charlie came back on the air after the song.

"I've been talking to Eb Groats from up north of the city limits. Eb tells me he was around when part of the building went up. Right, Eb?"

"Well, son, like I was telling you, we put that back wing up about '35. My first job, I wasn't more'n seventeen."

"Well, Eb, you did a great job."

"Hell, yes."

"Don't say hell, Eb. The FCC doesn't like it."

"My wife doesn't either. The hell with her."

"But about the city building, Eb."

"Well, you're right about one thing. That building was built to last. Any dang fool could see that."

"Even me."

"Even you. Even that other dang fool Rollie Whitcomb."

"Mayor Whitcomb seems pretty sold on the new building."

"Course, he does. His brother's gonna get the contract."

Charlie said, "What?" and Allie raised her head so fast she smacked it on the underside of the producer's desk.

"You check into it, boy. The contract will say Somebody or Other Construction, but you follow the trail back and you'll find Al Whitcomb's name on it."

Oh, no, not this. Allie rubbed the back of her head and thought fast.

"I think that's slander, Eb."

"Not if it's true, it ain't. I'm old, but I ain't stupid."

"That's for darn sure. Well, Eb, you've certainly made my first night on the job one to remember. And possibly my last night on the job, too. Thanks for calling. And call back and tell me I'm a fool again sometime, Eb. You sound just like my grandpa. I'm glad you were listening in."

"I wasn't. My great-grandson listens to that fool Harry the Howler and we kind of slopped on over into your show."

"Well, slop on over anytime."

"Will do, son. Good luck on savin' that building."

"Thanks. I'm going to need all the luck I can get." There was a click on the line. "Of course, I've already had more luck than any new guy in town deserves. My first caller is a great guy like Eb, and the first lady I met in town yesterday is the kind of woman a man never forgets, even when she says goodbye, which she just did today. Fortunately, I've had a lot of experience with rejection. Anyway, this is for that lady who said I insulted her in the bar yesterday. Trust me, honey, I meant it in the nicest possible way."

Allie shook her head when she heard Patsy Cline slide into "Crazy."

"Very funny, Charlie," she said into the mike. "About the city building—"

"I didn't mean to, believe me," he told her. "I thought it was just a nice, friendly kind of topic."

"Bill's a backer of Rollie Whitcomb."

Charlie laughed shortly. "He would be. He's just like my dad."

"Your dad backs mayors?"

"My dad buys mayors." Charlie swiveled away from the window to refill the cassette stack. "Oh, well, at least nobody's listening."

Just me. Allie watched Charlie pushing the slides happily for the next half hour, playing music and talking to three callers who wanted to put in their two cents about the city building. Things were going well. In fact, four callers in the first half hour of a new show was phenomenal.

They were safe.

But safe made for lousy radio.

She could fix that.

Of course, they didn't want to make enemies, but since nobody seemed too upset about the mayor's brother, that wasn't a problem. And Charlie was great with callers, absolutely brilliant. More people should know that. Of course, Charlie didn't want to be famous. But this was a civic issue. She had a civic duty.

And she wanted the show to be a hit.

"I'm a slime," she told Samsom, fast asleep in his basket. "A career-obsessed, pathetic slime." Then she picked up a clear phone line and punched in the mayor's phone number.

CHARLIE WAS FEELING pretty good. He liked Eb and the three people who'd called after Eb, the console was brand new and a piece of cake to run, and it didn't really matter whether he was a success or not at this hour of the night. And actually, it was fun. Once again his life was under control. He'd have all his days to track down that damn letter and figure out who wrote it, and then he could play radio at night until he finished the job and left in November.

Life didn't get much better.

Then Allie's voice came through his headphones. "Caller on line two."

"Who's this one?"

"The mayor."

He swung around to stare at her through the window, but she just shrugged and smiled and punched the button that transferred the call to him.

"Who the hell is this?"

"Uh, Charlie Tenniel." He shot an agonized glance at the digital readout on the console. Fifteen seconds till the last song was over.

"Well, what the hell is going on down there? Where's Bill? What is this garbage?"

He sounded like an overbearing, handshaking politician. Charlie had met a lot of them growing up and he hadn't liked them. Still, it wasn't his job to make waves. "We've been talking about the city building, sir."

"Well, stop it. It's none of your damn business."

Charlie took a deep breath. "Well, it's the taxpayers' business, since they're going to be paying for it."

"Screw the taxpayers. You shut up about that building or I'll have your job. I can do it, too, don't think I can't. Bill's a good friend of mine. You just shut up, boy."

Five seconds. Charlie knew he was going to regret it, but laying low had been a lost cause as soon as the Mayor had started yelling. "We're going to be on the air now, mayor, so whatever you say is broadcast. Might want to ease up on that 'screw the taxpayers' bit since most of them are voters, too."

"I don't *want*—"

"And welcome back, Tuttle," Charlie said into the mike. "We've got a real treat tonight. Mayor Rollie Whitcomb has called in to talk about the city building. You're on, Mayor."

"I'm what?"

"You're on the air."

"Oh. Well—"

"Now, you want to explain again how you feel about the taxpayers and the city building?"

Through the window he saw Allie put her head down on the producer's console. Rollie must have been right about Bill. Oh, well, win some, lose some. He went back to listening to the mayor tie himself in knots. Public speaking was evidently not what had gotten him into office. His sentences didn't seem to have any verbs, which was par for a politician. All nouns, no action.

When the mayor wound down, buried under his compound subjects, Charlie stepped in. "So what exactly was the rationale behind the new city building, Mayor? I understand the new building actually has less space than the old one."

That set Rollie off again, babbling about heating bills, big windows, all that marble, and the stairs. Rollie didn't seem to have a grasp as to why the last three were a problem, he just knew they were factors.

"Anything you want to say about your brother, the contractor?" Charlie asked him when he'd sputtered to a close.

"Fine businessman. Pillar of the community. Mason. Knights of Pythias. Proud to be in the family."

Rollie meandered on, while Charlie waited for a verb. "Does he have the contract for the city building?" Charlie asked when Rollie trailed off again.

"Of course not. I don't know. I don't award contracts. Building committee. Stalwart citizens. Pillars of the community."

Charlie gave up. "Well, thanks for calling, Mayor. I'm sure Tuttle is reassured now."

"Proud to do my duty," Rollie said.

Charlie punched the cassette button and shoved the slide up and music came through his headphones. Unfortunately, it was Paul Simon's "Still Crazy After All These Years."

He was screwed, as usual. He thought about it and began to laugh.

Allie sat stunned in the producer's chair, not sure whom she was in the most trouble with—the mayor, Bill or Charlie. She'd thought that maybe talking with the mayor would boost Charlie's credentials. The mayor could give his side of the situation and Charlie could discuss it with him. Serious talk radio. Maybe a nice mention in the *Tuttle Tribune* tomorrow since the mayor pretty much owned the paper.

And then Charlie turned out to be a hell-raiser. Asking about the mayor's brother. Sheesh.

"You still there, Tenniel?"

She adjusted her headphones. "Uh, no, he's not, Mayor Whitcomb. This is Alice McGuffey, the pro—"

"Well, you're fired. And so is he."

Then all she heard was a dial tone.

She sat back and tried to figure out the probable outcome of the mess she'd created. Bill wouldn't fire her, she was pretty sure. He wasn't that dumb, and if he was, Beattie wouldn't let him.

Charlie could be vulnerable, though. And it was her fault.

All right, she'd just go in first thing in the morning and tell Bill she'd called the mayor.

Then the phone rang and she got back to work.

At one, Allie shut down the phone lines at Charlie's request. By then he'd talked to eleven callers about the building, all of them telling him he was right and one asking if the mayor was drunk. "No, I think he always talks like that," Charlie said, and the caller said, "And we *voted* for him?" There were a few nonpolitical calls: one male caller wanted to know what he'd said to the lady in the bar, and four female callers offered to show him the city and let him insult them all he wanted. "Get me out of this," Charlie said to Allie from the booth, and she shut down the lines for the night.

"Go home," he told her through the mike. "Stewart's here if I need anything technical. I'm just going to play music from now on. I don't ever want to hear about the city building again."

Allie had been working since four, Charlie's show was off to a better than great start, and besides, guilt was making her groggy. She'd done her job and then some. "Thanks," she said. "I'll take you up on that."

She gave Samson to Charlie and told him how to feed him and then watched while he gave the puppy a bottle to the rhythm of Gloria Estefan. Samson was almost lost in Charlie's big hand, and Allie forgot her career entirely as she watched him try to drip the formula into the puppy's mouth. Sam tried to drink a little and then gave up, but Charlie kept on coaxing, his blond-brown hair shining in the booth light like brass as he bent over the little body, massaging Sam's tummy with his thumb. "C'mon, Sam," he coaxed softly, and Allie shut her eyes and prayed the puppy would make it.

She really didn't need any more trauma. She was due for a success here, and Sam might as well share it. "He's going to make it," she said out loud, and Charlie looked up at her and said, "Well, we'll give it our best shot. Go on. You're beat." And she nodded and left the booth.

Charlie sounded even better at home when she was in bed, wrapped in her quilt. His voice was sexy and soothing, and he played a lot of different music including one triple play of Lou Reed, Patsy Cline, and The Bangles, always leading so smoothly into the songs as part of his patter that it seemed like the music was part of what Charlie was saying.

She was almost disappointed when he wrapped up the show at two.

"Well, that's it for tonight, folks. Grady Bonner's coming up next with some background on crystals and healing and your sun sign's lucky numbers for tomorrow, and he tells me he's also going to be playing some whale songs a little later. Now, for those of you who haven't heard whale songs, that probably sounds like a joke, but keep an open mind and you'll hear music that is truly unearthly. And to get you over to Grady, here's Judy Collins doing her duet with a whale in "Farewell to Tarwathie." Listen closely out there, this is the music of the deep."

Collins's "Hunting the Whale" began and Allie closed her eyes and listened. The song was so lovely that the last notes seemed to hang in the air next to her.

Then she heard Grady's reedy voice saying, "This is Grady Bonner taking you into the hours when the city sleeps. If you missed Charlie Tenniel's show just before this, you missed what he said about our beautiful city building. There are so many old voices echoing through the old city building. Tearing it down would be ripping those voices apart. Go to the old building tomorrow, feel the power in it, and then go to the mayor and tell him that destroying that structure is destroying the spirit of public service in this city. And now, before I begin tonight's discussion on the healing power of the crystal, let's listen to a recording of some North Atlantic whales. This one's for you, Charlie."

Good for Charlie, Allie thought. *He's got Grady on his side.* She felt comforted by that. Grady might be a little strange, but his people instincts were excellent. If he liked Charlie, Charlie was good people.

She turned off her light and listened in the dark to the whale songs, and she drifted off in a dreamless sleep.

She hadn't been asleep more than half an hour when Charlie nudged her in the back.

Five

*"H*ey." Charlie sat next to her on the bed and propped his feet up. "Did you listen to the rest of the show?"

"Yes." Allie rolled over and stretched a little to wake up. "Now I know why Bill hired you. You're great."

"Thank you."

She squinted at him in the dim light from the window. He was dressed only in his sweatpants, and he was holding a carton and chewing something. She struggled to sit up, and he reached over her and turned on the lamp, blinding her.

"What are you eating?" She shielded her eyes until they adjusted to the light.

"Sweet-and-sour pork. From some place called Mrs. McCarthy's Chinese. Want some?"

"Yes. McCarthy's has good stuff, but Joe won't let me eat there." Allie yawned and took the fork from him and poked it into the take-out carton. "He says it's not authentic."

Charlie snorted. "Sure it is. Authentic Irish-Chinese."

Allie chewed the pork and then looked dubiously at the size of the carton. "Did you get anything else?"

"No. I didn't know you'd be hungry, too. There's plenty of this, though." He took the fork and the carton back.

He looked great in the lamplight, naked to the waist, his long legs stretched out on her bed. Allie hauled her mind back to the radio program and tried to make her voice noncommittal. "So what's your next move here?"

Charlie grinned at her. "Well, I figure if I can get your nightgown off, the rest will be easy."

Allie stomped down on the hot little thrill the thought evoked and looked at him with what she hoped was contempt.

Charlie said, "Joke. Sort of."

She shook her head. "Not your next move on me, you dang fool. The city building. Give me the fork."

"Ah, you liked Eb. So did I." Charlie passed the carton over. "I may wander up north and meet him. My kind of guy."

"The city building," Allie said around a mouthful of food.

"I think it should be saved, but I don't particularly want to do it. Especially if it's going to make people call me that much." He shook his head. "Some mighty pissed people out there when they heard about the mayor's brother. And the mayor didn't do himself any good, calling in like that." Charlie took the carton back. "I wonder if it's true?"

Allie put her chin on his shoulder to look into the carton. He had great shoulders and Chinese food. At the moment, he was the perfect man. "I wouldn't be surprised. Hurry up with the fork." She reached around his arm, enjoying the slide of her skin on his, and took the carton from him after he'd taken a bite.

Charlie chewed and swallowed. "If it is true, the mayor's an idiot."

Allie snorted. "Do you have any doubts?"

Charlie recaptured his carton. "I don't want to talk about the city building tomorrow night."

Allie looked at him, half-naked in the lamplight, and felt a growing hunger for more than Chinese. *No*, she told herself. "You're missing a great opportunity."

"Screen the callers."

Allie looked at him, dumbfounded. "You want me to tell them they can't talk about the city building?"

"I don't care what you tell them. Just don't put them on the line with me."

She looked at him in disgust. "You're a wimp." Okay, he was a sexy wimp, but he was still a wimp. She reached for the carton to distract herself. "Give me the fork."

"It's all gone." He put the carton on the floor.

"I'm still hungry."

Charlie grinned at her, and she forgot she was annoyed with him. After all, he'd done a great show. After all, he was Charlie. In her bed. Half-naked.

Turn back now, she told herself. *Get out of this bed.*

Charlie leaned toward her. "You're always hungry. You're the most orally fixated woman I've ever known. Not that I'm complaining."

Oh, boy. Allie threw back the covers and started to get out of bed, and he caught her nightgown and pulled her back. "Where are you going?"

She pried her gown out of his fingers. "I'm hungry. Really. I'm empty."

"No problem." Charlie pulled her down on top of him, and she meant to push herself away, but he was so warm, she leaned into him instead. He felt wonderful under her. "Empty I can solve," he told her. "And I'll make sure you get to sleep, too. Eventually." He kissed her neck.

She propped herself up on his chest and steeled herself to say no. "I thought we'd talked about this."

Charlie stroked her cheek with his finger. "We did, but you look awful good rumpled. How about one more time? I'll move out to the couch tomorrow, I swear."

"This is not a good idea." She pushed away from him and changed the subject to distract him. "You know, you have a great voice. I was concentrating on your body and your face before, and I didn't really appreciate your voice until I heard you on the air. It's incredible. I bet you were turning on women all over the city tonight."

He tugged her back down to him, and she shivered when he said, "How'd I do with you?"

"Not bad." She moved against his warmth. "Thanks for Patsy Cline."

"My pleasure. Kiss me."

Don't do it, she told herself, but she kissed him, anyway, and his mouth moving softly on hers distracted her while he pulled her nightgown up and ran his hands over her naked back. She felt the heat start again, and she stretched against it.

What could one more night hurt?

She pulled the nightgown over her head, and his hands were on her instantly, cupping her breasts, making her draw a sharp breath.

She touched him, too, then, stroking down his chest with her fingertips, over his sweatpants until she felt him shudder. He stripped off his pants, and she stroked him again, and she felt his fingers dig into the soft flesh of her hips as she moved to meet him. They tormented each other, touching and kissing and sliding together, gasping small laughs as they collided in heat until Allie thought she'd scream if he didn't take her. "Now," she said finally. "Please, now."

"Wait a minute," he said, and reached for the condom in his pants, and then he said, "Come here," and pulled her over on top of him. "Stay on top of me this time. You'll like it better."

He was lovely and hot under her, and she stretched against him, forgetting her panic from the night before. "I wasn't afraid of you," she said against his mouth. "It wasn't you."

"I know." Charlie's hands smoothed over her. "You just don't like being out of control."

"Maybe." Allie was distracted; he was moving under her now, pulling her hips up to his, spreading her thighs apart with his legs.

"Whenever you're ready." Charlie kissed her shoulder. "Just don't wait too long, or I'll lose my mind."

Allie propped herself above him, dizzy with heat. "What do you want me to do?"

He pulled her closer. "Just ease yourself over me and make me the happiest man in this city."

She laughed softly. "There are other guys in this city making love right now, you know."

"Not with you." He smiled up at her, and she wanted him so much she ached with it. "Allie, I want you so much."

Allie blinked at him, surprised out of her own thoughts. "Me?"

He laughed softly. "Yes, you. Can't you tell I'm interested?"

He was hard between her thighs, and she rocked a little against him and watched him close his eyes. "Yes," she told him, laughing again at how easy he was to distract. "I can tell. But I thought for a guy, it didn't make any difference who..."

His eyes snapped open. "You thought wrong." His hands were suddenly tight on her waist, as if he were trying to make her listen harder. "I'm going nuts right now only because I'm with you," he told her, and she lost her breath at the intensity in his voice. "You make me crazy. I've been thinking about you all day." He let his head sink into the pillow. "Now, will you please get a move on here? I'm not kidding about the crazy part."

She took a deep breath and found him with her hand. He held her hips so tightly she knew she'd have fingerprint bruises the next day, but it was erotic to have his hands on her that hard. She guided herself over him and eased him a little way into her, carefully, tentatively. He felt wonderful, and her heart pounded and she felt her blood begin to rush and she stopped, trying to keep from lurching out of control.

Charlie made a sound way back in his throat, but he didn't push. She was doing it all.

"Oh," she said and sank her hips down to his, and he felt so good that she moaned, and Charlie threw his head back on the pillow and bit his lip.

"Charlie?" she whispered.

"Don't mind me," he said through his teeth. "This is just ecstasy."

Allie moved against him slowly, holding him hard inside her, feeling her skin heat, trying to keep her breathing slow as she watched his face. He wasn't kidding. He was in ecstasy. *And I'm doing this,* she thought. She squeezed him with the muscles inside her and her heart pounded as she watched him suck in his breath. Then she moved her hips against his, and he moved to meet her, and her blood began to bubble. She licked her lips and breathed in and thought, *God, I'm powerful. No wonder men love sex so much.*

She eased herself up until she was sitting, straddling him until he was high inside her. He ran his hands up her body, cupping her breasts, and she leaned against his hands, relishing the pressure there and in the center of her body, and the prickling in her veins, and she began to move against him. She could feel the pressure growing, little flames of heat licking inside her as she rocked against him. The licking flames flared into a hot spiral, and she knew that it was going to explode, that she'd feel him everywhere, that she'd lose herself in him and be gone again, and she wanted it more than anything and still she clutched, just a little, as it began to go. Then Charlie arched up to hold her, dragging her down to his warmth, and she was wrapped safe in his arms as he moved convulsively inside her. "Come on, Allie," he breathed in her ear, and she pressed herself hard down against him and then everything did explode in a kaleidoscope of surge and flame, and she rocked against him over and over, sobbing, until he cried out in his own climax.

She clutched at him until even the tiny aftershocks inside her were gone, and when they were both breathing again, Allie whispered, "I don't want you to move to the couch," and Charlie held her tightly and said, "I'm not going to."

"BILL WANTS to see you," Karen called to Charlie when he strolled in late the next afternoon.

"I bet he does." Charlie stopped at the counter and grinned at her. "Did you bake cookies?"

"No, that's Mrs. Wexman. She brings them in for Grady and he shares."

Charlie bit into the cookie. Chocolate chip with pecans. "Good for Mrs. Wexman. What does Grady do to deserve this?"

"Drives her to chemotherapy." Karen blinked up at him. "Grady does that a lot for the people his mom met while she was going through it. We get a lot of stuff in here because of it. You should taste Mrs. Winthrop's almond cookies."

"He drives Mrs. Winthrop, too?"

Karen nodded. "He helps out with other stuff, too. Mrs. Winthrop came in one day all upset about her grandson yelling at her, and I called Grady, and he told her not to worry, that he'd take care of it. The next day, she brought in a devil's food cake."

"That's what I like, grateful women who bake." Charlie peered over the counter. "Where's Sam?"

Karen brought the basket up on the desk, and Charlie turned back the blanket to see Sam's little black head. "How's he doing?" He rubbed the puppy gently behind the ears, his broad index finger covering the back of Sam's head by itself, and Sam moaned a little.

"I'm scared for him." Karen sniffed. "He's so little, and he's not eating much, and—"

"I'll pour the stuff down him tonight." Charlie pulled the blanket back over Sam's head. "He's just getting the hang of it, that's all."

Karen caught his hand. "Charlie, this is so sweet of you."

"No, it isn't." Charlie retrieved his hand and picked up another cookie. "You'd have to have a heart of stone to refuse to feed Sam." He glanced at the clock behind her. "Which reminds me, I've got to go see Bill. Am I getting fired?"

"I doubt it." Karen put Sam's basket back under her desk. "But you're gonna have to listen to some yelling."

Charlie turned and almost fell over a stack of boxes next to the desk. "What's this?"

"Bumper stickers," Karen said. "Mark's idea. They're really popular. The college kids from Riverbend love them."

Charlie frowned. "College kids listen to Mark?"

"No," Karen said. "They just like the stickers."

Charlie put his cookie down and pried open the top of the first box and pulled out a sticker. It was neon blue with a slash of orange lettering that said WBBB: Turn Us ON! He turned back to Karen. "You're kidding."

She shrugged. "Who knows from kids?"

Charlie started to laugh. She couldn't be much older than twenty-five herself. "Well put, old lady," he told her and she grinned back at him.

"At least I'm not going nuts for a dumb bumper sticker," she said.

"Good point." He folded the sticker and shoved it in his pocket as he turned for the hallway. "Now for the yelling. Wish me luck."

"You won't need it," she called after him. "I heard your show. You were great."

Terrific. Just what he needed. A fan. He was really going to have to get a grip on things or Allie *would* make him a star.

"Come in," Bill yelled when Charlie tapped on his door. "Oh, it's you."

Charlie folded himself into the chair opposite the old man's desk, ready to listen to a litany of his faults. It would be like old home week, his dad all over again.

Bill looked out at Charlie under bushy white eyebrows. "The papers are calling about that mess last night. Don't talk to 'em."

"Wouldn't dream of it. Believe me, if I'd had any idea—"

Bill flapped a hand at him. "I'm not blaming you. Alice already told me it was her fault."

"Well, I was there, too," Charlie said mildly. "The city building was my idea."

"Yeah, but she called the mayor."

Charlie blinked. This was news. He and Allie were going to have to have a much longer talk than they'd managed the night before. He thought about the night before and stirred in his chair. A much longer talk out of bed where she couldn't distract him. He frowned at Bill, trying to bring his mind back to the problem. "She called the mayor?"

"Of course she called the mayor." Bill scowled at him. "You think Rollie Whitcomb was up listening to your show that late? She called him."

"It was only eleven," Charlie said. "I thought he might stay up that late."

"Only on poker nights." Bill's scowl deepened. "Which I won't be going back to if you don't stop stirring up trouble on the air. He wanted me to fire you, but I told him I couldn't. Unbreakable contract."

"We don't have a contract."

"Well, Rollie Whitcomb doesn't know that. But you *are* going to shut your trap about the city building. I didn't get you here to investigate political corruption. I got you here—"

"Wait a minute." Charlie sat up slowly. "You're going to pull the plug on this thing so you can play poker?"

"It's politics, boy." Bill leaned back in his chair. "You don't understand—"

"Sure I do." Charlie shook his head. "You and my dad. The get-along gang."

Bill's face turned dark. "Listen, boy"

"No." Charlie stood up. "I'm not going to shut up about corruption so you can play poker with the good old boys. I'm not going to bring it up, but if somebody calls in, I'm going to talk about it. Now, you can deal with that or you can fire me."

"*Sit down,*" Bill roared and Charlie sighed and sat down and listened to Bill's tirade, impervious from long practice of listening to his father. It was, in its volume and contempt, the same speech his father had given to him after Charlie had left business school—"I didn't raise my sons to be losers"—after he'd left the Air Force—"Damn good connections in the military, but you just piss 'em all away"—after he'd sold the computer-consulting firm that had become too fast-track for him—"You coulda been the Bill Gates of Lawrenceville, but no, you don't like the work"—and after any of the half-dozen odd careers he'd wandered into and out of on the road since he'd left Lawrenceville four years before—"Bum." Bill's theme was more along the lines of "Too damn dumb to know your ass from your elbow," but it was his father, all right.

This was what he got for doing favors for his father. His Father, Part Two. Blow Hard and Blow Harder.

"You understand me, boy?" Bill finished, his big white mustache quivering.

"Completely," Charlie said. "Now, are you going to fire me or are you going to let me talk to people about this tonight?"

Bill sat back into his chair. "This is not what I brought you here for."

"No," Charlie agreed. "This is a freebie. And I'm not interested in being Tuttle's favorite son, so it won't happen again. But I'm not walking away from this, Bill."

Bill stared off into space and tapped his fingers on the desk. "All right," he said finally.

Charlie relaxed an iota. "Now, about what you brought me here for. I found out Waldo isn't coming back. You didn't mention he'd shot up the booth."

"I don't give a rat's ass about Waldo." Bill scowled. "I want to know that that letter was bull."

Charlie sighed. "It's going to take a little while. I'm starting at ground zero since you didn't save the letter. I can imagine Allie doing damn near anything if she put her mind to it, but I can't imagine her as a crook. And Joe—" He broke off. "Joe's gay. Could that have been it?"

Bill waved the idea away. "Whole town knows Joe's gay. That all you've come up with?"

"Well, Mark doesn't seem to have the brains to break any law and get away with it, and Marcia's more likely to spit in somebody's face than sneak around, and Stewart doesn't have the focus. Karen's not the master-criminal type, although I suppose she'd make a nice dupe. You and Beattie have too much to lose. Unless Grady's been faith healing or Harry's been stealing car parts, I don't see many potential criminals here. 'Course, I haven't met everybody yet. I've only been here a day."

"Well, keep working on it."

Charlie sighed. "You know, it would have been a great help if you'd kept that letter."

"It didn't say that much." Bill looked away. "Just that something was going on here that I didn't know about. Some smart-ass, stirring up trouble. Couldn't even spell."

"That's not much help." Bill refused to meet his eyes and Charlie gave up. "All right, but I'm not making any guarantees. It's probably nothing. And in the meantime, I have to learn radio."

"That's why I gave you Alice." Bill finally looked back at him. "After I told everybody you were Ten, I had to, or you'd have died on the air and everybody would have known something was up." He scowled at Charlie. "You owe me for that. I had to promise Mark a raise just to get him to give her up."

Charlie blinked. "Mark didn't fire her?"

Bill snorted. "Of course not. He's not stupid. She's the best damn producer in the business. But Lisa's going to work out fine. Don't worry about it."

Great. Allie had lost her prime-time spot because of him. Somehow, he wasn't anxious to share that with her.

Bill went on talking. "Just do what Alice tells you to do. And stop whining about the city building."

"Why don't you just give me a list of all the graft your friends are involved in," Charlie suggested. "It'll help me steer clear of those topics."

"Very funny." Bill leaned forward, and the power in his eyes was no joke. "You leave politics alone, you hear?"

Charlie met his eyes. "And tonight?"

Bill sighed. "Don't bring it up. If somebody wants to talk, let 'em." He swung his head from side to side like a grumpy bear. "It would look real bad if we shut down on it now, anyway. Like we were covering up."

"Well, that's what I thought." Charlie stood up.

Bill snorted.

"Right," Charlie said.

ALLIE STOOD OUTSIDE the office and waited for Charlie, afraid the city building was dead in the water as a show topic. Bill hated controversy—page six in the handbook—and Charlie wanted a nice, quiet little call-in show that nobody listened to. After last night, her general inclination was to give Charlie anything he wanted, but this was her career on the line. Maybe she could seduce him into talking about it on the air...

She gave the idea careful consideration and discarded it. Charlie would cheerfully cooperate with being seduced, but then he'd still refuse to talk about it. He was as stubborn as...well, as she was.

Then she heard Bill's voice go up, and she put her ear to the door to try to make out the words. He was calling Charlie a lot of names for somebody who was agreeing with him.

Harry went by as she listened. "Getting anything good?"

"Shut up," she said. "I can't hear."

Harry went on and so did Bill, but in a minute Harry was back with his Lion King glass from the break room. "Try this."

The glass helped significantly. "He's yelling at Charlie about the city building," she told Harry as a payback for the glass.

Harry snorted. "Oh, that's a surprise. What's Charlie saying?"

Allie frowned. "Nothing. Bill's just raving."

"Charlie must be stonewalling. Let me hear."

Allie passed the glass over to Harry and leaned against the wall to think. Charlie wasn't telling Bill he was going to bury the story. So he was either doing it to twist Bill's tail, which would be dumb but entirely in character for Charlie, or he'd decided to keep pursuing the scandal. She sighed and pushed her glasses back up the bridge of her nose. That was really too much to hope for.

Karen came up behind them, basket in hand. "I thought you were in the booth," she said to Harry, and he shushed her.

"Beattie's doing the news," he said. "She wanted to." Then he went back to listening.

"Charlie still in there?" Karen asked Allie and she nodded, trying to press her ear to the sliver of door not blocked by Harry's bulk. Maybe Charlie really was defending the city building; maybe they could run with it tonight.

Imagine the people who would call in.

Imagine the ratings.

"This about the city building?" Stewart said from behind Karen.

"Shh," Karen said as she leaned around Allie. "What did he call Charlie?"

"A shit-for-brains moron," Harry reported. "He called me that once. It means he's winding down. Damn, he's stopped yelling. I can't hear."

"Is he fired?" Stewart asked and all three of them turned to him and said, "No!" and then they all turned back to the door.

Allie pressed her ear to the door. "What's going on?" She tugged on Harry's sleeve. "They're too quiet."

Harry shook his head. "Something about Waldo. I missed it." He listened for a couple of minutes. "They're talking too low."

"Give me the glass." Allie tugged again. The suspense was too great to bear. "Is Charlie saying he wants the city building on the show?"

Harry waved her away. "I told you, I can't hear 'em. They're talking low."

The door opened suddenly, and Harry's glass dropped like a stone in front of a surprised Charlie.

"Juice," Harry told him, hefting the glass. "Juice break. The news is on and..." He backed away. "Juice."

Karen smiled brightly. "The basket." She held it up in front of Charlie. "I was just going to give Harry the basket."

Allie met Charlie's eyes and smiled brightly. "I was just leaving," she said and turned back to her office.

"I was listening at the door," she heard Stewart tell Charlie. "You gotta talk louder next time."

"I'll remember that," Charlie said, and then she heard him coming after her. "You can run but you can't hide, McGuffey. We have things to discuss."

Allie took a quick left turn to head for the booth and safety. "I have to talk to Harry," she began, and then he caught her by the arm and dragged her back toward her office.

"Harry's drinking juice," he told her as he pulled her along. "You have to talk to me."

"YOU CALLED THE MAYOR," Charlie said when they were alone in her office. He really was annoyed at her, but she was so obviously figuring out all the angles while he talked that he wanted to laugh instead. When Allie thought, he could see the wheels go round, she put so much energy into it. He pulled his mind back to the problem at hand. "You punched your ambitious little finger on the buttons and you called the mayor."

Allie pushed her glasses up the bridge of her nose. "Well, I thought it was only right that he have a chance to respond to the allegations."

"Bull." Charlie leaned closer. "I do not want to be a star."

"But you do want to save the city building," Allie told him helpfully.

"As Bill would say, I don't give a rat's ass about the city building." Charlie did his damnedest to look stern, hampered by the suspicion that he looked a lot like Bill and his dad. "Don't do that again."

Allie nodded, the picture of obedience, and he knew he was losing. "So you won't talk about it tonight on the air, I guess."

"Unless somebody calls in and mentions it." Charlie narrowed his eyes at her. "They call us. We don't call them."

Allie nodded again. "No problem."

"Fine." Charlie looked at her suspiciously but she smiled back, innocent. He gave up and pulled the bumper sticker out of his pocket. "Now that that's settled, what is this?" He held the sticker up for her to see.

"A bumper sticker." Allie sat down and began to shuffle papers.

"No, I mean what does it mean?" Charlie leaned on the desk. "Karen said these are really popular."

Allie stopped shuffling and looked at him with palpable patience. "They are. Mark thought up the slogan—you know, turn on the radio—and everybody thought it was stupid, and then after we'd had them about a month, the high school and college kids started collecting them." Allie shrugged. "As long as it keeps WBBB in front of the community, who cares what it means?"

Charlie folded the sticker up again and put it back in his pocket. "How long ago was this? That they got popular?"

Allie shrugged. "I don't know. About a month maybe. A couple of weeks. Why?"

"It has occurred to you that they might be using it to refer to drugs."

Allie looked at him with exasperation. "No, Charlie, that never occurred to me. Gee, what an idea. Now if you don't mind, I've got things to do before you go on tonight."

"All right." Charlie gave up and turned to go. "I mean it about those calls. You don't call anybody. Ever again."

"I'll take care of everything." Allie smiled at him again, and Charlie closed his eyes.

"Somehow, that does not reassure me," he told her and then retreated back into the hall before he let her talk him into something he'd regret.

She was developing a real knack for that.

THE CALLS STARTED coming in before Harry went off the air, and Allie listened as Harry handled them with an intelligence that was eye-opening. Then right before the news, he said, "Well, I want to thank all of you who called in on the city building and remind you that Charlie Tenniel is up next, right after the news, and he's the man to talk to about this mess. If anybody can save the city building, Charlie can, even if he has to work all night. Which, actually, he does. The news is next, folks, and then…Charlie All Night!"

Charlie frowned at Allie. "Charlie All Night?"

Allie shrugged, trying to look innocent. "Harry and I thought it was catchy."

"Knock it off, Allie," he said, and she batted her eyes at him, too happy with the way things were going to care if he was mad or not.

When he took the booth over, Allie met Harry coming out.

"You were good tonight," she told him. "That was a nice intro for Charlie, but you were really good before that, too."

"I thought you didn't like the howling."

"I hate the howling." Allie folded her arms. "Why don't you just talk like you did tonight to those people on the phone?"

"Because usually there aren't any people on the phone." Harry snorted, and Allie wasn't sure whether his contempt was for her or for himself. "I'm not Charlie, honey. I don't do that philosophical stuff."

Fighting the urge to point out that Charlie had a way to go before he posed a major threat to Plato, Allie followed him out into the hall. "Harry, you don't have to be Charlie. Just be yourself. I thought about this today. Talk about things you like. Like…cars."

Harry stopped so suddenly she bumped into him. "Cars?" He considered it and shook his head before ambling down the hall again. "Nah."

"You could make it work, Harry," Allie said, still pursuing him. "You know a lot about cars and stereos and guy things."

Harry stopped again and Allie bumped into him again. "Guy things? Cut me a break."

"*Harry.*" The exasperation in her voice must have gotten to him because he turned around. "You can do this," she said slowly and distinctly. "I will help you."

Harry shook his head at her. "If anybody could, you could, Al, but I don't think so. I'm just not star material."

"Yes, you are," Allie said, but he turned away again. "Wait a minute." She caught his arm. "How's Sam?"

Harry shrugged again. "I got a little more formula down him. Not much. I don't think he's going to make it."

"Oh, no," Allie said and went back to the booth to see if she could tickle some more calories into the puppy.

BY ONE, Charlie had logged twenty-one calls: sixteen in favor of the city building, three in favor of impeaching the mayor and two women in favor of dating Charlie when he got off work. He was pretty sure he'd contained the controversy, but he was also pretty sure that the mayor and his brother had just lost a ton of money thanks to him.

So much for laying low.

Allie waved to him through the studio window. "Do you need me to stay around?" she said into her mike.

She looked tired, so Charlie shook his head at her. "Just shut the phones down. Sam and I are going to take it easy for the rest of the night." He tried to tickle the puppy into taking the bottle again, but it was no go.

He hated it, but they were going to lose him.

Allie came in to check on Sam before she left. "How is he?" she asked, but the tape was done, and Charlie set up the next triple play: Billy Joel, Heart and Tony Bennett. He listened to "River of Dreams" begin before he turned back to the Allie and the puppy.

"Not good." He took off the headphones and put them on the counter next to the basket. "See?" He tickled the puppy's chin and Sam moved his mouth weakly once. "I can't get him to take much. Harry said the same thing. I don't think he's going to make it, Al."

Allie lifted the tiny body out of the basket and put him on the counter to rub his stomach. "Maybe he's too warm. Maybe it makes him lethargic."

"He's a puppy. He should probably be in an incubator."

Sam began to move his legs feebly against the counter.

"He's cold," Charlie said, but Allie held the bottle to his mouth and Sam took it, making feeble sucking sounds, gulping down formula.

Charlie put his head down next to Sam, pushing the headphones away. "I'll be damned. He's taking it. No, wait, he's stopped."

"Wait a minute. Move your head." Allie shoved his head away from the puppy and pulled the headphones back close, and Sam began to suck again, weakly, but with a good rhythm.

"I don't believe it," Charlie said. "He likes Billy."

"Maybe it's the beat." Allie smiled down at the puppy. "Maybe it sounds like his mom's heart or something."

"Well, whatever it is, it's working." Samson sucked on like a champ and Charlie sat back, more relieved than he'd realized. Maybe Sam would make it, after all.

Allie bent over the puppy, cooing encouragement. Her rump was right in front of him. Practically an invitation. He pulled her into his lap, careful not to knock the bottle out of her hand or out of Sam's mouth, and wrapped his arms around her waist from behind. Her blue sweater was made of some kind of soft bubbly yarn, and she was warm against him, and he buried his face in the back of her neck and smelled the flowers in her shampoo. He spoke to her, mainly because he wanted to hear her voice. "How's the show so far?"

"Terrific, as always." Allie concentrated on Sam. "I can't believe this. He's drinking like a fraternity boy."

"What do you mean, 'as always.' This is just the second time we did this." Charlie tightened his arms at the thought.

"Well, we're good." Allie's voice went cold. "He's stopping. What's wrong?"

Charlie reached around her for the headphones and listened. "He must not like 'Friends in Low Places.' It's one of my favorites."

"Well, play Billy again, for heaven's sake." Allie squirmed around on his lap, exasperated. "He *drinks* when you play Billy."

Charlie swallowed and put the headphones back. "Stop moving around on me like that. It's distracting."

"Play Billy." Allie's voice brooked no disagreement.

"Burp him until this is done and then I'll put Billy back on again," Charlie said, surrendering. "Does it have to be 'River of Dreams'?"

"I don't know." Allie bent over the puppy, and Charlie let his hand trail down her back. "Better not mess with success. Play Billy."

"Right," Charlie said, and when Heart was done, he let Billy rip again, and Sam went back to the bottle like a trouper.

By the third play-through, Sam had fallen asleep and was back in his basket.

"I bet if we put headphones on his basket, he'd do better." Allie started to get up. "There's a pair—"

"Wait a minute." Charlie pulled her back into his lap, and when she turned to protest, he kissed her, wanting her softness against him and her mouth on his for just a moment. She relaxed against him, and he felt her tongue tease his mouth, and then he grinned and opened to her, cupping her breast hard in his hand while he bent her head back with the kiss and she wrapped her arms around him.

"Hello," she said a few minutes later, coming up for air. "What was that for? I'm in favor of it, but what was that for?"

"That was for me," Charlie told her, trying to get his breath back. "Go get those headphones now, or I'll take you right here in the booth."

"Oh." Allie stayed where she was for a moment and then grinned when he didn't move. "Talk's cheap, Tenniel."

He grabbed for her then but she slipped away from his hands, and he let her go because the song was over, and also because he had every intention of plying her with Chinese food later and of making love to her until she screamed.

"THIS IS GREAT," Allie said at two-thirty as they split a double order of garlic chicken, eating from the carton with two forks this time. "The show was really good tonight, right up to the end. I knew you were going to be a hit, but I had no idea it would be this fast. And I haven't even started on the publicity yet. This is wonderful."

Charlie stabbed his fork into the chicken. "No, it's not. I told you, I don't want to be famous, so just knock it off."

Allie gave an exasperated sigh. He really was impossible. It didn't matter because she was going to make him famous, anyway, but he was still impossible. "What's wrong with you? Why don't you want to be a success?"

Charlie ignored her. "Dump some rice in here, the garlic's really heavy."

"I bet I know what's wrong." Allie tipped the rice carton into the chicken.

"I do, too. There's not enough rice."

"No, you're afraid of success." Allie patted his hand, suddenly sympathetic. After all, he had hit the big time pretty quickly. "It's very common. You'll get used to it. Trust me."

Charlie moved the carton away from her, holding it behind him. "No, I won't. Look at me."

Allie obediently looked up at him, her fork poised in case he moved the carton back.

"I do not want to be successful," he said, speaking slowly and distinctly. "Successful screws with people's heads and makes them think they're above the law and can get away with anything. I'm not like that. I am not going to promote the show. I am not going to have my picture taken. And I am not going to ask any more questions that will get me in trouble. I just want a nice, quiet show. I'm a nice, quiet guy, and I want a nice, quiet show. Is that too much to ask?" He glared at Allie and she glared back at him, annoyed that he could be so wimpy.

"No," she snapped. "Certainly not. Anything I can do to help you on the road to obscurity?"

"Yes." Charlie moved the carton back within her reach. "Give me something nonexplosive to talk about tomorrow. Something nice and innocuous."

Allie stabbed her fork into the chicken. "Stewart drinks coffee from the break-room urn and doesn't pay for it and then he blames the money shortage on the technicians." She chomped down on her forkful of chicken and gazed balefully at him.

He rolled his eyes. "Well, that is fascinating, but I don't think Greater Tuttle will be interested. Come on, cooperate. You're my producer, produce. And move over. You're hogging the bed." Charlie shoved her over with his hip and looked into the carton. "Oh, there's rice on the bottom. Maybe we should dump this stuff out on plates."

"Whatever you want, Oh Great One."

"I want another topic for tomorrow's show," Charlie said.

"Okay, how about..." Allie leaned over his shoulder and scooped up some more chicken, trying to think of something stupid for him. "Sometimes Grady does his show stoned."

Charlie visibly corraled his patience. "I noticed. But I don't think

Tuttle will think that's news, either. I need a real topic here. Stop sulking and give me some help."

Allie shrugged. "Okay. The streetlights in Eastown are still out."

"Allie..."

She waved her fork at him. "You said, innocuous."

"Innocuous, not brain-dead." Charlie took the carton back. "I will let you have more of this when you come up with something good. Something people will talk to me about, so I won't get fired, but that does not involve newspaper headlines."

Allie looked at the carton with longing. "It's mean to keep moving the carton away. You know how I feel about food."

"Then think fast." He took a huge forkful of chicken and savored it while she watched.

"Food." She moved closer to him with her fork. "You were all mopey about the little grocery stores going out of business when we took you on that tour the other night."

Charlie moved the carton farther out of her way as he ate. "That's the best you can do?"

Allie nodded. "You wanted boring. Do a nostalgia thing. All we have now all over town are those damn FoodStops. Fluorescent lighting and house brands that taste like dog food." She eyed the carton. "I wonder if Samson would like Chinese? He was eating like a trooper when I left. Do you suppose anybody's noticed we're playing Billy Joel every hour?"

Charlie ignored her, lost in thought, and Allie grabbed the carton while he was distracted. "It doesn't sound very exciting," he said. "Maybe I'll do it."

Allie shook her head and scooped up some more chicken. "You're worthless. I could make you the biggest thing on midnight radio, but no, you want things quiet." She passed the carton over to him in disgust.

Charlie took another huge forkful and handed the carton back. "Old-time grocery stores." He chewed and then nodded. "All right. I'll do it. You can have the rest of that."

Allie poked her fork in the carton. "All that's left is rice."

"Too bad." He took the carton out of her hands and put it on the floor with their forks. Then he sat back and put his arm around her. "Now what are we going to do?"

Allie folded her arms. "You know, we're getting into a rut here."

"I know." Charlie leaned over her. She slid down into the bed away from him, and he followed her down, pinning her to her pillow. "A little take-out Chinese, a little interesting conversation, a little great sex." He slipped her nightgown off her shoulder and kissed her neck. "My kind of rut."

She savored his arm around her and his lips on her shoulder, but she kept her voice cool. "I have to get up and brush my teeth now. And then I think we should just sleep for once. We need some variety. This is getting boring."

"Variety." He moved his hand up her side, and she shivered. "Variety," he went on. "Fine. Tomorrow, I'll bring in a goat. But for tonight, I think we..."

Allie pulled away a little. "A goat?"

He blinked at her, surprised. "You've never done the goat trick?"

"The goat trick?" Allie blinked back at him. "Of course. I've done the goat trick. Thousands of times."

Charlie sat up. "What? I didn't think you were the kind of woman who'd do the goat trick *thousands* of times. I'm shocked."

"You'll get over it," Allie said.

"I'm over it now." Charlie moved back on top of her and kissed her, deep and long.

"Grocery stores are a dumb topic," Allie said when she came up for air.

"Quiet, woman," Charlie said and kissed her speechless.

CHARLIE'S NEXT EVENING began well. As far as he could tell in his poking around the station during the day, there was absolutely nothing illegal going on. The closest thing he had to a clue was that the college kids collected "Turn Us On" stickers. As a lead to an in-station drug ring, it was pretty flimsy, about as likely as a lead to an in-station prostitution ring. Still, he'd checked out the bandstand Joe had talked about before and all he'd found were mosquitoes and mud. No drugs.

He was beginning to suspect that the letter had been a hoax. He was also beginning to suspect that Bill thought it was a hoax, too. At least, he didn't seem to be particularly interested in how things were going. Beattie caught Charlie in the hall and grilled him on his living arrangements, his eating habits and his plans for his show, but Bill didn't even ask him what he was doing about the letter.

It was all highly suspicious, and Charlie intended to pursue it, but first he had to get his radio act together so he didn't make a fool of himself on the air. He shouldn't have cared about that, but he did. He also found himself caring about the people at the station, with the exception of Mark, and feeling relieved as he became surer that he wasn't going to have to bust anybody there. Joe combined the virtues of real friendship and great cooking, Karen was cheerful and extremely grateful, Grady was quiet and kind, Beattie looked at him with approval since she liked the city building and was now doing daily editorials on saving it and even Bill seemed to be warming to him. At least he hadn't called Charlie a moron again, even after the front-page story on the city building showed up in the *Tuttle Tribune*. Charlie particularly liked Harry, who, when not howling, was intelligent and, on this particular Thursday night, in a great mood.

"You're not going to believe this," Harry told him as soon as Charlie was in the booth. "Some woman called in and said she was having an argument with her boyfriend over leaving the car parked in neutral or in first, and asked my opinion."

"That's great," Charlie said, confused.

"No, it *was*." Harry's face was lit with excitement. "I explained it to her, and then about five minutes later some guy called in to talk about it, and then a little later some other woman called in with a carburetor problem, and then a couple of other people, and it was great." He leaned back in his chair, suffused with happiness. "I can't believe it. People called my show."

"Hey, if I had a car problem, I'd call you," Charlie offered. "You know what you're talking about."

"Yeah, but now *Tuttle* knows. This has been great." Harry got up and clapped Charlie on the back. "Really glad you're here, man."

"Oh." Charlie blinked. "Well, I am, too."

"*Five* people," Harry stood up and stretched. "*Great* show."

Charlie sat down in the vacated seat. The memory of the bumper stickers came back. Dumb idea, but… "Harry?"

Harry turned in the doorway.

"If you were going to buy drugs in Tuttle, where would you go?"

Harry's face sobered instantly. "I don't know. I hear the bandstand's the place to score."

Charlie nodded. "I'd heard that, too, but it's deserted most of the time."

"Drugs'll kill you in radio," Harry said. "Bad for your voice. Hard to concentrate."

"Right." Charlie gave up and turned to the console.

"Charlie?"

He looked back over his shoulder at Harry.

"Don't ask anybody else about the drug thing," Harry told him seriously. "This isn't that kind of place. People wouldn't understand."

Charlie nodded. "Right. Thanks."

"No problem." Harry hesitated and then left the booth.

Great. Now Harry thought he was a druggie. The things he did for his father and his father's friends. Oh, well. At least he had the show. It was a weird thought, but after only two nights, he was beginning to look forward to the show. It was fun, but it was more than that. It made him feel good. He didn't want to think about it too much because then he'd start cooperating with Allie, and he'd end up a star, after all.

That would be bad.

Of course, tonight's show about old grocery stores should pretty much kill that possibility.

Charlie put on the headphones, made sure "River of Dreams" was in one of the CD slots for Sam's dinner later, and watched the digital readout so he could slide in when the news was over.

Tonight was going to be one dull night on radio.

FOUR AND A HALF HOURS later, Allie sat propped up against her headboard and watched as Charlie sat down on the side of the bed and buried his face in his hands. He really was upset, and she really did sympathize, but she really was ecstatic. Two scandals in three days. His ratings were going to go through the roof.

"Price-fixing," Charlie said, his voice muffled by his hands.

"I didn't know," Allie said. "I swear, I didn't know."

Six

"Price-fixing drove the mom and pops out of business," Charlie repeated, and Allie tried to distract him.

"Maybe if we had some food—"

"It's illegal." He fell back onto the bed so that his head landed in her lap.

Allie loved the weight of his head on her thighs, so she began to stroke his hair so he'd stay there. What a wonderful night it had turned out to be. The callers alone had been spectacular.

Charlie kept his eyes closed, obsessing over the show. "That one old guy said they didn't do anything about it five years ago because they couldn't get enough evidence. Did you hear him say that?"

"Yes, Charlie." Allie said. "I can't believe all those people called in. Who would have thought so many of those little-grocery owners would have been listening at midnight like that?"

"Who would have thought?" Charlie turned his head to glare up at her. "Did you have anything to do with that?"

"Well..."

Charlie sat up. "Did you call them?"

"No!" Allie tried to look outraged, but it was hard since she was at least partially guilty. "I didn't know them. How would I have known them?"

"What did you do?" His tone brooked no babbling.

"What makes you think—"

"Because you play those phones the way Glenn Gould played the piano." He narrowed his eyes at her. "You called Harry's show and asked about carburetors and gears today, didn't you?"

Allie glared at him. "Don't you dare tell him that. I only called twice, all the others did it on their own."

Charlie glared back. "Well, that was swell of you. Now, what did you do to me tonight?"

She took a deep breath, and he said, "Allie? The truth."

Allie winced and surrendered. "Well, I did mention to the first guy who called in that if there were others like him, it would be a lot more effective if they called in, too."

"Terrific." Charlie collapsed back into her lap again. "Why don't you just shoot me? I have to play 'River of Dreams' every hour because of you and now this."

"You don't want Samson to die, do you?"

"Sam now eats like you do. I don't think death is an option anymore unless he ODs on formula."

Allie was already pursuing another train of thought. "You know that lawyer who called in about racketeering charges was something."

Charlie moaned, his face hopeless.

Allie took pity on him. It was cruel to be happy when he was in hell. "Well, people called in about other things, too, remember. There was that guy who wanted to know what poem of Tennyson's you quoted. And the lady who called in when you made fun of the way I eat and said all women should look like the ones in Rubens' paintings." Then she gave up and grinned in triumph. "And Johnson from the *Tribune*. I can't believe the paper is sending out an investigative reporter. Isn't it amazing how many people are listening to your show? It just shows how popular you are."

"I don't want to be popular," Charlie said through his teeth.

Allie shifted on the bed as she prepared to move in for the kill. He was becoming a household word against his will; if she could talk him into helping her, she could take him national. "You know, Charlie. This may just be God's way of telling you that you're destined for success. I mean, there are DJ's who would kill their mothers to get this kind of publicity, and you're just doing it by luck. After this, your ratings are going to go through the roof." He groaned and she stroked his hair again. "Just lie back and enjoy it, love. This is a free ride."

"We have to keep this as quiet as possible," he said.

Allie glared down at him, exasperated. "Why? This is great. I just don't see the problem." Then her expression grew wary as she thought of something. "Well, come to think of it, I might see one problem."

"What?"

"Well, gossip has it that the FoodStops are mob-connected."

Charlie sat up. "In Tuttle?"

Allie patted his shoulder. "It's probably just gossip."

"Oh, no. The mob would be just my luck." He heaved himself off the bed and started for the door.

"Where are you going?"

"To drown myself in the bathtub."

"Hey!" Allie protested. "Where's the food? You said you'd stop at McCarthy's on the way home."

"I didn't get any."

"Well then, where's the sex?"

Charlie opened the door and turned back to her. "You're not getting any, either. I'm depressed." He closed the door behind him.

Allie sat and listened through the wall until he turned the water on, and then she went in and seduced him in the tub so he wouldn't drown himself.

CHARLIE WAS STILL DOWN the next morning. He did snort at breakfast when he heard Mark on the radio introduce himself as "Mark All Morning"—"Well, he's trying," Allie told him—but then Joe passed him the *Tuttle Tribune* and the headline "Disk Jockey Sparks Investigation Into City Building" depressed him so much he only had two helpings of Joe's yeast-raised pancakes.

"I suppose this isn't the best time to tell you that you're doing a promotional appearance tomorrow," Allie said when he'd wiped the last of the syrup from his plate with the last of his pancake.

"In a pig's eye." Charlie stayed bent over his empty plate. "I told you—"

"You were interested in the college," Allie said as persuasively as she could. "Harry's going—"

Charlie's head came up. "The college?" He thought for a moment. The college kids were joking about the stickers. It was a lousy lead, but it was something. "All right. I'll do the college."

The phone rang and Joe went to get it, while Allie stared at him in surprise. "You'll do it?"

"Don't push your luck," he told her. "I'm not going to make a habit of this."

Allie nodded, obviously cheered he was going.

Then Joe came back and said, "That was Bill. He'd like to see both of you this afternoon at four."

"Oh, hell," Allie said.

"Very probably," Joe said.

ALLIE WINCED as Bill glared at them both with equal disgust. "What I want to know is who died and made you two Ralph Nader?"

"Ralph Nader's still alive," Allie said.

Charlie kicked her on the ankle. "It was an accident, Bill. We didn't know..."

"Well, then *shut up*," Bill roared at him.

"Now wait a minute." Allie stood up, determined not to give in. She had a show to save, and for once, she was in the right morally, too. "That FoodStop person bought up half a dozen grocery stores and then cut prices below cost just to ruin the little stores. And when they were all gone, he raised prices and he's been gouging Tuttle ever since. For five years. Anybody knows prices are cheaper in Riverbend, but only people with time and money can get there to stock up. He's preying on the poor and—"

"Sit *down*," Bill said and she sat.

"Do you know who the FoodStop person is?" Bill asked her with deceptive gentleness.

Allie stopped, sure she wasn't going to like finding out who the FoodStop person was. "No."

"Roger Preston."

Oh, terrific. Allie's chin came up. "Well, I hope you've won a lot of money off him in those poker games, because he's a crook."

Charlie slumped back in his chair. "You're kidding. Another poker player?"

"I'm gonna be playing solitaire if you two don't knock it off," Bill snarled. He stabbed a finger at Charlie. "This is *not* what I hired you for."

"Well, of course it is." Allie went back into action, protecting her star. "This is exactly what you hired him for. I can't wait to see the ratings."

"Young lady—"

"And Beattie loved it," Allie said, saving her killer shot for last. "Absolutely loved it."

Bill closed his eyes. "I wish she'd go back to the garden club."

"She's going to do an editorial on the news tonight," Allie said.

Bill's eyes flew open. "No, she is *not*."

"Well, you better tell her, then," Allie said.

Bill leaned forward, scowling at them so hard his eyebrows meshed into one white strip of fur across his forehead. "You let me handle Beattie. And from now on, *don't answer the phone*."

"But Bill—" Allie stopped midsentence when Charlie took her hand and jerked her up out of the chair.

"You got it," he told the older man. "No phones. We'll tell people they're down for the night. By Monday, everybody will have forgotten. Come on, Al."

"*Wait* a minute," Allie said, but he pulled her out of the office still protesting.

"We've got a great show here," she fumed at him. "And you're shooting it in the foot. Why can't you—"

"Repeat after me," he said as he dragged her down the hall past Marcia, the afternoon DJ, and Mark who were arguing about something. "Controversy is bad."

"Great show, Charlie," Marcia called back to them. "Everybody's talking about it."

"Terrific," Charlie muttered and picked up speed.

Allie looked back over her shoulder at Mark. He did not look happy. She tried not to feel good about that but it was hopeless, so she beamed at Mark as Charlie towed her away.

Life just kept getting better and better.

IT WAS ALMOST MIDNIGHT when Charlie saw Allie wave to him through the glass. He was still annoyed with her, but it was hard to maintain. It wasn't her fault he'd stumbled over the worst case of greed that Tuttle had ever seen.

He motioned her in.

"Nice boring show," she told him, and he rolled his eyes at her.

"Don't start. What have you got for me?"

Allie handed some papers over, and he frowned at them. "Here's the title for that guy who wanted the Tennyson allusion. It was really Wordsworth. And here's the print of Rubens' *Rape of the Sabines*. I forget why you wanted that. This is radio."

Charlie studied the print, a painting of ample bodies spilling all over a horse. "That woman last night who said it was okay you eat like a locust also said the problem with men is that all we look at are pictures of skinny women. She said if we put Rubens' work up instead of Hugh Hefner's, we'd all be better for it." He held the print up beside Allie so that he could see them together and squinted between her and the print. "You need to put on some weight."

"Good. I'll start now." She picked up what was left of the cheeseburger he'd brought into the booth with him and chomped into it. "You need anything else?"

"Nope." The tape ended and he went back to the mike. "And now, for all you William Wordsworth fans who have probably been trying to call in on our dysfunctional phones and tell me that yesterday's mystery quote was not Tennyson, 'Getting and spending we lay waste our powers' is from Wordsworth's *The World Is Too Much With Us*. Will dashed off that little ditty in 1807, but it's still relevant today."

A pickle oozed out of the cheeseburger Allie was eating and plopped onto her blouse, leaving a mustard trail on the white rayon as it toppled over the swell of her breast.

"Oh, great," Allie said next to the mike, and then winced at her mistake.

"And that was the voice of Alice McGuffey, my producer." Charlie grinned at her. "Usually this is a one-man show, but Allie just dropped a pickle with mustard on her blouse. What's the blouse made of, Al?"

"Rayon. Dry-clean only, hold the mustard."

"Anybody out there with a surefire method for getting mustard out of rayon, call in and save Allie's blouse. She doesn't get paid enough here to buy a new one. Oh, you can't call in, the phones are down. Well, write. And now a nostalgic wake-up call since it's after midnight, bedbugs—2 Live Crew."

Allie glared at him, and he shoved the cassette slide up while he tried to figure out what he'd done wrong this time.

"What?" he said to her. "It's not my fault you ripped off my hamburger and got slimed with mustard." He got out of his chair, stretched and sat down on the counter to get a better look at her. She was actually glowering. He moved back a little farther until his butt hit the soundboard. She was fun to watch when she was mad, but he was still a prudent man.

"2 Live Crew?" Allie sputtered. "You're playing 2 Live Crew?"

"Yes, Allie," Charlie said patiently. "I'm playing 2 Live Crew. It's my show. I do the playlist."

"I can't believe it." Allie smacked the hamburger down on the console. "And I thought you were an okay guy."

"I am an okay guy. I have testimonials." Charlie leaned back to enjoy the argument since for once it wasn't about making him a star.

Allie was visibly steaming. "2 Live Crew are sexist psychopaths and you give them airtime."

"Hey, it's a free country. The First Amendment..."

"The First Amendment doesn't give men the right to sing about attacking women. It doesn't give—"

"Well, actually, it does," Charlie said, and Allie turned bright red. "Hold it." Charlie warded her off with his hand. "Just hold it. You're saying I should censor what goes on the air?"

"This is your show," Allie steamed. "What you play reflects your tastes. You have a *responsibility*—"

"I have a responsibility to play music that appeals to a lot of different people. 2 Live Crew may not be my favorite group, but..."

"Oh. Right." Allie was so mad her eyebrows fused over her nose. "A lot of different music? So when are you going to play Barry Manilow?"

Charlie snorted. "I will die before I play Barry Manilow."

Allie leaned closer. "According to you, that's censorship."

"No, it's not," Charlie said, trying not to be annoyed. "I don't object to what he's saying. It's just lousy music."

"But you have a responsibility to play music that appeals to a lot of different people," Allie pressed on. "You just said so."

"Not Barry Manilow."

"So you'll play psychopathic music that advocates hurting women but you won't play pop music that advocates loving them."

"Allie, don't twist this—"

Allie jerked back from him, glaring. "You know what you are? You're just like Mark."

Charlie jerked his head back, outraged. "Hey, watch your mouth, woman."

"You have no respect for women. You're amused by the women's movement and you think—"

"I love women's movements. Come on, Allie…"

"Don't patronize me," Allie shouted. "I can't believe you're—"

"Ah, Allie, have a heart," Charlie said. "It's no big deal."

"—such a yuppie scum dweeb," Allie finished and stomped out of the room.

He started to follow her and then realized he couldn't leave the booth. "Allie, come back here."

Somebody moved toward the booth through the shadows of the production room, but it didn't look anything like Allie.

"Uh, Charlie." Stewart, the night engineer, looking more like a peeled egg then ever, came to stand in the doorway, looking sleepy but interested. "I was just in the break room, and I realized you probably didn't know."

"Know what?" Charlie frowned at him.

"You're on the air." Stewart shrugged. "It's good stuff, but —"

"The tape can't be over yet," Charlie looked around frantically.

"It never started."

"Oh, hell." Charlie put the headphones back on. Sure enough, no 2 Live Crew. He looked at the mike slide and closed his eyes when he saw it was up. "Uh, for those of you listening at home, Alice Mc-Guffey has just walked out in a huff. And for the record, she does a very nice huff. She overreacts, though. And now, let's try that 2 Live Crew again, shall we? This is for all you yuppie scum dweebs out there who dig rap. There must be at least two of you."

He punched the tape again and listened. Silence. "All right," he said into the mike, "seems we have a defective tape. Let's try Elvis since he was on deck next, anyway." He punched the next tape, shoved the slide up and heard absolutely nothing.

Then he looked at Stewart. "Go get me a tape. Any tape. Now." Then as Stewart disappeared, he spoke into the mike. "Well, it's a darn shame our phones are down because this would sure make one heck of a call-in topic. Send in those postcards, folks, and vote your preference, Manilow or Crew. Or maybe I'll try something different." He babbled on about some of the other choices he could have made, feeling like a fool and developing a real need for revenge on whoever had wiped his tapes. When Stewart came loping back and thrust a CD at him, he shoved it into the player. "Or we could play something good like this one."

Frank Sinatra began to sing "My Way."

Charlie looked at Stewart. "You're kidding."

"I like Frank." Stewart shoved a handful of CDs at him. "Here's more new ones. Want me to check to see if anything you've got in here has music on it?"

"That would be good." Charlie put his head in his hands. "This is a disaster."

Stewart dropped the new CDs on the counter and picked up the old tapes. "Not really. You had your mike slide shoved up so people could hear you talk. That's good."

Charlie looked at him as if he were demented, always a possibility with Stewart. "How is that good?"

"Because if you hadn't, you'da had yourself some dead air. Nothing's worse than dead air."

Charlie shook his head. "I suppose not. What's wrong with the tapes?"

Stewart picked up the one on the top of his stack and looked at it. "Doesn't look like anything's wrong. It's one of our old tapes, all right. Must go back five or six years. Maybe it was too old."

"I played it this afternoon," Charlie said.

Stewart shrugged. "Maybe somebody erased it. I'll check all of them, but I bet somebody did it on purpose. Not everybody likes you, you know. The mayor, for instance."

Charlie snorted. "You trying to tell me that Rollie Whitcomb snuck in here and erased my tapes so I'd have dead air? Come on. The man can barely drive a car."

Stewart shrugged again. "You asked."

Charlie tipped his head back to stare at the ceiling. "So Allie and I just broadcast our 2 Live Crew fight to greater Tuttle. All right. That's okay. I can't possibly get in trouble for this. Unless the FCC bars 'yuppie scum dweeb,' in which case, I pay the fine. I'm covered on this. I am not in trouble."

Somehow, though, he knew he was.

That was just the way his life was going.

Stewart left the booth. A few minutes later, while Charlie was figuring out the angles, the phone rang, and he picked it up out of habit.

WHEN CHARLIE GOT HOME that night, Allie was already in bed in the dark. He got a beer, undressed, and climbed in beside her, touching the cold can to her back.

"Get out," she said and drew away from him.

"It's the yuppie scum dweeb. Wake up." He drank a third of the beer in one gulp and then put the cold can against his forehead.

"Go sleep on the couch."

"Oh, no, Alice." He put the can on the table beside the bed, turned on the light and rolled her over to face him.

"You can't for a minute think I'm going to have sex with you." She tried to push him away. "You can't possibly…"

"After you left, Stewart, who has not been paying attention, noticed the phones were down. So he turned them on. We got over a dozen calls in less than an hour. Roughly speaking, fifty-five percent were in favor of you, forty-two percent were in favor of me and three per cent wanted to know exactly what a yuppie scum dweeb was."

"Send them your picture." Allie rolled away from him.

He rolled her back. "One person suggested baking soda for the mustard on your blouse."

"Why are we discussing this?" Allie asked, and the edge in her voice told him she was still mad and not just faking it.

Charlie sighed. "Because we have a meeting with Bill on Monday. For once in his worthless life, he was listening to the show to make sure we didn't do anything stupid, and you go berserk on the air." He shook his head and picked up his beer. "He was not happy when he talked with me."

Allie rolled back over and buried her face in her pillow. "Good. Maybe you'll get fired. Then you won't have to worry about success anymore, and you can stop screwing up my life and the lives of those around you by playing Nazi music."

"That does it." Charlie picked up his pillow and stood up, pulling the quilt with him.

"Hey!" Allie sat up and grabbed for the quilt, but he was too fast for her.

"If you want me, I'll be on the couch," he said over his shoulder.

"I may never want you again," Allie yelled after him.

"Ha." He turned to look down at her superciliously from the door. "You'll probably be out on the couch with me by morning."

"Ha yourself, you yuppie scum. Don't hold your breath waiting. Your brain needs all the oxygen it can get."

Charlie slammed the door behind him, and Allie flopped back down in the bed, put the pillow over her head and screamed with fury and frustration.

Seven

➤ ◀

Allie moved behind the scenes at the University of Riverbend campus the next day, making sure there were plenty of bumper stickers and station programs to hand out, that nobody hot-wired the sound system while Stewart slept in the back of the station van, and that none of the cassettes disappeared or were mysteriously wiped clean of music. If somebody was out to get them, she wanted to be there first.

The entire time she kept an eye on Charlie, studying him to make optimum use of future public appearances. She wasn't sure she was ready to forgive him, but she'd been relieved the night before when an hour after he'd stormed out of her bedroom, he'd come back, tossed his pillow on the bed and threw the quilt over her. "I figured you were cold without the quilt," he'd said and climbed in beside her. "Ha," she'd said, but she'd snuggled her back up next to his just the same.

Now, she watched him charm the crowd and felt her anger fade completely. Natural charisma, she decided, watching him lean over the portable broadcast counter to smile at a coed who was waving a bumper sticker for him to sign. Most of these kids didn't know who he was, since Tuttle graft was not uppermost in their minds as entertainment value. They'd just wandered by to pick up those dumb bumper stickers and stopped to listen to him as he sat slumped in his chair with his feet on the table. Charlie's patter was completely off the cuff and off the wall. It took a really focused person to ignore him, and not many college kids were focused on a Saturday afternoon.

Charlie was building an audience. *Yes,* Allie thought and forgave him completely, but she kept her mouth shut so as not to distract him. She had no idea why Charlie had agreed to two hours of college broadcasting, but she wasn't about to question her luck or, God forbid, point out to Charlie how well he was doing. Then Charlie called back good-naturedly to a heckler, and the crowd laughed, and Allie heard it as the sound of rising ratings.

AFTER TWO HOURS in the early-October afternoon sun, Charlie was ready to pack it in. He'd listened for any clue about crime or drugs in all the comments the kids had made as they'd drifted past, and he'd started animated conversations with everyone who came up to him, trying to leave openings for any clue they'd like to drop. After two hours, he'd found out exactly nothing. He had a bunch of drunk freshman fraternity guys hassling him off and on, and while they were easy to deflect, it wasn't his choice of the way to spend a great autumn afternoon. He'd also deflected more than enough young women who'd asked him what he was doing that night. "Sleeping with my producer" didn't seem to be a good answer, especially since, after last night, Allie might still be feeling hostile. Then he looked out over the crowd and grinned. Nope. He'd been a public-relations dream all afternoon. Given Allie's lust for success, there was a good chance she'd jump him in the van from gratitude. The thought led him to other thoughts of Allie in the windowless van with the doors closed and locked. He hadn't seen Allie naked for almost thirty-six hours. That was bad for him. Usually he wasn't this obsessive about sex, but Allie was different. It was easy to be obsessive about Allie. In fact, it was a pleasure to be obsessive about Allie. And the van had a bench seat in back, not wide but padded enough for Stewart to sleep on. Maybe he could get rid of Stewart....

"Quite a crowd," Mark said behind him and he sat up in surprise.

"What?" Charlie squinted at him in the sun. "Oh. Yeah. They're a great crowd. You up now?"

"Yes. Lisa's taking over from Allie." Mark surveyed the situation and frowned at him. "There are a lot of people here."

Charlie stood up. "Well, that was the idea. It's all yours." He clapped Mark on the shoulder. "Have a great time."

Mark ignored him and took over the mike as the last song ended.

"Hello, UR," he said into the mike. "This is Mark King, live from the University of Riverbend."

People started to drift away, and for a moment, Charlie felt sorry for Mark. Then he remembered who Mark was and his pity evaporated. This was the jerk who'd dumped Allie. This was the jerk who had probably sabotaged his show the night before. Even more important, this was the jerk who sooner or later was going to try to get Allie back to save his show. Annoyed, Charlie went down the steps to look for her, stopping twice along the way to tell groups of female students who'd asked that he was busy that night. Then he headed for the van, and someone hooted at him.

The bunch of drunk freshmen were back, hanging around the end of the platform. "Still givin' it away free?" one of them said.

Charlie stopped and raised an eyebrow. "Giving what away free? Bumper stickers?"

They all laughed and somebody said, "Bumper stickers. Yeah, right." Then one of them raised his fingers to his mouth and made a sucking sound. "You'll never get rich giving it away, man," one of them said.

"Forget it," the tallest one said. "He's stupid."

"Wait a minute." Charlie went toward them, but they faded into the crowd, laughing over their shoulders at him.

Giving it away free. The kid had mimed smoking, but giving pot away made no sense at all. Not even for Grady, their resident pot head. Charlie leaned against the van and thought about it. If he was looking for crime, he had to find a profit. That only made sense. So maybe somebody was giving away free samples, trying to hook paying buyers later? That ruled out Grady completely since he thought capitalism was a crime.

Unless he was faking it. Unless under all Grady's New Age babble beat a heart just like Charlie's dad's.

It was possible, but not probable. Grady's good nature was legendary. Someone would have noticed if he'd been leading a double life. Tuttle wasn't that big.

"Hey, we're through." Allie came up and leaned on the van next to him. "We are completely through until Monday night. More than forty-eight hours free. Can you believe it?"

"No." Her face was turned up to his, and he grinned at her and pushed her glasses up the bridge of her nose with his finger. "What do you want to do for forty-eight hours?"

Allie grinned back at him. "Watch videos. Eat Chinese. Feed Sam. Make love."

"Let's take those in reverse order." Charlie bent his head close to hers and watched her blush and smile. "It was very cold in that bed last night, and you're very cute today. Is the van empty or is Stewart still sleeping in there?"

"I don't make love in vans," Allie said primly.

"Of course not," Charlie said. "So is it empty or not?"

It was empty.

"That's a very narrow bench," Allie pointed out as Charlie sat down and pulled her onto his lap.

"I have a great sense of balance." He slid his hand under her T-shirt to cup her breast and listened to her soft gasp with a great deal of heated pleasure. "You don't really want to wait until we get home, do you? Think of the traffic."

He kissed her neck and she murmured, "Traffic would be bad," and then he tipped her gently down onto the seat as she wrapped herself around him. "Remind me to do these college things more often," he said as he unzipped her jeans. "I love doing remotes."

As FAR AS Allie was concerned, the weekend just got better after that. They rented videos Saturday night and stayed home with Joe and his date, critiquing the mistakes in *The African Queen* and *Casablanca.*

"Bad ending," Allie said when Ingrid Bergman left on the plane.

"A woman's got to do what a woman's got to do," Charlie told her.

"I think she's right," Joe's date, David, said. "*I* wouldn't have left Humphrey Bogart."

"You're a guy," Charlie said. "Women sacrifice. It's their job in life."

He complained loudly when Allie threw popcorn at him and then attacked her that night when they went to bed, tickling her until she giggled helplessly and then making love to her until she lost her mind. The next day, they had a picnic in the park and that night, Charlie dragged Allie off to see Arnold Schwarzenegger's newest exploding-head picture.

Allie had never been happier in her life. "You are one good time," she told Charlie.

Charlie grinned at her. "Let's take some Chinese food home to Joe and David."

But Joe was alone when they got home.

"CHINESE," Charlie called out when they came through the door and then stopped. Joe was standing in the middle of the living room and he didn't look happy.

"What's wrong?" Allie said.

"David and I were spending a nice quiet evening at home," Joe said, "when somebody knocked on the door."

Charlie put the take-out bag down on the coffee table. "What happened?"

Allie sank down on the sofa across from Joe. "Where's David?"

"He went home. Things got weird." Joe looked at Charlie. "Did you annoy anyone lately?"

"Just about everybody." Charlie sat down on the arm of the couch. "I'm not going to like this story, am I?"

Joe shook his head. "When I opened the door, this blonde was standing there, and she shrieked, 'Charlie!' and flung her arms around me."

At least nobody had tried to gun Joe down. There were worse things than being hugged by a blonde. Charlie grinned at Allie. "Happens to me all the time."

"Then she dropped her coat," Joe said. "She was naked."

Charlie stopped grinning. "That doesn't happen nearly as much."

"Then she grabbed me again and somebody took a picture. With a flash."

"That never happens to me." Charlie frowned at him. "What the hell?"

"I don't know," Joe said. "But it's not good."

Charlie glanced at Allie. She was glaring at him. "What?" he asked her.

"Is there something you're not telling me?" Allie said.

"Something blonde? No." Charlie looked at her with disgust. The last thing he needed was Allie getting jealous while he tried to figure out this newest wrinkle. "Come on, I spend every waking moment with you. Every sleeping moment, too, for that matter. When would I be dating blondes?"

"Well, something's going on with you," Allie said, getting up. "And I don't like it." She went in her room and shut the door.

Charlie looked at Joe. "Is this my fault?"

"I don't think so," Joe said. "But if it is, knock it off. You're screwing up my social life."

THE PICTURE OF JOE and the hooker was on the front page of Monday's *Tuttle Tribune.*

"I can't believe they printed that," Allie said as she stared at it over breakfast, trying to figure the public-relations angles. "Local DJ Patronizes Call Girl? How much of the paper does the mayor own?"

"God, I look like hell," Joe said over her shoulder. "In fact, I almost look like Charlie."

"Very funny." Charlie came into the kitchen and took the paper away from them to read the caption. "This is weird. They're setting themselves up for a lawsuit here. Somebody with clout must have got this in. Who have we annoyed that has clout?"

"Well, the mayor owns a chunk of the paper, and there's Roger Preston and all his friends." Joe took the paper back. "Good thing I warned David about this. He's not the jealous type, but this looks bad."

"Actually," Allie said, trying to look on the bright side. "It might help the ratings. It should definitely get us some callers."

"Great," Charlie said. "The Moral Majority calling in to tell me I'm the spawn of Satan. Yeah, I'm looking forward to that."

"Forget the Moral Majority," Joe said. "How about Bill?" The phone rang, and he got up to answer it. "Even as I speak. Do you want to talk to him?"

"No." Allie stood up and carried her plate to the sink. "We're already on the carpet for the 2 Live Crew mess. Tell him we'll see him this afternoon." She smiled at Charlie to reassure him. "It's all right. Bill's going to know that's Joe, not you, and that it has to be a setup. Really. It's all right."

Allie wasn't as sure later that afternoon.

Bill sat in his desk chair and swiveled back and forth, glaring at both of them. "I don't know what it is with you two," he began on a deceptively quiet note. "I don't know whether you're dumb or crazy or out to get me or what." He glared at Charlie. "I'm particularly glad I hired you, you dumb-ass."

Allie winced at the injustice. "Wait a minute. The Friday broadcast was all my fault. I know the rule is never to say anything in the booth that can't be broadcast. I broke it. It's my fault."

Charlie sighed. "No, it isn't. It's mine. I was the one who sat on the mike slide and moved it up so everyone heard us. She had every right to assume we were off the air. It was my fault."

Allie shook her head, trying to warn him off. Her job was safe but his might be in jeopardy. "I'm the producer. I should have checked. It was my fault..."

"No, it wasn't..."

"When you two are finished," Bill said, "I'd like to say a few words."

They both shut up.

"We logged a lot of calls Friday night." He stood up and began to pace. Allie found herself moving her head back and forth with him. "Even more calls over the weekend. A lot more than we ever have before. And now there's this mess with the hooker." He wheeled around suddenly and put his hands on the desk, looming over them. "*The press* would like to talk to you both."

Charlie shifted in his seat. "About the hooker—"

"I know about the hooker," Bill said. "Somebody's out to get you, son, but it's hard to tell who since you've pissed off so many people." He glared at Charlie. "Had to make waves, didn't you?"

"I don't think that was what I had in mind," Charlie began and Bill cut him off.

"You don't think at all, son. That's why we're in this mess. Just look at you on Friday. Playing songs about raping women." He snorted. "Making fun of Barry Manilow."

Charlie looked at Allie, and she closed her eyes in defeat. Bill was on her side. She must be wrong.

"And you," Bill said to her. "You and your women's movements. I've told you to keep that stuff off the air. The only good thing this fool said Friday night was when he made fun of you for that. And even that was dirty." He glared at Charlie again.

"Oh, hell, Bill." Charlie leaned back in his chair. "Fire us and get it over with."

Allie felt her heart rise in her throat but then Bill saved her.

"I'm not gonna fire you." He slapped the desk. "I need you. And besides, you're starting to make me money. Albert raised the ad rate on your show and it's still sold out. Damn it."

"You can fire me," Allie offered, not too worried he'd take her up on it. "Nobody knows I exist."

"The hell they don't." Bill glared at her, too. "You're famous now. I told you, *the press* wants to talk to you. Some fool woman wants to do a *human-interest* story on you two."

"Well, we don't want to talk to her." Allie stood up. "I'm not talking to anybody ever again."

"Sit *down*," Bill said and she sat down. "You're gonna have to go on again tonight."

"No," Allie and Charlie said together.

"And you're gonna talk nice to each other, and answer questions nice for the rest of the week, and then when everybody's really bored, you, Charlie, are gonna go back to being a solo DJ and you, Alice, are gonna go back to being a producer, and that's gonna be the end of it. Understand? Find something boring to talk about that you both agree on and talk about it for a week. There must be something that you both agree on."

Sex, Allie thought, but she kept her mouth shut. She looked over at Charlie who was fighting back a grin. He was turning into one hellacious one-night stand.

"Either of you got anything else to say?"

"No, sir," Allie said, and then she and Charlie escaped into the hall before he could start again. "I think Bill has slipped around the bend this time," she said when they were out of earshot.

"Well, he owns the bend," Charlie said. "Let's make this thing short and sweet. Think of something we talk about."

"The show," Allie said. "Chinese food. Sex."

"I don't think any of those are going to make a program," Charlie said. "What else do we talk about?"

Allie stopped, struck by the thought. "That's pretty much it. We don't talk much." She looked at him, appalled. "We don't really talk at all."

Charlie ignored her. "Maybe we can talk about music. You don't know anything about music, but I could talk about it, and you could say, 'Gee, Charlie, you're wonderful.' I like it." He looked at her without seeing her. "But this time, I'm double-checking the tapes. We're going to have music or I'm going to know why."

Allie left him in the tape library, carefully checking his tapes for the night. He might not want to be a star, but Charlie sure didn't want dead air, either. Whether he realized it or not, Charlie was getting sucked into radio.

And whether she'd realized it before or not, she was getting sucked into Charlie. She should have been delighted that all they talked about was the show and sex. That's what she wanted. A nice, uncomplicated, unemotional affair. Except that wasn't enough anymore. She'd gotten exactly what she'd asked for, and it wasn't enough, and she wasn't going to be able to get more because he didn't want more: he was leaving in November.

There it was, the thought she'd been ignoring all week. November. He was leaving in November. And no matter how hopeful she was, she knew how stubborn he was. Come November, unless she did something amazing, she was going to be left with an empty broadcast booth and an empty bed.

She wasn't sure she didn't have an empty bed already. If all they were was great sex, it was definitely an empty bed.

She tried to push the whole thing from her mind and went to get coffee. Her thoughts were depressing, and they got worse when Mark followed her into the break room.

"Allie!" The delight in his voice was mirrored on his face. He must want something, she told herself. He was never that happy to see anybody unless they could do something for him.

She steeled herself for the come-on. "What do you want?"

Mark spread his hands out, the picture of innocence. "I just wanted to talk to you."

Allie frowned at him. "Why?"

Mark put his hand on her arm. "I just miss you so much."

"Why? Did Lisa leave you?" She turned away from him and went over to the coffee urn, trying not to think about Charlie leaving her.

Mark followed her. "Allie, it's not the same. She's not you."

Allie laughed shortly. "No, she's ten years younger and twenty pounds lighter. And it's only taken you two months to notice." Allie turned back to him, her coffee in hand. "I talked to her Saturday at the remote. She's looking pretty frazzled, Mark. Cut her a break. She's still learning the job. Charlie's in the same spot." She stopped, realizing that while Charlie might be in the same spot, he was doing brilliantly. Not a good comparison for Lisa.

Mark moved closer. "Forget about Charlie. Let's go have dinner somewhere and talk."

Allie ducked around him and headed for the door. "We don't have anything to talk about."

Mark caught her arm, and she turned to see him with a soulful look on his face. "Let's have dinner. A long dinner."

Allie pulled her hand away, trying to compute what she'd just heard. "What?"

"I think we should see more of each other. A lot more, if you know what I mean." Mark moved closer, backing her against the wall. "We were good together, Allie."

Allie looked at him in amazement. "Are you kidding? We were lousy together. Are you propositioning me? I can't believe it." She shook her head. "You're propositioning me. No." She turned and opened the door and came face-to-face with Charlie.

"I was looking for you," he said to her. He glared at Mark. "What are you doing flirting with other disc jockeys?"

Mark smiled smoothly. "Allie and I go back a long way."

"As long as you stay back, I don't care." Charlie held the door for

Allie. "If you're finished here, we need to talk about this damn program."

"Fine," Allie said, annoyed with them both. Mark had dumped her and Charlie was leaving in November, but in the meantime they both thought they owned a part of her. And she knew which parts, too. Mark wanted her brain to save his show, and Charlie wanted her butt.

Well, the hell with both of them.

"What difference does the program make?" she said to Charlie, and he looked so stunned she felt vindicated. "You want to be a flop, remember?"

She took off down the hall and heard him follow her. "Are you all right?" he called after her. "This isn't like you."

"You're making me mad," she said. "You and Mark, both."

He followed her into her office. "Don't put me in the same sentence with Mark. What did I do?"

"All he thinks about is what I can do for him in radio," Allie said, slamming her coffee cup down on her desk and sloshing coffee on her papers. "And all you care about is what I can do for you in bed. The hell with both of you. I don't need you." She sat down and crossed her arms.

Charlie sat down across from her and watched her warily. "Uh, I don't know what brought this on, but I want you for more than sex. We're friends. You know that. Is Mark trying to get you back for his show?"

"I have friends," Allie told him. "Joe, and Harry, and Karen, and a lot more. They don't jump my body every chance they get."

Charlie's eyebrows rose. "Sorry. I'll stop."

"No, you won't," Allie said gloomily. "That's how you communicate. Men. The weaker sex. If you were a woman, you'd have the guts to talk to me, but since you're a guy you just want sex."

"Well, then say no," Charlie said, the exasperation plain in his voice. "You always seem pretty enthusiastic when I suggest it."

"I am enthusiastic," Allie said. "I love going to bed with you. But that's all we do."

"So what do you want?"

"I want to talk sometimes." She hated sounding wimpy, but there it was. "You know, really talk."

"Good." Charlie put a stack of disks on her desk. "We'll talk tonight on the show. You'll love it. Conversation and your career, a two-for-one deal."

Allie gazed at him for a moment, looking at the monster she'd created. She wanted to work on their relationship, he wanted to work on her career. Just what she needed in her already bleak life: irony. "Great," she said. "Tell me all about it."

FOUR HOURS LATER, Charlie leaned into the mike and said, "Well, here we are again, all phones working. And for those of you who were wondering, the guy being hugged by the blonde on the front page of the paper is not me. That's my roommate, Joe, and the reason he looks so surprised is that he's gay. Yes, folks, somebody's up to something here in old Tuttle. I don't mind, but Joe would appreciate it if whoever it is would quit sending hookers over to our apartment with cameras. They're ruining his reputation."

"Oh, he'll love that," Allie said softly as she petted Sam, careful not to speak into the mike.

"And now, back by popular request, is my producer, the poster girl for irrationality, Alice McGuffey."

"Hey," Allie said. "Let's try this introduction again."

Charlie shook his head. "You *are* the person who stood in your office today and announced to me that men were the weaker sex, right?"

Allie snorted. "That's not irrational. That's the truth."

Charlie laughed. "I can beat you at arm wrestling anytime, honey."

Allie's voice dripped with sarcasm. "Life is not about arm wrestling."

"What's life got to do with this?"

"What I said in the office was that women are stronger because they talk to each other, and men are weaker and concentrate on sex and ignore other more important things. Like establishing warm human relationships."

Charlie groaned. "Why do women always bring every discussion back to relationships?"

"Because relationships are the basis for life, you dweeb."

Charlie sounded wary. "Tell me you're not talking about marriage."

"I'm not talking about marriage," Allie said reasonably. "I'm talking about establishing warm connections with other people. Men don't do it."

"Hey. I have a warm connection with another person." Charlie wiggled his eyebrows at her.

"That's sex." Allie wiggled her eyebrows back and stuck out her tongue. "That's what men use as a substitute for relationships. But it's not the real thing."

"It feels real." Charlie scowled at her.

"Yeah, but can you keep the relationship going without it?"

Charlie looked at her, surprised. "My relationship with this woman is more than sex and she knows it."

"That's not the point." Allie leaned forward. "The point is that women can survive without all the physical stuff that men need because they know what's important is the human relationship. So they talk to each other. They don't get all the warmth in their lives from sex."

"Sex isn't important to you?" Charlie asked, disbelief heavy in his voice.

"Of course, it's important to me. But I wouldn't come unglued without it like you would."

"You wouldn't?" Charlie sat back. "Ha."

"No," Allie said primly. "As long as a woman is getting her emotional needs met by the ones she loves, she can handle sexual deprivation. But a man doesn't know how to get his emotional needs satisfied except through sex, so he'll get depressed and become irrational. Not that anyone would notice since men are pretty irrational most of the time, anyway—"

Charlie interrupted her. "I don't believe this. You're saying that if we stop sleeping together, I'll crack before you will because I don't have any friends and you do?"

Allie froze in her chair.

"Well?"

"Sort of," she said faintly. "Although I certainly wouldn't have put it that way on the air."

"What? Oh." Charlie winced as he realized what he'd done. "Well, the cat's out, so you might as well finish what you've started here. I can't believe you'd make such a sexist argument."

"Well, there's only one way to find out who's right." Allie stuck her chin out, daring him. "Today's October second, and as you know we were fighting last night, so we can count from there. Let's see which one of us is the most irrational by November first."

"What?" Charlie said, startled.

"You said it would be no problem." Allie shrugged. "Put your money where your...mouth is."

"Allie, that isn't funny."

Allie smiled at him, triumphant. "I rest my case. I knew you wouldn't even try it."

"Did you?" Charlie leaned back. "All right. Fine. We're celibate until November first. No problem."

"Really?" Allie said.

"Really," Charlie said.

The phone began to ring.

Allie laughed nervously and stood up, putting Sam back in his basket as she rose. "Well, I'd love to stay and chat with callers, but I've got to be a producer now. You started this, you talk about it."

He watched Allie leave the booth and then turned back to the mike. "She would pick a month with thirty-one days. Okay, folks, while Allie's hooking up the caller..." Somebody tapped him on the shoulder and he turned to see Stewart. "What?"

Stewart handed him a tape.

"Our engineer has just shown up with a tape in hand. Special request, Stewart? This isn't like you..." Charlie's voice trailed off as he read the label. "Oh, very funny. Okay, here's Stewart the comedian's request."

Charlie shoved in the cassette, and the Rolling Stones blared out "I Can't Get No Satisfaction." He flipped off the sound and swung around to face Stewart.

"So now how much trouble are we in with this one?"

"I'm not in any." Stewart grinned. "You're the one that's not going to get laid for a month in front of the whole city."

"Oh, big deal." Charlie stood up and stretched. "Lots of people go without for months, years, a lifetime. Priests do it."

"Yeah, but you're not a priest." Stewart turned to go. "Listen, if you need anybody to meet your emotional needs, don't come to me. I don't do that wimpy stuff."

"Thanks, Stewart," Charlie said. "I knew you'd be there for me."

ALLIE HAD HIS SHEETS and pillowcases on the couch for him when he got home.

"Here's another nice mess you've gotten us into, Ollie," she said, and he said, "Me? Wait a minute," but she'd already slammed her bedroom door behind her.

He sighed and stripped down to his shorts, too tired to argue. At least from now on he'd be getting some sleep. There was an improvement. Of course, if he had to choose between cataclysmic, head-banging sex and sleep, he'd choose the sex, but since the choice was now moot, he could see the bright side.

An hour later, he couldn't see the bright side.

He was so tired, he was punch-drunk, but he couldn't get to sleep. He tossed on the couch, tried sleeping sitting up, stretched out and took deep breaths, counted sheep, goats and German shepherds, and finally, as the numbers on the digital clock rolled around to 3:30, he gave up.

He picked up his pillow and went in to Allie.

She stirred when he threw his pillow on the bed, mumbled something and then fell back asleep.

"Glad to see you missed me," he told her body and then climbed in beside her, rolling so his back was to her and his rear end was warmly against hers.

He was asleep in less than a minute.

Beside him, Allie listened to him snore and gave herself the luxury of one wriggle against him. It was stupid to have missed just the weight of him in her bed, but she had. She smiled to herself and fell asleep for the first time that night.

WHEN HE WOKE UP the next morning, Charlie found he'd rolled over in the night and had wrapped himself around Allie, his leg slung over hers and his hand over her breast. It was definitely one of his favorite positions, and the temptation to throw the bet was overwhelming, especially when she stirred against him, stretching so that his lips were against her neck and her back slid against his front, and he went dizzy for a moment at the powdery, sleepy scent of her.

And then she woke up enough to mumble, "I knew you couldn't do it," and her voice was fat with sleep and satisfaction, and he remembered he'd have to concede in front of thousands of people, letting down not only his fans but his entire gender.

"Ha." He rolled out of bed. "No problem."

"Twenty-nine more days," Allie murmured to his retreating back. "And you're already groping me in the morning."

THE MORNING PAPER had a small notice at the bottom that due to misinformation, the picture in the previous day's paper was not of Charlie Tenniel, but was instead Charlie Tenniel's homosexual roommate.

"Now, this sort of makes me mad," Charlie said to Joe. "Is this their idea of a slur, to imply I'm gay? It's too subtle to tell."

"It's subtle enough to screw things up with David," Joe said. "He's already noticed that you and I are good friends. He just dealt with it because he thought you were sleeping with Allie."

"I am sleeping with Allie." Charlie put the paper down. "Which, by the way, I announced to Tuttle last night. You have no problems with David. Who's doing this newspaper stuff?"

"My guess? The mayor." Joe picked up his coffee cup. "The word is that the new city building is dead. You cost that man a lot of money. And then there's Roger Preston who is pretty sure to be indicted on price-fixing." He frowned. "You really did tell the world you were sleeping with Allie? That's not like you."

"It slipped." Charlie stared down at the paper. The mayor and Roger Preston were good guesses, but there were also these drug rumors about the station he kept tripping over. Anyone who wanted him fired would figure that bad publicity would make Bill get rid of him. Maybe he had another enemy. "Suppose it wasn't the mayor or Preston. Suppose it was somebody else who was mad at me. Who else would have this kind of clout?"

"I don't know." Joe stood up and carried his coffee cup to the sink. "I should think the mayor and Preston would be enough for anybody. Why did you tell the world about Allie?"

Charlie groaned, remembering. "We have a bet. We're going to be celibate for a month and see who gives in first."

Joe snorted with laughter. "That should be a close call. Whatever possessed you to do something like that?"

"Allie," Charlie said gloomily. "Ever since I met her, I've been doing one dumb thing after another."

"A smart man would leave her alone," Joe pointed out.

"Well, that's what I'm going to be doing for the next month," Charlie said.

Then Allie shuffled out, her hair all tousled. "You know, it took me forever to fall asleep last night. This is all your fault."

Charlie winced. "Thanks, I needed that." He tossed the paper to her and stood up to go. "Here. Read this. Things just keep getting better and better for us."

CHARLIE WAS SLIGHTLY more cheerful when he went on the air that night. "And a great big thank-you to all of you folks who called in last night to say that my significant other has rocks in her head and that men are much stronger than women. And for the other half of you who supported Allie, hey, just wait.

"I'd also like to thank Allie for wearing the most disgusting bathrobe she could find this morning and for not combing her hair before breakfast. Say what you will about the little lady, she plays fair. And now, just for Allie, here's the Pointer Sisters."

He shoved the slide up and "Slow Hand" began.

Harry ambled in on his way home. "You might want to keep your joviality level down a little," he said, passing over Charlie's coffee. "That way, when you get crazy later in the month, the change won't be so noticeable."

"So, you're on Allie's side," Charlie said. "I'm hurt."

"In general, no," Harry said. "In this case, yes. You'll never make it."

"Hey," Charlie said. "Look at me. Do I look tense?"

"It's only been forty-eight hours," Harry said. "Give it some time. I got a lot of money on Allie, but I'm not worried."

Charlie jerked his head up. "Money? They're making book on this in the station?"

"The hell with the station. They're making book on it on the street."

"Oh, great." Charlie slumped back into his chair. "So how am I doing?"

Harry shook his head. "You're a very long shot, my friend. If she gives in first, there are going to be some very rich gamblers in this city."

"What if we both make it to the thirty-first?"

"Practically no one's taking that one."

"A month is not that long," Charlie said.

Harry turned to go, grinning. "Tell me that on the thirtieth." He stopped at the door. "I probably shouldn't do this, since it might screw up my bet, but I'm pretty sure you're going to crack. So, if it gets bad, living with her, you can come stay at my place. I've got lots of room."

"This is going to be no problem," Charlie assured him.

"Yeah, well, the offer stands," Harry said.

Charlie watched Harry stop to talk to Allie on the way out. She grinned up at Harry and pushed her glasses back up the bridge of her nose, and Charlie felt the old warmth that he always felt when she was around. It wasn't as if he wasn't going to see her. It was just sex. He had things to investigate, anyway. He really didn't have time for her. No problem.

"No problem at all," Charlie said to the empty booth.

AFTER THE SHOW, Charlie went home and tried the couch again, lasting until four-thirty this time before he climbed into bed with Allie again, closing his eyes as he felt her body warm and soft next to his. And waking up with her was doubly painful the next morning when she stirred next to him, and he felt dizzy even though he was lying down.

You've got to get out of here, he told himself as he headed to the shower. Dieters did not live at the Sara Lee factory. He picked up the phone and dialed Harry.

HARRY LIVED in a split-level in a housing development full of tricycles and swing sets. Charlie dropped his duffel in the living room and looked around at the chintz furniture and flower paintings.

"You know," he told Harry. "This is not how I pictured you living. Flowered couches?"

"Sheila picked them out," Harry said. "Want a beer?"

"Always." Charlie followed him out to the kitchen. "Who's Sheila?"

"My wife."

Harry opened the refrigerator, and Charlie saw a twelve-pack, cheese spread and a piece of pizza. He spared one longing thought for the glory of Joe's refrigerator, and then took the beer Harry handed him. "You have a wife?"

"Well, I used to. I came home one day and found a note that she'd gone to her mother's."

"Oh." Charlie followed him back into the spotless living room. "Well, she must stop by to clean. The place looks great."

Harry stretched out in the recliner. "That's Mrs. Squibb. Comes by twice a week. Don't leave anything lying around. She throws it out."

"Oh," Charlie said again. "So your wife is...uh..."

"Gone," Harry said. "I waited a couple of weeks and called her, and she said, 'See, Harry, this is just what I meant. You don't even notice me.' And I told her I noticed her. I was just busy. The divorce papers came the next week." Harry shook his head. "I still think it was a mistake. And who knows, she might be back."

"Well, sure," Charlie said, still lost. "How long has she been gone?"

Harry frowned, counting back. "Uh, thirteen years."

Charlie stared at him for a minute, trying to decide if he was kidding or not. With Harry, it was hard to tell. "No offense, Harry, but if I were you, I'd make a contingency plan."

"I'm thinking about it." Harry stretched out in his chair, obviously a happy man. "What about you and Allie?"

"What about us?" Charlie said guardedly.

"You still leaving in November?"

"Yep." Charlie drank his beer. "What do you do for dinner around here?"

"Order out," Harry said. "You want pizza, burgers, or Chinese?"

"Not Chinese," Charlie said. "Anything but Chinese."

CHARLIE DECIDED that the only way to stay sane was to stay away from Allie. The bet was an excellent idea since he was leaving in November, anyway, so all he had to do was avoid her for the rest of the month, kiss her goodbye on November first, and leave her with great memories. At least he hoped her memories were great.

His were phenomenal.

But that way lay madness, so he deliberately shut her out of his mind and avoided her for the rest of the week, waving to her from the booth and making sure any conferences they had were in public. In his free time, he tried to track down the drug rumor and find out who'd sabotaged his tapes. The favorite for the last one was Mark, and Charlie would have loved to pin the drug charge on him, too—those were awfully expensive suits he was wearing on a DJ's salary—but he couldn't see Mark as the brains of a drug ring. Actually, he couldn't see Mark as the brains of a Jell-O ring.

When Saturday came, he took a day off from detecting and went fishing with Harry at Grady's.

It was really too late in the year to fish, but as Harry pointed out, catching fish wasn't that important, anyway. Grady's was just a good place to unwind. They had to take their own beer because Grady's place was nonalcoholic, but other than that, it was a bachelor's paradise.

Grady lived outside Tuttle on several acres of deliberate wilderness in a geodesic dome he'd built himself. "My father thought I was nuts," Grady told Charlie as he showed him around. "Now I think he kind of likes it. My mom thinks it's great." The interior was all natural wood and windows, and aside from a disquieting lack of corners, it was a very comfortable place, full of old, mismatched furniture and state-of-the-art computer and stereo equipment.

"Great setup," Charlie said, looking it over.

"My mom bought that stuff for me," Grady said. "She says I'm tough to buy for, so if I want something, she goes all out." He gazed around his dome lovingly. "It's a great place." Then he smiled at Charlie. "Come out anytime. Don't wait for Harry to bring you."

"Thanks," Charlie said, but then he stopped, distracted by what he saw out the window. Hidden from the driveway by the dome and a stand of trees but in clear view from Grady's back windows, was the biggest field of marijuana Charlie had ever seen. "Nice crop," he told Grady.

Grady shrugged. "Personal use."

You must have a habit the size of Texas, Charlie thought. If somebody was dealing drugs at the station, Grady had just moved up to the number-one suspect. But if he was doing it, what was he doing with the money? Aside from his stereo and computer, his place was furnished with hand-me-downs and Grady himself dressed like a bag lady. Charlie knew he was going to have to investigate it, but he hated the idea that it might be Grady. Grady was a truly nice guy.

But nice guy or not, if he was the problem, he was going down for it. That was what Charlie had come for. He spared a thought for Bill who would not be happy if his only son was busted, and then shoved the thought aside. He really didn't believe Grady was building a drug empire in Tuttle. Grady didn't believe in capitalism. He wasn't even sure Grady believed in money.

Harry came in the back door with two poles. "You ready?"

"Yep," Charlie said. "Lead me to them."

"Too bad Allie couldn't be here," Grady said. "She loves to fish."

"Yeah," Charlie said, shoving her firmly from his mind. "Too bad."

AFTER A WEEK at Harry's, Charlie was ready to crawl back to Allie on his hands and knees. And he'd have done it, too, if it had only been his honor at stake.

But the honor of all mankind?

Still, watching her sit outside the booth was torture. She had her hair yanked back in a ponytail, which made her face more moonlike than usual, and there were bags under her eyes as if she hadn't been sleeping, and she wasn't wearing any makeup for some reason, and he'd never wanted a woman more in his life. If he could have, he'd have taken her there on the production desk.

He closed his eyes at the thought of Allie round and warm, moving under him, his mouth on hers capturing her moans. Or Allie on top of him, her tongue caught between her teeth as she bore down on him, and his hand on the back of her neck bringing her mouth down to his. Or Allie sitting on the edge of the desk, her legs wrapped around him, her back arching her hips into him. Or—

The silence in his ears brought him back with a start, and he said something inane into the mike and punched in the next three songs. Then he took off his headphones and went out to see her.

"You look tired." He sat on the edge of the desk next to her chair, using every ounce of self-control he had not to touch her. "You okay?"

"Yeah." She leaned back in her chair and stretched as if her muscles ached, and he watched her breasts move under her sweater and restrained himself from leaping on her but not from imagining leaping on her. "I miss you," she said, and he snapped back to attention. "I miss you in my bed."

"I miss you, too," he told her when he had his breath back. "But I can't climb in your bed and just sleep with you. It drives me crazy standing up fully clothed in public with you."

"Really?" Her face folded into a smile, and he watched the lines there and reminded himself not to trace them with his finger. "That's nice," she said. "Thank you."

"You're welcome." The line of her cheek was so smooth. His hand went out, independent of his brain, and cupped her cheek, and she leaned into his palm, and he found himself moving toward her mouth, the lust to taste her as inescapable as gravity.

And then his lips were on hers, and her mouth was warm and hot and sweet, and her lower lip slid against his tongue, and his entire being was in his mouth, finding her, at last.

ALLIE SAT stunned as he kissed her, her head heavy on her neck, falling helplessly into him as his mouth moved on hers. His hand was gentle on her cheek, and he breathed into her mouth and she lived in his heat, moving her lips against his, letting the dizziness take her like a drug. And then he touched her lips with his tongue, and the air left her lungs as she sighed with surrender, only to gasp when he licked farther into her mouth, tangling with her tongue. She felt his kiss everywhere, in her breasts and her stomach and hotly between her legs, and she pressed her mouth back against his, spurred by the moan he made as she invaded his mouth.

Then he pulled back, his breath coming heavily, and said, "I can't stand this." He kissed her hard once, quickly, and moved away from her, back into the booth, while she leaned on the desk and tried to breathe.

"I'm sorry," he said over the mike when the door was closed behind him. "I didn't mean to. I just couldn't—"

"I'm not sorry," she told him. "But, oh, God, Charlie—"

"Go home," he said, and there was an edge in his voice. "Go home. The rest is just music. I can't talk to you anymore tonight. I can't talk to anybody. Go home."

AFTER A WEEK AND A HALF of sleeping without Charlie, Allie was ready to surrender. It wasn't the sex she missed so much, although she missed that so much she ached with it, it was Charlie. Charlie warm and laughing and safe and just there. She couldn't even face Chinese food anymore without getting turned on and feeling lonely.

They'd fought amiably over the end of *Casablanca* for that night's program, and then Allie left the booth, and Charlie put "River of Dreams" on and she watched as he cuddled Sam to his chest and began to feed him. Sam was growing like a horse, getting into everything, and she'd caught Charlie lecturing him earlier about chewing on electrical cords. They'd looked so funny, the tiny puppy looking up earnestly from Charlie's big hand, and Charlie scowling down at Sam, reasoning with him about electrocution, that she had to laugh. Charlie had looked up and grinned at her, and his grin hit her like a punch to the stomach.

She missed him.

This was a bad emotion, so she squelched it and went back to work, looking up again only when Charlie introduced a play for insomniacs. She could see Sam scampering over the console and Charlie reaching for him, tucking the squirming puppy under his chin while he punched up the next song. Then the Disney lullaby "Baby Mine" came up and he began to rock and pat Sam until the puppy curled up on his chest and went to sleep.

Watching a man pat a puppy was no reason to fall in love.

But she did, anyway, much against her better judgment and her will and her common sense. *Not this*, she thought. *Not him*. But there it was.

The phone rang and she grabbed it, grateful for anything that distracted her from this new disaster. She didn't want to be in love with anybody, especially not with Charlie I'm-Leaving-In-November Tenniel, especially not like this.

"Charlie All Night," she said into the receiver, and the caller said, "Yeah, let me talk to Charlie. I'm Doug."

The song ended and Allie said, "You have a caller. It's Doug, on one," and punched it in.

Charlie shifted Sam to his shoulder and spoke into the microphone. "Hey, Doug, what's up?"

"Well, that's what I was going to ask you. We were kind of wondering here why you keep playing 'River of Dreams' so much, and now a lullaby? We'd heard your station was wired, but this is weird."

She saw Charlie sit up. "Wired?"

"Well, you know. What gives? You a Billy Joel freak?"

Charlie relaxed a little. "Not me. We've got a puppy here at the station who wasn't doing too well at eating until we put on 'River of Dreams.' He really likes the rhythm. He's doing pretty good now, but we still play it once a night so he feels at home."

"You're kidding. You got a dog there?"

Allie watched Charlie look down at Samson and grin. "Well, you could stretch it and call Sam a dog, I guess. He's more like a Twinkie with paws and an appetite. And he was tearing up the booth a minute ago, so I put the lullaby on. Knocked him right out."

"Try 'Sweet Baby James,' man," Doug said. "My kid goes right to sleep when we play that."

"Great idea." Charlie moved Sam farther up on his shoulder and patted him as he stirred. "Maybe we should play a lullaby every night about this time. Put any kid who's fighting it to sleep."

Charlie talked on with Doug about rock lullabies, and Allie watched him, hopeless with love, until a nasty thought intruded.

He'd just announced the station had a dog to the listening public.

Bill didn't know the station had a dog. Beattie didn't even know.

They were in for another meeting.

And she couldn't even go home and crawl into bed with Charlie and talk about it.

Charlie punched up a song and continued to talk to Doug off the air, and Allie took her glasses off and put her head down on her desk and tried to figure out how her life had gotten so screwed up when she'd been doing all the right things.

BILL TRIED to throw his usual fit about Sam, but Charlie knocked him off-balance by bringing the puppy to the meeting.

"Good little dog," Bill said gruffly when he met Sam. "Probably good publicity. What the hell, let him stay."

"How did you know he'd say that?" Allie asked him when they'd escaped unscathed.

"Grady tipped me off," he told her. "Evidently, Bill's a sucker for dogs. Grady told me as long as Sam was in the room, Bill would fold."

"Well, good for Grady," Allie said.

Charlie lifted Sam up in front of his face and said, "You're in, kid, don't screw up," and when Sam licked Charlie's nose, he laughed. He laughed a lot more when Sam became the new Flavor of the Week after his picture showed up in the paper, and the local animal shelter called and asked to begin a This-Dog-Needs-A-Home segment the next week on Charlie's show.

They did still have a few problems. Somebody was still sabotaging the show, one night making crank calls that tied up the phone lines, the next swiping the ad tapes for the night. Charlie coped with all of it and avoided Allie like the plague, missing her so much that he couldn't sleep at night, telling himself that once November came and he was out of town, she'd just be a pleasant memory.

He kept telling himself that, but he didn't believe it. And it was getting harder and harder to stay away from her.

Charlie walked into the booth on Friday night, two days after he'd blown Sam's cover, grouchy because he was in a booth and Allie was ten feet away on the other side of a glass wall wearing a pink sweater that made him crazy.

Once inside the booth, though, he stopped in his tracks. "What is that god-awful smell?"

"Well." Harry leaned back in his chair. "It seems Mark got a dog."

"What?"

"A dog," Harry said. "At the pound. A Doberman-mix puppy. A man's dog. Called him King."

Charlie sat down on the edge of the console. "I don't believe this."

"And he brought King into the booth with him this morning so he could broadcast with him. Like we do with Samson. And after three hours, King scratched at the door to be let out."

Charlie snorted. "King obviously has a lot of stamina. I'd have been clawing at the door a lot sooner if I was trapped in a booth with Mark."

"But Mark ignored him, so King...uh, pooped."

Charlie grinned. "And then?"

"Mark yelled at him and scared him." Harry fought back a grin. "So King pooped again."

Charlie's grin widened. "Mark is an idiot."

"So then Mark waved the script at him, and King—"

"Pooped again." Charlie started to laugh.

"Then Marcia came in and threw a fit because of all the poop in the booth and because Mark was mistreating a puppy. She gave him ten minutes to get the booth clean, and she took the dog away from him."

Charlie looked alarmed. "Not back to the pound?"

Harry shook his head. "Nah. She said she needed a watchdog.

She took the dog outside and calmed it down, and then brought it back inside with her until her show was done."

"Good for Marcia. Although I can't picture her with a dog named King."

"Dorothy," Harry said. "The dog's name is now Dorothy. Mark missed a few details, as usual."

"You're kidding." Charlie closed his eyes. "What a dweeb. So then he cleaned up the booth—"

Harry snorted. "Fat chance. He made Lisa do it."

"Oh, great." Charlie shook his head. "Wait'll I tell Allie. She's not going to believe this."

"And then Lisa sprayed the place with that stinking pine disinfectant…"

Charlie nodded. "Which explains why this place smells like—"

"—somebody pooped a pine tree," Harry finished.

"Sounds like a good time to do a remote," Charlie said.

"I've been spending a lot of time out of here," Harry said. "Thank God I don't have a date tonight. This would not be an easy smell to explain."

"Pooped Pine, the cologne of Kings," Charlie said and they both started to laugh.

Allie came into the booth, and they stopped. "What's so funny?" she asked them. "And what is that horrible smell?"

Harry and Charlie looked at each other for a moment and then they both broke up again.

THE ONLY PROBLEM was that since the booth reeked, Charlie had to spend most of his time out of it. With Allie. He was supposed to be talking about the ads for the rest of the show, but Allie was wearing a silky pink sweater, and her curves were right there in front of him. She was saying something, but he couldn't hear because of the rushing in his ears.

He had to touch her. Touching was not sex. Touching was just touching. "What we need here is a definition of sex," Charlie said. "The bet said no sex. It didn't say no kissing." He took a deep breath. "I want to touch you."

Allie flushed pink and Charlie felt dizzy. Usually when she

blushed like that, it was because he was moving his hands on her. He thought of the nights he'd had with her the week before and thrown away, not memorizing every second of what it was like to touch her. How he hadn't concentrated on the feel of his tongue against her skin, the slide of her body against his as she arched against him, the heat and the wet and the—

"Oh, God," he said. "I really need to touch you."

Eight

Allie sat across from him and tried to control her breathing. *I really need to touch you.* He was making her insane over this stupid bet. If he wanted her, all he had to do was say, "You win."

Of course, all she had to do was say, "You win," and she could have him back. She could slide her hands down his back, bite into the muscle on his shoulder, lick her way into his mouth, arch her aching body into his hardness, and dear God, find some surcease for this endless need that was driving her crazy. She bit her lip to keep from saying it out loud.

And if she did that, he'd touch her like only Charlie could touch her, his hands on her breasts, hot and teasing, his mouth, moving lower...

She drew a breath, suddenly light-headed from not breathing before, suddenly wanting his mouth more than anything in the world. Her breasts felt hot and tight and made her crave his touch even more, and she moved her hands to press against them, trying to ease the itch and the throbbing there.

And Charlie said, "Don't do that, please don't do that," and she said, "You do it. I can't stand it anymore."

He got up slowly and came to her, and she stood and put her head on his shoulder. He finally touched her, smoothly his palms lightly over her breasts at first, then pressing against her, and then finally lowering his head to bite her gently through her sweater, and that's when she dug her fingers into his shoulders and cried out.

He kissed her then, licking into her mouth, and the relief was like drowning. She arched against him, feeling how hard he was against her stomach, and his hands pressed her breasts in exquisite relief while every cell in her body throbbed for him. She laced her fingers in his hair and pulled his mouth harder against hers, trying to drink him in, biting his lip, and his leg went between hers as he bent her back against the production table, moving against her, while she wrapped herself around him as tightly as she could.

He was heavy on top of her, wonderfully heavy, and she stretched up to him, trying to meld with him, using his weight to satiate her need to have him inside her. His lips were on her throat as his hands pulled her sweater down off her shoulders, and his tongue licked deep into her cleavage. She scraped her nails down his back and throbbed against him. He pulled her bra off her breast, and his mouth found her, hot and wet, and he sucked hard, and she cried out and tightened against him, blind with need. He shoved her skirt up and moved his hand between her legs, pressing against the nylon there, his fingers sliding under the elastic.

"Wait," she breathed. "You, too."

And he said, "No, this is just for you."

She moved away from his hand. "No." She pulled his head up to look into his eyes, and they both shook with passion. "No. Not unless it's for both of us. It has to be both of us."

"It is," he told her. "I love watching you come." His eyes were hot, and she wanted to drink them in with the rest of him and make them part of her, but she wanted him with her, too. They were in this together. They were in everything together.

"No." Allie drew a long, shuddering breath. "No. I want you so much I'm dying from it. But that's just sex. No. Both of us or nothing."

Charlie closed his eyes, and she slid out from under him, memorizing the feel of him as she did.

Charlie leaned on the table, gripping the edge, his biceps taut from tension. "We could end this damn bet by mutual consent. We could both give in."

Allie leaned back against the table, getting her breath under control while she tried to figure out why that was such a bad idea. It should have been a good idea. "Is that what you want?"

"It should be what I want." Charlie stood up and tipped his head back, staring at the ceiling instead of her. "I don't know why I'm so sold on this damn bet. It's making me insane."

"It's making us different," Allie said, and she knew that was why she'd pulled away. In the beginning, she and Charlie had been about sex. Now they were about something else. She knew it was love, but he was still getting there. So she'd give him time. "We're different now. It's just one more week."

Charlie met her eyes for an instant, and then turned and walked back to the booth.

Allie felt light-headed. Probably from not breathing, she decided and consciously filled her lungs with air. She was dying from not having him, but she didn't want him yet. She wanted him more than anything.

But not yet. Not until they both knew it was more than sex.

THREE WEEKS into the bet, Allie was trying to look on the bright side and failing. It should have been easy to look on the bright side. Charlie All Night was a huge hit. The paper ran stories about Charlie and the city building, Charlie and the FoodStop indictment, Charlie and Sam. Pictures of Charlie and Sam were particularly popular, and people had donated so much dog formula and food and puppy toys to the station that they were supplying the local animal-rescue groups daily. Even the sabotage was helping; when the ad tapes disappeared from the booth one night, Charlie had been forced to fake it. His ad-libs about how great McCarthy's cashew chicken was at two o'clock in the morning, how much Sam loved the formula he'd gotten from Paula's Pet Emporium, and how Harry swore by Gleason's Auto Parts, had started a trend. Now all the advertisers wanted Charlie ad-libbing ads. He was a radio natural.

And she was going crazy. For the first time in her adult life, her first thoughts on waking weren't about the radio station. They were about Charlie. She'd gotten what she wanted: they talked all the time now. About radio, about food, about politics, about books, about sports...they talked until she was ready to scream, "Shut up and kiss me!" And even if she did, he'd probably think it was a request and play Mary Chapin Carpenter. She was delighted her career was back in high gear, but she wanted Charlie back more.

She finally hit bottom one night after staring hopelessly at Charlie through the booth window for the entire show. She was a mess and she needed comfort, so she went home and knocked on Joe's door.

"Come in," he said, half-asleep, and she went in and sat on the side of his bed while he tried to focus on her.

"I know it's the middle of the night," she said. "I'm sorry."

"No problem." He yawned and moved over and she crawled in bed next to him, sinking down on his shoulder when he put his arm around her. "So what's up?"

"You were right," she said into his shoulder.

"I'm always right." He patted her. "Let me guess. This is about Charlie."

Allie nodded. "I'm in love with him. I really screwed up this time."

"Well, not necessarily." Joe shifted in the bed to make more room for her. "This could be a good thing. At least you've given up thinking a career is a life. And everybody should fall in love at least once in her life, so that's good, too."

"I was in love with Mark," Allie said miserably. "I served my time."

Joe scowled at her. "You were not in love with Mark. Mark was your career and you thought it would be efficient to have a relationship with him, too. That was your tidy streak talking." He stared off into space for a moment. "Now, Charlie is the worst possible match for you, so this must be love. Good for you, kid."

"Very funny." Allie wanted to stick out her chin and move away to show she wasn't kidding, but Joe's arm was too much of a comfort to lose. "What am I going to do?"

Joe shrugged. "Love him. What else can you do?"

Allie blinked, trying not to cry. "He's going to leave in November. Do you know how much that's going to hurt?"

"Do you have a choice? And anyway, it's not November yet. You've got some time. Things could change. As usual, you're focusing on the problem and not looking at the big picture."

"What big picture?" Allie slumped deeper into the bed. "There is no big picture. I love him and he's leaving in a week."

"You could leave with him, you know," Joe said, and Allie looked at him sharply. "Well, I'd miss you, but you'd write and come back to visit. It might not be a bad life, following Charlie around the country. You'd have a good time."

"And no career," Allie said stubbornly.

"It would be a choice," Joe said. "But at least it's a choice. And I think you're forgetting Charlie here, too."

Allie groaned. "Fat chance. He's all I think about anymore. I'm becoming *obsessed* with Charlie."

"Well, he's not exactly ignoring you." Allie blinked at him, and Joe went on. "I know he moved out, but that was the only sane thing he could do. He never takes his eyes off you when he's with you. He always knows exactly where you are. And..." Joe paused, and Allie waited hopefully for some killer point that would convince her falling in love with Charlie wasn't the dumbest thing she'd ever done in her life. "He's jealous as hell of Mark."

Allie slumped again. "Big deal. I want him to love me."

Joe rolled his eyes. "Well, Al, I'm pretty sure he does."

Allie sat up, "Then why doesn't he *say* so. Why doesn't he say, 'Allie, I love you and I'm not leaving you in November.' I'm not looking for a marriage proposal here. I'm just trying to get my option extended for another year."

Joe moved his arm away. "You know, if I didn't like you and Charlie so much, I'd enjoy watching the two of you be dumb about this. Allie, he's not going to tell you he loves you until he figures it out for himself."

Allie threw her hands up in exasperation. "Well, when's that going to be?"

"Hard telling," Joe said. "I like Charlie a lot, but he's not deep, and he really hates commitment. It may take him a while."

Allie flopped back onto the pillows. "Well, great. With my luck, he'll figure it out next spring when he's in Dubuque or Broken Arrow or someplace else I'm not."

"Then you make the first move. Tell him you love him. Tell him he loves you." Joe punched his pillow and slid back down into the bed. "Produce yourself a love affair."

"He would run like a rabbit." Allie sighed. "I'm sorry. You've got to get up and work in the morning. I shouldn't have bothered you." She started to climb out of bed.

"Don't be wimpy," Joe said from his pillow. "Of course you should have bothered me. You'll be okay. Charlie will get around to figuring out what he wants as soon as he finishes doing whatever it is he came to do."

Allie turned back to him. "What do you mean?"

Joe's voice was sleepy. "Well, he came here for something. What was it?"

Allie blinked at him. "To fill in for Waldo as a favor for Bill."

Joe yawned. "Then why is he asking so many questions?"

"Because..." Allie let her voice trail off. He *was* asking a lot of questions. She'd assumed it was for the show, but he didn't care about the show. Or did he? Maybe he was getting interested in radio. He was making sure nobody was sabotaging the show again. And he had her researching great topics for the show, like this drug legalization thing they were doing next week.

"Maybe he's starting to care about the show," she told Joe with hope in her voice.

Joe snored, and she gave up and went to bed, still miserably in love but vaguely comforted.

After all, November was still a week away.

"MARK TRIED to do a talk show with Lisa today," Harry told Charlie. "You've really got to start getting up earlier. You're missing some good stuff."

Charlie sat on the console. "Such as?"

"He decided they were going to discuss working relationships."

"Well, it's an okay topic," Charlie said.

"Yeah." Harry leaned back. "But Mark spent the whole time talking about Allie. Never let Lisa get a word in edgewise. She finally burst into tears and left the booth."

"We need to kick him," Charlie said. "I don't care how dumb he is, that was mean."

"Nah," Harry said. "He still doesn't know why she's upset. And she's staying with him. They deserve each other." He tilted the chair back to look up at Charlie. "I think he's planning on making his move on Allie again."

Charlie ignored the spurt of alarm he felt and shrugged. "She can take care of herself."

Harry shook his head. "Yeah, but you're not around to stick up for your interests much. You don't even see her outside of work."

"Come on," Charlie protested. "I see her five or six hours a day."

"At work," Harry said. "It sort of looks like, if you're not sleeping with her, why spend time with her?"

"Hey," Charlie said. "That's not—"

"That's what it looks like. And Mark has noticed. Probably mentioned it to Allie by now, too."

Allie came into the booth. "Here's the stuff you wanted," she told Charlie, handing him a stack of notes. "I got the—"

"You busy tomorrow night?" Charlie asked her.

"Uh, no." She blinked up at him.

"Let's get a video and some Chinese," he said. "Tell Joe."

"Joe's got a date. It'd be just us."

"Oh." Charlie shrugged. "Okay. Fine."

"Okay." Allie looked at him strangely again and left the booth.

"Good move," Harry told him.

"Right," Charlie said, but he thought, *Allie and me and Chinese food at her apartment. Oh, hell.*

HARRY CAME OUT of the booth, and Allie looked at him with suspicion. "What are you up to?"

"Me? Nothing." Harry grinned at her. "Have a good time tomorrow night."

"Did you put him up to that?"

"Nope. Thought of it on his own. 'Bout time, too, don't you think?"

Allie narrowed her eyes at him. "Harry, you wouldn't lie to me, would you?"

"Nope." Harry went off down the hall whistling.

Well, he was up to something. But she was going to see Charlie, outside the radio station, for an entire evening, so it really didn't matter.

For the first time in a long while, she began to look forward to the next day.

"YOU KNOW, Mark's up to something," Allie told Charlie during the news break.

"Oh, there's a surprise," Charlie said. "Of course he's up to something. He wants you back."

Allie blinked. "I don't think so. But I do think he's trying to ruin your show. I think he's the one—"

"Our show," Charlie corrected her. "It's our show. I know he's trying to ruin it. I found our missing promo tapes in his office. But he's also trying to get you back. I may have to hit him, after all."

"Why?" Allie looked at him in exasperation. "You're leaving next week. Why should you care?"

"Because I'd hate to think any woman could go from me to Mark," he said.

"Well, since you won't be here to watch, I don't see what difference it makes." Allie turned away from him in disgust. "You think I'm going to give up men just because you're leaving?"

Charlie watched through the booth windows as she stomped away. *Yeah,* he thought. *That's exactly what I want.* Then he picked up the headset and waited for the news to end while he mentally kicked himself for ever coming to Tuttle in the first place.

SATURDAY NIGHT, Charlie brought her *American Dreamer* because she'd said that was her favorite movie, and sat with her on the couch and laughed and felt better than he had since he'd moved out.

"I miss this." Charlie took her hand when the movie was over. "I miss watching videos and arguing with you over the Chinese food and waking up with you. I miss the physical stuff, too, but I miss this the most."

"I know." Allie tightened her hand on his, and he paid attention to the warmth of her grip and the softness of her skin pressed against his. "I want you here so I can tell you things, and so you can listen to Joe's jokes."

"Joe's jokes are the worst." Charlie grinned at her and watched her smile in response, watched the light in her eyes, and the way her cheeks bloomed with the smile, and the way her head tilted, just a little, toward him. "I miss Joe's jokes a lot."

"Mostly, I just miss having you here." She brushed her cheek against his shoulder, and he closed his eyes with pleasure. "You don't even have to watch the movie or listen to Joe's jokes. Just be here."

He opened his eyes then, and she was so right, so everything he wanted forever, and he wanted to say, "I love you, Allie," but it wasn't fair. He was leaving in a week. It wasn't fair.

It was true, but it wasn't fair.

Maybe Allie would like traveling. Maybe Allie would love him enough to leave with him in November.

"What's wrong?" she asked softly and he bent to hear her, and that brought him to her mouth and he kissed her, moving his lips gently against hers, feeling the surge in his throat and chest and groin, but feeling the swell in his heart more. Her hand came up to his cheek, and when the kiss was done she let her lips travel there and then kissed his eyelids and then his lips again, and he ached with love for her. "Why is it," he whispered against her cheek, "that we didn't start making love until we stopped sleeping together?"

She shook her head wordlessly and settled into his arms, and he held her and memorized the weight and the feel of her, and the scent of her hair, and soft rhythm of her heart against his, and he felt something break away inside him, the tension and the guardedness and everything that had kept him away from her.

A few minutes later, for the first time in almost three weeks, he fell dreamlessly asleep.

ON MONDAY, the *Tuttle Tribune* began a series on the history of the city building, killing forever any hopes the mayor might have had of building a new one, and making Charlie a household word once again.

"That's our boy," Joe said when he saw the first article, and Allie, remembering a warm, if platonic, weekend, said, "We can only hope."

Later that afternoon, Lisa came to see her. "It's awful, Allie," Lisa moaned to her in her office. "I can't do anything right. I hate it. No matter what I do, Mark thinks it isn't enough or it isn't done right or *something*."

"So quit." Allie stacked the notes she'd gathered for the drug legalization show and put them in a folder for Charlie who would actually read them on his own instead of insisting she explain them to him the way Mark had. Thank God, she wasn't stuck with Mark anymore. She felt positively sympathetic toward Lisa. "Leave him. You don't have to take that."

"But it's the *drive-time show*," Lisa wailed, and Allie was about to say, "So what?" when she remembered why that was important. At least, it had been important to her a month before. And if Lisa quit, Mark would offer her the producing spot again. He'd made that very clear. In fact, knowing Mark as she did, Allie had a sneaking suspicion he might be forcing Lisa to quit. Then Bill would ask her to step in to save the prime-time show.

She shook her head at the thought. Not in a million years. The hell with drive time. She was doing better in the middle of the night with the weirdos and Charlie, a redundant thought if there ever was one.

"The drive-time show isn't everything," she said to Lisa. "If you're this unhappy, leave. Ask Marcia to take you. She's not happy with her producer."

"And lose the drive-time show?" Lisa stood up. "Oh, no. I'm sticking it out." Lisa stomped out of the office, and Allie let her go. She had enough problems without counseling career-obsessed radio producers.

She had Charlie.

"YOU KNOW, I've been thinking," Harry said Tuesday afternoon in front of the TV. "You're still leaving in November, right?"

"Right," Charlie said with a lot more conviction than he felt.

"Well, then, I'm gonna make my move on Allie."

Charlie spilled his beer. "What?"

Harry held up his hand. "Not until you're gone, of course. Wouldn't dream of it. But once you're out of the picture...well, wouldn't you rather she was with me than with Mark?"

Charlie scowled at him. "That's Allie's business."

Harry nodded. "Exactly. So I thought I'd ask her to produce my show and then just see what developed. It's time I started thinking about getting married again. I've been thinking about it and you're right. I don't think Sheila's coming back."

Charlie took a deep breath. "Well, you never know—"

"Nope." Harry shook his head. "You were right. It's time I moved on with my life, got a contingency plan. I'd have never thought of it if it wasn't for you." He gave Charlie a serious nod. "Thanks, buddy."

"No problem," Charlie snarled and got up to get another beer, wondering why the hell he hadn't kept his mouth shut.

Back in the living room, Harry grinned and finished his beer.

WEDNESDAY MORNING, Allie met Joe in the kitchen for breakfast, stopping in her tracks when she saw the look on his face.

"This is bad," he said, and handed her the paper.

"Local DJ Former Drug Dealer," the headline flared at her. "Charlie 'Ten' Tenniel arrested for drug trafficking in Lawrenceville, disappears for months before arriving in Tuttle as the WBBB wonder boy. Do we want this element in our town?"

Allie looked up at Joe and shook her head. "No. Charlie did not deal drugs. He lived with us. He doesn't even smoke. His limit is two beers. He's not a druggie."

Joe sat down. "Look, they've screwed up before, but this time they have what looks like evidence. It was in the Lawrenceville paper. They have quotes from Lawrenceville reporters. There's some truth somewhere."

"Charlie doesn't do drugs," Allie said firmly. "I don't care what the paper says."

"All right." Joe sat back. "I've got to admit, that's my gut reaction, too. But…"

Allie met his eyes. "But nothing. He's innocent."

"But I wish you weren't so involved with him," Joe finished. "I don't want you hurt. You're unhappy enough because he's leaving. I don't want you to feel cheated, too."

"He's innocent." Allie frowned. "I know he's innocent."

CHARLIE MET HER in her office that afternoon. "I suppose you've seen the paper," he said, and she knew he was watching for her reaction.

"It's not you." She lifted her chin. "I don't know what's going on, but it's not you."

He leaned in the doorway. "There's a lot of evidence in that article, Allie. How can you be sure?"

"I know you." She snapped it out with more force than she'd meant to. "You're not that way. You wouldn't do that."

Charlie closed his eyes. "I do not deserve you, but I'm damn grateful just the same."

"Sure you deserve me," Allie said. "Anything you want to tell me before I start calling everybody I know in journalism to track this down?"

"No," Charlie said. "Don't call anyone. Just let this be."

Allie gawked at him. "Are you nuts? We have to stop this. We have to—"

"No," Charlie said. "I don't want it stopped."

Allie swallowed and tried again. "Charlie, this will be murder on the show. Drugs are not classy in Tuttle. This will kill us."

He winced. "I hadn't thought of that. I'm sorry, Al, I really am, but don't stop the story. Don't track it down. Let it play. It's important to me."

"Why?" The flatness of the question broke the mood they'd shared.

"You'll have to trust me on this," he told her, and her temper broke.

"I have to trust you that you're not a dealer, and I do," she said to him. "But you can't trust me with the truth."

"It's not my secret," Charlie said, and the only thing that kept her from screaming at him was how miserable he looked. "I'll tell you as soon as it's over, but it's not my secret."

"So I'm supposed to just sit here and let that damn article ruin us both while you keep somebody else's secret." Allie started to shake with rage and frustration. "What the hell is going on here?"

Charlie rubbed his hand over the back of his head. "Don't worry about it. This will be over soon. You'll be fine, I swear."

"Right," she snapped. "I'll be fine because I'll be breaking in a new guy in a week, and you'll be fine because you're leaving this mess behind you, right? We'll all be fine. Great."

"Allie," Charlie began, and she cut him off.

"Go away. Just go away. I don't want to talk about this anymore. Just leave."

"Allie, this is important." She ignored him, but he went on, anyway. "I want us to do the show about legalizing drugs tonight. I want you to be against it so I can argue for it."

She gaped at him. "Have you lost your mind? After this article…" Her voice trailed off. "You want people to think this is true." She sat back in her chair. *"Why?"*

"Just for a little while," he told her. "I'm almost there. This article could do it for me."

"Almost *where?*" Allie's annoyance blanked everything out. "You can't possibly think I'm going to help you ruin this show and my own reputation without some explanation here. Either tell me what's going on, or you're on your own tonight."

Charlie started to say something, and then he sighed, and said, "All right, that's fair, I'll do it myself," and left the office.

Allie put her head down on the desk. The show was ruined, Charlie didn't trust her, and he was still leaving in November.

And she couldn't think of a damn thing to do about any of it except go home and cry in Joe's arms.

THE NEXT MONDAY—after three polite work nights and one miserably lonely weekend, after the calls to the show had dropped off to hecklers who wanted to score off Charlie's arrest record and outraged citizens who wanted him off the air; after Charlie had disappeared for long stretches of time and the police had dropped by to see him—things hit bottom.

Charlie's wife showed up.

She was a little thing, dark and sort of wet with tears, and she was about seven or eight months' pregnant. Karen called Allie to the desk and pointed to her and said, "You're not going to like this. She's looking for Ten Tenniel. She says she's married to him."

Not possible, Allie told herself, but the list of possibilities for Charlie had been growing since he'd refused to defend himself on the drug charge. She still believed in him, but it was harder.

She went toward the girl. "Hello, I'm Alice McGuffey, Mr. Tenniel's producer and—"

"Where is he?" The girl stood up and looked at her defiantly. "He's my husband, and I want to see him."

"He's not here right now, but he should be in any time," Allie said. "Would you like to wait in my office?" She looked around to see Stewart and Lisa listening in from the hallway. "It's more private there."

"Where is he?" the girl demanded again, and then with his usual impeccable timing, Charlie came through the doors and stopped when he saw her. "Miranda?"

"Charlie?" She seemed as amazed as he was.

"Don't say anything," Charlie told her, taking her arm. "We can talk out here."

"Charlie?" Allie said, outraged.

Charlie shoved Miranda out into the hall and pointed at Allie. "You stay here and stop thinking dumb thoughts. You know me better than this. I'll be back as soon as I can."

"Wait a minute!" Allie said, incensed, but he was shoving Miranda into an elevator by then and she was left with her own murderous thoughts and Karen and Stewart and Lisa staring at her with sympathy and avid curiosity.

This time she was going to kill him.

But first she was going to find out what the hell was going on.

HE CAME INTO her office half an hour before the show and caught her dialing the phone.

"I know." He held up his hand to stop her from talking. "I'm a creep for leaving you like that. I had to call my dad and put Miranda on a bus home before I could explain. I know you're mad at me and I deserve it, but just let me explain."

"Oh, *now* you're going to explain." Allie slapped the phone down. "Well, that's just great."

"Allie, I'm not—"

"Ten Tenniel. I know. She's your brother's wife, right?"

Charlie sat down. "Well, sort of. They're not actually married. How did you figure it out?"

Allie shook her head, disgusted with him. "It wasn't hard once I woke up. You wouldn't let us call you Ten and that's what the Lawrenceville station was famous for. And you may be a natural on radio, but Harry was right. You didn't have any idea what you were doing that first night. So you came here pretending to be your brother, and since Bill knows your family, he knows that, too. So whatever secret you're keeping is Bill's, and this whole program thing was just a blind, and I've been killing myself to make you a success for nothing."

"Well, I told you not to do it," Charlie pointed out mildly. "Which part are you the most mad about?"

"That you didn't trust me," Allie said, her anger evaporating from the hurt. "You didn't trust me at all."

"It wasn't that." Charlie put his head in his hands. "I don't know how the hell this got so complicated. I trusted you. I knew it wasn't you from the beginning. But you go charging in on everything you do, and that was the wrong way to do this."

Allie leaned forward. "To do what? What do you mean it wasn't me?"

Charlie met her eyes. "Somebody's running drugs from the station. Bill got an anonymous letter and used it as an excuse to get me down here as a favor to my dad. He wanted to know about the letter because he thought it was a smear, and my dad wanted me to get a real job, so they cooked it up between them. And I bought it, and I've been trying to find a link between the mayor or Roger Preston or Mark and drugs. Nothing. So for the past week I've been letting the drug story slide, running around pretending to be a dealer, trying to figure things out. And last night, going over your drug legalization notes, I finally did."

"Who is it?" Allie asked when she found her voice. "I can't believe it. Who's dealing?"

"Grady," Charlie said. "It has to be Grady."

Nine

━►━◄━

"Are you out of your mind?" Allie looked at him in horror. "Grady is the last person to push drugs. He doesn't care about money. He—"

"He cares about his mother," Charlie said. "And Mrs. Winthrop and Mrs. Wexman and all the rest."

Allie shook her head. "I don't get it."

"I didn't get it either at first." Charlie looked so miserable she wanted to go to him, but not until he stopped saying stupid things about Grady. "Grady grows it behind his dome, but that wasn't enough because I knew Grady wouldn't deal drugs for money. But the fraternity kids said we were giving it away, and then I read your notes on drug legalization and the stuff you found on cancer patients. That's when it all fell into place."

Allie closed her eyes. "I remember. Pot helps people handle chemo." Then she had a thought and her eyes flew open again. "Grady gave Beattie pot?"

Charlie nodded. "He'd do anything to help her. And if Beattie knew it helped her, she'd insist on sharing it with others. They've been providing pot for the town's cancer patients. That's why Mrs. Winthrop's grandson got nasty with her. He wanted her stash."

"Oh, God." Allie put her head in her hands. "And that's why people bring Grady cookies and things. They're trying to say thank you." She tilted her head back and thought for a moment. "Well, okay. Now we know. All we have to do is keep out mouths shut about it—"

"No," Charlie said. "We can't. This is illegal."

Allie gaped at him. "You can't possibly be thinking of turning Grady in?"

He sighed. "You're not listening. I'm going to tell Grady I know, and he's going to turn himself in. It's illegal, Al. And he's running out of time. That little Winthrop brat sent the letter to Bill. Everybody at the college knows somebody here is dealing. And I've been asking questions. There was that newspaper piece about me being a pusher that made the police start watching me. They know who I've been talking to, and they know something's up. There's going to be hell to pay, and if Grady turns himself in, he's at least got that in his favor. It's too late for anything else."

"No." Allie came around the desk and headed for the door. "No. We can stop this. We can stonewall this. Grady is not going to jail."

Charlie caught her arm. "Don't say anything to anybody. Let me handle this."

"Like you've handled it so far?" Allie looked up at him, furious. "If you hadn't poked around, we'd be fine. Who is he hurting? He's helping people, and you're going to turn him in." Allie yanked her arm away from him. "This is the worst. You're just going to stand there and watch him go to prison."

"What do you want me to do?" Charlie said.

"You started this mess," she said. "You should fix it."

"I can't fix it. All I can do is see it through to the end."

Allie looked at him, uncomprehending. "I can't believe you're doing this. You're not even going to try to work something else out. You're just going to go ahead and do it your way."

"Allie—"

"Just like Bill," she said to him, knowing it would hurt him. "Just like your dad."

His mouth tightened, and then he left the office.

"Boy, I sure can pick them," she said to nobody in particular, and then devoted all her energy to not crying.

Mark stuck his head in the door. "Say, I just heard about Charlie's wife. That's a really bad break, Allie. Let me take you out to dinner." He smiled at her, looking as gorgeous as ever, and she wanted him dead, too.

"Get out of here," she snarled.

"Maybe tomorrow," he said and escaped out the door.

Allie went back to her chair and thought about tomorrow. She had to think of a plan. Soon.

CHARLIE WAITED until Grady came into the booth during the news at quarter to two before he said anything to him.

"You look like hell," Grady said when he saw him. "Take off, I'll take it from here."

"I can't." Charlie looked at him miserably. "I hate this. You have no idea how much I hate this."

Grady blinked at him. "What's wrong?"

Charlie sighed. "I know you give pot to cancer patients. In fact, a hell of a lot of Tuttle knows you give pot away, Grady. It's all over."

Grady pushed Sam's basket to one side and sat down on the counter. "Oh." Sam poked his head out, and Grady scratched him behind his ears. "Well, that depends. Are you going to turn me in?"

Charlie shook his head. "No, you're going to turn yourself in. That should work in your favor. With your dad's lawyers—"

"My dad will disown me," Grady said, but he didn't seem too upset at the thought. "What can I do to convince you this isn't the best way to do this?"

"Anything," Charlie said fervently. "You have no idea how much I want to be convinced. But this is going to blow any minute, Grady. Too many people know. You're a lot better off doing this yourself than waiting until they come for you."

Grady sat looking lost in thought for a moment. Then he met Charlie's eyes. "Can I have some time?"

"All you want," Charlie said. "But don't take too long. You'll lose the only advantage you have."

"How did you find out?" Grady asked him as he got up to go.

"The rumors. Your crop out in back. The chemo. The cookies and stuff. It finally all came together." Charlie shook his head. "I'm really sorry, Grady. I know you were doing it for a good reason."

"Which is why I don't want to stop." Grady sat down in the chair. "Let me think about this and I'll talk to you tomorrow."

"Great," Charlie said. "Something else to look forward to."

THE NEXT MORNING, Allie still hadn't thought of a plan even after talking the whole mess over with Joe.

"There's a mandatory prison sentence for possession," he told her. "And Bill isn't going to be much help once he finds out Grady's been getting his mother stoned."

"That's a stupid law," Allie said. "The stuff is medicinal, for heaven's sake."

Then Joe opened the paper, said, "Oh, hell," and handed it to her.

There was a picture of Charlie putting Miranda on the bus, captioned Local DJ Abandons Pregnant Wife. Allie stared at it grimly. She was furious with Charlie, but he didn't deserve this.

Then she had a new thought. How had the photographer known to be at the bus station? Somebody had tipped off the paper. Somebody at WBBB.

This one they couldn't blame on the mayor. She got dressed and went into the station early.

Allie was standing outside the booth when Mark came out at ten.

"Allie!" He all but ran over Lisa to get to her. "What a great surprise!"

"I decided to take you up on that lunch offer," Allie told him. "You free now?"

"We have a conference after every show," Lisa put in. "Sometimes they last a long time."

"Not today." Mark took Allie's arm. "We'll skip it today."

"But Mark," Lisa said.

"Forget it." Mark steered Allie toward the lobby. "This is just great. I've got a lot I want to tell you."

"Good," Allie said. "There's a lot I want to hear."

"It just hasn't been the same without you," Mark began when they were seated at the Settle Inn. "I've been—"

"You've been busy," Allie said. "That was you who played all those tricks on Charlie, wiping the tapes, stealing his promos, making the prank calls."

"Well..." Mark seemed at a loss. "I may have gone too far, but it was all—"

"And then you gave the story about Charlie's wife to the paper. That was a good one." Allie tried to keep her voice noncommittal.

He looked at her warily. "I might have mentioned it."

"Why?"

"Well, Lisa called me and told me about it, and I thought that the people of Tuttle should know what kind of guy he is." Mark shifted in his chair. "You know, leaving his wife pregnant and all. I thought you should know, too. He's not the kind of guy for you, Allie."

Allie fought down the urge to reach across the table and strangle him. "Oh? And what kind of guy is?"

Mark took a deep breath. "Well, me." He held up his hand to stop her protest. "I know I made a mistake when I broke up with you, but believe me, I know it now. I was stupid. You want me to come crawling back, I will. Whatever you say."

Allie shook her head at him in disgusted amazement. "And what about Lisa? She's been working her butt off for you."

"Lisa's a child." Mark settled back in his chair. "A lovely child, but still a child. The experience I've given her will look good on her résumé—"

"Oh, you want me back as a *producer*." Allie nodded. "I misunderstood."

"No, no! I want you back completely." Mark leaned forward. "I think we should get married."

"Married." Allie nodded. "Married. You're going to go back across the street and tell Lisa that you're dumping her as your producer and your girlfriend to marry me."

"Absolutely." Mark beamed at her. "I'm a big enough man to admit my mistakes."

"You're a dweeb." Allie stood up. "If you do anything else to sabotage Charlie's show, I will tell Bill and insist that he fire you. I mean it. Stay away from Charlie. And while you're at it, stay away from me."

"Allie!" Mark stood up to follow her.

"No." Allie put out her hand to stop him. "I can't believe you pulled this stuff just to save your career. What did you think you were doing?"

Mark blinked at her. "What you taught me to do. Make the show the best."

"I never taught you to sabotage other shows to do it," Allie said, appalled, but she knew he was right. The entire time she'd been with him, the show had been everything. She'd just forgotten to teach him morals before she'd left. "There's more to life than radio, Mark."

"Not to my life," he said, and she felt sorry for him because he was right again.

"Go make up with Lisa," she told him. "You're going to need her."

"HARRY TOLD ME you had lunch with Mark today," Charlie said when she walked into the booth at ten.

"Harry told you right." Allie handed him the notes and the promos.

"Have a good time?"

"He asked me to marry him." Allie turned and walked out of the booth to the production table.

"He *what?*" Charlie snapped over the headset.

"He offered me the producing slot, too," Allie said through her mike. "The news is almost over. Stand by."

"Screw the news," Charlie said. "Did you say yes?"

Allie glared at him. "What possible difference could it make to you since you're leaving tomorrow?"

"None," Charlie said. "Did you say yes?"

"No," Allie said. "I said no."

"Could we stop fighting and talk about this?" Charlie asked her once his heart was out of his throat.

"Why?" Allie looked at him miserably. "Nothing's changed. I told him to stop sabotaging your show, but I don't know why I bothered. You're leaving tomorrow. You're turning Grady in. It's all over, anyway."

Charlie looked at her just as miserably and said, "All right. Whatever you want." The news went off and he moved up the mike slide and said, "Good evening, Tuttle. You're with Charlie All Night—"

Allie took off her headphones. He could do the broadcast without her by now. It wasn't as if it mattered. It was his last show. He was going to be gone in another twenty-four hours and then she could put her life back together without him.

She could hardly wait.

THEY DID THE REST of the show with silence between them, Charlie just playing music. The worst was when he did a Paul Anka double play for Sam—"Puppy Love" and "Put Your Head On My Shoulder"—and patted the puppy on his own shoulder until Sam gave up and went to sleep. She loved him so much then, she hurt with it. He only stopped to talk once, this time about the use of marijuana in treating the nausea associated with chemotherapy. He made a good persuasive argument, and Allie knew he was doing it for Grady's sake, to prepare the way for Grady's defense, but it wasn't enough.

He was still going to turn Grady in.

She stayed until Grady showed up at quarter to two to take over the booth.

"Grady, I'm sorry," she told him when he came in. "If there's anything I can do…"

Grady shook his head. "Nope. I got myself into this. I'm ready."

"Oh, Grady," Allie said, but he'd already gone into the booth with Charlie.

Charlie plugged the news cassette in and she watched them as he gave Grady the chair and then leaned on the side of the booth to talk to him. Charlie looked like death, exhaustion and unhappiness making him haggard. For a moment, she relented because she loved him.

Then she went in to try one last time to convince him.

"You can't do this," she said when she was in the booth with them. "I've tried and tried to think of a way around this, but I can't. Joe says a prison sentence is mandatory. You can't do this."

Charlie closed his eyes against her. "It's the law. I know Grady did what he did because he loves his mother—"

"He saved her life," Allie broke in. "She couldn't eat. He saved—"

"But the law is the law," Charlie went on inexorably. "He broke it."

Allie looked at Grady for help. "I don't believe this. The law is stupid. In fact, the law is *wrong*—"

"Listen to me," Charlie said and the intensity in his voice stopped her in midsentence. "One of the biggest problems this country has is that people think a law is only a law if they agree with it. And if they don't, it's all right to kick guys like Joe out of the service and bomb abortion clinics because there's a *higher law* at work. And that's garbage, Allie. The law is the law. If you don't like it, change it. But don't break it and then start whining when there are consequences."

"But they won't change it," Allie snapped. "Politicians are such cowards when it comes to legalizing any drugs that they'd rather see people die than risk their careers. It's not going to change. And it's *wrong*."

"The law is the law," Charlie said. "You can't choose which part of it you like and which you're going to ignore. It's not a salad bar, Al. The whole thing stands, or the whole thing goes. And Grady broke the law."

"And you're going to turn him in." Allie stood there, her eyes blazing at him in contempt. "Good old by-the-book, my-way-is-law Charlie. I bet you look a whole lot like your father now."

Charlie winced, and Grady stood up and said, "Wait a minute." His voice was low and mild but it cut through her anger. "Thanks for the defense, Al. I appreciate it. But Charlie's right. Don't do the crime if you can't do the time." He turned to Charlie. "I'm only asking one favor."

Charlie nodded.

"Don't turn me in until tomorrow morning. Let me finish the show and tell my mom and dad first."

Charlie knew he was right, and he'd never felt worse in his life, knowing he was ruining Grady's life, knowing Allie would probably never speak to him again. It was a lot to pay for being right. "Of course I won't," he told Grady.

Grady looked him in the eye. "I won't run."

Charlie swallowed. "I know that. Oh, hell, Grady." He cast around for something to say.

Grady sat back down in the console chair. "It's not your problem anymore," he told Charlie as he picked up the headphones. "In fact, if I hadn't started doing this, you wouldn't have been here at all. So it's always been my problem. Sorry I dragged you into it."

"I'm sorry you did, too," Allie said.

366   *Jennifer Crusie*

Charlie looked at her. "I'm not sorry. I wouldn't trade these past weeks for anything."

"Well, I would," she said, and there were tears in her voice. "I'd trade them for Grady's freedom. You're going to send him to prison. Do you know how long he'll be there? Do you know how awful—"

"Allie, let it go," Grady said. "I'm not a kid. Stop treating me like one. This isn't Charlie's fault."

"Well, it sure looks that way to me," Allie said and walked out of the booth, and Charlie felt all the warmth and air leave the room with her.

He was right. He knew he was right.

But being right without Allie was lousy. And that was going to be the story for the rest of his life.

Grady rubbed his forehead. "She'll calm down. She'll see there was nothing else you could do."

"Will she?" Charlie sat on the edge of the console. "*I'm* not even sure there was nothing else I could do. You're not a criminal."

"Well, yeah, I am," Grady said. "I committed a crime. I'm pretty sure that makes me a criminal."

"And she was right about something else." Charlie looked unhappily at Grady. "I'm acting just like my father. And yours. Rigid."

Grady shook his head. "My dad told me about your brother. Your father covered up your brother's crime. You're doing the opposite. You're on the side of the angels."

"Pretty lousy angels." Charlie tipped his head back. "I know I'm right. My dad knew he was right. Bill always knows he's right. I'm everything I never wanted to be. I've spent my whole life refusing to have anything to do with people so that I'd never try to control anybody. And now I'm alone and still controlling people. What I should do is just leave town now. I know you'll tell Bill, so my job's done." He felt so tired his bones ached. "I should just go now."

"And leave everybody?" Grady looked incredulous. "Not say goodbye to Harry or Joe or Karen? Or Allie?"

Charlie laughed shortly. "I don't think Allie will talk to me long enough to let me say goodbye."

Grady watched him for a moment and then shrugged. "Then go. I'll tell them all you said so-long." He straightened as the music stopped and leaned in to the mike to begin his show intro, and Charlie backed out of the booth as soundlessly as possible. He listened to Grady for a few minutes, talking about herbal teas this time, and then he picked up his coat and left.

ALLIE DROVE around for a while, trying to make sense of what had happened. Charlie's arguments sounded right, but there were Grady and Beattie and Mrs. Winthrop, and they weren't wrong. So how could Charlie be right? There should have been a simple answer, and there wasn't.

She stopped and picked up cashew chicken and pot stickers because she was unhappy and starving and because it was what she wanted, for some reason.

Then she went home, and turned on Grady's show, and thought about the mess some more.

She wanted to hate Charlie for what he was going to do to Grady, but she didn't. She loved him. And tomorrow was November and he was leaving, and she'd be alone again, picking up the pieces he'd left behind him.

Well, not alone. She had Joe. And Harry. And Karen and Marcia, and even Mark and Lisa weren't a complete loss. And Bill and Beattie and most of all Grady. She'd be working her butt off for Grady because he deserved it. She'd find a way to keep him out of jail.

And she'd get the drive-time show back. Mark would take her back in a heartbeat: the last thing he needed was her making some new bozo the flavor of the month the way she'd done with Charlie. He still didn't get it that she hadn't done it alone. That they'd been a team.

Allie closed her eyes for a moment because it hurt so much to remember that. In the background, Grady was playing some weird chanting music. Who would play the weird stuff while Grady was in prison?

The doorbell rang, and Allie went to get it, assuming Joe had forgotten his key and grateful he was home to comfort her.

But when she opened the door, Charlie said, "Can we please talk about this?"

Allie stood silent, staring at him as he filled her doorway. She blinked back tears and tried to breathe. The worst thing she could do would be to cry all over him; he was her problem, not her solution. But he stood there, tall and broad and solid and safe, and he sure looked like all her solutions for the rest of her life.

And tomorrow was November and Grady was going to jail.

He came in and closed the door and took her hand and pulled her over to the couch. Then he sat down beside her, and she held herself rigid so she wouldn't lean into him, trying not to collapse against him, furious with him for what he was doing to Grady, loving him so much she was paralyzed with it.

"I don't want to leave it like this," Charlie said. "This is not the way we do things. Scream at me or something, but don't walk away from me."

Allie swallowed, and her voice came out strained. "I don't know what to scream. I know you're right. And I know you're wrong. And I'm so tired, and you're leaving anyway." She tipped her head back and stared at the cracks in the ceiling. One of the cracks curved around itself and looked vaguely like Australia so she concentrated on that. All her other thoughts hurt too much.

"My father got my brother off the hook on his drug charge," Charlie said. "Bought off the witnesses and slung Ten's butt into a rehab center. He got Ten so buried, he couldn't even call his girlfriend. But he solved the problem. My mother was not embarrassed. My brother was not jailed. And the law, well, the law is for the little people."

Allie turned at the pain in his voice. "Charlie, you don't have to—"

"Yeah, I do."

She could see how seriously he was looking at her, and she was too tired to argue. "All right. Tell me."

"He fixes everything the way he wants it." Charlie said. "He wanted Ten to be a success and he was. Only Ten had to deal drugs to get it. And he wanted me to settle down, so he sent me here. Bill didn't give a damn about that letter. He was doing my dad a favor, give his son a job, make him settle down. That's what my dad told Bill. I know it."

"Well, he didn't get what he wanted there," Allie said. "You're leaving tomorrow. You—"

"And I'm doing the same thing," Charlie went on. "I did what I was sent to do, fix Bill's little anonymous-letter problem." He looked at Allie. "I know I'm right on this. But it feels wrong. It feels like my father. It feels lousy."

"You're not your father." Allie's voice was firm. "You refuse to take any responsibility for anything. You never tell anybody what to do."

"Why does that sound so bad?" Charlie slumped back against the couch. "I thought it was a solution, but it's as bad as the problem." He shook his head. "I packed my car tonight. I figured my job was done, and I hated what was happening so I thought I'd just leave. Let you play opera until you found another schmuck to make into a star."

Allie latched on to his mistake. "I didn't make you a star. You did. Your personality and your brains and your talent."

"We did." He looked at her then. "We did it together."

Allie closed her eyes because it hurt too much to look at him. "Don't. It's over. You're leaving."

"No, I'm not," he told her. "I can't. I can't leave you. I love you. I can leave Tuttle, but I can't leave you. I don't ever want to spend another day without you." He leaned toward her, and his voice was taut. "I was going to leave this whole mess behind. I got in the car to go, and then I just sat there and thought, 'Where the hell am I going?' Because without you, there isn't anyplace else to go. You're all there is."

All the air had been sucked out of her lungs. Allie felt pain in her chest and heat behind her eyelids where tears pressed, and she couldn't move from all the emotion that was choking her.

When she didn't say anything, Charlie added, "Say something, please. I'm dying here."

She tried to suck some air into her lungs. She was having trouble breathing. And speaking. "I…" The words died.

Charlie took her hand. "I love you, Al. It's not about sex or the bet or the show. I love you. I don't know, with what I've done, if that's enough, but I do love you."

"It's enough," she said, and her voice broke. "It's enough." She swallowed. "I'm really mad at you, and I hate what you're doing to Grady..."

"I know."

"But I love you," she said, and as she said it, any doubts she had disappeared forever. "I love you so much sometimes I get dizzy when I look at you. I feel good when I'm with you. I feel right. I think you're wrong here, but I don't think I could stand life without you."

He bent to kiss her, and she held her breath and felt his lips on hers, warm and gentle and everything he was, and she kissed him then, with all the love she had for him, memorizing him, breathing with him as his mouth grew hot on hers.

"Don't ever leave me," he said against her lips, and she almost laughed because she wasn't the one with the need to leave, but then the chanting on the radio stopped and Grady's voice broke in.

"This will be my last show for a while, Tuttle," he said, and they both turned to listen to him, their heads close. "I've been breaking the law, and tomorrow morning, I'm turning myself in. I had a long talk with a friend tonight, and he pointed out that the law is a fine thing, even when it's wrong. It's the only defense we have against anarchy, against the strong overwhelming the weak. And if it's wrong, well, then it's our job to change it. I've been giving away marijuana to chemotherapy patients because it helps them withstand the nausea the treatments cause, but it's against the law. I think it's time this law was changed, and tonight's the only night I have left to talk about it before I go to jail. If you're listening and you have an opinion, call in. The number is—"

"Grady is the only person I know who could make his arrest a call-in topic," Allie said when she'd recovered her voice. "What do you suppose he's been doing for the past hour while all that music played?"

Charlie let go of her. "He's been talking to his father. I called Bill and told him."

Allie sat up. "You *what?*"

Charlie sighed. "I called Bill and told him that Grady was doing something important that had probably saved Beattie's life, and that now it was Bill's turn to stick his neck out. He yelled a lot, but I think he saw the light at the end. I think he's going to fight for Grady. When I hung up, he was making a plan. If nothing else, it should be interesting to see what happens next." He picked up the chicken carton from the table in front of them and began to eat, and when Allie stole a look at him, he looked almost relaxed.

All right. It wouldn't have been her way of handling it, but at least he was handling it. Getting involved. And he might just be right. "I bet Bill's not the only one making a plan," she told him, picking up the pot stickers. "I bet Beattie's working on a beaut."

"You should have gotten more food," Charlie said. "This chicken is going to be gone in no time."

They sat close on the couch and finished the chicken and the pot stickers while they listened to Grady and his callers, all of whom seemed ready to march on city hall to spring him if necessary. Of course, they were all Grady's callers, and anyone who would listen to Grady at three in the morning was already fanatically loyal, but it did reassure Allie. Even more reassuring was having Charlie near. She finally fell asleep on Charlie's shoulder while he listened to Grady's show, and she didn't wake up until he shook her at five-thirty.

"Come on," he told her softly. "Let's go back in and see if Grady needs help after the show."

Ten
➤ ◄

The station was crowded when they got there at five forty-five. The lobby teemed with two TV crews, print journalists, the sheriff, a grim Bill and Beattie and a bemused Mark.

"What is this?" Mark caught Allie's arm as she came through the door behind Charlie. Charlie looked back and rolled his eyes at Mark, but he kept on going into the station hallway. "What's all the publicity for?" Mark asked. "What did Charlie do now?"

"Nothing." Allie pulled her arm away. "Grady confessed to giving away marijuana to cancer patients. He's going to be arrested."

Mark got a faraway look in his eye. Probably planning on confessing to possession of oregano. How anyone could get that caught up in a career—

She stopped. Thank God for Charlie. If it hadn't been for him, she'd still be with Mark. In fact, she'd probably *be* Mark.

"I've got to go," she told Mark and went into the station to find Charlie and thank him.

SHE FOUND HIM in the booth with Grady.

"There's quite a crowd in the lobby," Charlie was telling him. "Anything I can do? Whatever you want, you got it."

"Nope." Grady leaned back in his chair, Sam on his lap happily chewing on the sleeve of Grady's sweatshirt. "I've got ten minutes of Hildegarde of Bingen on now, and then I'll say my goodbyes and go to jail."

"Oh, Grady," Allie sat down on the floor of the booth. "I still wish you hadn't said anything. We could have—"

"No, this is going to be great." Grady's voice sounded so self-satisfied that Allie jerked her head up to see if he could possibly be that happy.

He was.

"This is exactly the forum we need," Grady told her. "We need to get this stuff legalized for medical treatment. Now we have a cause. They're going to have to arrest me and my mother and probably a half-dozen cancer patients. Think of the publicity when Mrs. Winthrop goes to jail. Your celibate bet made the tri-state news. This will have to go national."

Allie went back to the part that scared her the most. "Grady, you're going to jail."

Grady grinned at her. "Not for long. You don't know my dad. Hell, I didn't know my dad. He yelled at first, but he had a plan worked out, and then Mom got on the other line, and by the time she was finished, he was ready to run me for governor. He's all gung ho, getting lawyers and filing motions and calling the press. He says there's bail and appeals and no end of lawyer red tape he can throw at them to keep me out. And the whole time, Mom and I will be giving interviews, making statements..." He trailed off as his grin widened. "I bet Dad will even let me keep my show once he gets over the shock."

"He's over it now," Charlie told him from where he was leaning on the side of the booth. "He's arguing with the sheriff in front of the TV cameras. This is going to be a circus."

Grady leaned back in his chair. "This is great."

Allie stood up, suddenly reassured. "No, it's not, but I'll help, anyway." She started out of the booth, and Charlie caught her arm.

"What are you doing?"

Allie smiled at him, buoyed by Grady's optimism and the fact that Charlie was touching her again. "You know all those people I was going to call to try to stop your drug story? They work both ways. I'll have Grady on the national news by tomorrow."

"Oh, right," Charlie snorted. "Even you—"

Allie stopped him in midsentence. "Want to bet?"

"No." Charlie shook his head. "Absolutely not. I'm not betting anything with you ever again."

"That's what I thought," Allie said and left the booth to make some phone calls.

THREE HOURS LATER, Grady had been arrested and bailed out, and Charlie was alone with Bill in his office.

"Things didn't turn out quite the way I'd planned," Charlie told him.

Bill sighed and sat heavily in his chair. "The two of them. Running a charity drug ring. And now they're in hog heaven, and the poor old sheriff has to go through the motions. If they'd kept their damn mouths shut…"

"At least now you know," Charlie said. "The anonymous-letter mystery's over."

"Oh, yeah, I'm real glad about that." Bill leaned back in his chair and glared at him. "So I guess this means you're leaving."

"Nope," Charlie said. "I'm staying. You can tell my dad he won."

Bill started and then tried to look innocent. "What's your dad got to do with this?"

Charlie shook his head. "Forget it. I figured it out a while back. You called Dad and told him you had an anonymous letter, and he told you he wanted me settled down and you cooked this up together. Favor for an old friend, right? You didn't give a damn about that letter."

"I told him I couldn't make you stay if you didn't want to." Bill scowled at him. "Then you went and made yourself a hit. And me some money. It's your fault."

"No, it's Allie's." Charlie sighed. "She wanted to make me a star."

"Well, I got to tell you, son, I'm real glad she did."

Charlie looked up in surprise at the emotion in the older man's voice. "I am, too." He blinked at the thought. He really was glad.

That's what hanging around with Allie had done for him. Made him career crazy.

"You're sure gonna make the nights interesting around here," Bill went on, and Charlie shook his head.

"No, that'll be the mornings. I want the drive-time spot."

Bill frowned at him. "Can't do it. That's Mark King's show."

Charlie shrugged. "Then I'm out of here. And so is Allie."

Bill's eyebrows shot up. "Alice? She's not leaving."

"We're getting married, Bill. Whither I goest, she goest. And if we don't get the drive-time show, we're going." Charlie mentally crossed his fingers, hoping Bill wouldn't call his bluff. Allie was too independent to follow anybody anywhere, but Bill didn't have to know that.

Bill glared at him. "What the hell am I going to do with Mark?"

"I am not the person to ask that," Charlie said as he stood up. "You wouldn't like my suggestions."

"All right." Bill ground his teeth a little. "All right. You got it."

"Thank you very much." Charlie turned back as he got to the door. "And good luck with Grady and Beattie. Let me know if there's anything I can do."

Bill sat back in his chair. "We can handle it. It's a family problem."

Charlie leaned in the doorway. "Well, to tell you the truth, Bill, I kind of think of you and Grady and Beattie as family now. So if you need anything..."

Bill's face softened and he nodded. "I'll call you."

"Thanks. I'd like that."

Charlie looked in Allie's office, but she was long gone, her phone calls made while he was helping Grady.

He knew where she'd be, and he tried not to think about it on his way out to the car.

Now was no time to have a heart attack from lust.

ALLIE OPENED the door of her apartment when he knocked, and just the sight of him made her weak-kneed. Coming home to bed had been a mistake. It was November first, and Grady was where he wanted to be, and the bet was over, and she wanted him. She didn't want to lose the closeness they'd had, but she wanted him with a craving that went beyond lust.

So when she opened the door, and he was standing there, broad and safe and male and Charlie, her knees went, and she tried to pretend it didn't matter. "Come on in," she said and then went back into her bedroom and crawled under her quilt. "I can't believe this," she told him when he followed her. "I can't believe this last twenty-four hours happened. I can't believe this last *month* happened."

Charlie slumped at the foot of the bed, and Allie fought back her disappointment. He was supposed to be under the quilt with her.

"It happened," he told her. "The last thing I heard as I went through the lobby was Mark, on the air, telling the world he'd inhaled in the seventies."

Allie was so surprised, she forgot to lust for a minute. "Inhaled what?"

"I don't know." Charlie rubbed his neck. "I don't care. I'm just glad it's over. I just want some sleep."

Sleep. Well, it was a start. She moved over a couple of inches to make room for him. "You can get some sleep here if you want."

He was still for a moment. "Here?"

She nodded.

"Allie, if I climb into bed with you, I'm going to want more than sleep."

Her heart did a little heated lurch in her chest. *Thank God.* Now, if only things didn't change. "I've been thinking," she said to him. "All last night, and this morning while I was on the phone. And I don't know what I think about this Grady mess. I don't even know which one of us is right. But I do know that you did what you thought was right even though I tried hard to change your mind." She smiled tentatively at him. "And I'm pretty impressed with that, that you'd give up everything to do what you thought was right. And I know that you've been right on some other things this month, too. Not everything, but some things. And I know I love you, and you love me, and after that...well, I think we can work this out." She swallowed. "What do you think?"

Charlie's eyes met hers. "Will you marry me?"

Allie almost fell out of bed.

"I already told Bill we were getting married, so I'm going to look like a real fool if you say no." He leaned forward. "Make an honest man out of me. Marry me."

Allie stopped breathing. Marriage. That was permanent enough. And since it was Charlie asking, it was forever. She'd have to follow him all over the country, and they'd probably have all their kids in different states, and she'd never have a career again.

But she'd have good times. And laughter.

And Charlie.

She drew a deep breath. "Can we get a Winnebago?"

He blinked at her. "Well, yeah. Sure. I guess." He frowned at her. "Why would you want a Winnebago?"

"So it'll be like home while we're traveling," Allie said. "Like a house."

Charlie's frown deepened. "Traveling where?"

"Wherever it is that we're going. It's November."

He started to laugh, and she wanted to kill him. "Forget the Winnebago. We're not going anywhere. I told Bill I wanted a full-time job. Medical insurance. Pension plan. Paternity leave. We're adopting Sam. I'm settling down."

Some days, you get everything you ask for. Unbelievable. Allie sank back against the pillows. "Oh. Oh, good." She closed her eyes in relieved wonder. "Oh, Charlie, I do love you, and I'd follow you anywhere, but I'd really rather—"

"Stay here and make me a star." Charlie grinned at her. "I know, babe. You've got it."

Allie loved him so much she thought she'd die of it. And he was still a whole bed-length away from her. She tried to glare at him. "Will you please come here and kiss me? You just proposed. You're supposed to kiss me."

His grin disappeared. "I'm not going to stop with a kiss. I want a lot more than that."

Allie took a deep breath. "You've got it."

His eyes met hers and he didn't move. "This is unbelievable," he told her. "I feel like a kid on a first date."

"It's not like we haven't done this before." Allie tried to smile at him. "It's not like it's our first time."

"Yes, it is." Charlie moved up until he was sitting on the side of the bed, his hands on each side of her, and she put her hand on his arm, grateful to finally be touching him. "It's our first time for this," he said, his eyes looking deep into hers. "What we had before was fun, but it wasn't this. This is our first time."

She couldn't move her eyes from his. "I know." She moved her hand to his cheek, barely touching him. "I know. I want you so much. I couldn't bear to lose you now."

She hadn't meant to sound so vulnerable, but she couldn't call back the words. He closed his eyes, and then he shook his head. "You won't lose me. Things have changed, but they'll be better. They're already better. If you don't want to move this fast, we can wait to make love. Until you're sure."

"I'm sure," Allie said. "I'm just…nervous."

"I know. I am, too. But I want you so much…"

He leaned forward then and kissed her softly, lingering, and the heat from his mouth went straight into her bones and called back all the cravings she'd ignored for too long.

"Oh, come to bed," she whispered. "I can't wait any longer."

He stood then and undressed, deliberately, not like the old exuberant Charlie who had stripped at the speed of light and then pulled her to him like a teenager in heat. When he slid into bed beside her, he didn't touch her; he just supported himself on one elbow and looked down at her as if she was something irreplaceable.

"This must be what wedding nights used to be like," he said. "Terrifying. Incredible."

Allie put her hand on his chest to feel his warmth and felt him stiffen at her touch. She'd forgotten exactly how good he could feel under her hand, how hard his chest was, how hot his skin burned, like a brand on her palm. She let her hand trail down his chest and put her cheek against him and listened to his heart pound, and he slowly slid his arm around her waist and pulled her close as he eased himself under her, onto the pillows.

Charlie tipped her face to his, and she almost suffocated from love, just watching him look at her as if he was memorizing her. There was so much love in his face, she thought she'd drown in it, and when he finally did pull her head down to kiss her, she did drown. His mouth was gentle at first, and then more insistent, his tongue invading her, and her hands clenched his shoulders as he grew more demanding. She felt her body deepen in heat against his, her blood growing thick and hot as his mouth took her away, and she willed herself to remember that it was him with her and not to melt into senselessness. She felt him pull at her nightgown and helped him strip it off, closing her eyes as the cool air fell on her body, opening them as the heat from his hands reclaimed her. She licked at the base of his neck, and then down his chest to his nipples, feeling how hard and smooth he was under her lips, hearing his breathing break as she touched him.

Then he bent his head, and she felt the sweet chill of his mouth on her breast, and then the chill turned to heat. She raked her fingers through his hair and pulled his head against her, savoring the ache of his mouth on her. The heat and the ache and the torment were everywhere, and as he moved under her, she fell into him, becoming part of him, wanting him everywhere against her, inside her. Even simple pleasures like the brush of his cheek against her skin became charged with electricity and love.

"I love you," she whispered to him, and he said, "I didn't know this existed. I didn't know until you."

"Make love to me." Allie tried to move against him, but he rolled her gently onto her back and began to kiss her neck. "I want you inside me," she said, arching into him. "I've waited so long. Don't make me wait longer."

"Just a little bit," he said against her throat. "Just a little bit." His cheek was on her breast and then his tongue traced down the seam of her stomach, and her nerves fluttered and she forgot how to breathe.

"Soon," he said, when his hands were on her hips, and her hips flexed on their own, tightening under his grip. "I just need to taste you. I need this first." His fingers found her, and she moaned and stretched to ease the ache, then he licked his tongue inside her, and she jerked under the shock and grabbed the headboard above her in desperation, holding on to it as if it were sanity.

"You taste so sweet, Allie," she heard him whisper, and she moaned at the thought while his breath tantalized her thighs. She gripped the headboard until her knuckles went white, trying to stay with him, but his whisper pounded inside her and she couldn't breathe because the heat was everywhere. "You're so sweet."

And then he licked inside her again and again, and she writhed in his grasp, and he moved his mouth harder against her, holding her hips harder against him, and she couldn't twist away, didn't want to twist away, had to twist away as the heat screamed through her veins until she cried out, "Oh, Charlie, *now*," and he whispered,

"Soon," and drove her on and on until she went over the edge, ecstatically out of control.

He moved back beside her then while she throbbed against him and the aftershocks of her climax wracked her. He whispered that she was beautiful, most beautiful when she was coming, and she breathed, "It's not enough. I need you inside me." And he closed his eyes and then moved over her, his lips saying her name soundlessly, his thighs moving her legs apart. She ached so for him that she moaned with it, her veins bursting under her skin. "Oh, please," she said, clutching him to her, and he said, "Look at me," and when she did, loving him so much she was insane with it, drowning in the heat and love she saw in his eyes, he moved into her, filling her, and they both stopped breathing for that moment, their eyes locked on each other, their bodies tensed together as the shock flooded them both.

And then they moved together, breathed together, and the heat rushed through them, and Allie surged and bloomed, feeling Charlie in her fingertips, in her heart, in her brain, as his warmth and light and love moved through her, and she fell into her climax, screaming with it, feeling him surge against her over and over, beyond measured rhythm, and his shuddering moans brought her back into the aching spiral again and again until she thought she'd die of ecstasy.

And when they were both quiet, both breathing again, holding each other in the early-morning sunlight, Charlie kissed her and said, "I love you, Allie. I'll never stop loving you."

She nodded against his cheek, weak with spent passion. "I know. This is forever."

She felt him relax, and then moments later he was asleep in her arms, and she held him tightly until she fell asleep, too.

IT WAS AFTERNOON when she woke up, and Charlie woke, too, when she stirred. He pulled her close and she closed her eyes when he kissed her forehead. "I forgot to tell you the good news," he whispered. "We've got a new show."

Allie frowned at him, still half-asleep. "What new show?"

"Bill gave us the drive-time spot," he murmured into her hair. "The one at 6:00 a.m. You're back where you wanted to be."

Allie sat up, suddenly awake and appalled. "Did you say 6:00 a.m.? In the morning a.m.? Are you nuts?"

Charlie blinked and pushed himself up beside her on one arm. "I thought that was what you wanted. Back on top."

Allie looked exasperated. "I can be on top at night."

He grinned at her and moved his hand to her breast and said, "Anytime," and she grinned, too, covering his hand with hers. "You know what I mean," she told him. "I like the ten-to-two people. They're bizarre. Let Mark have the drive-time show. At least until Marcia takes it away from him, which should be any day now. We belong at night, Charlie." She looked at him anxiously. "Don't you think so?"

"Well, yes." Charlie started to laugh and collapsed back into the bed, pulling her on top of him. "Wait'll I tell Bill."

Allie propped herself up on his chest, enjoying the way her breasts squashed against him. "I can't believe you even considered the morning show."

Charlie sighed. "I thought I was giving you what you wanted."

"You always give me what I want. Which reminds me…" Allie moved her face to his until they were nose-to-nose, stretching and feeling the long hard length of his body against hers. He'd be hers for the rest of her life. She almost died just thinking about it. Then his hand moved lazily down her back to her rear end, and she brought her mind back to the subject at hand. "I have an idea for a new show," Allie told him. "It'll run forever. Audience of one. I'm thinking of calling it Charlie All Afternoon. And the playlist—"

"I do my own playlist," Charlie told her and kissed her to start the program.